The Inheritance of
Solomon Farthing

Also by Mary Paulson-Ellis

THE OTHER MRS WALKER

MARY PAULSON-ELLIS

The Inheritance of Solomon Farthing

MANTLE

First published 2019 by Mantle
an imprint of Pan Macmillan
20 New Wharf Road, London N1 9RR
Associated companies throughout the world
www.panmacmillan.com

ISBN 978-1-4472-9394-1

A CIP catalogue record for this book is available from the British Library.

Typeset by Palimpsest Book Production Limited, Falkirk, Stirlingshire
Printed and bound by CPI Group (UK) Ltd, Croydon, CR0 4YY

Visit **www.panmacmillan.com** to read more about all our books
and to buy them. You will also find features, author interviews and
news of any author events, and you can sign up for e-newsletters
so that you're always first to hear about our new releases.

For Jack,
with love

And for my dad,
the best of men

Solomon Grundy
Born on Monday
Christened on Tuesday
Married on Wednesday
Took ill on Thursday
Worse on Friday
Died on Saturday
Buried on Sunday
That was the end of Solomon Grundy

Traditional

'*The First World War, if you boil it down, what was it?*
Nothing but a family row.'

Harry Patch

THE BEGINNING

PART ONE
The Debt

PART TWO
The Pawn

PART THREE
The Bet

PART FOUR
The Charge

PART FIVE
The Reckoning

PART SIX
The Inheritance

PART SEVEN
The Legacy

THE END

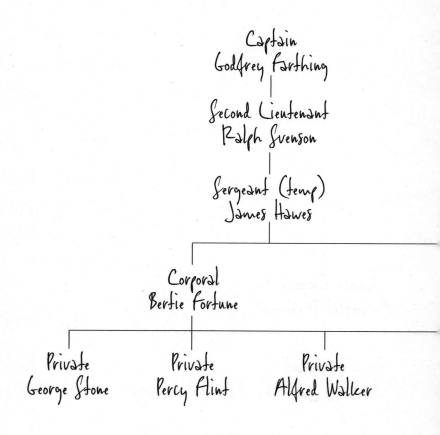

Captain
Godfrey Farthing

Second Lieutenant
Ralph Svenson

Sergeant (temp)
James Hawes

Corporal
Bertie Fortune

Private
George Stone

Private
Percy Flint

Private
Alfred Walker

Lance Corporal
Archibald Methven

Private Edward
(Jackdaw) Jackson

Private
Arthur Promise

THE BEGINNING

In the end there was one, but there should have been two, dead men laid out amongst the walnut shells, skin already blue. A great rose bloomed over the dead man's heart, there on his second-best shirt, bright amongst the decay. Those who were left looked away, thinking of the one who should have been there but was not, lungs like wings of ice holding him to the bottom of a river where none of them would have to follow now. Above them birds perched silent amongst the branches. The sky hung grey on the horizon. It was morning. Dawn would be here soon.

In the end they drew lots to decide who would choose first:

A wishbone;

A tanner;

A reel of pink cotton.

Before the rest came rummaging, too. Into breast pockets. And hip pockets. And pockets tucked away by the kidneys and the groin. The dead man lay unprotesting as the men dipped their hands in. Everything was sticky. They wiped their palms on damp khaki wool and fingered the rest of the treasure:

Two dice;

That piece of green ribbon;

A canvas pocketbook filled with needles and pins.

They all smelled it. Cordite. And the bullet that was inside the dead man now.

In the end they buried him before they walked away. Not deep, but a dip in the ground scraped out beneath a scattering of walnut shells, like the shallow form of a hare. Their hearts were beating – *one two one two* – as they scratched at the hole. They didn't leave a marker; only the mud on their boots told the tale. And the treasure that came last from the dead man's pockets:

Pawn ticket no.125.

That small square of blue.

In the end the men who were left went ahead, single file across the fields, no sound but the *clink* and *jink* of weaponry as they walked. None of them looked back to see where they had come from. None of them looked ahead to see where they might go. Only one of them stayed behind to pray.

A thread of pink stained the sky as he closed his eyes, standing once more in the shadow of that rubbish dump, remembering fields of buttercups and two kinds of clover. Of air flowing pure as the river at the bottom of the hill. Then there were the whispers of the men as they drew from their pockets – a dice, a penny, a thick stub of pencil. The card in his wallet, *I am quite well* the only words not yet crossed out.

He wondered then what the card would say once it was done. Who it would be sent to. And opened his eyes as light touched his skin. Dawn was spreading low on the horizon. It was November. The end would be here soon.

PART ONE

The Debt

Solomon Farthing
b.1950 d.

2016

One

They called him Old Mortality. After the book. But he hadn't expected to end like this. Face down on a mattress that smelt of urine. Nothing between him and the ground but a cold concrete bunk. It was May, dawn breaking over the city of Edinburgh. But Solomon Farthing could not draw back the curtains to see it, for he was already in the gutter – no money, no friends, no estimation – the last of him dribbling onto the stone floor of a police cell, not even a bottle of Fino to wash away the indignities of his life.

'Wakey, wakey, you bastards! Rise and shine for glory.'

Outside he could hear the clatter of a police station waking to its daily business. Inside he could feel the judder of his heart. Solomon pressed at the soft fat around his nipple. He was not a well man, of that he was certain, a mess of memory lapses and confusions, skin grown irritable on the inside and the out. His most recent predicament did not help, though it was all of his own creation, lying in a police cell without any laces to tie up his shoes. What would his grandfather have made of it, a man for whom respectability was embodied in the buttoning or unbuttoning of a collar. And yet here was his offspring, sixty-six and counting, his shirt hung loose, the edges of his trousers muddy. Also the knees.

There was the sudden shuffle of heavy boots, two police officers coming down the corridor, banging on each metal door as they passed.

'Time to get up, gentlemen.'

Solomon levered himself into a sitting position, licked his palm and ran it across his hair. He was hoping for DI Roberts, ex-Enquiry Team, bag carrier for DCI Franklin, come to read him the Riot Act by way of admonition. A warning. A minor fine. A rap on the knuckles. Or, if the dice rolled in his favour, a straight pass through the doors of Gayfield police station into an elegant Edinburgh square. That old haunt of prostitutes and rent boys, first home for all those first-generation immigrants come to the Athens of the North to polish their dreams. Transformed now, of course. Five hundred thousand for three bedrooms and counting. Whatever its murky past, Edinburgh always did find a way of lifting one up in the end.

Solomon pulled his wrinkled fuchsia socks straight at the ankle, attempted to smooth away the creases accumulated after a weekend of sleeping in his clothes. When exactly had he taken the wrong path? he wondered. An Edinburgh Man with at least a semblance of a profession, given to riding the ebb and flow of life to his advantage, lost now like some sort of child abandoned in a storm. His appeal to the only relative he had left in the city – an aunt who wasn't really his aunt – had elicited nothing but silence. No calls to a solicitor. No demands for early release. Not even a clean set of clothes. Solomon took a surreptitious sniff at one underarm after another, waited for salvation to arrive in the form of a police officer for whom he might have done a favour, once, long ago. It wasn't that many years since he had known all the officers in the city – by their first names, too:

You scratch my back and I'll scratch yours.

An ability to charm, one of Solomon Farthing's more valuable qualities, though even he knew it was hanging by a single thread now.

But when the hatch was lowered Solomon did not recognize the blank eyes gazing at him through the hole in the door. Female. Young. Discerning. Everything he was not. The PC looked at him for a moment longer than was comfortable, then vanished before Solomon could make any sort of appeal. A shit. A shave. A *good morning.* Not to mention breakfast. Nothing more than the ordinary courtesies of life.

In the cell next door a moan rose up, the same elemental groaning that had kept him awake for most of the weekend.

'Oh man, oh man, oh man. You fucker.'

There was a pause. Solomon waited (the illusion of hope). Then the repeat.

'Oh man, oh man, oh man . . .'

You fucker.

What more was there to say?

The misdemeanour had begun in the ordinary manner. An attempt to make money. A scramble to be first. What else was there when it came to being an Heir Hunter, pursuer of all that remained when someone died without a will.

Property was the key, particularly in a city like Edinburgh. Three bedrooms for sale; five hundred thousand pounds to share amongst those who were left. The return was commission. Ten per cent. Twenty per cent. Sometimes even thirty, if things were going well. The important thing – the crucial thing – was to chase the estates that were worth half a million and counting. And to get there first.

The house had been abandoned, at least that was what Solomon had been told. A substantial property in a quiet residential street, owner long since deceased. Generous driveway. French windows unlocked at the back. It was a tip-off from Freddy Dodds, normally the most reliable of Solomon's Edinburgh Men, someone who fed him information in return for a first go at whatever riches might not be missed. Solomon's plan had been simple, a typical Heir Hunter's scam. A quick recce inside the empty property to establish its worth, then claim the estate the next day before the crown office got involved, offer to assist any next of kin he dug up with disposal of the remains. Five hundred thousand for three bedrooms and counting. Possession of an empty property with no apparent owner – nine tenths of the law where an Heir Hunter was concerned. It should have been an easy night's work.

The first problem had been the streetlight shining on the very gap Solomon needed to disappear along to access the rear of the house. He stood on the opposite side of the road, breathing in a lilac's heady night-time scent, trying to look as though he was a man who appreciated nature rather than one who would smile as he robbed you of all you had been left. To leave. Or to remain. That was what it amounted to. Solomon's instinct was the former. But despite being the laissez-faire type – *what could be done today can always be left until tomorrow* – Solomon knew that this time he did not have any time to waste.

His second problem was the French doors that would not open once he did decide to make his move, no longer unlocked from the inside out as Dodds had assured him would be the case.

The third was the absence of an open window any larger than a porthole to scramble through when the motion sensors set off their phosphorescent flare. The whole garden flung into sudden slices of dazzle and shadow. It was the tendency to self-preservation that propelled Solomon forwards. Head first, of course.

He got stuck halfway.

'Fuck!'

Ripped the sleeve of his second-best shirt. Found himself slithering onto the floor of a cold WC. He came to rest with his head jammed against the toilet bowl, wondered how on earth his life had come to this. A man whose upbringing had been predicated on the polishing of shoes every Sunday, side by side in the scullery with his grandfather. Thank God the old man was long dead, more than forty years in the grave.

Solomon felt as though he was in the grave himself as he hauled himself to his feet and stared into the gloom of a mirror hanging above the tiny cloakroom sink. He looked old. He looked dissolute. He looked drunk. All things that were true. His left hand would not stop fluttering as he held it under a trickle of cold water from the tap, splashed at his face. There was no towel to wipe his hands dry, so he used the tail of his second-best shirt instead. Then he stood listening at the door as though he really was a child again, before stepping into the dark run of the hall.

The house was waiting for him – a potential treasure trove ready to offer its secrets to whomever might ask first. Canteens of silver cutlery, perhaps. Family portraits in curlicues of gilt. A necklace made of pearls. The kind of thing Dodds was interested in. Not to mention

Solomon's particular concern, three bedrooms, walk-in condition, every estate agent's dream. He crept along trying each door as he came to it, a silent opening and closing of rooms belonging to a dead man, his own reflection looming now and then from a mirror over a fake electric grate. Every inch of the house was carpeted – the rooms, the corridors, the walk-in cupboards – Solomon's tired leather shoes sinking into the pile as though discovering a luxury they had been promised once but never received. He could tell already the house was virgin territory, no other Heir Hunters yet arrived to muddy his patch.

He peered into a linen press, ran his hand along the top of all the door frames, slid open every drawer in the kitchen in the hope of a spare set of keys. But it never occurred to Solomon Farthing that the former occupant might still be in residence, stretched out in the front room across the end of two brocade chairs.

'Christ!

Solomon's heart practically leapt from his chest when he pushed open the living-room door and saw the wooden coffin with its shiny brass handles. Then again when he heard a reply.

'Who's there?'

Female. Loud. Alerting. A woman holding vigil, starting up as Solomon jerked the living-room door closed.

Sitting in.

Wasn't that what they called it? Solomon didn't wait to do any sort of introduction, made his escape instead. His heart was beating a wild *one two* as he heard the woman call after him.

'Solomon Farthing?'

Found the French windows open this time, as though they had been all along.

He fell on the patio. Then again on the grass. Made it to the local cemetery then out the other side, by way of diversion, before the blue lights came flashing to take him away. It wasn't until they put him in the squad car, torn cuff flapping aimless about his wrist, that Solomon realized he had lost it. That lucky silver charm he carried always in his pocket – all that remained of his childhood glittering now between a dead man's floorboards. A regimental cap badge, lion raising its paw. Also the motto of the London Scottish:

Strike Sure.

Two

The Sheriff Court was in the heart of the city. Five minutes'
walk from the castle with its soldiers and its cannons. Four
from the Kirk with its memorial to the fallen. Two from
the graveyard where Edinburgh's finest once used locks
and bars to keep the dead in. All of these sites now swarmed
with tourists. Edinburgh always did have a way with the
departed – liked to keep them alive if it could.

Solomon was driven to his own grubby destiny in the
back of a squad car, the same inscrutable officer who had
eyeballed him through the metal slot early that morning,
pinioning him once again.

PC Noble.

That was what the desk sergeant at Gayfield had called
her. How much better for the city could it get?

PC Noble looked about fifteen to Solomon Farthing.
Then again, he probably looked near death to her. He tried
to make conversation as they slid their way through the
morning traffic. Might as well cultivate the young, he
thought, now that the old had forsaken him.

'Do you live in Edinburgh?' he asked.

PC Noble glanced at him in the rear-view mirror, then
looked away.

'Maybe.'

Maybe. What kind of answer was that?

Despite it still being somewhat early the holding area

beneath the courts was already busy, a long queue of the city's finest waiting to be judged. Not solicitors or accountants, bank managers or financiers who knew how to fleece a man of all his life savings while sharing a pint. But another type of Edinburgh Man, just like Solomon, who had not shaved that morning, or changed their underwear from several nights before. Solomon picked a seat in the cell as far from the rest as possible, the smell of the great unwashed saturating the air. Next to him the wall was inscribed with a thousand furious epithets scratched and scored beneath a thin wash of paint. F words and C words and words that described a desire to violate in every possible manner. Solomon liked to imagine he'd manage a more eloquent dissection of his circumstances should it come to that. An elegy to what had gone wrong, and what might yet go right, written out on prison paper while all around him the dispossessed swirled and swore. After all, incarceration might yet have its advantages. For what was freedom but a state of mind? And his mind had been pressed recently, beset by worries about what he owed, to whom, and why. Prison could be the making of him, a place to stand and stare.

And yet . . .

'Enjoy your weekend?'

One of Solomon's fellow prisoners slid towards him along the bench, settled in uncomfortable proximity, knee pressed to knee. The man was young enough to be Solomon's grandson, grey-skinned enough to have spent his short life supping on every drug of choice. Solomon blinked as the young man grinned, revealing a full set of pristine crowns almost blinding in their newness. What had happened to the originals? Solomon thought. And how had such a man paid for their replacements? He didn't have to wait long to find out.

'Dodds says hello,' said the young man, leaning close, the faintest whiff of decay on his breath. 'Suggests you come for tea.'

Solomon felt it at once, that *one two* starting gun in his chest, smelled again the lilac and its heady night-time bloom. Not a friendly tip-off, then, from one professional to another. But a message. A warning. Perhaps even a threat. Freddy Dodds was an Edinburgh Man of many and varied persuasions, reliable for info, but not a person to cross in any way.

Solomon closed his eyes, dipped one fluttering hand into his jacket pocket to grasp for his silver charm, remembered all of his luck was in the clutches of a dead man now. He twisted away from Dodds's emissary towards the wall with its F words and its C words, prayed that his case would be dealt with soon. But as with everything in Solomon Farthing's life at the present, it was not to be.

Three hours and thirty-seven minutes later, after Assault, Drugs, Theft, Mugging, and general bad behaviour all round, Solomon's name was called by the clerk.

'Solomon Farthing!'

And finally he stepped into the dock.

Needless to say, this being Edinburgh the sheriff knew Solomon Farthing and Solomon Farthing knew the sheriff, too.

'Farthing,' she said. 'How nice to see you again.'

The opposite of what she really meant.

The last time Solomon had met the sheriff was at the Residents Association Garden Party for the crescent where they both lived. One long balmy afternoon quaffing free drink amongst the azaleas and decorating the raffle prizes with sticky fingerprints. Over the years the Garden Party had proved a fruitful fishing ground for an Heir Hunter – all those singular Edinburgh folks with their million-pound homes, thought they'd go on forever so forgot to make a will. Solomon had got drunk and spilled barbecue sauce down the sheriff's blouse as he attempted to take advantage. Realized now that the favour was about to be repaid.

Charge: Drunk. Disorderly. Breach of the Peace. All because of a scuffle at Gayfield police station once he'd been lifted from the street. A shout. Demands from Solomon to call a certain DCI Franklin from her bed. A wrangling and a twisting as two officers attempted to grab him. Then the kick, somebody yelping, the reckless flail of a fist (his own) connecting with flesh (not his own). Not to mention Breaking and Entering . . . with Intent to Steal.

Solomon began to sweat as the clerk read through the disposals. Five years at Her Majesty's pleasure. A ten-thousand-pound fine. Or worse, a community sentence – sent out to sweep the city's gutters of little bags of dog shit while wearing one of those fetching fluorescent vests. What would his grandfather have said, Solomon thought, a man for whom the wearing of a uniform was a matter of honour rather than a mark of bad behaviour all round? He glanced down at his current attire, could practically feel the stink emanating from beneath his crumpled tweed.

Whatever had life come to when he did not even have anyone in this city who could lend him a clean shirt.

The sheriff cleared her throat and Solomon raised his eyes to the bench wondering whether to plead guilty and throw himself on her mercy (or at least on the fact that she was a neighbour), found the clerk of the court handing her a note instead. The sheriff frowned as she unfolded the small square of paper and studied its contents. When she looked up it was no longer Solomon Farthing she was concerned with, but someone at the back of the court. Solomon turned to look too, caught the flap of a peach-lined coat disappearing through the swing of a just-closing door. When he turned back the sheriff was adjusting her spectacles in preparation for annunciation. Solomon closed his eyes, a young boy again praying next to his grandfather, for freedom, or something like it. Then she said it.

'Case dismissed.'

Outside the city was flying its flags for summer, rather like the cuffs on Solomon's shirt. He looked left. Then right. Then over his shoulder and back again, wondered whether it would be Dodds (or some other creditor) who would call in his debt first. Despite having spent a lifetime taking it from others, Solomon now found that he owed money in every nook and cranny of the city, an ever-expanding and yet unsustainable debt:

That large bill at the off-licence and another at the deli;

A tab to settle at his local in Jamaica Street (growing long now, unlike the patience of the landlord, which Solomon knew was growing very short);

The former client suing him in the small claims court

– three grand's worth of an inheritance that Solomon had already spent;

The Mini stolen from his aunt who wasn't really his aunt, an Edinburgh Lady, just like the sheriff, knew where all the bodies came from, and where they were buried, too.

Then there were the debts arising from his passion for the puggies, Lucky Sevens spinning always in his eyes. The turn of one playing card after another, the thrill with which he had tossed the dice across the baize, shovelling money he did not have into Freddy Dodds's coffers. Five thousand or thereabouts, if Solomon dared to count it. How was he to know that all the opportunities to gamble in this city belonged to Freddy Dodds one way or another? Something Solomon hadn't realized until it was too late.

Now, as he exited the black gates of the Sheriff Court and hurried across George IV Bridge towards the statue of Greyfriars Bobby, Solomon Farthing could feel his hand begin again with its flutter against his muddy corduroys. He had feasted on Edinburgh for a long time, but it seemed that Edinburgh might be about to feast on him.

The statue of the famously faithful dog was surrounded by tourists taking photographs, mainly of themselves. It was a new tradition, rubbing the little dog's nose in the hope of good fortune – only started in the last five years and already the council was trying to ban it. But in the absence of his silver charm, Solomon would take any luck he could get.

'Spare some change, sir.'

A man was sitting on the pavement near the bottom of the statue. A beggar. One of Edinburgh's regulars. And next to him another small dog, alive this time. Solomon pulled his trouser pockets inside out.

'Sorry, Mr Scott. Nothing doing, I'm afraid.'

'Solomon Farthing,' said the beggar. 'Haven't seen you for a while.'

'Hard times, Mr Scott. Hard times.'

The beggar shuffled along a little, indicated that Solomon could share his cardboard if he wished. Why not, Solomon thought. Rich man. Poor man. Beggar man. Thief. He'd been three of them already in his life. Might as well add the fourth. He squatted next to the beggar, felt the touch of a dog's nose cold on his wrist. The dog was wearing a spotted kerchief, as though he were the gentleman and all the rest the knaves.

'How's tricks, Mr Scott?' Solomon asked. 'Good business?'

'So, so,' the beggar replied. 'Worried about the vote. What might happen after.'

Remain or Leave. All anyone was talking about this summer. The same question Solomon was asking himself now. Stay in Edinburgh and face up to his troubles. Or do what he had always done before. Flee. The dog circled and went to sniff at some nearby railings. A passer-by dropped a coin onto the cardboard at Solomon's feet. One pound. Only four thousand, nine hundred and ninety-nine to go. Plus whatever interest Dodds wished to charge, of course. The pound coin glinted in the sunlight, as though it contained real gold rather than fake. But Solomon resisted.

'After you, Mr Scott. After you,' he said.

Begging was a profession in Edinburgh. There was an

established hierarchy, Solomon Farthing at the bottom once again. Like any good Edinburgh Man the beggar did not demur, lifted the coin and tucked it into one of his many pockets.

'Not sure begging will get you what you need.'

Two black boots. Size five. The voice female. Young. Discerning. The inscrutable PC Noble returned to taunt Solomon with those impenetrable eyes. Despite the mud dried now on cuff and knee, he attempted a dignified demeanour.

'Something I can help you with, officer?'

'You forgot these,' PC Noble replied.

She was holding out a small plastic bag, transparent, so that everyone in the city could see at a glance what Solomon Farthing was worth now:

A packet of orange tic tacs, almost empty;

A Nokia with no charge;

The half-shell of a walnut rubbed to its bones.

He stretched his hand to take the bag, but PC Noble dropped it at his feet instead.

'Don't bother to get up.'

She really was magnificent.

Solomon tipped the contents onto the pavement – all his worldly goods tumbled at the feet of Greyfriars Bobby. It made a certain kind of sense. The dog with the kerchief returned to sniff at each of the items, gave the walnut shell a cursory lick. Solomon slid the dead Nokia into his jacket pocket, along with the tic tacs, realized PC Noble was offering him something else, too.

'You forgot this.'

Small. And white. A business card. The sort of thing a

proper Edinburgh Man might carry. Or an Edinburgh Lady, of course.

On one side, in neat black print, the card said:

DCI Franklin.

On the other, scribbled in biro,

You owe me.

Solomon Farthing felt it then, that flutter in his hand. There was a reckoning to be had, and it was coming sooner than he had anticipated it might.

Three

Seven thirty-two a.m. and Solomon woke from a dream of dark water for a meeting that was due to start at eight. Pain pressed in behind his left eye as he turned with a groan, wondering if this was the moment his universe might explode. Aneurism in the brain. *Pop*. All over. No one to look after him but that dreadful Penny woman from the Office for Lost People, come to pick over what was left of his life like some sort of carrion poking through the bones.

He'd phoned DCI Franklin the day before, as instructed, lifted the receiver like a boy expecting trouble, only to be offered something else instead.

'I've got a case you might be interested in,' DCI Franklin had said. 'Fresh. Not even gone to UH yet.'

Ultimus Haeres, the Last Heir – his usual hunting ground.

'It has your name all over it. No win no fee.'

No win no fee used to get Solomon's heart jumping. Now he worried it might tip him off the scales of life for good.

'What sort of case?' he'd asked.

The DCI had been evasive. 'You'll find out if you say yes.'

'A favour, then.'

She'd laughed at that, the short bark of a fox in the

25

night. 'We both know it's the other way around. I'll pick you up at eight.'

Solomon got dressed as best he could in the time he had left, drenched himself with patchouli body spray picked up cheap from the local Scotmid to disguise the fact that he hadn't managed to shower. The grandfather clock in the hall began to strike the hour as he attempted to smooth his reflection in its glass.

Ding

Ding

Ding.

Eight a.m. and counting, small sun rising. Quick lick of his thumb across a mud stain on his shoe, then up through his hair. He would surprise the DCI with his punctuality. But when Solomon opened the front door she was outside already, waiting to surprise him.

He'd looked her up, of course, DCI Franklin and all her antecedents. A fox to catch a fox, wasn't that the idea? Insurance, Solomon called it, the ability to dig for family secrets, a perk of his profession. He used to do it for all those from whom he might one day require a favour.

You scratch my back and I'll scratch yours.

Needless to say DCI Franklin's relatives had turned out to be run-of-the-mill charlatans and pretenders like most ordinary folk. A few names changed here, a bit of slipperiness on dates of birth there, a patina of legitimacy. Nothing that any reputable Heir Hunter hadn't dealt in every time he opened a new case. It wasn't that long ago people wanted to hide anything disreputable or illegal, nothing to show but one perfect generation after the next.

But even in Edinburgh – a place as dirty underneath as it liked to appear clean on the surface – Solomon knew that things were beginning to change. Nowadays all the amateurs revelled in whatever squalor they could find. Adultery. Bigamy. Madness of a virulent sort. Wore their genealogical discoveries like a badge of triumph, as though they added colour to otherwise colourless lives. It had destroyed Solomon's job really, this absence of shame. That and the Internet, of course. Opened all of Pandora's boxes at once without so much as a specialist like him to intervene.

And yet . . .

There had been one thing where the DCI was concerned. A baby boy carried off by a nurse years ago, before his mother even had the chance to touch his tiny toes.

A favour, the DCI had called it when she asked him to look. Just as she was repaying Solomon with another favour, now. One last chance to turn the wheel of fortune in a more favourable direction, as he had spun it for her. A little digging here. A few questions there. Then stand aside and watch the DCI's long-lost son surface, as though he had been waiting for her to find him all along. Solomon had heard through the city grapevine that the DCI was in touch with the boy now, a young man grown glorious off the back of both his mothers. He was glad. Solomon had a lot of time for DCI Franklin. What did it mean to lose a child, he often wondered, because you made a mistake once when you were still a child yourself.

Now, as he made to open the passenger door at the front of the DCI's car, she didn't say a thing to greet him, just indicated with a silent incline of her head that he should get into the back. As they pulled away from the kerb, Solomon sank low into the leather, wondered what the neighbours would say as they watched him being escorted from the premises by somebody whose car alone suggested three letters before her name. That elegant Edinburgh crescent full of elegant Edinburgh Men. Accountants and Financiers. Solicitors and Advocates. Not to mention a sheriff somewhere on the opposing side. Though she was an Edinburgh Lady, of course, a whole different breed. Why was it, Solomon thought as the DCI's car glided away, that he always ended up surrounded by the law?

They proceeded at a stately pace towards their destination, no sense of urgency despite the early morning call. All the way along Solomon could smell it – fresh earth and a thousand sticky buds blooming. Unlike him, the city's sap was rising now.

'Bit early for a case conference, isn't it?' he said as they passed a group of children making their way to school.

'Not exactly in a position to choose, are you?' the DCI replied.

It wasn't a question so much as a statement of the facts. What did the DCI know about his current circumstances? Then again, this was Edinburgh. What did the DCI not know about what went on in her patch.

'Besides, you owe me for that fuss you made at Gayfield.' F words and C words and words that DCI Franklin must have heard a million times. 'You should know by now not to take my name in vain.'

Solomon flushed. Embarrassment, or the after-effects

of a bottle of Fino drunk to the last the night before, he couldn't be sure. He shrank even further into the leather as the car took a left turn down a road that seemed all too familiar. Generous driveway. French windows at the back. The sudden cloying scent of a lilac bush blooming in the night. Whatever Solomon had been expecting, it was not a return to the home of a dead man little more than forty-eight hours since he had broken into it himself.

But the real scene of the crime turned out not to be the site of his recent Breaking and Entering, rather a nursing home built on the brow of a hill in Edinburgh's south-east. The home specialized in soldiers – a last resting place for the old guard, counting them out one by one, just as once their officers had counted them in. The Reckoning, that was what Solomon's grandfather used to call it, a roll call of those who were still living after the battle's end, compared to those who had been lost.

The entrance to the home was adorned with a centenary banner:

1916–2016 Celebrating 100 years of serving the troops.

'Started life as a hospital for the limbless,' said DCI Franklin as she pulled into a space marked *reserved*.

Another form of reckoning, Solomon thought as he clambered from the back seat. The naming of body parts after a shell has fallen:

One arm;

Two arms;

Two legs;

Five fingers.

All that was left of a man on which he could rebuild.

Inside, the home was full of people who still had most

of their limbs but were wandering the corridors as though they knew where they were going, when (rather like him) Solomon knew that they did not. A little shudder rippled through him. Despite his job and everything that came with it, Solomon didn't really like the elderly. The terrible stink and cloy of old age.

The DCI flashed her badge and set off down a long corridor. Solomon followed, before being intercepted by an elderly man wearing slippers and a tracksuit embroidered with some sort of crest. The old man winked at Solomon as he attempted to pass.

'Hello, sailor. Want to go below?'

His eyes a sudden, startling blue. Solomon blinked as the man's attendant, a young woman with hair like molasses, laughed and touched her patient's shoulder.

'Come on now, Mr R. You know he's not your type.'

What did she know, Solomon thought, as the old chap was led away. He always had enjoyed the company of servicemen. They had a good sense of humour, dark and degraded. Liked a drink, too.

As he continued down the corridor in pursuit of the DCI, Solomon found his old instincts kicking in. Eyes left. Eyes right. Looking for anything that would tell him who to target first. A hint of hidden wealth, of absent family members waiting to be hunted. Or even better, the smell of loneliness, that whiff which meant any relatives he did find would be distant and untethered, the sort to sign straight away if they were offered the right price. Whatever their generally unhealthy appearance, Solomon knew there was money to be made in an old folks' home. All those properties worth a million left empty by decrepitude, just waiting to be plucked. Perhaps Solomon could chat to Mr R. over a lunch of peas and omelette, identify a likely candidate for his next foray into the past. When he caught up with DCI Franklin at the door to one of the bedrooms, the look on her face suggested she knew exactly what he had been thinking, didn't like where it might lead.

'After you,' she said opening the door without even knocking.

It reminded Solomon of his entry to that cell at Gayfield – a place from which there might be no escape.

The dead man's name was Thomas Methven. At least that was what DCI Franklin said. Solomon wondered how long that name would stick given the blank slate of their surroundings. A bed. A wardrobe. A chair. Not even an antimacassar. Nothing to indicate that a life had taken place here, let alone a death.

'How old?' he asked.

'Ninety-five, maybe, ninety-six,' said the DCI. 'No one's quite sure. Wife died twenty years ago or so. No children that we're aware of.'

'Siblings?'

'Only child.'

Solomon couldn't resist a small smile at the idea of a big space all around the dead man on whatever family tree might grow from his demise.

'What about his next of kin?' he said. 'Have they been informed?'

'There aren't any,' said the DCI. 'At least none that anyone knows about. That's where you come in.'

That, and the money, of course.

Fifty thousand in used notes. That was what it amounted to. The treasure Thomas Methven had left behind.

'Sewn inside his burial suit,' said the DCI.

'What?' Solomon had come across lots of odd things in his career as an Heir Hunter. But he'd never heard of that before. Money for a funeral worn like a second skin.

'The undertaker found it when she came to dress him,' said DCI Franklin. 'Called the home. They called us. Said it was about fifty thousand, give or take.'

Despite the early morning hour, Solomon felt a sudden tingle inside at the prospect of this case. Fifty thousand. In cash. Twenty per cent of which would start to sort his problem very nicely indeed, thank you very much.

'Don't suppose he left any instructions about what to do with it?' he asked.

Where there was a will there was a way, but not for an Heir Hunter. A will was the last thing Solomon wanted to stumble across.

'Not that we can find,' said the DCI. 'No idea where the money came from or where it should go. The home thought he was an indigent. They were about to call Margaret Penny at the Office for Lost People and get them to arrange the cremation when I stepped in.'

Fifty thousand up in smoke, thought Solomon, saved by the DCI to live another day.

'Why don't you investigate yourself?' he asked.

The DCI leaned against the doorframe. She seemed tired all of a sudden. 'It's legit. The death's non-suspicious, signed off by the GP. No reason to pursue it further than the sudden death report.'

Solomon understood at once what she meant. Cuts.

Cuts. And more cuts. That was what it amounted to. Till they were all sliced down to the marrow, let alone the bone. He'd heard all about the demise of the Edinburgh Enquiry Team, those specialists in non-suspicious death, dispersed to the four winds, north, south, east and west. All the experts were gathered at a flashy new crime campus on the other side of the country now. Glasgow always had worn whatever wealth it had on its sleeve. Whereas Edinburgh (rather like the deceased Thomas Methven) preferred to keep it under wraps.

'Why not just pass it over to UH?' he said. 'Let them deal with it.'

A cursory trawl for potential inheritors by the crown office, then publish it on their lists and watch the vultures like him pile in.

'We will if you can't find a living relative,' said DCI Franklin. 'Thought you might like to have a go first.'

Solomon smiled.

You scratch my back and I'll scratch yours.

'Where's the money now?' he asked sliding open every one of Thomas Methven's empty drawers with a casual air.

'In the nursing-home safe,' said the DCI.

'Don't you want to secure it?'

'We will if you can't find anyone to claim it,' she said. 'Till then it's lost property, nothing more.'

Finders Keepers, thought Solomon.

'How long do I have?' he asked.

'Four days.'

'Four days!'

'Only so much I can do to detain the paperwork.'

And Solomon knew exactly what paperwork meant. Margaret Penny of the Office for Lost People wading in and wanting to know why an old man's last wishes hadn't been respected. Fifty thousand up in smoke inside Thomas Methven's burial suit because she was a stickler for the rules. He fiddled with the edge of the nylon net curtains hanging at the window, looked out over the deceased's last view of the world. Would it be to his advantage to play hard to get? he wondered. But when Solomon turned back, the DCI was dipping a hand into her pocket, as though fishing for a lucky charm recovered from between a dead man's floorboards.

'There is one more thing that recommends you.'

Solomon blanched, tried to joke. 'Family silver?'

DCI Franklin smiled then as though she'd known all along it was the right thing to involve him. She pulled her hand from her pocket, held the treasure out. Not a silver cap badge with a lion raising its paw. But a pawn ticket, no.125. That small slip of blue.

1918

One

It was November, the beginning of an uneventful month, nothing but cold mornings and ice fringing the shaving bucket, air that covered them all in a blanket of dew the moment they ventured out. The rain was falling again as though to turn the world into a river, water running with abandon through the pond beyond the farmhouse – in one side, out the other – each small channel joining with the next until it had become something to wade through whenever one of them wanted the latrine.

Captain Godfrey Farthing stared out of the farmhouse window at the pools gathering in the yard. It was just like the river they were supposed to be crossing, he thought, if only the order would come. A stretch of water a mile or so away, flat and unexceptional, bordered by willows not yet destroyed by machine-gun fire. Godfrey had been on reconnaissance to survey their embarkation point. Found it all disappointingly ordinary. Saplings and stubby reed beds, a grassy field on the opposite bank with no distinguishing features other than the likelihood that this was where the enemy would shoot them all down.

He'd come away wondering whether it really was worth the effort, wriggling in reverse through the dips and troughs of the intervening marsh until his uniform was soaked and stained. As he'd walked back to the farmhouse where what remained of his unit had made their billet, all

Godfrey could imagine was the impossibility of traversing such a flat and undistinguished piece of land without exposing his men wholesale to the enemy. They'd probably drown in some drainage ditch along the way, floundering beneath a shower of bullets before they even got their chance. It would be a stupid death, unnecessary, like a toddler fallen into a neighbour's ornamental pool. But then again, wasn't that what the war had become now? Something stupid to do every day because, well, they hadn't been instructed to do anything else.

The whole thing reminded him of Private Beach.

I'll be seeing you, then.

Speaking his goodbye as though he was going home for tea rather than into the great lacuna of death. It was not until much later that Godfrey wondered if in fact Beach's words had been more prescient than he realized.

I'll be seeing you, then.

If only he had listened. Too late now.

'You know the end is coming.' Second Lieutenant Ralph Svenson tipped his chair as though he was at school again declaiming amongst the sixth-formers (which he had been, not long since). 'A matter of days now, maybe a week.'

Godfrey refused to look up from the postcard he was supposed to be writing to his mother. 'We've heard that one before.'

It said everything about the difference between them that Second Lieutenant Ralph Svenson tipped his chair without thinking, while Captain Godfrey Farthing couldn't bear to watch.

They had been waiting almost ten days already and still

no orders had reached them, not even of the most trivial kind. No drilling instructions or supply counts. No demands to dig ditches where no ditches were required. It was as though they had been forgotten, sent forwards to make camp, then abandoned, nothing left for the section to do but sit tight as the war rolled on in front. Godfrey knew he ought to send a messenger, ask why the rest of his company had not joined them yet. But as each morning dawned greyer than the next, he had found himself putting it off, then off again, one day pooling quietly into the next.

'No, but really.' Ralph tipped forwards now, leaning towards Godfrey across the table as though to emphasize what he had to say. 'I think it might be true this time.' Tapped with his fingers on the edge of Godfrey's postcard.

Godfrey stared at the boy's scrubbed nails. *Dear Mother, they say the end is coming* . . . Slid the card a fraction away from Ralph Svenson's hand.

Second Lieutenant Svenson was a boy really, only nineteen, but still a commissioned officer, not been in the war six months. He'd arrived too late for any sort of real action, with a grin as wide as the Channel and that scent of lemon oil he liked to slick through his hair. He was the new subaltern, an unwelcome reminder that Godfrey had already forgotten the name of his last. That was what happened when all your men disappeared. You got reassigned to the company of strangers; had to go back to the start. Godfrey knew he should have taken the boy under his wing, been a sort of father-figure. But he found he could not. Ralph had a way about him that resisted instruction. Also something that was lost to Godfrey now – the exhausting eagerness of youth.

Ralph withdrew his hand, sulking, tilted his chair again and fiddled with something in his pocket as he stared out of the window with those strange translucent eyes. Godfrey knew that his Second was bored. A young man hardened by a few weeks in a drill square, abandoned to lounge around in the muck.

'It's not fair,' the boy had complained only the day before, fed up with parading the men to no purpose. 'They've left us here to rot.'

Ralph hadn't taken part in any battles yet. No crouching in a muddy dip waiting to be sliced by shrapnel. No running at the enemy with bayonets fixed. That was why he liked to feast on rumours of the end. Second Lieutenant Ralph Svenson was hoping they would not come true yet.

The farmhouse they had commandeered was a lavish affair – practically Versailles after everything that had gone before. The rats. The dugouts. The low stink of gas. Foxholes with finger bones poking from the sides. By contrast their new billet had stone walls and a roof thick with tiles, windows that still had both shutters and glass. There were outbuildings big enough for a horse and a cow, had there been any livestock left. There was a barn for the men to bunk in. A grain store in which Private Flint had strung the washing wall to wall. Also the worn stub of a boot-scrape at the front entrance, as though what mattered above all else here was at least an attempt at keeping clean.

While they waited Godfrey had set himself and Ralph up in the parlour. Fireplace with a wooden mantel. Narrow settle set along one wall. A table stained with the ring of a vase. Also a small crucifix hanging to the left of the door.

Godfrey liked to touch the crucifix before he went to bed each night. A reminder of all that was past for him now. And what might still be to come.

There was even a rose bush in the garden – the promise of spring, Godfrey had thought when they first arrived, if any of them lasted long enough to see. Great blowsy things in pink and orange, perhaps, scattering fragrant petals to the summer winds.

Beach would have declared it a palace.

Now that's really something.

First spoken as they crouched beneath the third day of a bombardment that turned out later to be useless for all concerned.

As they had approached the farmhouse that first day, single file along the muddy lane, Godfrey had thought it a palace, too. Yet still he had anticipated pushing open the door to find disaster. A man sprawled on the hearth with a bullet through his face. A woman slumped over the kitchen table, throat sliced, skirt hitched high. It was how they all encountered the new these days – as though they could taste death before it landed, that urge rising within them to run back to what they all understood best. The mud. The guns. The relentless train rides to disaster. The knowledge that the end was coming whether they liked it or not.

But then the chicken had appeared, strolling around the corner of the grain store, followed by another and another, a whole flock of them scraping and pecking about Captain Godfrey Farthing's feet. The chicken had turned its black eye upon Godfrey as though to ask a question, made him think of Beach's eyes the morning that he died.

Then he had caught the lazy flap of an apron on a clothes line; a row of winter cabbages wrapped in scraps of sacking to protect them from the frost. Who looked after their cabbages, he thought, if they themselves had been ravaged? The men obviously agreed, because behind him Godfrey had heard them walking faster then, two-by-two down the lane, breath clouding in the cold air of yet another year winding towards its end.

In the parlour, Second Lieutenant Ralph Svenson got up all of a sudden and retrieved a rough wooden cup from the mantel. He placed it on the table before Godfrey, then delved into his uniform and produced a pair of dice.

'Two sixes and it'll be over in a week.'

Ralph called the dice his lucky charm, wouldn't go anywhere without them. Godfrey had refrained from pointing out that his Second was putting his trust in something random. Might as well take his chances raising his head above the parapet of a front-line trench to check the direction of the wind.

Now he ignored Ralph's request and considered what to write on the blank expanse of his postcard.

Dear Mother . . .

'Two fives, ten days.'

We are all going on fine here . . .

'Two threes, a month.'

The weather is wet . . .

'C'mon, Farthing,' Ralph grumbled. 'Aren't you even going to take a punt?'

Godfrey gripped at his stub of pencil. 'You know I don't gamble.'

'We all gamble.'

Godfrey blinked. Ralph Svenson was wrong about a lot of things, but he was right about that. 'All right. Two fives, then.'

Ralph grinned, shook the wooden cup as though he was mixing some sort of cocktail, tumbled the dice onto the table.

A six and a three. No win. Not even close.

At once Ralph began again, rattling off the various combinations he was sure would secure the correct result. Two threes. A five and a one. Two sixes followed by a two and a four together. He threw to bet on when the war might end – in a week, in a fortnight, in a month. At least that was what he told Godfrey. But Godfrey knew it was the other way around. Ralph threw in the hope of one last battle; some reason to flash his pistol before the other side strung whatever white linen they had left above the line.

It was almost admirable, Godfrey thought now, Ralph's belief in his ability to summon the result that he desired, even if that was the extension of the war long enough for him to fire his gun. The boy did it in the same way he might order up a cocktail.

Gin fizz, cherry on the side, please.

With a simple wave of his hand. A bit like Godfrey's ability to summon Beach.

I'll be seeing you, then.

Those flat grey eyes.

Godfrey looked again at the blank card beneath his hand, Ralph's dice spinning once again. He had never tasted a cocktail until he came to France. Then it had been just the one in a bar a few miles back from the line that first year. An intoxicating mix of brandy and champagne that had sent him spinning, too. He'd never wanted a second in case it didn't live up to the first. But recently he had started to wonder if this was some sort of handicap to living. Enjoyment wasn't a sin, was it? Or anticipation? The end might come, after all. But after that, there would always be something else.

There was a sudden commotion outside in the yard, men shouting, others laughing, a flurry of squawks and flaps. Ralph stopped with the dice and cup.

'It's time,' he said.

For the end, thought Godfrey, if only for the poultry. His Second Lieutenant stood, pushed his chair in towards the parlour table.

'Want to join us?'

Godfrey looked at the blank piece of card before him, nothing written on it but the date, *5 November*. Then at his second. Ralph's eyes were pale, very clear, like Godfrey imagined a glacier might be if he ever had the opportunity to see one close.

> *Dear Mother and Father,*
> *We are all going on fine here. The weather is wet, but we have plenty to eat and the conditions are favourable. Yesterday I walked into the village and drank a cocktail.*

It couldn't be any worse than what had happened so far, could it, thought Godfrey, the sudden fizz of bubbles on his tongue.

'I think I'll go for a walk,' he said, putting down his pencil. 'Clear my head.'

'If you're certain.'

Ralph was already at the door, one eager hand through his hair, the other tugging at his tunic, disappearing into the stone passageway with a shout to the men outside.

'I'm coming.'

The clamour from the yard growing louder, someone shouting in turn.

'Catch the bugger!'

Ralph calling excited instructions.

'This way. Over here now.'

Nothing more than a leader amongst boys.

Godfrey slipped the postcard into his top pocket, the pencil in beside, buttoned them both down. He got up from the table with its water stain, lifted his coat from the back of his parlour chair. He would leave the men to their fun, go out the back so as not to get in the way of their game. They liked to play with life and death, even if it was just a chicken, throw the dice and decide which one would be next. But if the end really was coming, Godfrey Farthing wasn't sure that he wanted any part of it yet.

Two

The real game had begun the second night after they'd arrived, light fallen from the sky as seven men spread themselves amongst the ground sheets, across the barn's stone floor:

Hawes, the temporary sergeant;

Private Flint;

Private Walker;

Corporal Bertie Fortune;

Private Jackson, known as Jackdaw;

Private Promise;

And Lance Corporal Archie Methven, the accountant. The man who kept them all straight.

Seven o'clock and already dark outside, their cook, George Stone, cleaning up after dinner in the farmhouse kitchen, and it was Percy Flint who had brought out the cards. Hair slick. Cuffs turned neat. His parting a white arrow on his scalp.

'Six playing,' Flint said. 'Me. Walker. Fortune. Promise. Jackdaw. Hawes. The accountant to hold the bank.'

Gambling was forbidden in the army, but everybody did it. One more way to get through the day, until the next one dawned.

'Not me.'

James Hawes, the temporary sergeant, was sitting a bit away from the others, reading a book with a faded red cover, thick arms, and a splatter of freckles across the back of his neck. When he'd first arrived over two years before, James Hawes had joined in every game. Now he almost never gambled, turned and turned the pages instead.

'Five, then,' said Flint. 'Walker, Fortune, Jackdaw, Promise. Me to deal.' Percy Flint liked to lay out the parameters. Transactional arrangements were where he came to the fore.

The men who were going to play gathered around a small area swept clean of grit and straw with the sweep of Flint's sleeve.

'Give us a light, Fortune,' Flint instructed, sifting the cards between one hand, then the next.

Corporal Bertie Fortune had dug a paraffin lamp from an outbuilding during a foraging trip the day before. With his quick grin and easy wink, Fortune was the section's fixer, could get anything anyone wanted, as long as a man was prepared to pay. He fiddled now with the lamp's wick, crouching close and pulling at the ends of his neat moustache as he waited to see if the match would take. The flame puttered, then rose with its sudden glow, Fortune sitting back with a satisfied nod. The lamp was faulty, gave off a strong stink of fumes. But the barn was high roofed, its wooden skeleton far above. Outside the rain was falling again. Inside it was warm, everywhere the sweet scent of cut hay.

Percy Flint shuffled the cards, one hand slicing over another, before neatening the edges again and beginning the deal. He tossed the cards towards each man, one by one, letting them land where they would. The players scooped their share from the floor, each taking a quick look, before rummaging in their pockets for whatever they were prepared to bet first.

A matchstick.

A button.

A spool of pink cotton.

Trust Percy Flint to have the one thing that reminded them all of the French girls who used to serve *vin blanc* at the bars behind the line.

'What did you swap that for, Flint?' said Private Alfred Walker.

'Don't ask,' Flint replied with a smirk.

The men laughed. Flint was older than the rest. One of the married conscripts who'd held out as long as possible before being driven to the recruiting officer's door by shame.

'Had to leave the wife at home to do it all alone,' he'd whined when he first arrived, to anyone who might listen.

But Flint knew and they all knew that he should have come earlier. A quick return for a cheap pack of fags, humping around the back of an estaminet. That was Percy Flint's main currency. War and its dirty consolations had turned out to be the perfect playground for a man like him.

'Play on now, if you're ready.'

Archibald Methven, the accountant, sat back from the inner circle, holding his notebook, keeping an eye on the score as the men began. One ace. One ten of spades. One five. Three to make fifteen. Back to the ace again. Methven was a quiet man, steady, old enough to be put in charge of the armoury or anything else that needed counting. How many bullets were spare. Who had a knobstick. What man had managed to acquire a knife. They all knew Archie Methven had a beauty himself, taken from an alley man one night when Fortune and Beach had visited them in their trench. Beach had come back with a ribbon the colour of an Irish summer, had tied it to his pack like a pennant on a lance. Whereas Bertie Fortune had bartered his stolen knife with Archie Methven, who knew what for. The men had been trying to persuade Methven to swap the knife ever since. But the accountant did not give up his prizes easily. Liked to keep them tucked into his gasbag, just in case.

The men played in silence for a while, nothing but the smoky gutter of the lamp and the *spitter spatter* of raindrops on the barn's roof to accompany the scuffle of their cards. It was Bertie Fortune who started it, the section's lucky man.

'Any of you lot heard the rumour?'

Mention of the *chitter chatter* that had been going up and down the line for weeks now. That the end was coming, sooner rather than not.

'I'll believe that when the captain gets it in black and white.' Flint spat into the shadow behind the circle, always the pessimist. 'Until then it isn't over. Why else did they send us here if it wasn't to have another go?'

'To eat the chickens before anyone else could,' Alfred Walker replied, grinning.

Private Alfred Walker was the joker of the section, barely twenty-one and always after the main chance, a soldier by profession but a petty thief by inclination. And habit, too. Alfred Walker always whistled as he polished his rifle, wore his hair a bit longer than was regulation.

He liked to duck his head beneath the pump each morning, shake silver droplets all across the yard, laughing in a way that made them all want to join in.

'One chicken a week,' said Archie Methven now, licking his pencil and making a mark in his notebook. 'That's what the captain's ordered.'

'Who says?' said Walker.

'Stone. He's in charge of the rations.'

George Stone had taken to the kitchen as though he was born to it, plucking the apron from the washing line that first morning and folding it around himself like some sort of skirt. Stone was an old sweat, one of those who had been in the army before this latest war began, seen it all before.

'Christ,' said Alfred Walker now, throwing down his latest hand. 'It'll take us forever to get through them, then.'

'I think that's the point,' said Archie Methven.

'Need to petition for better rations.'

Bertie Fortune gestured to the two boys crouched together on the far side of the circle, Privates Jackson and Promise, knees almost touching, one dark, one fair.

'You, Jackdaw,' he said pointing towards the darker boy. 'You could do with feeding up.'

Jackdaw grinned at that, tossed a black cowl of hair from his forehead, pretended to puff out his chest. 'You calling me skinny?'

'Like a tent pole.'

'A bean stick.'

'A chicken bone sucked dry.'

Jackdaw laughed at the banter, black eyes a-sparkle. 'I will, then.'

'He doesn't need extra rations. He's getting his fill in the hayloft.'

Flint's voice was low, but they all heard him. Arthur Promise, the fairer of the two boys, blushed and looked away. There was a sour moment of silence. Jackdaw broke it with a jibe of his own.

'You're just frustrated, Flint. Not getting your usual.'

Everybody laughed then, even Hawes in his corner. Flint couldn't help himself. Spent most of the last year avoiding any action via thirty-day stints in the military hospital for VD.

'Now, now,' said Bertie Fortune, ever the one to try and broker a deal. 'Keep it clean, why don't you.'

He glanced towards the two boys on the opposite side of the circle, watching as Arthur Promise put his hand on Jackdaw's arm for a moment, before taking it away. Jackdaw and Promise were A4 conscripts – the last round to be drafted in. 'A' class, meaning fit to serve, but no longer allowed to wait until they were nineteen to see the inside of a front-line trench. The A4 boys had been sent over because all the rest were crippled or dead; two weeks' training then into the big spring push, only eighteen and already up to their armpits in the battlefield, been inseparable ever since. It amazed Bertie Fortune that they were still alive.

Percy Flint scowled and gathered in the cards, shuffled and began to deal once more. The men played in silence for a while, nothing but the murmurs of satisfaction or dismay as the betting rose and fell. It was Alfred Walker who started the chat again, laying an eight of diamonds to win a trick, gathering in the small bets with a quick grin as the others threw in their hands.

'I'm going to America,' he said as they waited for Archie Methven to make his calculations. 'When it's all done. '

'What d'you want to go there for?' said Bertie Fortune. 'Plenty of money in England if you know where to look.'

'All right for you, Fortune. You can smell money before it's even minted. What you going back to anyway?'

'Rag-and-bone man,' said Fortune as though it was the industry of kings. 'I'm going to be rich.'

'Don't forget us when you make it,' laughed Walker. 'Every one a deserving cause.'

'What about you, Promise?' said Bertie Fortune, looking across the circle towards the fairer A4 boy. 'What do you want to do?'

They all knew that Jackdaw and Promise had never even had a job before they joined the army. Eighteen and barely minted, didn't know any sort of life other than marching and shooting and doing what they were told.

'I don't know,' said Promise, face rosy from the heat of the paraffin lamp. 'Something with boys, perhaps. Maybe a teacher?'

Flint snorted. 'You'll fit right in, then.'

'Well, we all know what you'll do when you get home, Flint,' Hawes growled from his corner. 'No need to give us the sordid details.'

But this time Flint didn't rise, tapped the cards on the floor to square the pack and said, 'I'll go back to work, won't I. Go on the same as before.'

'What did you do before?' asked Bertie Fortune.

'Delivery driver.'

Alfred Walker whistled. 'What, one in each port?'

Flint flicked a bit of dirty straw in the petty thief's direction.

'You wish,' he said. 'At least I'll be getting some. Whereas you'll be wasting your dreams on a promised land that'll probably never arrive.'

'Got to dream.' Alfred Walker grinned, tossing a penny he had won into the air, before slipping it into his pocket. 'Otherwise what's the point.'

'The point is nothing's going to be different when it's done,' said Percy Flint. 'It'll just be the same as always, won't it. Some men'll make all the money and the rest of us'll starve.'

'It'll have to be different though, won't it?' Promise's voice was clear as a schoolboy's. 'After everything that's happened.'

'Don't be an idiot.' Flint was frowning. 'Some men were born to give instruction and others to take it. That's just the way it is.'

'What about you then, Hawes,' said Bertie Fortune, looking over his shoulder towards the temporary sergeant sitting in the shadows. 'Back to the meat?'

Hawes had worked in an abattoir before the war, his arms thick with the muscles of a man who used to saw meat for a living. But they all knew he couldn't stand the sight of blood now.

'Get through tomorrow with my feet dry.' Hawes turned a page of his book. 'No point dreaming about what might never come.'

It was then that Second Lieutenant Ralph Svenson stepped into the light.

'I shall stay in the army,' he said. 'Become a brigadier.'

The men froze like rabbits caught by a poacher in the

night, nothing to see but the glitter of their eyes. Officers did not normally join the ranks for their evening recreation. It was Bertie Fortune who spoke first.

'Anything we can help you with, sir?'

Fortune always had known how to speak to a superior. Second Lieutenant Svenson might only be nineteen, but he wore the officer's stripe.

Ralph gestured with his hand. 'No need to get up.'

Though none of them had given any indication that they might. The young officer blushed slightly.

'I thought I might play,' he said. 'If you don't mind.'

Captain Farthing had warned him against it when Ralph first arrived off the boat from England, dice in his hand. Best leave the men to their own games, that was what he had said. But Ralph didn't see why the men should have all the fun while he sat alone in a parlour. That was not what he considered life.

'I could take a hand now,' he said coming closer. 'Then tomorrow we could play for a chicken. I fancy the red.'

A fat thing. A feast on scaly legs. Strutting around the yard with her feathers plumped as though she owned the place. There was silence for a moment. The men knew they would soon be dreaming of chicken, didn't want to wait a week each time when any moment they might be ordered out. They all looked to Archie Methven, the accountant who kept the bank. Gambling for matchsticks and buttons was one thing. Gambling for fresh breast meat a whole other game.

Methven looked at Ralph from across the small circle, then glanced towards Bertie Fortune. They all knew officers were dangerous territory. But officers often had

the best treasure, too. For a moment there was nothing
but the sound of the rain *pitter pattering* on the roof. Then
Bertie Fortune coughed, leaned back and gave a slight nod
of his head.

At once Ralph moved to sit amongst the men, didn't
even wait to be invited. Alfred Walker shifted to make
space. Percy Flint grimaced, turned his body away. Jackdaw
and Promise seemed to meld even closer together on the
far side of the circle. Bertie Fortune was touching his
moustache again as though uncertain as to whether he had
done the right thing. Behind him Archie Methven wrote
a new name in his little book, then looked up, pencil in
hand, waiting for the game to begin once more. It was
Ralph who broke the silence this time.

'What do you want to do?' he said to Methven. 'When
it's all over.'

The accountant paused, pencil poised over the blank
page of his notebook. Then he said it.

'I want to see my son grow up.'

Three

Godfrey approached the trees just as the men should be cutting the throat of the chicken. One man to hold it down, one to chop with the knife, James Hawes turning away as the blood spurted out.

It had become a routine over the last ten days, the bets on which bird it would be this time. The black one. The red one. The one with the crooked beak. After that, the chase. As far as Godfrey could tell, they were down to the last five or six now. It had been foolishness on his part to let them eat the meat so soon. But Second Lieutenant Svenson had pled their case. And who could blame the men when they had no idea whether the feast would continue indefinitely or end tomorrow, the rest of the company marching towards them down the muddy lane, all the chickens slaughtered in a fifteen-minute frenzy of killing and blood.

The trees were tall, a walk away behind a fold in the land, discovered on the third day as Godfrey Farthing wriggled away from the river through the watery marsh. They had been planted in a ring, the patch of land within as still and silent as the inside of a church. The moment Godfrey had first stepped into the hidden circle, he'd known that this would be his place.

He made no attempt to conceal his approach now, walked swiftly across the ruts and dips of the empty fields towards the isolated grove. He had come several times and never seen anyone arrive or leave. No men out walking the hedgerows. No women collecting brambles or roots.

'They went with the Germans,' Ralph had said that very first evening, upstairs in the attic room they had requisitioned for themselves. 'The farmer and his wife.'

'How do you know?' Godfrey had asked.

'I met a man on the road. From the village.'

Ten miles back across the fields, a hamlet in the middle of what had been enemy territory until the last few weeks. Ralph had twisted his head away, not looking at Godfrey as he said it.

'We could have some fun there until we join the rest of the company.'

'We're not going to join the company,' Godfrey replied.

'Why not?'

Godfrey had turned away himself then. 'We're to wait here for them to join us.'

Now, as he reached the ring of trees, Godfrey was glad that the rest had never arrived to spoil his sanctuary, a haven in amongst the muck. He imagined the land beneath the trees as it might be when spring finally came. Girls from the village fractured by sunlight. Boys saved from slaughter by the fact of their youth. Then later the other women arriving as the sun was going down, standing in amongst the shadows with the only men who were left. Old men. And men who were not able. Perhaps even the enemy if the price was good enough. Lying together within the hidden circle making something of all they had lost.

It seemed a shame that they had all gone now, disappeared from their land as the enemy had disappeared, too. The war had been reduced to a strange kind of absence now that it was nearly done, Godfrey thought. Something ephemeral that he found difficult to pin his thoughts on, as though it had all been some sort of dream. But Godfrey Farthing was still wary. War, he knew, had a way about it, like gas lying in the bottom of a trench. Just when one thought it was over, it rose again to bite.

In the yard, Ralph laid down the rules for the latest game of chicken. No cross bets. No multiples. One mark only per man. All the section gathered around, eager to join the fun. Second Lieutenant Ralph Svenson had proved a valuable source of treasure over the last ten days. Shillings rather than pennies. Boot laces rather than string. Once even an Oxo cube, won by Flint who wouldn't let anyone share.

Only James Hawes, the temporary sergeant, still refused to play.

'Not my kind of game, sir.'

The second week of his resistance. Ralph was not amused. He stood before Hawes in the mud now, hair smoothed back, thumbs hooked on belt loops, frowning at the temporary sergeant.

'It might have to be, Hawes. When we receive the orders.'

'Hoping it won't come to that, sir.'

'We all have to do our duty.'

Hawes didn't reply, big hands stuffed into his pockets, freckles bright amongst the grey. The temporary sergeant had fought several battles already. Duty would not be the reason he took part in any more. Ralph flicked his strange eyes away, then back again.

'You're not afraid, are you, Hawes?' he pressed.

Hawes scowled, muttered something beneath his breath.

Ralph stepped closer. 'What did you say?'

Hawes refused to raise his eyes from the ground. 'Nothing – sir.'

'Yes, you did.'

'Nothing important.'

The younger man flushed, a sudden colour rising in his cheeks. 'It's important to me.'

The ex-abattoir man paused then, lifted his gaze to fix it on the Second. 'I said, I'm not the coward around here.'

Ralph's face shone hot in the damp. They all knew he had never fought in any battles, whatever the rank on his sleeve. It was Bertie Fortune who stepped between them, held out a helmet turned upside down to make a bowl.

'Throw in your bets, gentlemen, or it'll get too dark to play.'

A button.

A centime.

A stub from a candle.

Asked the question they all wanted the answer to.

'What will you be betting today, sir? How about those Woodbines none of us seem able to get our hands on?'

Ralph frowned as Hawes took advantage of the lucky man's intervention to turn away. 'Let's keep them for a big game, shall we, Fortune.'

'When might that be, then, sir?'

All the men looked forward to a big game. It was when the real treasure appeared. For a moment Ralph's eyes shone pale in the grey light, a kind of absence at their centre.

'When we get the orders,' he said.

'What if we never get the orders, sir?'

'Then you lot will never get the chance to win.'

Fortune smiled at that, offered up his makeshift bowl again. Ralph rummaged in his pocket for a penny to toss in, then hesitated, drew out something else instead. A regimental cap badge belonging to a member of the London Scottish, a tiny lion at its centre raising its paw. Also the motto:

Strike Sure.

The men jostled to see the shiny little thing lying in Second Lieutenant Svenson's palm. A cap badge was proper treasure, could be bartered for all sorts.

Walker whistled. 'That's a beauty.'

Jackdaw jiggled on the spot. 'I'd like a shot at it.'

Just like his namesake, Jackdaw loved to collect shiny things. But the older men were frowning now, Bertie Fortune and Archie Methven, eyes fixed on the tiny treasure as though they recognized it from somewhere but couldn't understand how it had arrived here.

'Where's it from?' asked Promise.

Second Lieutenant Svenson did not belong to the London Scottish as far as they knew. Methven glanced at Fortune, the two men looking at each other for a moment before Bertie turned to the young officer.

'Yes, sir. Where did you get it?'

Ralph didn't reply, blinked twice at the section's lucky man. 'Fancy it, do you, Fortune? Could buy a lot of stuff with this.'

It was Percy Flint who interrupted. 'Who cares where it comes from. Let's get on with the game.'

Ralph was the one who was smiling now, staring back at Bertie Fortune with his strange eyes as though daring him to ask again.

'I'll bet it if Hawes plays,' he said.

Fortune flicked his gaze to where Hawes stood at the periphery of the group, half in, half out of the circle, hands still thrust deep in his pockets.

'I'm not sure the sergeant wants to play this time, sir.'

'Afraid he'll have to wield the knife?' said Ralph.

'No, but—'

'I know a coward when I see one, Fortune.' Ralph flipped the silver cap badge from one finger to the next. 'Even if I haven't fired my gun.'

'Let's see it, then.'

James Hawes spoke so quietly that none of the men were sure they'd heard at first. They shifted as the temporary sergeant pushed forward to see what the second lieutenant held in his palm. Fortune put a hand on Hawes's sleeve as though to restrain him.

'No need, James . . .'

But Hawes shook him off, a rough gesture. All of them saw how the temporary sergeant's neck coloured a deep raw crimson as he stared down at the little cap badge. There was silence, nothing but the *scritch* and *coo* of the remaining chickens to remind the men of what they were betting for. Then Hawes withdrew his fist from his pocket, held it out towards Ralph.

'I'll play then,' he said. 'For this.'

Opened his fingers to reveal a tarnished coin in the

centre of his palm. A sixpence. A tanner. Something cheap in return for something precious – not a good deal. The men all stared at the dirty sixpence in Hawes's hand. Then they looked at the second lieutenant to see what he might do. Ralph hesitated, curled his fingers around the cap badge as though he had not really meant to offer it after all. Hawes spoke again, voice low.

'I said, I'll play.'

'I heard you.'

Ralph pushed a hand through his hair, suddenly aware of his fluster. He hesitated, then tossed the cap badge into the upturned helmet as though it was nothing, where it landed with a soft *cling*. The men breathed, began to disperse. Hawes rolled his sleeves up his thick arms. A cap badge for a tanner. It wasn't a good return. But Second Lieutenant Ralph Svenson never could resist a bet.

Up on the rise in the land, Godfrey Farthing looked out across a thousand walnut shells scattered beneath the ring of trees. The shells were black and decomposed, like the bones of a thousand men. Godfrey had walked into the circle that first time before he realized, felt them crunch beneath his boots.

He crouched and picked a half-shell from the ground, found his fingers stained as though with ink.

Dear Mother and Father . . .

Slid it into his pocket next to the one that was still whole.

The farmhouse had been deserted when they first arrived. No farmer with a fatal wound in his chest. No wife in a sticky puddle of her own warm blood. Instead there had been a stone floor swept clean, a scrubbed table, knives in the drawer. In the corner of the kitchen Godfrey had found a basket full of walnuts, dribbled his hand amongst them before sliding one into his pocket, wondered how they had survived.

The rain *pitter pattered* through the naked branches above Godfrey's head. He tilted his face to feel the drops cold on his cheeks, opened his mouth wide to catch a few. It was a game he used to play when he was a boy, counting how many he could capture, one frozen sting on his tongue after another, the taste of being alive. He dropped his head again, glanced at his wristwatch, hair covered in a maze of tiny silver beads. Four twenty-three p.m. and the skies beginning to turn. The watch-strap was damp, still felt odd against his skin, a gift from his father that last time he'd been home.

'Don't forget to wind it,' the old man had said as Godfrey first strapped it on. 'Hopefully it will keep time.'

Neither of them had mentioned the kind of time Godfrey might need to measure – counting down the minutes until he blew the whistle and sent all his boys scrabbling to their deaths. Like most fathers and sons, nothing that mattered was ever spoken between them. But now, as Godfrey saw how the circlet of gold glinted in what remained of the light, he remembered the care with which his father had showed him how to wind the grand-father clock when he was young, and realized that perhaps his father had spoken after all.

Across the silent space there was a sudden movement, something flitting across Godfrey's vision like a chicken disappearing into the barn. At once he stilled, his body alert to every possibility, everything shaded, the afternoon mist closing in. But it was nothing more than a rabbit foraging for its supper, as the men in the yard would be foraging for theirs. Godfrey smiled, leaned his hand against the trunk of the nearest tree. He would not tell Ralph that he had seen a living creature this close to the farmhouse. Second Lieutenant Svenson would bring his revolver and shoot up the whole countryside in pursuit of the game. He had been waiting for months to fire it in anything other than training. Wanted to return home clad in the blood of the enemy, rather than the ever-present mud.

Godfrey stirred at the decomposing matter on the ground with his boot, thought of all those soldiers sifted into the loam. The chickens would have forgotten already that there was one less of them than there had been an hour before; returned to their pecking and their preening, their squabbling after any leftover seed. They were the perfect creatures for war, Godfrey thought. Small brains. Dealt with what was in front of them rather than anything that was past. Probably didn't contemplate the future either – roast, boiled, stewed or fried. George Stone had done every variation over the last couple of weeks, then tossed the bones into the pot for stock. Life had a way of going on despite what men did to it. There was something pleasing in that.

Godfrey took a last glance across the circle of trees wondering if it might be better to live the life of a chicken than to be a man at war. Then he saw it again, that movement in the undergrowth, and realized it was not a rabbit at all, but a boy, standing silent on the opposite edge of the trees. The boy was wearing a uniform, but he appeared too young for battle. Godfrey raised a hand by way of salute, but the boy did not respond. Then Godfrey blinked and when he looked again the boy was gone.

Down at the farmhouse they had played for an hour, a yard full of men breathless from the chase, mud and chicken shit smeared across their breeches and their boots. George Stone had already gone inside to start the preparations for that night's supper. Jackdaw was on his arse in the mud, Alfred Walker laughing and offering a hand to haul him up. James Hawes stood to one side, his hands on his knees, panting in an attempt to get some breath into his lungs. Percy Flint brushed at a smear of dirt on the shirt he had washed only the day before.

'Fuck's sake.'

Arthur Promise stood by the pump with a yellow chicken cradled in his arms. He was the winner this time.

In the entrance to the barn, protected from the rain, Archie Methven made a note in his little book as Bertie Fortune itemized the winnings. A couple of pennies. Three hand-rolled tabs. A walnut from Stone. The tanner from Hawes. Also that little silver cap badge with a lion raising its paw.

Strike Sure.

Second Lieutenant Ralph Svenson came to stand by the barn door, dirt all across his brow, colour high as he stared at the array of treasures lined along the helmet's upturned rim.

'Sorry, sir,' said Fortune. 'Better luck next time.'

Ralph flushed, pushed hair from his forehead. Then before Bertie Fortune could protest, he scooped the little bets into his hands.

'I'll do the honours this time, shall I?'

Sauntered across to where Promise stood beaming by the pump with a yellow chicken beneath his arm. Ralph held out the winnings for Promise to take. The A4 boy hesitated, then reached out to claim his prize. The chicken struggled and flapped as Promise picked each little object from Ralph's hand, stuffed them one by one into his trouser pocket. Until he came to the silver cap badge. Second Lieutenant Ralph Svenson closed his fingers over that particular treasure, slid the badge into his own pocket instead.

Promise hesitated, suddenly confused. Jackdaw came over to stand next to his friend.

'Hey. He won that fair and square, didn't he.'

Ralph smiled, slouched a little in front of the two other lads.

'I changed my mind.'

'You can't do that!'

Jackdaw was annoyed, but Promise was silent, the yellow chicken squawking and pecking at his sleeve. Bertie Fortune came over.

'Is there a problem?'

'He won't pay his debt,' said Jackdaw, gesturing to the second lieutenant.

Fortune flicked a warning glance towards the darker A4 boy. Then he turned towards Ralph.

'You sure about this, sir? You did offer it.'

Ralph gazed at the section's lucky man, a faint scent of citrus hanging in the air.

'Quite sure, Fortune. Thank you.'

'Got to pay our debts, sir.'

'Of course.' Ralph dipped his head. 'How about this instead?'

He leaned towards Promise and tucked a silver shilling into the top pocket of the A4 boy's tunic, buttoned the thing down. Promise blushed a furious pink. Jackdaw protested.

'Hang on . . .'

Bertie Fortune took his hands from his pockets.

'Sir . . .'

But Ralph ignored them all, grabbed the chicken from Promise's arms, then stepped back, holding the creature aloft by its neck.

'Right, then, men,' he called. 'Who wants to slit its throat this time?'

'I'll do it.'

Alfred Walker, always ready to play with the knife, darted over to retrieve it from George Stone where he stood at the farmhouse door waiting to see how the game might end.

'What about the cap badge?'

Jackdaw's voice was querulous, like a child's.

'Get on with it, can't you, whoever's doing it,' said Flint. 'Bloody freezing out here.'

Ralph ignored them both. 'I think Hawes should do it this time. He hasn't done us the honour yet.'

The men turned to where James Hawes was standing in the entrance to the barn, breath regained, holding his red book against his chest. They all saw how his fingers *tipple tappled* against the book's cover. Bertie Fortune stepped towards Ralph.

'I think we should sort the debt first, sir,' he said in a low voice.

But Ralph waved him away. 'That's done, Fortune. I've

paid Promise something else instead. Now it's Hawes's turn.'

'Wait . . .'

Jackdaw pushed forwards, but Archie Methven moved to stand in front of him.

'I'll do it, sir.'

The section's accountant, offering to clear Hawes's debt.

'No.' Ralph dismissed Methven, as he did the rest. 'Hawes will do it. After all, he's the expert. Aren't you, Hawes?'

No one spoke as the two men fixed eyes across the yard. The young officer grinned and squeezed at the chicken's neck. The chicken flapped and struggled, scaly feet scrabbling against the air.

'Don't make the poor thing wait any longer, Hawes,' Ralph called. 'Wouldn't want it to suffer.'

The men all stared at Hawes. To be afraid of blood was one thing. To disobey a direct order from an officer was a capital offence. There was silence for a moment, then a sudden blur across the yard, the knife grabbed from Alfred Walker's hand, a flash of silver. One swift slice and the chicken's head was severed from its body, blood spurting high to splash all over the second lieutenant. On his shirt. On his face. In his hair. All its sticky warmth.

Flint swore.

'Fuck!'

Jackdaw squealed. Alfred Walker laughed in disbelief. James Hawes turned and retched into a pile of dirty straw. The knife clattered to the base of the pump as Promise dropped it and stepped away. Then they all watched in silence as the chicken ran its last and most frantic dance across the mud, before it fell, too.

*

The rain came on stronger as Godfrey turned for home, the *spitter spatter* of a thousand droplets decorating his uniform with a thousand dark spots. When he got back he would take the half-walnut shell from his pocket and set it to sail on the flooded pond, he thought, see where the water took it. Then he would remove his dirty boots, sit again at the table in the parlour and begin once more.

Dear Mother and Father . . .

Look out through the rain to where roses would bloom next summer if the war would let them, sweet perfume in his nostrils, a bowl of them on the parlour table, heads dipped towards the stain.

He was almost back in the yard when the boy appeared again, ambling towards him down that muddy lane this time. The boy was fair, hair bright amongst the grey. He was carrying a pack almost as big as himself, a rifle slung across his chest, though he was only sixteen, by the looks of him, perhaps not even that. At his feet there was a small dog, some sort of terrier with a rough coat and mud on its paws. Godfrey felt his body suddenly hot beneath his tunic. What soldier brings a dog to war? he thought.

He closed his eyes, heard the raindrops dripping from the eaves, the tick of his wristwatch suddenly loud. But when he opened them again the boy was still there, standing three feet in front now, eyes grey like Beach's had been on that final morning. The boy saluted, held out an envelope.

'Sir.'

Godfrey stared at the small rectangle of paper. He knew at once what it was. The end had come at last.

1995

Methven

It was the year they separated the men from the boys. Lined them in front of the coaches, grinning and prodding with rifle butts as the women pressed around. Thomas Methven had never expected to see that again in his lifetime. Yet here it was, two days' drive across the continent to a land somewhere on the fringes of Europe, stuffed now with men holding guns. He could have been one of them, Methven thought as he watched the drama unfold on the small television set in his kitchen. A pensioner driven to his death from a suburb of Srebrenica, in a minibus belonging to a neighbour, helped on board by a Dutchman wearing a blue cap and a rifle only ever pointed down.

He pressed mute on the television remote, looked away towards the remains of his breakfast. Marmalade. Flora. A single teacup and a half-pint of milk. The ordinary things. Also a shoebox, the last item waiting to be unpacked. The box was a simple thing, with a lid that had been taped up years before as though there was nothing dangerous inside. The tape had lost all its stick, left a silvery residue on Methven's hands as he peeled what remained away. Like those house moths his wife used to wage war on when they got amongst the jumpers, turned to dust with a single rub of finger against thumb.

*

Two weeks after they had burned Thomas Methven's wife in the furnace at Mortonhall and he had started in the garage. Moved from there to the spare rooms. Then to the bookshelves, and the cupboards in the kitchen. After that the lounge. Then he had clambered into the attic with its bin bags and its cardboard cartons, thrown the lot through the hatch into the hall below. Two weeks of spreading their belongings like butter across the charity shops of Edinburgh to bring succour to the poor, no room for anything that reminded him of what was gone and could not be replaced. All that was left of Methven's life would be ahead of him now – that was what he had decided. Not something to look back on with regret.

He'd dug everything up because time was running out, a trickle of seconds and minutes passing through the hourglass as though they would never stop. He was old now, well over seventy, would be lucky to enjoy another twenty years. But he only had to remember his wife's face nestled amongst the satin lining of her coffin to know that he might have a lot less time than that.

Thomas Methven pushed back his chair now, put the marmalade in the fridge, followed by the margarine and the milk. Then he swept crumbs from the tabletop with his cuff, to clear a proper space. The shoebox had once contained a pair of new leather sandals in turquoise, the label still stuck to the outside. He remembered his wife wearing the shoes for her cousin's wedding, turning on her heel before the mirror in the hall. She had smelled of sweet peas then, wore coral-shaded lipstick. The box was one of the things he had meant to sort through before she died, thought he would have time. Realized now it might already be too late.

He removed the lid and peered inside, before lifting out the contents one by one, laying them along the edge of his kitchen table as though he was starting an inventory of sorts. First was a shopping list written on the back of an anniversary card, *To my darling*. Milk. Pickle. Tea. Next a coral-shaded lipstick rubbed to a stub, like his wife had been rubbed down, too. Then there was a clipping from the *Edinburgh Evening News* – a picture of him amongst his roses.

First prize.

After that a note that he recognized – the one where he had written, *Sorry*. And inside the fold, three dried rose petals, brown and fragile. Also a photograph of the two of them together, young people grinning at the camera as though they had all the time in the world.

Thomas Methven lifted the photograph close, peered into the grey of a life long past. His wife was wearing a dress that flared from the waist. He had hair pushed back from his brow and fixed with brilliantine. They were standing on the promenade at Hastings holding hands. It had been their honeymoon. Somewhere as far away as they could imagine, before they came home to Edinburgh and never left again. He remembered the argument about whether to go further – across the Channel to France, perhaps, take a look at the tapestry with the king who got an arrow in his eye during another battle long ago. It was his wife who had wanted to go, step off the white cliffs into a different kind of world. But he had been away once before and come home, had no reason to explore any further. What was the world, he used to say, if it could not be glimpsed in the faces of the roses he had spent a lifetime growing along the path to their front door.

Now, as he laid the photograph on the table along with all the rest, he considered whether in fact they should have travelled further. Then there would have been so much more. A whole lifetime of experiences spread out in black and white and Technicolor, the two of them ageing square by square by square. He looked into the shoebox again, hoping for another reminder that once his wife had been here. A handkerchief, perhaps. Her wristwatch. But under the detritus of a life well lived, there was something different. The remnants of a war.

There was a quiver in Thomas Methven's hand as he lifted the rest of the box's contents into the light, to lie amongst the crumbs.

A stub of pencil.

A plaque like a huge bronze penny: Britannia holding out her wreath.

Also a pawn ticket, no.125. That small square of blue. He knew at once what these things were. The remains of his father. All that was left of a man on which his son could rebuild.

At the bottom of the shoebox was a notebook the size of a man's palm. The book was stiff and crinkled with age, as though it had got damp once and never quite recovered. He lifted it out with care, noted the slight tremor in his right hand again, getting much worse now. He ran one shaky finger over the front cover, then opened it and read the name on the inside page:

Methven.

As though he might have written it himself.

The notebook was all faded inside, with its blue horizontals and its red verticals at the far edge where the reckoning was due. Methven turned the first page, fingers sweaty on the brittle paper. He recognized the contents immediately. A profit-and-loss account.

Several names were listed, only ever written in pencil, never in ink. *P. Flint. A. Walker.* Someone called *Jackdaw.* An *Arthur Promise* and a *George Stone.* Also a soldier called *Bertie Fortune* – a lucky man indeed.

Vertical columns indicated what each man had put in and what had gone out again, written in his father's neat hand:

A wishbone;

A tanner;

A reel of pink cotton.

Typical of soldiers to have something with which to sew their clothes. He traced the passage of each object from one man to the next, like his own passage across the northern oceans when he was a young man, there and back and there again, each time a slightly different path.

He turned a few more of the stiff pages, came to a series of entries over consecutive dates culminating in one for a cap badge owing to the man called Arthur Promise. For a chicken. The yellow. Unpaid. After that there seemed to be one more game, all its ins and outs, before the writing in the notebook ended with a double line at the bottom of the last entry, as though to mark a reconciliation of what had gone before. Always pay your debts, that was what his mother had said, whatever happens. She had been very particular about that.

And Thomas Methven could see at once that every one

of these debts had been settled, a thick grey pencil line cancelling them out, but in a different hand. He wondered what game it was the men had played that ended with everything back where it had been at the beginning, turned to see what came next – a new round, perhaps – found the pages blank.

Thomas Methven knew that his father had been a soldier once. A tall man with serious eyes, standing in his uniform with his hand upon a table, small son by his side – a photograph his mother kept on her mantelpiece until the day she died. His father had been a man who loved to till the soil, as his son did, that was what she said. Always digging in his garden, before he was sent to till the soil of a foreign land to see what might grow there. Methven had heard all the stories. How his father had gone to war, though he did not have to. How he had kept a strict record of his earnings, so that there might be some savings once he returned. How he had looked after the little things, even when he was away, so that the bigger things might look after themselves. Nothing left of him now but a Dead Man's Penny. Methven ran one finger over the inscription on the bronze plaque.

For Freedom and Honour.

Remembered his mother muttering as she shoved it into a drawer in the kitchen. *Murderers.* That was what she called them. A life-long pacifist, his mother, always wore the white poppy, never the red.

But when war came round again, as it must, Thomas Methven had grasped it with both hands, too. Signed for a sailor, never did go home. Stood instead on the deck of a rolling boat on the great northern ocean, ice on the lanyards, chickens in the hold, taking his turn at the watch. He remembered how huge the sky had been, as dark sometimes as a piece of velvet laid across his eyes. Other times ablaze with the luminous path of the Milky Way. He could hear it still, that constant roaring in his ears, a young man again peering through the waves in the darkness, the whip of sleet on his cheeks. At night now he missed his hat with its fur earflaps, his petrol-scented oilskin falling almost to the tips of his boot. He had been warm then, he thought, not cold like he felt now, deep inside his bones. Then he saw again the rolling of the boy amongst the surf, the bright splash of a sou'wester, glimpsed once, then vanished, the empty churn of the ocean as the boat steamed on ahead.

Thomas Methven looked again at the list of small treasures bet by men long dead. Then at the pawn ticket on the edge of his kitchen table, wondered what exactly it might redeem. He could still hear the soft slap and scuffle of cards as his fellow sailors played for pennies beneath the fo'c'sle, the happy exclamations when one triumphed, the swearing when all the others lost. Exchanging pinches of tobacco for a sliver of soap or an extra biscuit. Those postcards that came from Russia, 2d a time to buy. Just like his father, Thomas Methven understood how sometimes the simplest things were worth the most.

He laid the notebook aside, next to the pencil and the plaque and the little pawn ticket, peered into the shoebox again. There was a neat lining of newspaper laid on the bottom, date printed along the perforated edge. June 1971. The era of all change. Decimalization. The turn of old money into new. Methven and his wife had been all alone in the world then. No children. No brothers or sisters. His mother not long in the ground, too. He had been his own man at last; come to Edinburgh with nothing and made good all on his own. Spent a lifetime adding up the numbers for an insurance company in the certainty that it would have made his father proud.

The tremor in Methven's hand worsened now as he contemplated lifting the edge of the newspaper to see what lay beneath, wondered if the letter might be hiding in the box, too. 1971 and sitting in the cinema with that envelope burning a hole through the inside pocket of his jacket. He remembered the figures on the screen looming large, dust swirling in the projector's beam as the letter pressed against his heart, holding his wife's hand in the dark as though they were newlyweds again, wondering whether to confess.

The letter had arrived two days before, sliding onto his doormat in Edinburgh as though it was nothing more than an ordinary bill, nothing to indicate the incendiary nature of what it contained. He had read it and put it in his pocket. Then later he had put it further away than that. Couldn't remember where, now, maybe torn into little pieces and scattered in the compost – where he planned to bury the Dead Man's Penny, once the breakfast things were cleared. Blood money. That was what the offer in the letter had amounted to. One man's legacy to his only son. But Thomas Methven always had been a man who grew roses and thought only of the future, not someone beholden to his past.

He looked out of the kitchen window now to where his roses were just starting to unfurl. The pride of the street, that was what his wife used to call them, great blooms in orange and pink. Ever since she had died he had found himself talking to the roses, telling them about this and that, about the war that was in the news. Sometimes, after he had picked greenfly from the stems and applied feed where it was needed, he came inside and wept. Sat in his armchair in front of the fire in the lounge, face wet with remembering everything he could no longer get back. He wondered often about digging the roses from the ground, dragging them from the earth, all their long roots cut through with one slice of his spade. It felt wrong now that they should bloom and bloom and bloom again, while his wife and everything that had gone before her would only ever decay.

He turned back to the television set, where a man in khaki was laughing as another wearing nothing but a dirty tracksuit put the barrel of a gun into the mouth of a boy. The boy could have been twelve, but might also have been fifteen. Thomas Methven knew straight away that if it was the first then the boy would survive; and if it was the second he would not. He saw again a boy he once knew rolling twice in the heave and froth of the northern ocean before he disappeared. Then his wife's mouth, coral against the satin. Also his father, a man so long dead Methven could not remember what he looked like. Felt the tears rise.

He missed his father. He'd missed him as a boy and now he missed him again. Every day. With a pain at the very centre of his chest that never seemed to grow any smaller, only larger and larger, till it had become a mountain that he could never climb. Thomas Methven knew he was supposed to be strong, a man who could tend to it all, including the roses. And yet every day he sat in his chair in his empty living room and found himself crying like a child; felt his father close, like a second skin, now that he was old himself.

What was it about the past, that it would never leave a man alone?

PART TWO

The Pawn

Solomon Farthing
b.1950 d.

Thomas Methven
b.1920/21 d.2016

2016

One

The tree began with a single name.

Thomas Alexander Methven.

Then the dates.

b.1920/21 d.2016.

A whole life encapsulated in fewer than all the letters of the alphabet. What was it about death, Solomon Farthing thought, that it left one so easily reduced?

His initial foray in pursuit of Thomas Methven (deceased) had brought him to New Register House – that hallowed hall at the east end of Princes Street where all the actual records were stored. Solomon knew that most Heir Hunters had it at their fingertips these days, digital portals to every possible record there could be when it came to hunting the deceased. Census reports. Passenger lists. The database of the Salvation Army. Also the Mormons – the biggest of the lot. But Solomon had always preferred the hand-made approach. One line after another written out with a fountain pen in black ink following a visit to the ledgers in Births Marriages and Deaths.

The nursing home had given him the information he needed to begin. A name. An approximate d.o.b. A copy of the death certificate, too. A GP had signed off the latter, but that didn't mean a thing. *Cash for Ash.* That was what they used to call it. Sending in a junior doctor to sign for the deceased, one hundred and fifty quid and no questions asked. Illegal in Scotland now, though not in the south. Another sign of their divided nation, perhaps. Either way, paperwork lied, of that Solomon was certain. Or at least it never told the complete, unvarnished truth.

He'd arrived at New Register House with a stolen dog on a string, discovered on his doorstep only that morning when he returned from his trip to the nursing home in a squad car summoned by DCI Franklin, but driven by PC Noble, of course. PC Noble had delivered Solomon right to his front door in the crescent, refusing to acknowledge his suggestion that she drop him somewhere further down the street. When they arrived, there had been a small dog wearing a blue kerchief sitting on the step. PC Noble had glanced at Solomon in the rear-view mirror.

'Is that your dog?' she'd asked.

Assaulting a police officer. Housebreaking with Intent. Kidnap (or was it Dognap). How ironic if all the charges that could have been pinned on Solomon Farthing came down to the taking of a creature he didn't even want.

'Probably a neighbour's,' he'd said.

'What's his name?'

'Who, the neighbour?'

PC Noble's look had been enough to shrivel Solomon's most intimate organs. Nobody in Edinburgh spoke to their neighbour.

'The dog.'

'How should I know?'

'Maybe you should give him one. Make him feel at home.'

Solomon hadn't replied, heaved himself from the back of the squad car and tried to ignore the dog as it trotted forwards to wait for him. PC Noble had scrolled down the window.

'The DCI said to call her if you find anything. And next time you might want to shower first. You stink like a teenager.'

She'd been laughing as the squad car pulled away.

And yet . . .

As Solomon had stood on his doorstep with a dog that didn't belong to him at his feet, it hadn't been lilac he could smell, or even his own sweat. But a man already swimming towards him from out of the past, fifty thousand in used notes clutched in his fist for whoever might pull him to shore first.

At New Register House, Solomon handed the dog over to the security guard sitting by the entrance, an old acquaintance from years of ducking and diving through the archives. He planned to return the dog to its owner at the feet of Greyfriars Bobby once he'd done his initial search. He'd tied a string to its kerchief in an attempt to assert some authority on his walk into town, found the dog leading him instead.

The security guard owed Solomon a favour. The Heir Hunter had rescued the man's aunt from a charlatan just like himself once, turned up at the optimum moment when the guy was snug on her sofa, eating Rich Tea, about to fleece her for forty per cent. The aunt had gone to the Caribbean on what Solomon had saved her. He'd only charged ten per cent that time, knew that he'd been on the side of the angels. It had been a good day's work.

Once inside, Solomon made his way to the Finders'

Room, not a friendly place despite being housed in a building with a splendid copper dome not far from the city's heart. Thirty computers in an L-shaped space, office lights blinking, every workstation taken except for two saved for urgent business by the police. The only sound was the ripple of fingertips on keyboards. Solomon Farthing's idea of hell.

He ignored the eyes glancing at him now from over the other monitors, as he settled to his allocated station. Everybody here behaved as though they did not know anyone else in the room. But they were all familiar to each other, professionals and serious hobbyists with bent-over backs and suspicious stares. Occasionally an interloper appeared, an enthusiastic amateur exclaiming:

They're here!

As they raised their heads from a census record to share the discovery that their great-grandparents really had been alive once. But generally it was the usual suspects, clocking each other in and clocking each other out.

Solomon knew that they would all be working on the latest list from the QLTR. The Queen's and Lord Treasurer's Remembrancer, looking after all those ownerless goods. Assets from dissolved companies. The things missing persons left behind. Lost or abandoned property. Not to mention Treasure Trove.

Quod nullis est fit domini Regis.

That which belongs to no one becomes the King's.

Well, not if Solomon Farthing had anything to do with it, or any of his fellow Heir Hunters, given the number of them hunched over the monitors now. They would all be digging into whichever abandoned estate had the biggest sum of money as yet unclaimed. But they would have no interest in conferring. It said something about the nature of his industry that no one wanted to share.

Solomon's first attempt to get to know his dead client had taken place early that morning – by the bins, round the back of the nursing home, once DCI Franklin had abandoned him to await the arrival of PC Noble instead. A small gathering of care-workers indulging in an early morning smoke, happy to tell Solomon Farthing what they knew.

They'd begun with introductions. Kassia. Pawel. Nico. Estelle. What would they do if the vote went Leave, Solomon had thought as he shook hands. Or, more important, what would he and the rest of the country do once they left. They all remembered Thomas Methven, a veteran of particular charm and erudition, who slid away as Edinburgh's cherry trees began to drop their flowers.

'Everyone wanted to sit next to him at the card table,' said Kassia. 'They used to argue about who would play his hand in bridge.'

'He only did it to be polite,' said Estelle. 'Didn't really approve of gambling.'

'He liked to watch though. Write up the odds.'

'He was old style,' said Nico. 'A gentleman. Made sure the debts were paid.'

The women nodded as Nico puffed out a cloud of dewberry smoke, the memory of Mr Methven suddenly shiny in their eyes. Solomon wondered if he could fake a soldier's career so that these people might take care of him, too, at the end. He hadn't been to war, of course, one of the lucky generation who never had been called to serve.

But there was always his grandfather's legacy to lean on, Captain Godfrey Farthing, an officer whose job it had been to blow the whistle and send all those young men to their deaths. Up and out. Trench to trench. Look the other man in the eye as you stab him in the gut with your shiny bayonet. That might do, Solomon thought, if he had to make something up.

'He was sweet,' said Pawel. 'Mr Methven. He liked to tell stories.'

'What sort of stories?' asked Solomon.

'War stories mostly. Aren't they the best?'

Estelle, it seemed, had a thirst for blood.

'He was in the navy, wasn't he?' said Kassia. 'Arctic convoys. He talked about shooting the chickens when they didn't have anything left to eat.'

'Do they have chickens in the navy?' said Pawel.

Only in tins, Solomon thought.

'He preferred Oxtail,' said Nico.

'Oxtail?'

'Soup. The only thing he could manage in the end.'

'He liked the navy,' said Pawel. 'All the boys together.'

'Just like Mr R.,' Estelle smiled.

The four care assistants laughed. Solomon remembered the old sailor with the slippers who had accosted him when he first arrived, eyes the colour of the Aegean like a glorious boy from Solomon's youth. Kassia took a reel of cotton from her pocket, held it out for Solomon to see.

'He used to sew their buttonholes for them,' she said. 'That was what he told me. This was in his room when he died.'

'I didn't know boys could sew,' said Estelle.

'Boys can do anything,' said Pawel, taking the spool of thread from Kassia to look at before slipping it into his pocket. 'If you give them a chance.'

Solomon was disappointed to see the reel of cotton disappear. It might have come in useful, given the current state of his attire. He pulled at his jacket sleeve to hide the flap of one loose cuff.

'Did he talk much about his past?' he asked.

'He always mentioned the cold,' said Nico. 'The ice. How it got to him.'

'He had a coat made of fur,' said Estelle.

'I thought that was a hat?' said Kassia.

Perhaps both, they agreed.

The huddle of care workers were silent for a moment as they contemplated the soldiering required of a previous generation, turned their faces to the sun.

'Do you know what happened to the rest of Mr Methven's things?' Solomon asked.

The care workers all frowned, sucked on their cigarettes, shrugged. Thomas Methven had been old when he died, almost a hundred. By the time one got to that age, there was almost nothing left. Solomon rummaged in his pocket, brought out all that remained of the family silver. Pawn ticket, no.125. That small square of blue.

'Do any of you recognize this?'

The care assistants peered at the slip of paper, shook their heads. Except Pawel.

'Yes,' he said. 'Well, he showed it to me once. Said it belonged to his father.'

'Did he ever talk about his father?' asked Solomon. 'Where he came from?'

Pawel shrugged again, lids low over lovely brown eyes. 'Not that I remember.'

'He never had any children, did he,' said Estelle, quick jut of her lower jaw as she released a perfect smoke ring.

'Said he wished he had done,' replied Nico. '*What's a man without a boy?* That was what he used to say.'

'He never said that to me,' Kassia said.

'You're a girl.'

'What's a man without a girl,' said Estelle, tossing her cigarette into a bush. Kassia put out her cigarette too, pinched off the coal, popped the tab back into the box.

'All he had at the end was that suit they dressed him in for his funeral,' she said.

'What was it like?' asked Solomon.

'Old-fashioned,' said Nico.

'Gorgeous,' said Estelle.

'Blue,' said Kassia.

A proper burial gown.

An hour of search and counter search and Solomon came out of New Register House to find the dog lying waiting for him beneath the security guard's desk. Next to it was an empty Macdonald's carton, a strong smell of burger lingering in the air. The guard looked up as Solomon approached.

'Get what you needed?'

'Sort of.' Solomon pulled a face, patting at the inside pocket of his jacket containing a crumpled piece of paper with the beginnings of the Methven family tree. 'You?'

They both looked at the dog.

'Aye, no bother.'

The security man handed over the piece of string and Solomon felt lighter somehow, like a child carrying a birthday balloon. He glanced left, then right, to make sure none of Freddy Dodds's men had followed him, set off down the steps of New Register House towards the anonymity of Princes Street. He almost made it before he saw him. Colin Dunlop of Dunlop, Dunlop & Dunlop People Search lounging by the gate.

Colin Dunlop was the modern face of the industry now, an Heir Hunter who looked as though he belonged in the Edinburgh club. Suit, check. Striped shirt, check. Silk tie, check. Even polished shoes. Despite knowing all the tricks in the Heir Hunter bible, Colin Dunlop had joined the ranks of Edinburgh's finest. Solicitors and Surveyors. Estate Agents and Accountants. Edinburgh Men who talked up the price over a pint after the rugby, then shook hands all round so that they could keep it in the club. But Solomon knew that Colin Dunlop had started out scrapping on the same doorsteps as he had, understood how to sniff out a punt.

Solomon wiped sweat from his palms down the sides of his jacket, attempted to straighten the tweed. The last thing he needed was a competitor getting in on the act. Four days the DCI had given him. More like twenty-four hours, if Colin Dunlop was on his tail. But despite his clammy hands, Solomon knew that he would have to stop and speak. It was what this city demanded, an ability to pass the time of day without descending into a fight.

Colin Dunlop was smoking a cigarette – a sure sign that he was not a true Edinburgh Man at heart.

'Hello, Solomon,' he said, smoke dribbling from his mouth. 'Nice to see you.'

Typical of this city, Solomon thought. Start the conversation with something that was probably an untruth. Still, he played along, as any Edinburgh Man must.

'Dunlop,' he said, 'lovely to see you, too.'

Shook the hand that his competitor held out. After which they got down to the real business.

'You on a case, then?' Colin Dunlop sucked on his tab.

Yes, no, maybe, Solomon thought, decided obfuscation was best.

'Favour . . . for a friend. Bit of family history.'

Colin Dunlop flicked ash towards the ground that lay between them, landed a sprinkle on the toe of Solomon's shoe.

'Heard the DCI requested a visit.'

Christ! What was it with Edinburgh that all of one's secrets leaked? But in an unusual display of camaraderie, or perhaps just because he enjoyed slow torture, Solomon's competitor didn't press his hand.

'Asked you to look after her dog, did she?'

Solomon hadn't even known DCI Franklin had a dog. But camouflage was camouflage, whatever shape it took.

'Er, yes. Something like that,' he said.

They both looked down at the dog, which uttered a small whine and sidled behind Solomon's left leg. Colin Dunlop took another drag of his cigarette, till the tip glowed red.

'Your aunt wants to see you, by the way. Said it was urgent.'

Solomon felt sweat gather between his shoulder blades at this reminder that he had 'borrowed' his aunt's Mini without asking some time ago and not returned it yet.

'You her messenger boy now?'

Colin Dunlop just laughed. 'A favour. For a friend.'

Of course, thought Solomon.

You scratch my back and I'll scratch yours.

He wondered for a moment what exactly his aunt who wasn't really his aunt needed from Colin Dunlop. Decided it was probably best not to find out. He tugged at the string in the hope that the dog was ready to leave now, attempted to move past. But Colin Dunlop wasn't finished yet.

'I'm on a case myself,' he said. 'Something bigger than usual.'

The typical Heir Hunter's boast.

'Oh yes?'

'You might find it interesting.'

'Bit tied up at the moment.'

They both looked at the string in Solomon's hand. Then Colin Dunlop shrugged, tossed the cigarette into the street in front of them.

'Have it your own way.' Reached to crush the still-smoking butt with the toe of his polished brogue. 'I had a dog once. Got rid of it. Bit the hand that fed.'

As Colin Dunlop disappeared into New Register House, laughing as he leapt up the steps two, by two, by two, Solomon Farthing knew that the hand which normally fed him had delivered something of a similar result. Thomas Methven (deceased), a charlatan of a different kind. A ninety-something old man, died in a nursing home of natural causes, nothing suspicious. Just another ordinary case of someone with no immediate next of kin.

And yet . . .

However hard Solomon searched, there had been no birth certificate to match the d.o.b. given on the death certificate. No children of the right name anywhere in the records to match the relevant dates. In fact, there had been no sign of how his new client had begun at all. Solomon had no idea why, but just as he had surmised at the nursing home, Thomas Methven wasn't really Thomas Methven. He was someone else instead.

Two

Godfrey Farthing's shop hadn't changed in the forty years since Solomon had last been there. Down a close off the tail end of the Royal Mile, barely the toss of a fag butt from the city's mortuary, all those indigents lying in its fridges, waiting to be claimed. Solomon approached the shop as though by stealth, hoping to avoid the attentions of his creditors. It always had been a race to the finish line in his industry, and he had not crossed first for some time now. But as he made his way along the narrow street, Solomon knew that he had one advantage. A pawn ticket belonging to a dead man tucked into his top pocket – the only clue to the truth.

The door to his grandfather's shop was shuttered, window covered by a griddle of metal, thick layer of dirt coating every inch of the glass. The padlock was rusted, an orange stain on the ground where it had bled out from the rain. Solomon lifted it to see, let it fall back with a clatter. It didn't matter that he no longer had a key with which to gain entry. He wasn't planning on going in the front.

He left the dog tied to the grating in the hope that it might bark should any suspicious-looking men come along. Temptation Lane. That was what his aunt used to call this place, an ancient passageway that once had a playhouse at the head and a brothel at the foot. The playhouse was long gone, but the brothel still existed, windows covered, door permanently ajar. It was called a sauna now – a classic Edinburgh sleight of hand. Scratch the glitter of the city's tourist industry and it quickly gave way to dirt.

Solomon glanced over his shoulder to check that he was alone as he wove his way further along the close, tall buildings looming on both sides. He emerged into a tiny courtyard where his aunt who wasn't really his aunt had once lived in a tenement flat on the far side. She had been fifteen when Solomon first arrived in the city, and always ordered to look out for him when she'd rather have been somewhere else instead.

Solomon made for an anonymous entrance in the opposite corner, all dead leaves and rubbish blown in, somewhere he had stayed for little more than a decade but still the only place he had ever called home. A panic of woodlice scattered as he forced the flimsy back door. One kick, then another, a shove with his shoulder and he was in. At once the damp took hold, that familiar chill which ran to the centre of his bones. Welcome home, Solomon thought, staring into the dark.

Solomon had first come to Edinburgh when he was seven years old, mother gone, father gone, too. A boy with nothing but a borrowed suitcase and a lucky silver charm in his pocket.

Strike Sure.

He'd arrived to the swirl of steam and bustle that was Waverley station, never been to Scotland before. It had been raining, a steady fall splashing over the sets and running through the open gutters as he hurried through a mishmash of Edinburgh streets after the grandfather he had only just met. The whole city had shimmered like some sort of dark mirror, each street lamp a halo in amongst the murk. His grandfather had led Solomon through the dark wynds and passageways, striding forwards, forwards, always forwards, until they arrived in the same narrow close Solomon had walked down now.

He remembered holding the silver cap badge tight in his pocket as he tilted his head to search for the moon high above in a patch of dark sky. Caught the glint of three golden balls hanging from a sign instead. Like three golden eggs, he had thought then, the promise of treasure. The mark of a pawnshop, he knew now, somewhere much more concerned with the ordinary stuff of life.

For a moment Solomon was a boy of seven years old again, rather than a man not far from ten times that. Then he stepped through the back doorway into shadow, the stink of eggs boiling and the burn of a single-bar fire catching in his throat.

Inside it was as though the past forty years had come and gone with nothing in between. Solomon moved along the passageway of his old home, the tips of his fingers touching now and then at cold plaster that crumbled as he passed. To his left there was a room which once housed an open fire and a grandfather clock that ticked in the gloom. Off that was the box room in which he had slept, light seeping from the casement to cast shadows onto the distempered walls. Opposite was his grandfather's bedroom, nothing but a crucifix on the wall and a narrow bed, no books but the Bible and one with the red-woven cover which appeared after Godfrey Farthing died.

Solomon had no idea what they had done with his grandfather once he coughed his last. Buried or cremated? Scattered, or left beneath some patch of overgrown grass? He could barely recall his grandfather's funeral, other than digging through a box of shoes in the back of the shop in the hope of finding a matching pair. Just like Solomon's father, Godfrey Farthing had got lost somewhere along the way. Not even two generations, and already the family remains were dispersed, north, south, east and west.

To Solomon's right an archway indicated the entrance to the scullery where he and his grandfather had washed that first night, Solomon sitting on the draining board, legs dangling, as he waited his turn to take off his shirt. Solomon felt for the light switch, flicked it back and forth in the hope of catching the glitter of the taps. But when he looked towards the ceiling he saw that all the bulbs had been removed.

He moved further along the passage, feeling his way until he came to the room that had always been full of odd things too big, or too ordinary, for the front of the shop. Piles of clothes. Blankets folded and stacked. Baskets of shoes tied into pairs with string. He remembered the fizz of the old light bulb as it warmed, waiting for his eyes to adjust when he was sent in to dig. When he was young, Solomon's heart used to beat quick in his tight little chest at the thought of what could be hidden there, and what might be revealed. The cold shiver of a fur coat. A row of Sunday gabardine. Once even a stuffed otter in a glass case, high on a shelf, watching him from inside its painted landscape. All disappeared into the coffers of his aunt once his grandfather breathed his last. Solomon stretched a hand to push at the door, but he didn't need a light to see. Inside the room would be empty, his own past robbed from him, just as he had spent a lifetime robbing others of theirs.

The main body of the pawnshop was just as Solomon had last seen it more than forty years ago. There was the sign on the back of the door saying *Open*, even though it wasn't. The wooden counter inset with baize. The bell that once called for attention.

Ding

Ding

Ding

The glass cabinet where once his grandfather had laid out all his most valuable goods still stood at the far end of the counter, though it was empty now, too. No more wristwatches or silver cigarette cases, rings embedded with gemstones that scattered the shop with sparkles when Solomon turned them to the light. Blood spatter for the rubies. The rainbow of opal. Emeralds like a river full of weed. There had even been a pistol once, with pearl inlay on its handle. A ladies' gun, that was what his grandfather called it. All these years later Solomon could still feel the gun's cool imprint on his palm.

It was all gone now, of course, the currency of Solomon's childhood swept away with the rise of bank loans and credit, nobody needing to barter stuff for cash once they could borrow it instead. There had been a hundred or more pawnshops in the city when his grandfather started. Down to one or two by the time he'd met his end.

Solomon's aunt who wasn't really his aunt had taken over the shop in return for a settling of the old man's debts, everything valuable that was left sold off or melted down:

A shirt without a collar;

A fur coat made of squirrel;

A brass cornet, dented at the end.

All that had remained of Solomon Farthing's inheritance, such as it was.

Solomon had been looking for a new life himself back then, so he'd let his aunt take the lot. Departed soon after with a boy just like him riding pillion. Andrew, his eyes the colour of the Aegean, clasping Solomon around the waist as they roared and bumped over the sets on the High Street to a place where sun sliced through their eyelids of a morning as they drank tea from patterned glass. They had spent a happy few years ducking and diving through the backstreets of every city they came to, before it all went wrong. Solomon had abandoned Andrew eventually, just like all the rest. Crawled home thirty years later, middle-aged, with his pockets empty, to camp out in that basement flat in the crescent, rackety and full of draughts. Solomon looked after the flat for a man who let him stay because then he could pretend that he stayed there too.

Domiciled for tax purposes.

That was what the owner called it. Accountancy. The other way in this city that money moved around.

Through the back, off the main shop floor, Solomon parted the bead curtain that hung across the entrance to what had once been his grandfather's office – a cubbyhole with just enough space for a desk and a swivel chair. Also a safe. The office was much smaller than Solomon remembered. He felt enormous suddenly as he edged his way in, as though at any moment he might knock something from the wall.

His grandfather's chair lurched to one side as Solomon sat, rather like the drunk man he had become now that he was old himself. He dipped into the top pocket of his jacket, took out the remnants of his latest client, laid it on the edge of his grandfather's desk:

Pawn ticket no.125.

All that was left of a man on which Solomon Farthing could rebuild.

There was nothing to suggest that the ticket found in Thomas Methven's room at the nursing home had come from Godfrey Farthing's shop. But there was no harm in checking. Heir Hunting was full of false trails, but Solomon knew from experience that there was never a dead end on a family tree, only another branch to explore.

He bent now to the safe beneath the desk, turned the dial to its familiar numbers and waited for the *click click click*. It opened on his first attempt, Solomon putting one hand inside to fumble left and right. He came out with nothing but a single coin. An old-fashioned sixpence. Enough for a sherbet dip or a fistful of liquorice laces when Solomon was a boy. Not worth anything now.

Solomon slid the tanner onto the surface of the desk next to Thomas Methven's pawn ticket, put his hand further inside the tiny tomb. This time he came out with proper treasure – a box with a flip lid and faux-leather covering, all mottled now. He placed the box on the desk in front of him, heart beating *one two* at the realization that despite forty years having come and gone, the treasure might still be here. Then he flipped the lid, discovered the contents intact.

The box contained a hundred filing cards (or thereabouts) arranged by number, each with the name and address of a client. Also a description of whatever the original owners had left behind in return for cash and that small paper slip:

One gabardine overcoat;

Two earrings, seed pearls;

A pair of leather shoes with buckles.

Amongst other things. The cards were a mishmash of ticket stubs and crossings out, new information scribbled in the margins as one colour ticket was matched to another, blue next to pink. Godfrey Farthing's customers had been loyal before they petered away, coming back again and again as their lives progressed through births, marriages and deaths. They used to borrow against anything they could do without, taking cash in return for a lace collar, sometimes even a simple Sunday suit.

A service.

That was what his grandfather had called it.

Moneylending for the poor.

That was what his aunt had said.

But Solomon knew even then there was more to it than that. His grandfather's box contained all of his neighbours' secrets. Also their lies.

The cards smelled of mildew and mould now, each one marked with the stamp of greasy fingerprints from the constant taking out and putting back. Solomon always had been able to tell the best customers by the way the edges of some cards had furred over the years, while others stayed sharp.

He knew that each exchange marked on the cards had been matched by a line in a ledger – a list of everything his grandfather once owed and everything that was owed to him, tallied at the end of each night. *The Reckoning*, his grandfather used to call it as he sat at the table in the living room totting up the figures. *The Books* was what his aunt had said when she took ownership herself. The ledger's contents had taught Solomon the value of things long before he might otherwise have understood. How one year a simple gold wedding ring could be worth five shillings; and the next nothing but a farthing. How the best customers were the ones who came back again and again, even if they only ever bartered a shoe. It had proved useful in his subsequent profession, a young man buying and selling whatever he could get his hands on amongst the backstreets of a dozen cities, long before he got into the business of hijacking a family's ancestors and selling them back for a fee.

When his grandfather died, Solomon had not understood why his aunt might be interested in taking on the ledger. He had gone through it himself in search of his inheritance, discovered to his disappointment that there was a lot more *Out* than *In*. It was only much later that he understood. Just like Freddy Dodds, it wasn't the money she had wanted, so much as the names – all those people prepared to borrow their way through life.

Out front, without even a growl of warning from the dog, there was the sudden rattle of metal on glass. Through the sway of the bead curtain Solomon glimpsed a face pushed to the dirty window. He laid his hand across the flip-top box as though to protect the only inheritance he had left. Freddy Dodds, perhaps, come to claim what was his; or Colin Dunlop of Dunlop, Dunlop & Dunlop, come to steal something that was not.

The face outside shifted and morphed as Solomon leaned back in his grandfather's old chair, attempting to hide. His hand fluttered at the sudden thought that it might not be Freddy Dodds or Colin Dunlop who had followed him here, but an associate hired to do the job instead. A man with a pristine set of crowns, ready with a crowbar and a brick, two jobs folded into one. Freddy Dodds's empire always had relied on muscle. And Heir Hunting was an unscrupulous industry in some quarters, nothing ventured, nothing to pay the rent.

Blood thumped in Solomon's temples as he felt again the loss of his lucky silver charm. Where was the DCI when he needed her? Or even better, that inscrutable PC. Then, at last, he heard his salvation. A rapid scrabbling on the cobbles. A frenzied yapping. Followed by a curse.

'Fuck!'

A scuffling.

'Bloody bastard!'

More frantic barking. Then the faintest echo of footsteps heading away along the close. Solomon waited, heart beating its swift tattoo against his ribs. Then he began once again with his grandfather's box.

His searching was clumsy this time, a rapid shuffle from first to last in pursuit of anything that might match Thomas Methven's pawn ticket, no.125. A long shot, but one which could yet pay off. The first card in the box was the record for a fox stole, pawned once and never reclaimed, sold on to a man called Alfred Walker with an address in London some time not long after the first war. Solomon riffled through the rest of the cards, one by one. A coat made of squirrel. An otter in a case. But nothing to match Thomas Methven's pawn ticket, no.125.

At the very back of the box, the last two cards were pretending to be one, pressed together like the pages of an uncut book, camouflage of a sort. Solomon ran his thumbnail between the two cards, prised them apart. The newer card was from 1971. An era of all change. Also the year Solomon's grandfather had breathed his last.

The edge of the card was sharp rather than frayed. A record that had been put in the box once and never redeemed. Solomon lifted it close to see the date:

June, 1971.

Also the name:

Hawes, J.

Recognized the writing at once. Andrew's, with its odd 'i's and 't's, writing out the last exchange that ever took place in Godfrey Farthing's shop. An old itinerant who came in when Solomon's grandfather was near the end and left behind a suit. Blue like a starling's egg, lining dark as midnight. Perfect for a burial, that was what he said. Except when they had tried it on Godfrey Farthing after he was gone, the suit had been too short.

Solomon put the most recent card back in the box, turned to the older one instead. For a moment he was disappointed. There was no pink ticket pinned to the edge of the old card to match the one left behind by Thomas

Methven. But there was something else taped to the surface. An advertisement cut from the classifieds of some provincial newspaper many years before. Solomon peered at the clipping, saw something scribbled in the margin:

Methven.

Written in pencil, in Godfrey Farthing's hand. Then he read the advertisement itself:

WANTED: Home for a baby boy, 6 months old. Total surrender.

As though signalling the end of a war.

Three

The National Library of Scotland was an austere kind of place. Twelve floors in the centre of the city, only five of them above ground, its blank edifice of stone no hint of all the treasures it contained within. Old books. And new books. And books with hand-painted pages and gold leaf on the spines. Not to mention every kind of newspaper, map, manuscript, business directory, film or photograph one could possibly imagine. Amongst other things. But Solomon Farthing had not come to browse amongst the smorgasbord of the printed word the library had to offer. He had come to dig in the stacks where all the real secrets were held.

Solomon didn't bother making for the library's main entrance. Instead he cut through the dark chasm of the Cowgate, in search of an anonymous-looking metal door beneath the great curve of George IV Bridge. There was one advantage to Edinburgh's dark passageways, he thought as he hurried along with his head down. They kept the opposition guessing. Not just Freddy Dodds looking for repayment, five thousand and counting. Or his aunt who wasn't really his aunt pursuing him by proxy until he returned her car. But his adversary, Colin Dunlop, intent on cooking up some sort of Heir Hunter duel: let Solomon Farthing do all the leg work on Thomas Methven (deceased), then ride in at the last to take the glory. Plus commission on fifty thousand in cash, of course.

The dog scuttled along behind, close to Solomon's feet as though it, too, wished to avoid being seen. Greyfriars Bobby was only a two-minute walk up Candlemaker Row from where they were headed. Solomon attempted to look inconspicuous as he rapped on the metal door. Freddy Dodds's spies were everywhere in Edinburgh, one way or another, but it wasn't too difficult for a man of Solomon's age and demeanour to go unnoticed in this stretch of the Cowgate. It always had been rolling with men who drank Crazy Jack cider for breakfast and sloped around with dogs on string. Still Solomon was relieved when he heard the familiar screech of metal on concrete as the door was finally opened from the inside.

'Solomon Farthing,' said the man on the other side, a file of paperwork tucked beneath his arm. 'Welcome to the Void.'

Mr Michaels was an Edinburgh Man of a different type from those like Dunlop who wore the suits. He was more on the academic side of the city, hair grown thin and a cycling helmet permanently rattling at his side. Mr Michaels was a member of the National Library's Collection Support Service. Or a Book Fetcher, as they were more commonly known. He walked miles every day, up the library corridors and down the library stairs, searching out the written word. They were said to be able to navigate in the dark, the Book Fetchers, so familiar were they with the innards of the national collection, even the bits that could only be handled with gloves.

Mr Michaels had become one of Solomon's best contacts, ever since their first encounter in that corner of a rambling north-side cemetery where men like them often took their evening walks.

'After the book?' Michaels had asked, eyes gleaming for a moment in the twilight when Solomon admitted to his nickname, as they stood amongst the graves.

Old Mortality.

The man who cleaned the stones.

After that the innards of the National Library were often placed at Solomon's disposal. It turned out that Mr Michaels was not only a Book Fetcher, but also an expert of a literary sort, a man who had spent ten years or more failing to complete a PhD on Walter Scott.

Now, he led Solomon and the dog away from the drunks of the Cowgate and through the slit trench that marked the boundary between the bowels of the National Library and the founding stones of the city's George IV Bridge. Above them the void soared several floors into blackness. Beneath them their feet traversed the remains of a long-abandoned Edinburgh street. As he followed Mr Michaels, Solomon felt contentment settle on him like dust falling from a mantelpiece. There was no way any of his pursuers could find him in here. Besides, everybody knew that all of the city's best secrets were hidden in the dark.

Mr Michaels's hideaway was on the seventh floor below ground, a cubbyhole in the furthest corner of the stacks. There were no windows to let in the light, only a million pipes running hither and thither above their heads. Edinburgh was warm outside now, but it could be cold as Hades once winter spread itself around. But in here Solomon knew that the curators didn't take anything for granted. Everything was temperature controlled.

As he and Mr Michaels made themselves at home, the dog wandered away to dig for treasure of its own, nothing but the sound of its claws *tip tapping* in some hidden recess the further it went. Mr Michaels leaned against the great metal shelves and nibbled on a forbidden flapjack, while Solomon perched himself on an empty book trolley beneath a sign that declared, *Disaster Box*. A reasonable summary of his life to date. He took a packet of cheese and onion crisps from his jacket pocket, pulled open the top.

'So what's the story?' he asked.

'Your Mr Methven,' said Mr Michaels brushing flapjack crumbs from his T-shirt. 'Nothing much, I'm afraid, given the very short time I had to compile it. But a few morsels.'

'Tasty, I hope.' Solomon stuffed a handful of crisps into his mouth.

'That's for you to say, isn't it. I just come up with the facts.'

Down in the depths of the National Library, Mr Michaels recited the headlines from his report.

'Thomas Alexander Methven. Born in 1920, or perhaps 1921.'

Two possible lies to begin with, thought Solomon. Not a bad start.

'Died in the Old Soldiers' Nursing Home in south-east Edinburgh. Birthplace unknown.'

And two that were true. So a balanced sort of life.

'Came to Edinburgh as a young man. Got a job as a clerk at the Edinburgh Assurance Company after the war. Stayed there his whole life.'

Acumen and perspicacity. Not to mention a head for

figures. Thrift, investment and sound husbandry of money. All the skills Solomon's grandfather had wanted him to have. All the things he did not.

'How do you know where he worked?' he said now, spraying a few crisp crumbs down the front of his tweed jacket.

'I checked his war record,' said Mr Michaels. 'Turned up on his demob papers. Then I looked in the relevant business directory for the city. Amazing what you can find in there.'

'Don't suppose there was an address for his parents?'

Mr Michaels shook his head.

'No sign of that, not mentioned at all. But when he first enlisted he was renting a room down the Canongate, by the old Holyrood Square. Wasn't that where your grandfather used to have his shop?'

Solomon licked his palm and wiped it on his trousers.

'Roughly speaking,' he said.

Sometimes he wondered if Mr Michaels knew more about his past than he did. Like many of his kind, Solomon had never researched his own ancestors. Family trees were dangerous territory. Why else did Heir Hunters make sure to avoid their own?

'Who did he give as next of kin on his war papers then?' he asked.

'No one,' said Mr Michaels. 'Maybe he was an orphan by then.'

Like me, thought Solomon, tipping the last of the crisps into his mouth and crumpling the packet. Nothing but a boy adrift in the world.

'He had a house not far from you in later life, though,' said Mr Michaels.

In a suburb where all the men had gold-plated pensions and were members of the Probus. For a moment Solomon's left hand fluttered at the prospect of fifty thousand turning to five hundred thousand between one mouthful and the next.

'Don't suppose he owned it, did he?'

Mr Michaels flashed a grin at Solomon as though he knew exactly what the Heir Hunter was thinking.

'Yes. But he sold it about twenty years ago. Used up all the capital on his nursing home fees, as far as I can tell.'

'So any cash must be more recent, then?'

Mr Michaels glanced at Solomon. It wasn't like an Heir Hunter to question where his latest pay cheque might come from.

'If it was on his person when he died, then it's part of his estate, isn't it? No questions asked.'

'Just curious.'

Solomon licked at the tip of each greasy finger. If he was going on a wild goose chase, he wanted to be prepared for the worst. Mr Michaels tapped at the paperwork in his folder.

'Don't suppose you want to see a picture, do you?'

'Oh yes.'

Solomon levered himself off the book trolley with an eager jolt. He was an old-style Heir Hunter, liked to see who he was dealing with face-to-face if he could. The Book Fetcher turned the final page of his report to reveal a grainy photograph, a man standing amongst an array of roses.

First Prize.

Copied from an old edition of the *Edinburgh Evening News.*

'He was a stalwart of the fruit and veg shows,' said Mr
Michaels, indicating the caption beneath the photograph –
Mr Thomas Methven triumphs again. 'Entered every year.'

Solomon stared down at the face of his dead client,
open like a flower to the sun. A man in his sixties then
(as Solomon was now), probably lived a good life and
prospered (as Solomon had not). Dead now, though,
Solomon thought, reduced to clinker soon enough if that
Penny woman from the Office for Lost People got her
hands on him, did her job well.

And yet . . .

'He looks cheerful, doesn't he?' said Mr Michaels.

And Solomon had to admit that Thomas Methven did.

Mr Michaels flipped the cover of the folder closed. By
way of reply, Solomon pulled something from his jacket
pocket as though he too was a magician of sorts. He laid
it on the edge of the grey metal shelf.

'What's this?' said the Book Fetcher.

'Mr Methven's legacy,' said Solomon.

Pawn ticket no.125. The relic of a long and cheerful life.

Mr Michaels wiped both hands on his T-shirt as though
he knew he was about to handle treasure, picked up the
little slip of blue paper and held it to the light. They both
saw it then – two tiny pinholes, each with a thin rime of
rust, as though the ticket had been attached to something
once, long since removed. Mr Michaels turned the ticket
over, then over again.

'Quite old,' he said. 'Pre-war, if I had to guess.'

'Thomas Methven was in the war,' said Solomon. 'On
the Arctic convoys.'

Ice on the lanyards. Chickens in the hold.

But Mr Michaels shook his head. 'First, I mean, not second.'

'Oh.'

Solomon felt his feet suddenly hot in his fuchsia socks at the thought of his grandfather as a young man, shiny leather strap and brass buttons, blowing a whistle so that his men might go over the top. Both of them looked again at the slip of paper.

'I wonder what it might redeem?' said Mr Michaels.

'Now,' said Solomon, discarding his empty crisp packet on the book trolley next to him. 'That's where it gets interesting.'

He pulled another slip of paper from his pocket. A cutting from a newspaper this time. *WANTED: Home for a baby boy, 6 months old.* Mr Michaels took the clipping with delicate but eager fingers.

'*The Scotsman* used to be covered in these,' he said. 'Adverts. Hundreds of them. All over the front page.'

New Goods. Young Bachelors. Articles for Sale.

'Not babies, though, surely,' said Solomon.

'Read once about a baby given away in return for a gramophone. That was in Dundee though. Different rules apply.'

'Is this from *The Scotsman*, then?' asked Solomon.

Mr Michaels turned the scrap of newsprint over one way, then back. It took him less than thirty seconds to decide.

'No. Wrong typeface. And paper quality.'

'Where do you think it does come from if it isn't *The Scotsman*?'

'Now that's something I can help you with.' Mr

Michaels's eyes shone for a moment as he pointed to a PO Box number written on the bottom of the advertisement. 'Borders. My speciality. If I had to guess.'

There was the sudden *tip tap* of small claws on lino getting nearer. Solomon and Mr Michaels looked at the dog as it reappeared, began to lick the evidence of their misbehaviour in the food department from the floor. Not only camouflage, Solomon thought, but a way to keep the scene of the crime clean.

Mr Michaels slid the small blue pawn ticket and the newspaper cutting into the folder of paperwork containing Thomas Methven's known history, such as it was, handed the lot to Solomon. Then he led the Heir Hunter back through the Void to the National Library's emergency exit, the dog trotting behind. Both men stopped in the darkness when they got to the door, to say their goodbyes, nothing but the smell of damp and brick dust all around, the scent of Edinburgh's deep past. The Book Fetcher bent to give the dog a quick fondle about the ears.

'By the way,' he said, 'Dunlop was asking if I'd seen you.'

Solomon felt heat rise again beneath his jacket. 'What did you say?'

'Nothing, like you asked.'

Solomon looked at the dog, standing quite still now to receive the adoration that it seemed to think was its due. Then he slipped a hand into his jacket pocket, pulled out treasure of a different sort and offered it to Mr Michaels because he felt the Book Fetcher was due something, too.

'This is for you,' said Solomon. 'As a thank you. It's a decent edition, I think.'

A book with a red woven cover, rather stained now. Mr Michaels took the book like a man who was used to handling paper worth a thousand pounds a page, cradled it in his fingertips, before turning to the spine.

Old Mortality.

Stamped in gold.

'Where did you get it?' he asked.

'It was my grandfather's,' said Solomon. 'Bit missing from the end, I'm afraid. But I thought you would probably know that by heart.'

Mr Michaels grinned. 'You always did appreciate my interests.'

Solomon smiled, too. There was something very satisfying about passing on one's inheritance to someone who would appreciate it more.

The two men shook hands before Mr Michaels dragged again at the metal door with its squeal of metal on stone, released Solomon and the dog back onto the dark streets of Edinburgh. As Solomon slipped past him into the shadows of the Cowgate, the Book Fetcher touched him on the sleeve.

'I'd be careful, if I were you,' he said.

'Why's that?' asked Solomon.

'Your dead man's legacy.'

'What about it?'

'If it's business, that's one thing,' said Mr Michaels, sliding the emergency exit closed until there was only a slit between them. 'But if it's family business, that's something else.'

1918

One

It was a suicide mission. Godfrey understood that the moment he opened the envelope and read the note. Instructions from the Company Commander to take his men and cross the river, engage the enemy on the far side as best they could. They were to hold their ground whatever happened. There would be no back-up. There would be no relief. They had been designated the forlorn brigade – the first to go over and the last to return. It was the end, but not as Godfrey had hoped for, turned by the stroke of a general's pen to dust.

The boy waited for his orders like a good soldier, upright beneath the weight of his pack, the dog waiting too. Godfrey crumpled the note, shoved it into his pocket, become aware once more of the *drip drip* of raindrops from the eaves of the house. Suddenly there was water all over the yard, pools of it, rivers running around his feet. He turned from the boy back towards the farm.

'Dismiss.'

Thinking of the roses that would never bloom for them now. The least he could do was return this boy to the safety of his own unit, let him have the future he deserved. But the boy did not fall out and march away to safety. Instead he followed Godfrey to the door.

'Sir.'

'What?'

'I've been instructed to join you, make up the numbers.'
The dog tight about his feet.

Godfrey laughed, unbelieving. Eleven men to the slaughter then, not ten. As though that might somehow make a difference. Godfrey looked at the mud smeared on the new recruit's boots, tasted the acrid stink of a gun fired too close. The certainty he had craved was upon him and it wasn't as sweet as he had hoped.

He dismissed the boy once more, directed him to the barn to find a place to lay his groundsheet, instructed him to ask Percy Flint about washing and George Stone about food. The boy had walked ten miles or more, he said, until he found them, everyone else far ahead now across valley and field. Godfrey and his men had been left behind in their forgotten Eden, just as Ralph had feared.

The men in the barn were sorting the washing in silence when the new boy appeared – shirts and trousers rubbed down after their encounter with the chicken, the rest of their clothes dragged from the line in the grain store and folded into rough piles. It was the first time in months they had managed to wash their entire wardrobe, greybacks pilfered from dead men, undergarments of odd proportions, socks of every possible yarn and knit. But still the mud clogged every seam.

'Who's this, then?' said Percy Flint, ever the first to scent fresh blood. He came to stand before the new arrival, hands in the pockets of his breeches, hair neatened with a slick of eau de cologne courtesy of a deal with Bertie Fortune – a splash in the hand in return for a sliver of fancy soap.

'Alec,' said the boy, dropping his pack to the stone floor. 'Alec Sutherland.'

'Where you from, Alec?'

'Fusiliers, "A" Company.'

From the borderlands, where England touched the north.

The rest of the men left the clothes where they lay, gathered round at that. All except Hawes who hunched on his bunk, knees to chest, turning the pages of his book, a constant twitching in both hands now.

'"A" Company,' said Alfred Walker. 'I thought they were all gone. Got blasted a few weeks back.'

'They did,' said Alec, lifting his rifle over his head and propping it against his pack. 'I'm one of the few that's left.'

'What you doing here, then?' said Bertie Fortune.

'Brought orders.'

'What orders?'

'How should I know?'

'You must have some idea,' said Flint. 'If they sent you all this way.'

Alec just shrugged, looked around for where he might lay out his stuff.

'You can put it next to ours,' said Jackdaw. 'In the corner.'

'Though we sleep in the loft,' said Promise. 'There's plenty of room for one more if you like.'

Promise was naked from the waist up, ribs like a ladder, had taken off his shirt still smeared with blood from his encounter with the yellow chicken not an hour before. Flint flicked hayseed from his tunic.

'All the boys together,' he muttered.

'Give it a rest, Flint, can't you,' said Fortune. He turned

back to the new arrival. 'Bit young for war, aren't you?'

Alec smiled. 'I know how to point a gun. If that's what you're asking.'

'We all know how to point a gun, son,' Hawes growled from his corner. 'It's who you point it at that counts.'

Alec shrugged again, lifted his pack towards the quarter of the barn where Jackdaw and Promise had laid their stuff. Jackdaw stuck out his hand, wrist extending beyond the cuff of his shirt like the bone from a chicken.

'I'm Jackdaw,' he said. 'This is Arthur Promise.'

'Alec.'

The three boys grinned, shook hands.

'Eh up,' muttered Alfred Walker from his stance by the door. 'Here comes trouble.'

Second Lieutenant Svenson approaching across the yard.

In the parlour, Godfrey laid the contents of his pockets on the table. A pencil and a blank postcard. A half-walnut shell he had meant to set sail on the pond. Another still whole. Also the orders, smoothed now with the heel of his hand. With two fingers he pressed at a spot above his heart, felt the ache begin. He would tell the men about the orders later, that was what he thought. Tomorrow, perhaps. Let them have the fun of a new recruit first, someone to distract their attention with stories of where he had come from and what he had got up to. Godfrey would take a moment to consider, before it all came down.

He went to the settle pushed back against the parlour wall and lifted its seat to reveal a wooden lockbox hidden inside. There was a real tremor in his left hand as he lifted the box out and laid it on the parlour table. Just like Hawes, he thought, as bad as it had ever been, despite the absence of the guns. In the kitchen there was the sudden *clank* and *clatter* of pans as George Stone began his preparations for their evening meal. The old sweat knew how to turn out a feast, that was something. Winter cabbages cooked to a soupy broth. Eggs, warm and speckled. A store of wizened potatoes recovered from the cellar, fried in small batches to a sort of hash. Even that first night Stone had produced a meal the likes of which none of them had seen for months. Roasted walnuts. Potatoes mashed and served with gravy. Chicken turned on a spit. The men had competed for the wishbone when the meat was done, dice tumbling over and over on the table from Ralph's wooden cup. Bertie Fortune had won, of course. Fortune always had the luck.

'Got to live up to the name,' he'd said.

Grinning as he swept his treasure into his hand. The men might grumble, but Godfrey knew they didn't really mind. Bertie Fortune had a way of spreading his luck around, you only had to ask.

The little brass key Godfrey had taken from a string around his neck rattled in the matching hole on the lockbox, refusing to turn for a moment until he heard at last that soft *click* as the mechanism released. The flutter in Godfrey's fingers was still there as he lifted everything out. The men's pay books. The pouch with the tobacco ration. His cigarette tin, all scratched and dented, ten Capstans neatly lined inside. Then there was the map with the river they were meant to be crossing marked in blue.

Godfrey took out his service notebook, flipped open a clean page and wrote the date, *5 November*, stared at the blunt tip of his pencil as he wondered what to write next. That the orders had arrived? That they were ready? Forty-eight hours till he must lead an attack across the river, one last stand. Then he laid the pencil down, left the page blank.

At the bottom of the box lay the letters every soldier was made to write, just in case. A missive from a petty thief to his girl. From an A4 boy to his mother. From a lucky man to his wife. Beneath them were Godfrey's own letters to his parents.

We are all going along fine here . . .

And underneath that, the one Archie Methven had written to his son.

Godfrey remembered that second night at the farmhouse after the rain had stopped, a thin layer of silver running across the surface of the yard. How he'd stood in the cold outside the barn and heard them talking. Arthur Promise, the A4 boy who wanted to be a teacher. Alfred Walker, with his dreams of sailing to the promised land. Bertie Fortune, of course, who was going home to become a rag-and-bone king. And Archibald Methven, the section's accountant, who wanted nothing more than to see his son grow up. Interrupted by a boy who would rather march them to the top of the hill to be shot, than see them all live to fight another day. Godfrey Farthing had never understood it before, the certainty that there would be life, when before there had only ever been the certainty of death. But as he'd listened to his men whispering about the future, he had felt his own heart spin at the thought that one day he too might leave all this behind and start somewhere afresh.

There was a sudden *skiff skaff* at the front entrance as Ralph returned from wherever he had been. Tossing the dice, no doubt, making fools of the men. Godfrey listened, hand hovering over the open lockbox, as his young lieutenant scraped his boots on the metal stub by the door, then creaked up the wooden stairs to the attic to lie on his bed. Godfrey could smell the bones of the latest chicken stewing in the kitchen, yellow feathers drifting on the flagstones. Ralph would be delighted with the orders, he thought as he returned his service notebook to the wooden box, followed by the map and his tobacco tin, the pouch with the ration, locked it all down. A chance at last to demonstrate his prowess with his revolver. And not just on a bird that could not fight back.

But Godfrey had been in a forlorn brigade before, every man from the unit killed except for three who were wounded beyond repair. And him, of course, walking through it all, then walking back, returned whole-skinned to the right side of the wire as though he'd been out for nothing more than a country stroll. It seemed like another lifetime now, a time when Beach was still alive and they had lived like rats in a sewer. Godfrey had not expected to survive that, yet here he was waiting once again for another disaster to unfold.

In the barn, the remains of Godfrey's unit stood in silence, a semi-circle of men grown thin and ragged with the never-ending war. Flint and Fortune, Alfred Walker and Jackdaw, the darker of the two A4 boys, Archie Methven the accountant, who kept them all straight. Hawes, the temporary sergeant, stayed in his corner turning the pages of his book, refused to look anyone in the eye. Arthur Promise was crouched amongst the chiff chaff, husks and sawdust all about his feet. He was scrubbing and scrubbing at another shirt, now, Second Lieutenant Svenson's second-best khaki, chicken blood all along the collar. Promise's knuckles were raw with the cold of it, fair hair flopped across his brow so that none of the rest could see his face.

'Best thing to do is forget it.'

Bertie Fortune with his wise counsel pulling at the corner of his neat moustache as he stood at the centre of the group.

'Why should he?'

Jackdaw, with his *chitter chatter*, was all jerks and nerves.

'Because he's an officer, you idiot.'

Flint had his shirt sleeves rolled tight on his forearms.

'He owes Promise.' Jackdaw insisted, wouldn't leave it alone. 'The rest of us have to pay, don't we. Why shouldn't he?'

'He's a fucking officer.' Flint came to stand right in front of Jackdaw, small vein throbbing in his forehead just beneath the parting. 'Don't you get it? They never have to pay if they don't want to.'

'Back off, Flint,' said Bertie Fortune. 'It's not the boy's fault.'

'What the fuck was that with the knife, then?' Flint said.

They all shifted to look at Promise hunched over his bucket. Alfred Walker giggled suddenly at the memory of Second Lieutenant Svenson with blood across his cheek. The rest of the men were silent.

'What did he want, anyway?' said Archie Methven, a man used to calculating the odds.

'He wants to know that Promise won't make a fuss.' Jackdaw's eyes shot black in the gloom. 'Why else did he come in here.'

'To flash his badge, of course,' said Flint. 'Get you all worked up.'

That little silver pin with a lion at its centre: *Strike Sure*.

'Where did he get it anyway?' said Walker, rubbing a hand across his hair. 'It's not his mob, is it? The London Scottish.'

'Must have won it from someone,' said Methven, touching the pocket where he kept his notebook, all the *Ins* and *Outs*. 'He likes to toss the dice, hadn't you noticed?'

'Never should have let him play in the first place.'

The men all turned to where James Hawes sat propped against his gasbag, that book with the woven red cover open in his lap.

'What would you know, Hawes.' Flint spat onto the stone floor. 'You're the one who started it with that bloody tanner. Should have offered a better prize and then maybe he'd have let the badge go.'

Hawes turned a single page of his book, let it fall.

'He'll never let the badge go,' he said, his voice low.

'He probably stole it from somewhere.'

Jackdaw's answer was bitter. Archie Methven glanced at Bertie Fortune then, their eyes meeting for a second before they both looked towards Hawes. But the temporary sergeant had his head bent over his book again, wasn't going to get involved.

'Bloody coward,' muttered Flint, staring at Hawes, too.

'Should have joined in from the start like all the rest. Or can't you bear to play anymore?'

'Shut up, Flint.' There was a cold bite to Bertie Fortune's reply. 'You don't know what you're talking about.'

'He wanted to know the orders.'

The voice came from another corner of the barn. Alec, the new recruit, laying out the final touches to his billet – fleabag, gasbag, rifle and pack. The men all turned towards the new boy, the bright flax of his hair. There was silence for a moment, nothing but the sound of raindrops high on the roof.

'What did you tell him, then?' said Flint.

Alec stopped with his sorting, stared at the married conscript for a second – Percy Flint with his hair slicked and his shirt buttoned to the collar – before looking away.

'Nothing,' he said.

'Fuck's sake,' Flint swore. 'Why not, if he asked you?'

Alec turned back to his fleabag then, with its cover and its makeshift pillow, a small dog curled at the foot.

'Because he's not the one in charge.'

After supper, Godfrey asked Alec to join him in the parlour, a boy washed in from somewhere obscure and shifting, not even certain about which battalion he belonged to now that things were nearly done.

'Northumberland Fusiliers,' he said when Godfrey enquired. 'Twenty-third to start with, sir. Not sure which now.'

Godfrey wasn't surprised. Ever since the summer when they had all begun to move so fast men had become displaced and lost and found again with amazing regularity, the whole territory full of wandering soldiers from disbanded regiments trying to catch up with the next. In this section alone Fortune and Flint were originally from London outfits, Hawes and Stone from Manchester or some other northern city. Jackdaw and Promise from God knows where. Ralph was from one of the Home Counties, no good for anything but taking tea on the lawn.

'And have you seen much fighting?' Godfrey asked.

'Aye, sir, a bit.'

'Been out long?'

'Nine months, sir.'

Since spring. Since Jerry pushed to within a few miles of Paris, plundering and looting all the way. No wonder it hadn't lasted. Godfrey had seen the look of the men from the other side who'd been captured, shirts off as they were paraded through the streets. Could play their ribs like a piano. And their faces, too.

'And what's your patch of the north like?' he said.

Alec grinned, a quick flash of teeth. 'All work and no play.'

Godfrey smiled, too. 'In the hayfields?'

The new recruit nodded. A country boy, then, used to fields and hedgerows. Godfrey tried to remember being a boy himself. Days perched on hard wooden benches watching dust circle in the sunlight. A clock ticking in the parlour. The sound of his mother on the stair.

'Your mother must be proud,' he said.

But Alec didn't answer, a quick flush on his cheeks, looked away instead. Godfrey didn't press it, glanced towards the wooden settle, thought of all those postcards he still wrote to a man and a woman who'd been long dead before he discovered the fact. Swept away by a motorcar on the parade at Hastings, over a year ago now. It had been an accident – death within the sound of the guns. Like drowning in a drainage ditch beneath a spatter of enemy bullets, nowhere near the main event. His father's solicitor had written to tell him. But the letter had got lost, or diverted. Or Godfrey had got lost, or diverted. Each heading in opposite directions, just at the moment when they needed to meet up. When the letter finally reached him, his parents had been dead for a couple of months. Eight weeks in which he had sent at least a half-dozen postcards.

Dear Mother and Father, we are all going on fine here . . .

Godfrey had read the solicitor's letter and put it in his pocket. He never said a word. Not to the Company Commander. Not to any of the other officers. And not to Ralph, either. Made no request for leave. What would he do at home but stand over yet another grave? After all, the worst had happened long before his mother and his father fell beneath the wheels of a charabanc, Godfrey marching away as a young man, returning twelve months later as something else. An old man, sitting opposite another old man, who had fiddled with his watch chain because he hadn't known how to put it all to voice.

'Sir?'

Godfrey looked at his new recruit. The boy's eyes reminded him of Beach, another young man assigned to his protection, dead in less than six weeks. He rose from his chair, came round to perch on the edge of the parlour table, felt the orders shift in his breast pocket, just above that ache beneath his skin.

'Anything you're particularly good at, son?'

'I can sew a bit, sir, if that's useful.'

'Might be.' Godfrey thought of the buttons loose on his greatcoat, Flint's spool of pink thread. 'Do you like to gamble?'

Alec shook his head. 'Not really, sir.'

Godfrey slid from the table, stood close to the new recruit, as a father might to a son.

'And did you read the orders?'

Alec flicked his eyes to his new captain's face, then away. 'No, sir.'

But Godfrey knew at once that he had.

Two

6 November, rain still threatening from the east, and Godfrey Farthing woke to the sound of men in the yard, talking and joking as though nothing untoward had happened, the grey light of morning seeping through the parlour window at the front. He rolled from the narrow settle with a groan, stared at his boots standing neat by the door. When was it in the night he had risen to remove them? He tried to remember the message he had received the day before – touched a hand to a paper in his tunic pocket – and what he had decided must happen next.

In the kitchen, George Stone the old sweat was wearing the apron again. He stood over the stove dishing up a treat – two or three of the few remaining eggs scrambled in a smear of chicken fat, another remnant of the yellow slaughtered by Promise the day before.

'Do you want some, sir?'

It was Bertie Fortune who asked, holding out a battered mess tin to Godfrey – on breakfast duty for today.

'Where's Second Lieutenant Svenson?' said Godfrey.

'Chatting up the new recruit. He's got the others with him.'

Godfrey took the tin, went and stood in the porch doorway to see. The men were gathered in a tight circle in the middle of the yard, their backs to him, breath pluming above them in the air. All except James Hawes, who sat alone by the entrance to the barn shovelling egg into his mouth with a spoon that *clitter clattered* on the edges of his tin. Hawes looked sick, thought Godfrey, full of tics and jerks, wouldn't last much longer before it all came down.

In the centre of the circle of men sat Alec, the new recruit, scraping up mouthfuls of egg, too. And next to him, his dog.

'I give him six months.'

It was Percy Flint, the sexual adventurer, who was setting the odds, tossing down a matchstick burnt black at one end by way of a casual bet.

'We won't have six months.'

Archie Methven, ever the realist. Knew that if the orders ever came, the chances were none of them would live to see spring.

'It'll be over by then anyway.'

Alfred Walker with his prediction. And, perhaps, his dreams.

'That's what they said about Christmas the first year.'

Promise's fair skin had a bloom to it in the cold morning air.

'What would you know about it, Promise?'

Second Lieutenant Ralph Svenson appeared from the back of the circle, tunic unbuttoned, chewing on a match-stick of his own. The men all took a step to the side as though to widen the circle and allow Ralph through. Although to Godfrey's eyes, it could have also been so that they could move away. Ralph's cheeks were high-coloured, too. Like a baby, thought Godfrey, freshly woken for the day. The men hesitated, as though waiting to see what Ralph might do. But when he didn't say anything more, it was Alfred Walker who took up the refrain again, the chancer of the company, always ready with a joke or a game. Walker dug into his pocket for a penny.

'Six days,' he said. 'That's how long it'll last.'

Flipped the coin with his thumb, caught it, pronounced 'heads'.

They all laughed at that. Alfred Walker with his fantasies. As though he could toss a coin and in less than a week it would all be done. Walker turned to Archie Methven, the accountant.

'I'm serious, six days. Write it up, Methven. In your book.'

But the accountant just shook his head, smiling. 'Book's for proper games, Walker. None of your on-the-fly stuff.'

'Six minutes,' called Flint, fag tight between his fingers, never a man to let a bet alone.

All the men turned to look at Alec then, as though the matter was settled. For a moment Godfrey thought that it was the new recruit's life they were betting on, a boy fresh to the field like Beach had once been, just waiting for one of the other men to reach for his bayonet and stick it into the boy's belly for the pleasure of winning a bet. Godfrey felt a queer turn in his stomach at the thought. Then the dog rolled its head, let out a yowl and the men laughed, Godfrey realizing with relief that it wasn't the new recruit whose life they had been betting on, but his dog's.

Alec ferreted in his tin for a blob of egg, held it out for the dog to take. The men all watched as the dog licked at the boy's fingertips, then stood and stretched, sniffed about a bit before nosing its way to the edge of the circle, waiting for them to let it pass. They stared down at the creature as they parted, watching in silence as it sauntered towards the barn. Then Ralph spat the matchstick he'd been chewing from between his teeth and reached a hand to where his Webley sat against his hip.

'How about six seconds,' he said. 'We could do it now. Save ourselves the trouble later.'

Withdrew the gun from its holster and lifted the pistol as though sighting it at Promise, cocked the safety off.

The men were suddenly still. No sound but the water running into the pond and out again, Godfrey Farthing's blood so loud in his ears he thought everyone must hear. He looked towards Hawes to see if he might intervene, caught the flicker of panic in the temporary sergeant's eyes. How quickly things changed, Godfrey thought, once a gun appeared.

Ralph cast his pale eyes at the A4 boy. Promise's face turned to chalk, shadows huge beneath his cheekbones. 'What's the matter, Promise? I thought you liked blood sports.'

Then he laughed, pointed the revolver towards the retreating dog instead.

'Lieutenant Svenson!'

It wasn't like Godfrey to shout. But when he did, everybody listened. The men scattered at once, leaving Alec spooning egg from a mess tin as though nothing untoward had happened, Ralph standing over him with his weapon still drawn. Godfrey looked at his feet in their khaki socks. He was not inclined to dirty them for a young officer who had learned nothing so far about war.

'Lieutenant Svenson. A moment.'

Ralph came over to stand in the doorway to the farm-house, re-holstering his pistol as he did so, face eager. Second Lieutenant Svenson was wearing his boots this morning, as though he knew that something had changed.

'Just a lark,' he said, running a hand through his hair as though to smooth it.

'It's not a game, you know.'

Godfrey's reply was sharp, a warning for his second who had never known what it meant to walk towards the guns. Ralph blushed.

'Yes, sir.'

Then followed Godfrey inside.

All the time they were in the parlour, Godfrey could feel the square of paper in his pocket burning into his chest, like the envelope they used to pin across the heart of a condemned man to ensure a clean shot. He had meant to lock the orders into his wooden box with all the rest, but when the moment came, he had not.

Ralph sat at the parlour table without being asked, tipped back in the chair, excitement lighting his eyes.

'They've come, then,' he said. 'The orders.'

It wasn't a question. Godfrey remained standing in his woollen socks.

'What was that all about in the yard?'

'I told you. A bit of fun.'

'It isn't fun to unsheathe your weapon when there hasn't been a command.'

'Just shining it.'

Godfrey sat, began to pull on his boots. Once he was

done, Ralph let the feet of the chair clatter to the floor, stood abruptly, heels together, saluted.

'Sir, orders, sir.'

'Oh for God's sake . . .'

Ralph dropped his arm. 'But he did bring some, didn't he – the boy, I mean.'

As though he was not a boy himself.

Godfrey felt a great weariness inside then. War required precision in the matters of the soul, he had learned that at least, after everything that had passed. But he had become blunted by years of the need to go forwards, forwards, always forwards, whereas Ralph was fresh to the kill.

'Sit down, Ralph, can't you.'

'But we are going to fight, sir?'

The colour was high on the boy's cheeks.

'Why are you so keen to christen your weapon, Ralph?'

'It's our duty, isn't it.'

'Even when it will all be over in a week or two?'

'You don't know that.'

'Only yesterday it was you telling me that it would be soon.'

'But it's not over yet,' said Ralph. 'Is it? Unless that's the news the boy brought.'

But even Godfrey Farthing could not lie about that. He lifted his hand to his pocket, hooked a finger beneath the flap as though to draw the papers out. Then he thought of Beach with his grey eyes, dropped his hand to his side.

'They were nothing,' he said. 'A request for a supply inventory, that's all.'

Ralph was silent for a moment. 'May I see them, sir? The orders, I mean.'

'They were addressed to me, Ralph.'

'We're both officers, aren't we?'

Godfrey looked up at that, the sudden stink of lemon oil in his nostrils.

'Then why do you spend all your time gambling with the men?' he exclaimed.

'Because. It occupies the time.' Ralph slid his hands into his pockets. 'Besides they enjoy it, don't they. It helps to pass things around.'

'And what things might that be?'

Ralph shifted then, a flicker of doubt in his strange eyes. 'I just thought they needed something to do. Can't march forever to no end.'

'You'd like that, though, wouldn't you?'

'What?' Ralph was perplexed.

'March them to the top of the hill,' said Godfrey, a chilly edge to his voice. 'And march down what's left.'

Ralph flushed then, bright-cheeked at the accusation. 'It's only what we're here for.'

And who was Godfrey Farthing to argue with that.

Down in the cellar once breakfast was cleared, Godfrey and his lucky man, Fortune, checked through all that remained of the rations to see exactly how long they might last. The supplies were low, Godfrey sweating slightly beneath his tunic as he watched Bertie Fortune count them out and count them in again, realizing just how far he had let things go. Less than half a sack of bran. Three tins of M & V – the standard meat and vegetables. Two brown-paper packets of char. Two tins of Nestlé's Condensed Milk. Some tackety biscuits and a jar of pozzie – plum and apple.

A single tin of Lyle's waiting for the moment when they all needed something sweet. It wouldn't keep them going much more than a few days, Godfrey thought, hands hot where he gripped his supply list, and only then if they were lucky, now that the chickens were diminished, too.

Godfrey peered at the almost empty shelves in the gloom, wondered if Fortune would take the bait if he asked. Bertie Fortune had become Godfrey's eyes and ears in the section, because he could not rely on Ralph. He watched as his lucky man scraped flour from the bottom of the sack. Four cupfuls. After, Fortune wiped his hands down the front of his tunic, leaving two white lungs. Best to know the enemy inside out, Godfrey thought then, if one wanted to survive.

'So tell me,' he said, voice casual. 'What happened yesterday while I was gone?'

Fortune rubbed his hands again, on the sides of his trousers this time, wouldn't look at his captain.

'What do you mean, sir?'

'You know what I mean, Fortune. One more dead chicken and Promise can barely look at Lieutenant Svenson.'

Fortune shifted, kept his eyes on the tins.

'Ask the accountant,' he said. 'He holds the book.'

'I'm asking you.'

Fortune nudged at one of the Nestlés. 'Promise won something from the lieutenant, sir. In a bet. Over a chicken.'

'Christ,' said Godfrey. 'I warned him about too much gambling with the men.'

'It was Hawes's idea.'

'Hawes . . .' Godfrey frowned at the thought of his

temporary sergeant getting involved in a bet with his second. 'I thought he didn't play anymore. Too busy reading that book.'

'*Old Mortality*,' said Fortune.

'What! Where on earth did he get that from?'

Bertie Fortune refused to look at his captain. 'It belonged to Beach, I think. He liked adventure stories. Hawes has had it ever since.'

Godfrey felt the tips of his fingers suddenly cold, a silence growing between them in the dim expanse of the cellar, before he tried again.

'So what's the problem, then?'

Bertie Fortune sighed. 'The lieutenant wouldn't hand over the prize, sir. The men don't like someone who doesn't pay their debts.'

Godfrey swore, a low curse. 'Bloody hell. What did Hawes do about it?'

It was the temporary sergeant's job to keep the men in order, whether he liked it or not. Bertie Fortune smoothed a finger across his moustache.

'Nothing, sir. Promise got in there first.'

One swipe of the knife and sticky blood all over. Godfrey was silent. Both men knew that Hawes couldn't stand the sight of blood. Not anymore. Fortune leaned on the edge of the shelf, shifted the single jar of pozzie to the centre, then back again.

'You should organize a big game, sir. Winner takes all. Now that the chickens are almost done. Let Promise try to win it back.'

'Why would I do that, Bertie?' said Godfrey. 'You know I don't like gambling.'

'Everybody does it.'

Fortune was right, of course. Godfrey had spent his whole life in the army with soldiers whose spare time went in scrounging and bartering. Tobacco nips and bullet casings. Tossing the dice for Crown and Anchor, backs up against the wall. Godfrey had seen fights break out over a plum, the fruit smashed and bruised beyond repair, yet still borne away triumphantly by the winner. He knew that men who had little fought over everything if they had the chance. That was why he had let Ralph lead the men out in pursuit of the chickens – in the hope that they would focus their minds on the birds, rather than anything else.

'What makes you think a big game will help?' he said now.

'They're jumpy, sir,' said Bertie Fortune. 'Since the new boy arrived. Nervous about what might come next. It would help take their minds off it, give them something else to do while we wait.'

'We're all bloody nervous about what might come next, Fortune. That's nothing new.'

'It is this time.'

Godfrey understood. They were all waiting to hear the bells sound in the nearest village, heavy peals ringing out over the empty fields even though it wasn't a Sunday, knowing that it meant the end had come at last. Bertie Fortune turned to face his captain.

'They've been wondering about the orders, sir. What was in them.'

'You're wondering, you mean.'

Godfrey's tone was dry. They had been together more

than two years now, Captain Farthing and his lucky man, seen all there was to see.

'Aye, sir,' Bertie Fortune admitted. 'I'm wondering. Whether it's all going to be over. Or whether my letter will be winging its way to the wife.'

Godfrey felt the tremble in his fingers as he thought of the letters stacked in his wooden lockbox, all that might be left of them if he followed the orders through. Then he jabbed his hand towards the stores in the cellar, its cool walls and beaten earth floor scented with long-lost turnips lifted from the fields.

'These are the orders, Fortune. Counting the supplies.'

Bertie Fortune looked away then, before he said it. 'One last roll of the dice, sir. Never did hurt.'

Three

That afternoon, Captain Godfrey Farthing stood at the bottom of the fold in the land turning and turning the walnut he kept in his pocket, feeling for all its shallow tunnels and grooves. Next to him Alec, the new recruit, was foraging in a clump of brambles, the dog digging alongside. Godfrey imagined the small berries in the boy's palm, stained and sweet, wondered if he would ever be able to eat something like that again without tasting decay.

They had come in search of wild offerings. Mushrooms, and the last fruit of a season, beech nuts safe inside their prickled shells. Also to check for burrows, those small holes that hinted at a honeycomb of tunnels beneath their feet. It was Stone who had sent them, the old sweat coming to stand at the parlour door once Godfrey and Fortune had finished in the cellar – the revised list in his hand.

'Need to start getting in new supplies,' he'd said. 'Now the chickens are nearly done.'

'Down to the last two, are we?'

Godfrey had been joking, thought there must be at least five. But he saw at once from the look on Stone's face that it was true, Ralph's game led to its inevitable conclusion now that the end was near. Godfrey had felt queer again then, as though the orders had come at just the right moment, paradise about to be lost.

'You could always go for rabbit, sir,' George Stone had said, seeing his captain's confusion. 'Set some traps.'

All those warm bodies cloaked in fur, sleeping top-to-tail beneath the earth like Godfrey's men used to sleep top-to-tail in their trench. Now he watched as Alec dipped amongst the tangle of undergrowth to lay the first trap.

'Tell me more about your farm,' he said. 'Where you come from.'

'It's just a farm, sir,' said Alec, setting the coil of wire, then stepping back. 'Animals. And fields like these, two kinds of clover in the summer. A river at the bottom of the hill.'

Godfrey smiled. 'Did you grow up there?'

'When I was young.'

'Is that where you learned to trap rabbits?'

'Aye, sir.'

'I knew a boy like you once,' said Godfrey. 'He came from the city. But his family were from the north.'

'Of England, sir?'

'Scotland, I think.'

The mountains and the burns.

'What was his name?'

'Beach.' Godfrey hesitated. 'William.'

The boy glanced at his captain. It wasn't usual for an officer to use an infantryman's first name. 'What happened to him, sir?'

'He was shot,' said Godfrey, starting to walk on now. 'Died of his wounds.'

Down in the yard, the men were taking a bath. Any receptacle they could find, Hawes in charge, Second Lieutenant Svenson to supervise. Might as well go clean to the slaughter,

Godfrey had thought as he handed down the instruction, should it come to that. It began to rain as the men lined up the tubs, Ralph lounging in the doorway to the farmhouse as he watched the men drag them across the yard to the pump. A low cattle trough. A couple of buckets. A barrel of some description just big enough for one of the slighter lads to dip into up to his neck. There was a proper tin bath hanging in the back room of the farmhouse, but Ralph would not offer it to the men. He would bathe in it himself later, a slow descent into warm water, a thousand tiny bubbles silvering his thighs.

Jackdaw and Promise took turns to pump, skinny arms flexing in the wet, shoulder blades like knives. Hawes joked as he watched the A4 boys work, water gushing in spasms from the wide mouth of the pump.

'This'll build you up, lads.'

But even he could see how out of breath the work made them, Jackdaw and Promise not as fit as they had once been, nothing but spit and bone between them now.

George Stone went to and fro from the kitchen with the big kettle full of hot water, adding it to each container before Percy Flint and Archie Methven hauled them into the barn. Ralph sauntered across the lagoon of mud to watch in silence as the small section undressed, his face all shadow and scowl. Godfrey Farthing had forced his second to hand over his lucky dice in punishment for pointing his weapon at Promise. Ralph felt naked without them, unmoored, like the men before him now.

As the section disrobed, piling their clothes in neat heaps by each tub, Ralph fiddled with the silver cap badge in his pocket, turning the little thing over, then over again. What was it that made Captain Farthing dislike him so much, he wondered. A man not that much older than Ralph was himself – the same age his brother would have been if he'd survived, buried now beneath an ever-shifting battlefield, never would come home again to drink tea or bash on the piano, challenge Ralph to a game of tennis on the lawn.

When Ralph had crammed himself into the train carriage along with all the other new officers, the smell of freshly pressed khaki filling the air, he had imagined card games round a table in the billet, laughing and tossing his dice with the older men as they told tales about what they had seen. But when he arrived, Ralph had found that Captain Godfrey Farthing was a man who barely spoke, kept his treasure locked away in that wooden box, never did agree to join his second in a game. An officer who did everything he could to keep his head down, and those of his men, too. It wasn't fair, Ralph thought now, rubbing his thumb over the lion with its paw raised ready for battle, that after weeks of waiting for something to happen the captain had taken the new recruit on reconnaissance, while Second Lieutenant Ralph Svenson had been left behind to watch old men and boys take off their clothes.

The mist lay thick on the fields as Godfrey and Alec Sutherland stood side by side beneath the ring of trees looking out across the broken walnut shells, black and de-composed. An hour or more of walking and their pockets were already filled with treasure. Berries and haws. Nuts dug from the earth where they had fallen. Nothing but the smell of earth and loam. What would it be like to be buried here, Godfrey thought, once the end had come?

Alec's dog panted by their feet for a moment, then wandered away across the walnut shells, sniffing at one here, licking another there. Neither man attempted to stop him, watched in silence until the dog disappeared into the undergrowth on the opposite side. It was Alec who started to talk of what might happen once they reached the other side, too.

'What will you do next, sir?' he said. 'When it's over, I mean.'

'I don't know. Go home, I suppose.' Though where was home, Godfrey wondered, now that his parents were in the ground. He turned to the boy. 'What about you? Back to your mother? She won't want to let you go again, I bet.'

Alec looked embarrassed, a slight flush on the back of his neck.

'I never had a mother, sir.'

'Everyone has a mother, don't they?'

Godfrey had meant it as a joke, but Alec flinched and Godfrey felt bad. After all, he didn't have a mother either. Not anymore.

'I didn't mean to pry,' he said.

'I have a girl, sir.' The boy spoke as though to make up for the absence of a mother. 'She lives next door to the farm.'

'What's her name?'

'Daisy.' Alec blushed. 'Haven't heard from her for a while, though.'

Godfrey thought of all those letters in his lockbox. Perhaps the boy had one that he wanted to add.

'I can keep a message for her, if you like,' he said. 'Just in case.'

Alec hesitated, brushed the tip of his boot against a blackened walnut shell. 'Mebbe.'

'Or anything else you want to keep safe.'

The boy raised his hand then, as though by instinct, touched the pocket over his heart. Godfrey wondered what it was that Alec kept there as treasure, felt again the orders burning in his top pocket. He made as though to put his hand on the boy's shoulder, dropped his arm to his side.

'And what are you and your girl hoping to do once this thing is done?' he asked.

'We want to get married, sir,' Alec replied. 'See a bit of the world.'

'What, like France or Belgium?'

Alec grinned then. 'Something like that.'

A boy like Godfrey had once been, then, keen for adventure, his sweetheart left behind amongst the hay.

'Well,' Godfrey said. 'You've seen some of that and then some. Time to go home and settle down for a bit first, don't you think. Start a family when you're ready.'

'Aye.' Alec shuffled, looked at his boots amongst the debris of the walnut shells. 'Is that what you would do, sir?'

Yes, thought Godfrey. Yes. Though he hadn't imagined it before, the idea of a son.

'Maybe I'll drink a cocktail first,' he said. 'To celebrate.'

Champagne. With brandy at its heart.

'I've never had anything like that,' said Alec.

Godfrey smiled. 'We could drink one together. Toast the future.'

'I might prefer a pint, sir.'

Godfrey laughed. 'Drunk many of those, have you?'

Alec flushed slightly. 'A few.'

Godfrey imagined the two of them then, sitting together at a table in a pub somewhere in the north, the dog at their feet, froth on the boy's top lip as he took his first sup. He could almost taste it, too, the sweet fizz of bubbles on his tongue.

Then the dog began to bark.

Despite the rain outside, the atmosphere in the barn was high, the men larking as they took turns in the water, splashing and tossing a thin ration of soap from one to the next. The soap was like a sickle moon after more than ten days of waiting for the orders to arrive, almost gone now. But Percy Flint had a private cake of his own, unwrapped from a single piece of waxy paper the week before to the envy of all the other men. Flint's soap smelled of lavender, was stamped with the image of a woman's face. He had probably bartered it with Bertie Fortune, Ralph reckoned. For something equally precious in return.

Flint lounged in the cattle trough as though he was bathing in a spa, a leisurely wash around his dick and his balls. He balanced the fancy soap on the lip of the trough – didn't want it to get coated in grit and chiff chaff. Ralph knew he would not share it with the other men, unless they had something to give him in return.

'Perfect for the ladies,' Alfred Walker shouted from where he lathered and splashed in his own bucket.

'You wish,' said Flint flipping him a lazy 'V'.

Walker talked big-time about the sweetheart he was going to marry when this war was done. But all the men knew he probably hadn't even kissed a girl yet. Walker shook out his hair, flecks of foam spattering across the barn's cold floor like the first specks of snow they were expecting any day now.

'At least we'll be clean for when the bells ring,' he said.

'Who says the bells are going to ring?' drawled Flint.

'Why else did the captain order baths?' Walker flicked water towards the married conscript. 'That's the orders the new recruit brought, don't you think?'

'Or for going over.'

There was a lull in the men's chat as Percy Flint offered his prediction.

'Offer Alec your soap when he gets back and then maybe we'll find out.' It was Jackdaw who made the suggestion.

'Why don't we just ask the captain?' said Promise.

'He won't tell, will he,' sneered Flint. 'Likes to play his cards close to his chest.'

Bertie Fortune's voice cut through the rest. 'Nothing more than a supply count.'

'How do you know, Fortune?'

'Just do, Flint. Just do.'

'What about you, sir?' said Archie Methven, standing next to the cattle trough with a towel draped about his neck. 'Do you know what the orders are?'

'None of your business, Methven,' said Ralph turning away. But they all saw the flush upon his neck.

The men who had bathed already began to dress, the skin of their fingers wrinkled like the walnuts Stone served them for dessert after every dinner, their feet sprinkled with a dusting of Boric powder so that they slipped and squeaked inside their heavy boots. How squalid they were, thought Ralph, filthy on face and neck, pale as dead men underneath, their skin riddled with lice bites, blotched with shadows and scars. Like the wound Ralph had glimpsed beneath Godfrey Farthing's shirt. A small pucker of skin, just above his heart, that seemed to ache in the damp if the captain's constant pressing at it was anything to go by. Ralph had noticed it when he and Godfrey passed on their way to and from their tin bath in the back room, the flicker of a candle high on a shelf shimmering across the captain's pale skin. Ralph had lain in the bath after, staring at the roses on the greasy wallpaper, wondering how the captain had got the wound. Something to do with Hawes – that was what Fortune had suggested, called their temporary sergeant the bravest of them all. But Ralph was too afraid to ask.

He looked now across the wide expanse of the barn towards where James Hawes was handing out towels taken from the wash line in the grain store. Hawes had kept his clothes on, as befitted a temporary sergeant, no need to expose himself to the men any more than he had been already the day before. But he stank, Ralph thought, bad enough to make his own mother turn away. All the men smelled bad, in fact, a stench of decay hanging on them however much they washed beneath the pump each morning or got caught in the rain. Except for him, of course. Second Lieutenant Ralph Svenson only ever smelt of lemon oil, a sweet note of citrus following wherever he led.

Ralph watched as Hawes helped Jackdaw clamber into the barrel, the boy dipping his head right under the water like a child on a trip to the seaside, before rising like a nymph emerging from the waves. This was who was left to win the war, Ralph thought. A4 conscripts and sexual adventurers. George Stone, the old sweat who wouldn't remove his apron and Alfred Walker, the petty thief, always stuffing his pockets. Bertie Fortune, the entrepreneur who could get anything anybody wanted as long as they paid. Not forgetting James Hawes, of course, the temporary sergeant who could no longer stand the sight of blood. Not the bravest of them, thought Ralph, not anymore.

Across the barn, Jackdaw splashed some more before he clambered out, made way for Promise, a broad beam on Hawes's solid face as he handed the darker A4 boy a towel. Jackdaw began a vigorous rubbing down of his whole body as Hawes disappeared towards the grain store to get another. Jackdaw was a skinny thing, scrawny, but he didn't mind it all being on show. Walker whistled a few bars of 'Mademoiselle' till the others joined in, Jackdaw laughing and striking a pose. Legs like a lady's, thought Ralph. He would let the A4 boys lead, when the orders came.

He sauntered over to where Promise was still dipped into the barrel, all the others out and dressing now. Flint was attempting to comb a parting into his hair, frowning at himself in a bashed-out piece of tin.

'Are you coming out, Promise?' Ralph said. 'Or are you going to lounge in there all day?'

He took the silver cap badge from his pocket, flipped it between his fingers as though it was nothing more than a toy. Promise's face was suddenly all angles and dips. Jackdaw couldn't help himself, came slapping over in his bare feet, towel flapping.

'That doesn't belong to you . . . sir.'

Ralph turned the little badge over once, then twice, more slowly this time.

'It doesn't belong to you either, does it, Jackdaw? But your pal can come and get it if he wants.'

Jackdaw didn't reply. The men all stopped what they were doing, looked towards Promise. The A4 boy huddled naked in his barrel, the water grey now, silted with pubic hair, dead lice floating on the surface.

'Come on, Promise,' Ralph laughed. 'We've seen it all before.'

Promise shook his head, shivering as the already tepid water cooled even more.

'Well, if you don't want to get out,' said Ralph, 'you can do some more swimming.'

He reached a hand to the A4 boy's fair scalp and pushed him under. Promise scrabbled blind, water slopping over the top of the barrel, before, at last, he rose again, gasping for air. But Ralph was waiting.

'In you go again.'

Pressing his hand to Promise's head once more, holding him down as he struggled in the water, spluttering and choking, Bertie Fortune restraining a half-naked Jackdaw as Ralph laughed.

'What's going on?'

James Hawes came into the barn from the grain store, a fresh towel for Promise folded on his arm. Ralph removed his hand and Promise rose from the barrel, coughing and hacking, fair hair plastered dark with the dirty water, thin body shivering and shivering as he hunched in the filthy soup.

'Diving practice,' said Ralph.

Flint laughed. Promise and Jackdaw stayed silent, the other men too. Hawes frowned. Ralph stepped away from the barrel as the temporary sergeant came close, offered Promise a hand. The A4 boy looked scared for a moment, before he took hold of Hawes's thick fingers, held on tight as he stepped over the high lip of the barrel and onto the barn's cold floor.

Hawes draped the towel around Promise's shoulders, stood in front of the boy.

'Something I can help you with, sir?' he said.

'No, thanks,' said Ralph, giving the little silver cap badge a twirl before sliding it back into his pocket. 'Unless you want to give us a hand slaying the rest of the chickens, Hawes. Two still to go, if anyone's up for it, Promise to lead.'

The freckles on Hawes's neck were suddenly raw in the falling light as he slid his eyes towards the A4 boy, then away. All the men saw it, that look in their temporary sergeant's eyes as he dipped his head, turned towards the darkest corner of the barn. Fear. Or something like it. The inability to quell the panic in his heart.

Up on the hill, afternoon mist pressing down, Godfrey and Alec found what the dog had discovered hidden in amongst the brambles on the far side of the ring of trees. Alec grabbed the dog, pulling it away as Godfrey parted the undergrowth to see. There amongst the dead grass and leaves piled high lay the remains of a creature, scattered amongst the decay. A rabbit pegged to the earth by an old trap, wire all rusted and black, a mess of blood and fur.

Godfrey could see at once what had happened. The

rabbit had gnawed its leg off. Through the fur. Through the meat. Through the sinew and the bone. Not much of it left now but a foot abandoned in the grass, a self-inflicted wound. Like Beach, Godfrey thought, the sudden burn of bile in his throat. Like all the other men. He pressed the sleeve of his greatcoat to his mouth. But Alec was already crouching close enough to touch the thing.

'Good luck,' he said, eyes shining in the late afternoon light, as though they would all be safe now.

Godfrey looked at Alec then, hair bright amongst the brambles, small dog panting at his feet. Was it wrong, he thought, to consider it love? To admit that he was a little in love with all his men. Beach with his flat grey eyes. Hawes the ex-meat-man with his fear of blood. And now this new boy, not even old enough to wield a gun. Godfrey couldn't pretend to make sense of it, after all the things he had seen, after everything that had been done. But he did understand one thing: whatever happened next, these men had become all he lived for now.

He stared out beyond the trees to the horizon, felt Ralph's two dice in his pocket, understood suddenly how his second must feel when he itched to throw. Not once. Not twice. But again and again until it came up with the right result. Godfrey would never have allowed it, even one month ago, even two weeks, a gamble on which might come first: court martial for refusing to carry out a direct order; or the ending of the war. But what harm could it do now, he thought. One last roll of the dice as Fortune had suggested. Winner takes all.

1971

Hawes

Hawes had found God. Not gradually. Or by persuasion. Or by regular visits to his parish church. But like in the Old Testament. A revelation. A fiery conversion. From this mortal life to the next.

A young man still when it happened, more than forty years before, one minute Hawes had been walking along the sea front at Hastings, the next he had been up to his waist in the waves. The grey churn of the English Channel had swilled and frothed around him, far behind faint shouts of warning like the short cries of a seagull floating on the air. Far in front the line of the horizon. And beyond that the terrible lair of France.

The sea had been freezing, water in every orifice, that great heave and swell. Hawes remembered gulping and thrashing, going under, as though he might never rise again. Then coming up for air, in a rush, like two A4 boys rising from a barrel. Before dipping down again. Washing. And washing. And washing again, in an attempt to get himself clean. They'd had to drag him out in the end, lay him on the pebbles that shucked back and forth around him, rattling like a dead man's final call. Above him the sky had been grey like Beach's eyes the night before the bombs came down.

When he'd found himself on dry ground once more, Hawes had made straight for the nearest church to sit amongst the pews, water pooling on the flags beneath his feet as once mud had pooled around the bones he'd volunteered to pull from the mire. The church had been quiet, like that moment before dawn when everything is waiting. He'd slid a hymn book from the wooden ledge in front of him, a prayer falling out:

Our Father who art in heaven . . .

Printed on a card about the size of the ones they used to carry in the pockets of their tunics:

I have been admitted into hospital
I am sick
I have received your parcel.

Like the one the captain had been left with in the end. Hawes remembered the constant tremor in his fingers as he bent to pick the prayer card from the floor, the thick clod in his throat as though he had swallowed a lump of clay. What was it the chaplain had said about absolution as Hawes and the other volunteers dug and dug and dug again once the war was done, men falling into putrid pieces in their hands?

. . . Forgive us our trespasses, as we forgive those who trespass against us . . .

Hawes had known then what he must do, where he must go. But life took its time, that was what Hawes had discovered. And so did he. Until there was no time left.

1971 and James Hawes finally arrived in the Athens of the North on a morning light with spring. He was old now, just like his captain, hadn't been home since that baptism in Hastings all those years before. He had abandoned everything long ago to wander the byways and the highways with his orange box and his placard, till he was nothing but a rag-and-bone man himself. When he needed money he would stop in a town square, or a high street, pull all kinds of everything from his jacket – razor blades or chamois leathers, reels of pink thread – calling to his customers about what they could get if they just took the leap. They would stand for up to an hour sometimes waiting to see what might come next, a cheap gold chain or a discourse on the Fall. He had a way about him of compelling attention, as though he had experienced everything they were too afraid to try for themselves.

At nights, in summer, he slept in dry ditches or beneath great trees, watching the world turn above him. In winter he would find the corner of a barn where he could roll himself in a blanket and dream of chickens in a shed. Whenever he could, he slept beneath the pews of a church, or under the lychgate where they used to shelter the coffins until the clergyman arrived. Hawes knew that he smelled like those who had lain there before him. Decaying. Damp to his bones. But there was also the soft scent of beeswax, those notes of old pine. He kept his feet dry and didn't plan for tomorrow. What was the point of worrying about the next day, when the next day might never come.

When he arrived, Hawes found Edinburgh was full of its own beauty, grey buildings warm in the sun, flags and spires flying as though in a perpetual dance. Hawes had been to Scotland before, when the second war was barely over. But it had been cold at night and sometimes the people even colder, depending on where one went. Or perhaps it had been that old disease which had stopped him doing then what he had come for now. Fear, rising through his body at the thought of what he must say.

But age was pressing on Hawes now, a new decade come round again, the year already pulsing with argument and disorder, division in the air. He could feel time flowing away from him like sand through the hourglass, the stone he had carried in his mouth for all these years too large for him to swallow any more.

He wound his way through the closes and passageways of the elegant city, asking here and there. It wasn't hard to find the place that he required. Pawnbrokers used to be ten a penny when he first went on the road, three gold balls hanging from every street corner. Not anymore. He found it in a narrow street off the Mile, down a close. He peered through the metal grating over the window of Godfrey Farthing's shop, watching for a moment as two young men laughed together over some odd bits and bobs, one dark, one fair. The boys reminded Hawes of Jackdaw and Promise, the way their bodies bent towards each other even when they didn't touch.

The bell rang as he made his way inside.

Ding

Ding

Ding.

It was the darker boy who looked up first, adorned like some sort of peacock, beads and leather strung around his wrists and his neck. Hawes smiled when he saw the young man's attire. This boy was a product of the new generation, shirt unbuttoned at the collar, everything flapping about cuffs and waist. Whereas Hawes was wearing his blue suit with the dark lining, neat lapels and three buttons fastened. The suit was old now, but he had made sure to get it cleaned.

'How old are you, son?' he asked as he came to stand on the opposite side of the baize counter.

'What?' The darker boy frowned. 'Twenty-one.'

Twenty-one. Not much younger than Hawes had once been hugging this boy's grandfather to him at the bottom of a trench, blood in his eye. Nothing left of either of them now but skin and hollow bones. Like one of those new-fangled ha'pennies someone had given him only the other day, '71 and light as a pigeon's feather when you tossed it in the air.

'What's your name, son?' he asked.

'Solomon.'

Solomon Farthing. Hawes smiled then, a mouth full of gaps and teeth worn to stumps. What kind of man would the boy become, he thought, with a name like that? Someone who would end with wisdom or riches? Or neither. Or both. Hawes laid the tips of his fingers along the edge of the baize counter, nails embedded with the grime of long years spent digging in the earth.

'I'm here to see your grandfather,' he said.

His captain lying in the back room, awaiting absolution. Or maybe that was what James Hawes had come for himself.

'He's not well,' said the boy his eyes huge suddenly, dark, like the copper pennies that were now obsolete.

'That's why I came,' said Hawes. 'To see him at the end.'

Through the back of the pawnshop, in a single room with a crucifix hanging on the wall, Godfrey Farthing breathed in and breathed out as though he had a child's rattle in his throat. The room was dim, lit by a low-wattage bulb. It smelled of iodine and that familiar scent of a man only a few steps from death.

Hawes lifted a plain wooden chair from behind the door and positioned it next to his captain's bed. Godfrey Farthing's eyes were closed, sunk into his face as though he was nothing but a skull already. Just like the ones Hawes had dug from the fields of France in '19, everyone else gone home to drink tea at a kitchen table instead of outside in a yard. Left volunteers like him to give the dead the graves they deserved. Digging and digging and digging again till they found whatever remained. No blood this time, but everything else. Teeth scattered in an oily pool. A clavicle dug into the ground like a spade. How resilient the human body was, Hawes had thought as he pulled those boys from the ground one small piece after another, scraping for their dog tags and their pocket books, anything to identify who they had once been. And how frail, with its capacity for smash and fracture, one bullet to the skull and everything gone forever. Hawes never could wash it away after – the ever-present stink of putrefaction. Only twenty-three and his whole life already beholden to the past.

Hawes placed his hand on Godfrey Farthing's hand now, felt all its angles and planes.

'Not too many of us left, old man.'

Fortune gone.

Jackdaw.

And all the rest.

He pressed his finger to the old man's skin, left an indent.

'Remember the chickens.'

Godfrey Farthing's eyes opened suddenly, two black points burning through Hawes's seven layers of skin. Inside Hawes a great swell rose, like the sea that time at Hastings, the stone in his throat suddenly huge, as though he might not be able to get the words out just when it mattered the most. His heart began to beat like a rabbit caught in a sack as he gripped the old man's hand tight. Then he crouched close, began to whisper in his captain's ear.

Our Father who art in heaven . . .

A young man again retching into dirty straw.

. . . Give us this day our daily bread . . .

A chicken without a head running past him to the grain store.

And forgive us our trespasses . . .

Six bullets dribbled into his hand.

As we forgive those who trespass against us . . .

A boy's eyes shining bright amongst the grey.

Hawes sat with his captain for more than an hour whispering his confession, counting them out and counting them in again. Jackdaw. Flint. Walker and Promise. Not forgetting the new recruit, Alec. And Ralph, the second lieutenant, of course. It was like the counting of the young men's bones once the whole thing was over, excavated from the mud one fibula at a time.

The rattle was quieter in Godfrey Farthing's throat when Hawes finally stopped. He let go his captain's hand and placed it beneath the cover, slid an old prayer card from his pocket and laid it on the bedside cabinet, its edges soft now with all the time that had passed. He watched his captain as the seconds between each breath grew long. Then he took something else from inside his jacket, fingers *tap tapping* on its red woven cover for a moment, before he placed it beside the card. Hawes pulled his captain's sheet neat one final time, crossed himself and turned towards the door. The boy, Solomon, was watching from the entrance, fear beating in his young heart, no doubt, as it used to beat inside Hawes. Hawes opened his mouth to speak.

'He'll be away soon now, son. Best you sit with him.'

Found that his throat was clear.

Out front, one each side of the counter, Hawes faced the other young man while through the back Solomon Farthing said goodbye to the only family he had ever really known.

'What's your name, son?'

'Andrew.'

'Like the fisherman.'

'What?'

So godless these boys. Didn't know their Bible, or any of the other stuff a man needed when he was faced with a gun. The boy was wearing a long coat made of heavy wool, brass buttons sewn with thread that had once been pink. Hawes smiled. He recognized where the coat had come from, even if this young man did not.

'Do you have any memorabilia I can look at?' he asked. 'War stuff.'

'War stuff?'

'Medals and that.'

Andrew shook his head. Hawes smiled again.

'Try under the counter.'

What he was after was always under the counter. The boy crouched to look, appeared again holding a box covered in a thick skein of dust. He lifted the lid for Hawes to see and the old man dipped his hands in amongst those familiar things. Cap badges and bullet casings. A couple of old postcards with messages stitched in silk thread, once vibrant, now dull. Then the medals, stripes on the ribbons faded long since, just like the shine on the brass. There were quite a few medals, stretching back over several wars. Hawes dug through them like he once dug in the mire, until he found three together at the bottom of the box, laid them on the counter for Andrew to see.

'Pip, Squeak and Wilfred,' he said, pointing to each in turn.

A Star. A War medal. One for Victory, too.

'Sorry?' Andrew frowned.

'That's what we called them, son,' said Hawes. 'After the cartoon in the *Mirror*. A dog. A penguin. A rabbit. And *Their Luvly Adventures*.'

Then he laughed.

'I like this one.'

Andrew touched the Victory medal with its angel of the huge wings. Though Hawes suspected that the boy liked it most because of the rainbow ribbon on which it was hung. Both of the young men were the sort to like colourful things, that was what Hawes could tell.

'That one was named for the rabbit, son,' he said. 'The star's the dog.'

Hawes had a sudden memory of a small dog lying on a blanket in the corner of a barn, eyes like tiny mirrors. Wondered what had become of him.

'Are you looking for anything in particular?' Andrew asked.

Hawes sifted through the box again, one small metal disc sliding over another.

'Nothing in particular,' he replied.

But he knew it should be there, a silver cross with small crowns on the four tips, north, south, east, and west. But there was nothing like that here. When he looked up again Andrew was holding the Victory medal to his chest as though to see how it fared against his coat, before he placed it on the counter next to the rest. Hawes stopped with his searching, pointed to the medals laid on the baize.

'How much?' he said. 'For these three.'

'They're free. You might as well take them,' said Andrew. 'The shop's getting cleared.'

That was what happened when old men died, thought Hawes. Everything else got scattered. But he shook his head.

'Got to pay, son. Not right otherwise.'

Andrew shrugged and Hawes foraged in his trouser pocket, found a sixpence, tossed it down. The boy laughed.

'Not legal tender anymore.'

'Still is for now,' Hawes said. 'It got a reprieve, didn't you hear? Or you can put it in your shoe, keep it till you get married.'

The boy blushed. 'Not sure I'll be getting married.'

Andrew's hair touched his shoulders. Hawes's hair touched his shoulders, too. They could have been related if Hawes had ever had a son. The old man smiled. Unlike him Hawes knew that this boy was born to be a lucky man if he wanted, hadn't arrived in the world until both the wars were done. He ran his hand across the front of his suit. Then he slid the jacket from his shoulders and laid it over the baize.

'What will you take for this?' he said. 'It's my lucky suit. But I won't be needing it anymore.'

Andrew touched the suit's lapels, its mix of wool woven with silk, blue as a starling's egg, the fabric fragile now. 'I don't know. I don't really wear suits.'

'But the old man will need one soon.'

The boy glanced towards the room at the back where Solomon Farthing was sitting with his grandfather. Hawes turned the flap of the jacket to reveal a dark lining.

'Perfect burial gown.'

Andrew shifted as though embarrassed by the thought of death.

'But what about the trousers?' he asked.

'You can have them too.'

'What will you wear?'

Hawes laughed, a rough growl. 'There must be another pair here I can have, don't you think.' He indicated the young man's coat. 'And I'll give you a pound for that.'

Andrew grinned then. 'Done.'

He turned to a flip-top box on the counter, opened it and removed a card, edges sharp and clean.

'What's the name?' he said.

'Hawes, James.'

And the boy wrote it out. *Hawes, J. One suit, blue, three buttons.* He offered Hawes a numbered slip in return, like any good pawnshop, should the old man ever wish to redeem the suit again. Hawes stared at the small square of paper in the boy's hand. Then he shook his head.

'No need for that, son. I won't be coming back.'

Hawes left as he had arrived, three notes on the bell sounding his departure.

Ding
Ding
Ding.

Like the three medals pinned across his chest now. A Star. A War medal. And one for Victory, too. He took away a coat that hung to his ankles, khaki wool heavy on his shoulders like a blanket after the storm. The art of the deal, that was what Hawes was all about. Come in as one thing, leave as something new. He left behind a blue suit hanging on a rail. And a prayer card slipped onto a dead man's bedside table.

Our Father who art in heaven . . . forgive us our trespasses as we forgive those who trespass against us.

Also a book, its pages worn away to almost nothing, the red woven cover stained with seawater, amongst other things. The book was by Walter Scott.

Old Mortality.

Battle pages ripped out at the end.

PART THREE

The Bet

Godfrey Farthing
b.1893 d.1971
|
Thomas Methven
b.1920/21 d.2016
|
Solomon Farthing
b.1950 d.

2016

One

Solomon Farthing drove south as though on a last adventure, fleeing the dark streets of Edinburgh towards the truth about Thomas Methven (deceased). He was heading for a Borders town, one of those places full of people with slippery ancestors, never pledged to any nation other than their kin.

Solomon had rescued the Mini stolen from his aunt from its state of abandon outside his favourite local cemetery – a great expanse that stretched from the leafiness of an Inverleith suburb, to the dark covered walkways of the Water of Leith. He'd squeezed in behind the steering wheel, knees almost to his chin, cast Mr Michaels's folder of information onto the passenger seat beside him, and a small thank you heavenwards as the engine started first time. The floor of the Mini was dotted with holes, the bonnet tied together with string, but still it went along, rather like him, an ancient chariot with rust for wings.

The car had coughed its way to the city bypass, then on to the open road. Now the dog was riding the back seat like it was a roller-coaster, small ears flapping in the breeze. It raised its nose to the air and yowled as they clattered along the B-roads, Solomon singing, too:

'*It's a long way to Tipperary . . .*'

Like his grandfather might have once sung, marching his men to their deaths down those long flat roads in France.

Solomon's destination was a village not far from the invisible line that divided the north from the south. On arrival, he clambered from his aunt's Mini into the sweet scent of clematis and spring roses, an unexpected delight. But Solomon Farthing had not come to smell the blossoms. He had come in search of the *Borders Observatory* – the area's local rag.

The office for the *Borders Observatory* was an anonymous-looking shopfront halfway along the small high street, with a door that announced Solomon's arrival just like the bell at Godfrey Farthing's pawnshop used to welcome his customers.

Ding

Ding

Ding.

The bell was followed by a voice, disembodied:

'No junk mail, circulars or fliers. Any news, just leave it on the counter. If you're a hawker, I don't have cash of any sort.'

A counter ran the width of the shop, a Formica-covered bulwark against the daily intrusion of people come to dish the dirt on their neighbours or advertise for a cow. Beyond it Solomon could hear the sound of old-fashioned typewriter keys being hammered by the two-finger dance. He smiled. Here was a fellow traveller, someone for whom the word 'computer' was probably synonymous with 'death'.

He looked around for some other way to rouse the furious typist, found a small dome of brass on the counter, stared at it for a moment, then down at the dog. The dog stared back, impassive. The typewriter keys clattered. Solomon knew he ought not, but he couldn't resist.

Ting, ting.

Then the explosion.

'Bloody hell, what did I say!'

The journalist, proprietor, editor and sole shareholder of the *Borders Observatory* was in his seventies, hair a-fly upon the top of his head. He appeared on the far side of the counter as though World War Three had just broken out.

'Are you deaf?'

'What?'

'You are, then.'

Solomon decided deflection was the best course.

'Solomon Farthing,' he said, tucking his folder beneath one arm and holding out his hand. The man glowered at it. Solomon withdrew. Men here obviously didn't shake hands with strangers. He must remember he was not in Edinburgh now.

'What d'you want?' the man said. 'I'm busy.'

A typical Borders greeting, prepare a getaway before the terms of business have even been agreed. Solomon held an ace though.

'I'm interested in your archive.'

The man's eyes gleamed then, if only for a second.

'The archive, you say?'

'I'm trying to track down the story behind this.'

Solomon placed the newspaper clipping retrieved from his grandfather's pawnshop on the counter. A scrap of a thing, yellowed with age as any surviving offspring would be, too.

WANTED: Home for a baby boy, 6 months old. Total surrender.

The man frowned at the clipping like one might at a museum exhibit. Then he lifted the Formica barrier with a slow grin, held out his arm.

'I think you'd better come in, sir. Come in. You're most welcome.'

To a place of treasure trove or lost property, a hoarder's paradise full to the brim with newsprint, the repository for a million different stories of a million different lives.

The room behind the shopfront of the *Borders Observatory* must once have been for living in, if living meant coming second to the printed word. Everything was covered in piles of newspapers and magazines, books, journals, pamphlets and reading material of all distinctions. This man must be a roaming encyclopaedia, Solomon thought as he stepped gingerly across the threshold, if he had spent his life immersed in this stuff.

It was clear that the room had functioned as head (and probably only) office of the *Borders Observatory* for some time. Coal dust marked every corner. Animal hair of some description clung to every surface, though there was no suggestion now of any office pet. Solomon had achieved the inner sanctum, but every potential movement carried the threat of a tsunami of the printed word. He looked across the crowded room to a crowded mantelpiece, discovered the dog had woven its way through the mayhem to stand in front of it, too. On the mantelpiece was a case displaying three greenfinches, feet curled in a way that suggested rigor mortis.

Father. Son. And Holy Ghost.

'I enjoy birdwatching,' the man called, as though he

had known Solomon would be studying the wildlife. 'Best thing in the world, birds, the way they flit about.'

Not these ones, thought Solomon, staring mournfully at the finches.

'Bought them in Edinburgh.' The man reappeared at Solomon's side, holding out a mug in which slopped some brown-looking liquid. 'Do you know it?'

'I have some familiarity.'

Solomon did not want to admit to being a resident of the Athens of the North until he had ascertained this Border man's inclinations.

'I do.' The man edged towards the safety of an armchair, plopped into its cocoon of cushions. 'Den of Satan.'

'Ah.'

'Only joking.' He wheezed in a way that made Solomon realize he must be laughing. 'That's Glasgow, of course.'

Walter Pringle was a man who had seen it all.

'I cover everything,' he said.

Fetes. Car crashes. Agricultural affairs.

'Even murder, if we're lucky enough.' Pringle grinned. 'Usually shootings. All those farmers with their guns.'

Solomon blinked, remembering that pucker of skin over an old man's heart, a bullet wound first glimpsed the night he arrived in Edinburgh, perched on the draining board in the scullery watching as his newly discovered grandfather washed in the sink. Godfrey Farthing's body had been as pale as a grub dug from the earth, scar glistening in the light cast from the thirty-watt bulb, tiny blue ghost shifting beneath. Solomon had wanted to touch the scar then, just like later he wanted to touch the ladies' gun with the pearl inlay on the handle. But instead he'd sat in silence, shivering in short trousers, waited for his turn to take off his shirt.

Walter Pringle gestured towards his typewriter.

'Been at it since I was a boy,' he said. 'Used to do the deliveries and line up the slugs. Hot fingers on cold metal. Of course it was an empire then. Adverts for all sorts.'

Martins for quality bread. The Pavilion for variety. Coal deliveries and spring goods.

'Nothing but a village news-sheet now.' Pringle poked a finger at the scrap of newsprint lying on the arm of his chair. 'But this pre-dates even me. 1920. Maybe 1919.'

Solomon was amazed. 'How can you be so precise?'

Pringle sat back in his armchair and took a slurp of his coffee. 'There's an art to it. Reading the classifieds. When was the last time you ordered flannels?'

'Flannels?'

Solomon's grandfather used to wear an ancient pair of flannels, trousers shiny about the bottom and baggy about the knees. Despite being surrounded by other people's clothing, Godfrey Farthing never had been a man to let go of his own. Pringle was pointing at something printed on the cutting. Not an advert for the disposal of a child, but an offer for home-sewn flannel trousers, followed by a short text bordered in black.

I.M. Horace Chicken. Aged 20. Much loved.

'Used to get them a lot,' he said. 'When my father was a boy. Memorial ads. It's the combination of flannels and died of his wounds, that tells you.'

1919 or 1920, perhaps. An advert from a time when Thomas Methven (deceased) was only just beginning. And

Solomon's grandfather, Godfrey Farthing, was still a young man. A soldier returned from war dressed in khaki like all the rest, looking for a new pair of trousers, perhaps, with which to rejoin the world. But Solomon felt certain that flannels were not the reason this particular scrap of newsprint had been kept for all these years.

'It is one of yours, though?' he said.

'Oh, aye,' Pringle replied. 'It's one of ours all right. Can tell from the PO Box number.'

'I don't suppose you have a record of who placed it, do you?'

'Might do.' Walter Pringle smiled then, as though at last Solomon had asked the right question. 'But you'll have to come outside for that.'

Out back the Borders' Fourth Estate owned a whole series of sheds, each one more dilapidated than the next. Solomon could just imagine what Walter Pringle's neighbours must make of this shambles – an eyesore amongst their blossoms. Then again, it was an eyesore that contained all their history. And all their secrets, too.

'I did a follow-up story on them once,' Pringle was saying as he led Solomon and the dog along a crooked garden path. 'The classifieds. Fifty years on, what happened next.'

Trumpet for Sale. French lessons. Feathers for a hat.

'Tried to track down people who'd answered the ads. Never did do any good, of course. Vanished like robins in summer.'

Pringle tilted his face to the sweet air for a moment as though considering where robins flew in summer, before pushing further along the ever-narrowing track.

'How did you know where the replies came from?' Solomon asked, stumbling on what looked like a molehill, mud on the hem of his trousers once again.

'Used the office as the PO Box,' said Pringle over his shoulder. 'My job to open all the requests. And file the responses. Never know when a juicy story might present itself.'

He turned to grin at Solomon, a sudden glimpse of crowded teeth.

'I like dipping into the personal ads. All of life in there.'

Solomon understood. He used to like dipping into the personal ads, too. London in the seventies. *Married men. Make-a-million. Boys available for rent.* A whole world of skin and sweat and dirty smells as far from the grey of Edinburgh as it was possible to be. Andrew never did find out, as far as Solomon knew. He'd enjoyed it for a time, ten years or more, before all the men like him began to fall. Black scabs blooming across their shoulders. Those sudden onsets of pneumonia. Then the drop into an early grave. Young men like Andrew brought down by the joys of liberation. Drink. And drugs. Sex. Love, too. Just the normal stuff of life. Solomon's generation living as though there would always be a tomorrow, only to discover that sometimes when you wanted it most, tomorrow didn't necessarily arrive.

Solomon put his sleeve to his nose as they pushed past a huge and sprawling buddleia, sticky scent and a thousand tiny purple flowers clinging to his tweed. When he came out the other side, he discovered that finally they had reached the very last shed in the row. The shed was a ramshackle thing, door all rippled with the damp, the interior chilly after the balmy air outside. The dog shivered as it followed the men inside. But Solomon felt it immediately once he stepped across the threshold – nostalgia colouring his bones.

The shed was filled to the brim with ledgers, row after row, from the warped wooden floor, to the ancient felt roof. Rather like the great books stored beneath the dome at New Register House: Red for Birth, Green for Marriage, Black for Death, of course. Solomon closed his eyes for a moment, breathed in animal hide and the scent of ancient paper spores. He could tell that he was getting closer to the centre of things now that a ledger was involved.

It was Walter Pringle who did the heavy lifting, balanced on an ancient wooden chair that looked as though it belonged in a French cafe rather than an archive, pulling one old book from the shelves after the next. The ledgers were heavy, pages glued together with damp. Mr Michaels the Book Fetcher would have had conniptions. But the Borders' Fourth Estate was in his element, reliving the glory days of the newspaper before automation came along.

They found the information in the fourth ledger they tried, working their way into the year from January, coming upon it in spring. There, along a neat horizontal line in blue, Walter Pringle's father had written out the words that whoever placed the ad wished to be printed:

WANTED: Home for a baby boy, 6 months old. Total surrender.

Followed by a date:

May 1919.

Pringle grinned as he pointed at the latter. 'Told you so.'

Solomon laid the newspaper clipping alongside to see the match. Proof, he thought. But of what, he couldn't be certain, only that Thomas Methven's pawn ticket had led him here.

'Do we know who placed it?' he asked.

Pringle was already shaking his head as he studied the entry.

'Father usually took a name and phone number, but not everybody wanted to leave one. There is this, though.'

He indicated a figure at the far edge of the page, contained within a column demarcated by two vertical lines in red. *6d.* Someone had paid sixpence. A tanner for the inconvenience of giving up a son. Solomon dipped a hand into his jacket pocket, felt for the little tarnished coin he had retrieved from the safe in his grandfather's pawn-shop, nestled next to pawn ticket no.125. Why was it always the recording of money, he thought, that meant all the other things survived? Next to Solomon the dog leaned in against his leg, a sudden patch of warmth.

Walter Pringle peered closer at the ledger, nose almost touching the page.

'Here's something,' he said, indicating the faintest of pencil marks made long ago. 'Initials. *G. F.* Mean anything to you?'

'What!'

Solomon's heart danced a sudden *one two* jig at the thought of what he might be about to uncover. Was this how his grandfather and his father had become estranged? The latter adopted out by the former before they'd had the chance to get to know each other first? Godfrey Farthing had been an old man when Solomon first met him, never did reveal anything about his past other than the fact that he was once a soldier. A hero, Solomon had always supposed, like they all were. Someone who had been through it all and survived.

Then again, perhaps this lost child belonged to another branch of the Farthing family tree Solomon had never taken the time to research. A line that ran parallel to Solomon's own, connected by blood at the top, divided by secrets at the bottom. Solomon had a sudden vision of DCI Franklin and the boy who had been spirited away from her, returned now as a young man so that their pasts could be reconfigured. Perhaps he and the DCI had more in common than he had thought.

Solomon took the crumpled piece of paper on which he had started to draw Thomas Methven's family tree from his folder, leaned against the page of Walter Pringle's ledger and was about to write *1919* in the space where his client's d.o.b. should be, followed by a question mark. Then he looked again at the wording for the advert, counted back six months and wrote *1918* instead. Then he moved his pen to the space where the name of his client's father should appear. He tried to imagine what DCI Franklin would say if it turned out that all of the fifty thousand belonged to him, Thomas Methven and his grandfather connected by more than just a small slip of blue.

It took Walter Pringle to puncture his flight of fancy – like any good Borders man would. 'It seems the ad was cancelled,' he said. 'G. F. didn't even claim the refund.'

Solomon frowned, bent to see where the 6d required to place this particular advertisement had been struck through.

'Why would they cancel?' he said.

'Maybe they changed their minds,' Pringle replied. 'Got cold feet.'

And Solomon reconfigured the image of his own grandfather in khaki handing over a baby on a village green, to make way for someone else instead. He lifted the little newspaper cutting from the page of the ledger, held it up for a moment to look at his grandfather's writing neat along the edge.

'It doesn't say anything about a Thomas Methven, does it?'

'Ah, now. Why didn't you say earlier.' Pringle's eyes gleamed then like a falcon spotting its prey. 'If that's who you're after, you'll need to go to church.'

Two

The church was a small thing, a single storey of ancient stone perched on a rise at the edge of the village, a bell at one end of the gable and a cross on the other in reply. The graveyard surrounding it was filled with ancient stones leaning here and there like the few teeth left in an old man's mouth. It reminded Solomon of his namesake – *Old Mortality* – travelling the borderlands on his white pony, scraping at graves just like these until they were clear once again. As he entered by the small gate he bent and scratched at one of the memorials with his fingernail to see what might be revealed. The name he uncovered made his left hand flutter.

Methven, 1896.

The door to the church had been painted red once, long ago. An invitation, Solomon thought as he approached to try the handle. Or, perhaps, a warning. Border Men always had been suspicious. Unlike Edinburgh Men, who knew that whatever came their way they were likely to prevail.

Inside the church smelled of wood shavings and poison put down for the mice. The walls were white, paint peeling in great damp curls. There was a simple choir stall and a solitary lectern at the front, a few wooden pews on either side of the aisle. The aisle itself was paved with stones belonging to the long-since departed, as though they did not mind being walked upon now that they were dead.

The dog pattered its way across them to stand in front of the modest altar. But Solomon stayed at the back of the church to study the names, Methvens repeating themselves over and over as one generation made way for the next.

There was the sudden shuffle of footsteps on flagstones, a cough that reverberated around the cold walls. Solomon turned to find an old man standing at the door, jumper unravelling at the hem. The man coughed again – the kind that results from smoking with joy for more than sixty years.

'Who're you looking for?' he said by way of introduction.

'Methven,' said Solomon.

'Aye, that's me. Who's asking?'

And Solomon understood that he had arrived at the source.

'Mr Methven,' he said. 'Solomon Farthing.'

Didn't offer his hand this time.

'Aye,' said the man. 'Pringle said you were on your way. It's Archibald and Mabel you'll be wanting.'

Somehow it didn't surprise Solomon that a Border Man might know his business before he'd even got to it himself.

'You stay here.' The old man indicated one of the pews. 'I'll go get the others.'

'The others?'

The minister. The elders. The people who kept the accounts. Or whoever it was in this parish that knew exactly who had been born, and who had died. And where the bodies were buried now.

The late afternoon sun cast long shadows on the floor as Solomon Farthing settled himself on a pew at the back of the church to await the old Mr Methven's return, a pattern of diamonds stretching across one man's grave to reach the foot of the next. The dog trotted back up the aisle to lie by Solomon's feet, the familiar creak of wood joints easing as Solomon shifted, the murmur of a hundred boys inside his head.

Our Father who art in heaven . . . give us this day our daily bread . . .

The stillness reminded Solomon of the church his grandfather used to take him to in Edinburgh when he was young. Every Sunday, up the Mile and down again, into the gloom of Old St Paul's. Old St Paul's was high church – incense and candles dripping, vaulted ceiling hung with lamps. But it was dark, too, everywhere grey stone rising. Also that chapel to the side, a memorial to the fallen, names hammered into the stone. A message board for the Sick and the Departed. And a martyrs' cross hanging on the wall.

He had always touched that cross – Solomon's grandfather – when they arrived, then again when they left. He had liked things gloomy, Godfrey Farthing, that was what Solomon had learned as he was growing up. Whereas he always had been drawn to excess. Mary slick with varnish. Children rimmed with gold. But sitting in this plain little church, the triangles of light its only adornment, Solomon found he preferred it now, just as his grandfather had once preferred it, too. The austere. The stripping of everything to the kernel. A church with not much in it but silence and an air of all that was past.

Five minutes later the clue to Thomas Methven's past returned as some sort of posse: three men identifiable as related by the way they tended to scratch at the top of their ears when asked a question they did not have the answer for. Mr Methven of the smoker's cough did the introductions.

'I'm the older Methven,' he said. 'And this here's another Thomas. Known to us as Tom.'

Tom was a middle-aged gentleman who wore a green padded jacket.

'Not your Thomas, though,' he said. 'Heard from Pringle he was dead.'

A younger man in a boiler suit with dirt smeared across the front pushed forwards, held out a hand.

'Archie,' he said with a broad smile as Solomon returned the unexpected gesture.

Archie was wearing wellington boots, a trail of mud in his wake. Farmer boy, thought Solomon. Unlike his Thomas Methven, who had lived out his entire life in the city, never did leave it behind. The three men trooped to the front of the church, Solomon following, perched themselves along the edge of the nearest pew like three crows on a wire. A few minutes passed. Nobody spoke.

'Are we waiting for someone else?' said Solomon eventually.

'Aye, son,' said the older Mr Methven. 'The oracle.'

All the men chuckled at that.

The oracle arrived a few minutes later with a rush and a bang of the door, a huge bag over her shoulder, hair all over her shoulders, too.

'Sorry, sorry!'

She scurried up the aisle as though she was late for a baptism or a wake. The three men levered themselves from the edge of the pew and stood as though they had been awaiting a wedding and now the bride had arrived.

'How's things?' said Tom once the oracle reached them.

'Oh –' the woman flapped her hands – 'the usual. Births, marriages, deaths, salvation.'

And she laughed. She offered her hand to Solomon.

'The Reverend Jennie Methven. Welcome to my patch.'

Solomon knew he should not have been surprised. Women ran everything these days. But still, he was.

'Pleased to meet you,' he said.

'You too,' said the Reverend Jennie, shaking Solomon's fluttering fingers as though she was used to being in charge. 'Now, it's a Thomas Methven you're enquiring about, I understand, died recently in Edinburgh?'

'Yes,' said Solomon, thinking that Walter Pringle had done his job well. 'And his parents. Or any other relative I can find.'

'Well, you've come to the right place, then. Plenty of Methvens around here.' The oracle laughed again, the men too. She dumped her bag on the flagstones. 'And when was your man born?'

Solomon scrabbled in his pocket for the scrap of paper on which he had written out the roots of Thomas Methven's family tree.

Thomas Methven b. ~~*1920/21*~~*, 1918? d. 2016.*

The Reverend Jennie nodded as though it was normal to have this degree of latitude when it came to date of birth. She crouched to where her bag was slumped at the foot of the lectern, pulled out a roll of paper, let the thing unfurl.

The tree was huge. Methvens here. Methvens there. Methvens everywhere. And all their extended kin. Solomon stared at the scroll, all its horizontals, all its verticals, all its little boxes containing a myriad of human lives.

'Crikey,' he said. 'Did you draw this?'

The Reverend Jennie smiled. 'Something of a hobby.'

But Solomon knew a fellow traveller when he met one. 'Ever thought of becoming a probate researcher? You can make money from this sort of thing.'

'You mean an Heir Hunter.'

Solomon felt hot suddenly beneath his crumpled shirt. Heir Hunter. Angel to the Intestate. Ambulance chaser of the dead. He had been called all sorts of names over the years, most of them to his face.

The Reverend Jennie, it turned out, was the chronicler of the Methven family history. Any piece of information dragged from the past, down it went on her chart. Solomon had met a few amateur genealogists in his time. They were indefatigable, never gave up. But this was extraordinary. Six generations of Methvens spread about his feet.

The three living Methven men got down on their knees, Reverend Jennie gesturing to Solomon to get down on his, too. The dog pattered over to sniff at the edge of the chart, sat next to Solomon with a quick thump of its tail. Once they were settled, the Reverend Jennie began to point out possible candidates:

Thomas George Methven: born to be a farmer, ended as an engineer.

Thomas Sinclair Methven: had five children, two of them called Thomas, too.

Thomas Abel Methven: never married, died with one leg.

Tommy 'the Ginger' Methven: known for some reason as Fred.

She knew all the stories, all the jingle and the brass.

And yet . . .

Whichever way her fingers wandered along the horizontals and up the verticals, they always returned to the same small square amidst the mass.

Thomas Archibald Methven, b. 1913.

'Told you,' said the older Mr Methven with a firm nod of his head. 'Archibald and Mabel.'

Pointed to the names of the child's parents inscribed above. *Archibald Methven & Mabel Methven née Kerr.* But inside Solomon could already feel his stomach falling, falling, knew that he had pursued the wrong branch.

'It's not him,' he said. 'Wrong date of birth. I already discounted a Thomas Methven with these dates in my initial search at Register House. Too old even for my client.'

'Plus the problem that he's been dead for almost a hundred years,' said Archie.

Thomas Archibald Methven, b. 1913. d. 1918.

Buried in the grass outside.

The men all leaned back then, the older Methven scratching at the top of his ear. The Reverend Jennie frowned.

'Are you sure your dates are correct?' she said to Solomon. 'I have verified everything here.'

Yes, no, maybe, thought Solomon.

'I don't doubt it,' he replied.

Never argue with an amateur genealogist. That's what he had learned.

'Well, let's double check, shall we?'

Reverend Jennie turned to a hole in the stone wall

behind her, drew out a huge book thick with pages cut rough at the edges, a metal clasp holding the bottom to the top. The book looked like a Bible, all the family names inscribed in the front. But it was much more interesting than that.

'It used to be the official record,' she said settling it on top of the Methven family tree. 'Births, marriages and deaths till the 1850s. Just baptisms after. All the ins and outs.'

She unlocked the clasp with a tiny key foraged from inside her capacious handbag, began to turn the pages, stroking each one before she flipped it over as though putting the past and all the people in it to bed. As Solomon watched he felt his whole body suddenly soft, his knees, his shoulders, the insides of his gut, nothing to hear inside the church but the sound of pages turning; and outside, the call of a blackbird in a hedge. This was what he loved most about his profession – that moment when the dead waited for the living to wake them, bring them home again.

It didn't take the oracle long to find the good news, pressing her fingertip to a line written in flowing copper-plate and exclaiming like the interlopers at New Register House.

'Here he is!'

There on the parish record, one hundred years past or thereabouts, proof that water had been dribbled over the head of a *Thomas Archibald Methven* in just the way that Solomon Farthing liked to dribble the finest Fino down his throat. The posse of Methvens leaned close, craning to see one of their ancestors brought back into the light.

Thomas Archibald Methven. b. June 1913. bpt. July 1913. d. 1918. The boy's name struck through on the register, followed by the initials of his mother, Mabel, as though to confirm the awful fact, a last kiss in ink.

'Only five,' said Archie. 'Poor wee bugger.'

'What did he die of?' asked Tom. 'Does it say?'

'Got the Spanish, didn't he –' the older Mr Methven nodded his head as though he knew all about the Spanish – 'just like all the rest.'

'You're right.' Reverend Jennie pointed at a word, *Influenza*, inscribed next to the child's dates. 'He liked to keep a thorough record, my predecessor. Used to add comments sometimes. Gossip mostly.'

'P' for Poorhouse.

'D' for Drunk.

The older Methven coughed into his sleeve. 'Sometimes true.'

The Reverend Jennie turned the pages of the book some more, one year further on, then the next, flipping over several pages at once and running her finger over the baptismal records, just to check. But then she closed the book with a heavy *flop*, shook her head.

'No sign of any other Thomas Methven, I'm afraid. Nor in 1919 or 1920.'

She locked the clasp once again with a tiny *click*, heaved the book back into its hiding place, satisfied that her version of events had prevailed. The older Mr Methven hawked in his throat, made as though to spit onto the flagstones, changed his mind and swallowed it instead.

'He wants Archibald's and Mabel's other son,' he declared. 'Went out one day, came back with him in the dark.'

Tom laughed. 'That old wives' tale.'

'You calling your grandmother old?'

'She might have got it wrong.'

'The cousins say it, too,' said Archie.

'Aye, but they're by marriage only,' said Tom, rubbing at the top of his ear.

'What's that got to do with it?'

'Hearsay. Gets in the way of facts.'

Reverend Jennie agreed. 'I've never found any proof of that story.'

'What story?' Solomon asked.

'That Mabel took someone else's child and brought him up as her own.'

Solomon started, touched at his top pocket where a small newspaper clipping sat next to a blue pawn ticket, wondered whether to reveal what had brought him to this altar. But something stopped him. Like any good Heir Hunter, Solomon Farthing knew to be evasive at just the moment all might be revealed.

'What makes you think your Thomas Methven comes from here anyway?' the Reverend Jennie asked.

Solomon could tell that she was suspicious, her nose was twitching like a small dog ferreting out a chicken bone.

'Just a hunch,' he replied.

'Well, there is something else I've always wondered about.'

Reverend Jennie got up from the flagstones and indicated the Bible on the lectern. A huge thing, ornate and solid, pages fine as tissue, closely printed with the Word. Solomon and the Methven troika gathered around as the oracle flipped the pages once again. This time she turned straight to the very back, to a flyleaf all freckled with the years that had passed.

'I've always thought it must be some sort of alternative record,' she said. 'Off the books, so to speak.' She tapped one finger at a list of names and dates in faint brown ink. 'An unofficial register. Of the wayward of the parish.'

Bastards. And poor boys. Not forgetting the foundlings, of course. They all held their breath as the Reverend Jennie studied each name with care:

Alice Brown

Mary McLeod

John Purvis

Until she got almost to the bottom.

'Well I never,' she said then, tucking some wayward strands of hair behind her ears. 'Here he is.'

Thomas Methven. bpt. June 1919.

The Methven men almost knocked heads as they crowded in to stare at the second entry.

'Well, I'll be,' said Tom. 'It is true, then.'

For next to the child's name was that of the boy's mother. *Mabel Methven née Kerr*, making her mark once again. The older Methven nodded twice this time, as though he had known all along.

'Told you so. Says it here, clear as cuckoo spit.'

A second Thomas Methven smuggled out of the night, came in as one thing, left as something else. Solomon could feel the hair on his neck prickling at the thought that his dead client's pawn ticket had led him to the very font where he had been named – a child born somewhere unknown, turned into a Methven by the simple act of pouring water on his head.

'I'll need to take a copy,' he said, fumbling for his piece of paper on which to inscribe the good news. 'To prove that this is my Thomas Methven, if it comes to that.'

He could almost taste it now. Twenty per cent commission on fifty thousand, plus expenses, of course. Cash in clean, crisp notes. But they were canny, the Methven clan. Knew when to ask.

'So there might be money in it, then?' said Archie, a bland smile belying the determination of his stare.

Solomon flushed, feet hot inside his fuchsia socks.

'I don't know,' he said. 'Depends if it is him. I'll have to trace his parents' line first, see how many have a rightful claim.'

They all looked at Reverend Jennie's family tree spread along the aisle. Hundreds. Possibly thousands. If her chart was to be believed. The brothers would be lucky if they got the price of a pint between them by the time the dispersal came. But the older Mr Methven already had other ideas.

'We won't get nothing,' he said, coughing into his sleeve.

'Why not?'

Solomon was surprised. It wasn't like a potential beneficiary to give up his claim before it had even begun.

'Weren't right, were it. Put the first in the ground one day, come back with the second the next.'

'Aye,' said Tom, agreeing with his father for once. 'The Kerrs always were a tricksy lot. Back and forth across that border like they owned it, buying and selling whatever they could get their hands on, no questions asked.'

'Proper Borders folk those Kerrs,' Archie agreed.

Thieves. And raiders. Each side of the frontier a personal fiefdom, no concern for where it might start and where it might end.

'Are you not Borders folk?' Solomon asked.

The three men shook their heads in unison, an adamant gesture.

'No, son, we're from Fife originally,' said the older Mr Methven. 'Grandparents came down to work, never went back.'

'When was that?'

Tom frowned, looked to his father. 'Before the war?'

'Aye, well before the war,' said the older Methven.

'In the twenties?' said Solomon.

'No, son. The first.'

They all turned to stare at the date on the flyleaf of the Bible, the six-month gap between the first Thomas Methven dying and the second showing up. Solomon's hand fluttered against his corduroys as he thought again of his grandfather in khaki.

'Did Archibald Methven go to war?' he asked.

'They all went, didn't they,' said the older Mr Methven. 'Silly fools. Should have stayed behind and seen to the earth when they got the chance.'

'I've got a photo,' said Tom, pulling something from his jacket and holding it out for the rest to see. 'Thought it might be useful.'

Black and white. A serious man standing with his hand upon a table, small boy by his side.

'Aye, that's them,' said the older Methven. 'Archibald and Tom.'

'Don't suppose you know what happened to him, do you?' asked Solomon, studying the man who'd gone for a soldier, just as his grandfather had, too.

'He got shot, didn't he,' said Tom. 'That's what granny always said.'

'A bloody mess,' said the older Methven. 'That was the story.'

'I thought it was an accident,' said Archie.

'No, son. Deliberate.'

All those farmers and their guns.

'The beginning of the end, either way,' said Tom, a mournful touch to his voice.

They all paused then, looked towards the church's own small memorial to its fallen, names carved in wood along the edges of the choir stall, the older Methven's eyes suddenly rheumy, even Archie with a shine to his. Then they looked back at Reverend Jennie's chart. *Archibald Methven & Mabel Methven née Kerr.* And their long-lost son. All gone now. It was Archie who said it.

'Maybe the second child wasn't his.'

'Trust you to think of that,' said Tom.

But the elder Mr Methven wiped his face with his sleeve and nodded as though it was only to be expected.

'Could be, son. Could be. It was a war, wasn't it. All sorts went on then. Mother always did say the second boy was different.'

'In what way?' said Solomon.

'Went a-wandering, didn't he. Disappeared to Edinburgh, never came back.'

'No Methven ever goes a-wandering,' agreed Tom.

Archie laughed. But Solomon thought it was a fair

judgement given how many were buried beneath the flag-stones on which they were standing now.

'Where might the child have come from, then?' he said. 'If he didn't come from here.'

The older Methven jerked his head in the rough direction of south.

'Across that border, probably. Best way to keep something quiet hereabouts. But you want to be careful if you're headed that way. It's a war in those parts.'

'What is?' asked Solomon.

'Immigration. They're not too sure about foreigners right now.'

Of course, the vote. To leave. Or to remain. A divided nation. It was left to the minister to point the way forward.

'I would try the school first,' said Reverend Jennie.

'A school?'

'Aye, son,' said the older Mr Methven, pointing to the land beyond the diamond window panes. 'For foundlings. Thirty miles that way. You can't miss it. Been bringing up lost boys there for more than a hundred and fifty years.'

Three

Solomon drove south as instructed, sliding over the border into a foreign land of moors and beaches swept clean by the wind, following the siren call of a dead man clothed in fifty thousand as it drew him towards the hidden foothills of his youth. As he hunkered over the wheel of his aunt's ancient Mini, he could feel an urgent pressing in his chest. What was it he was about to uncover? Adventure. Or the beginning of the fall. In his pocket a pawn ticket burned against his heart, a newspaper cutting inscribed with his grandfather's handwriting pressed close.

The dog lay low on the back seat, whimpering as the little car rattled and bucked, cold air whistling a tune through the floor:

It's a long way to Tipperary . . .

As though Godfrey Farthing was whistling to Solomon, drawing his grandson ever closer towards a school for foundling boys: a place for children who had somehow lost their parents, or parents who had somehow lost their child.

They arrived as the sun was almost gone from the sky, a long northern evening stretching out like the shadows of the trees that had once lined the route. The school appeared like a ghost at the end of the never-ending drive, a building folded into the turn of a river valley, hidden from all who might want to see. Solomon drove the Mini right into the courtyard with its gravel and its weeds, parked in the shadow of that familiar plinth. A memorial to all those young men who had lost their lives on some distant battlefield, nothing left of them but this spear of dark granite reaching for the sky. What was it about death amongst the stench that people found so alluring?

And yet . . .

Was this not where Solomon Farthing had acquired his calling?

Old Mortality.

Digging out the names of the dead until they were alive once more.

Solomon knew the moment he arrived that he had been to this place before. That spring in '57, after his father was lost in the great rope of the Thames. Went straight down. *Like an arrow*. That was what they'd told him. Caught in its muddy churn. His father had been trying to save a young woman. Or perhaps he had been drunk. Or maybe he hadn't wanted to live after the loss of Solomon's mother to some disease that ate her lungs before her son was barely six years old. All of the three were possible, Solomon could see that in himself now. Yet even sixty years later he wished that his father might have waited, stood on the parapet imagining a future, rather than contemplating the past.

He had been seven years old, abandoned on the doorstep of their London home expecting his father to return at any moment, sensing even then that perhaps his father never would. Eventually, he had let himself into their flat with the key he carried on a string beneath his shirt, found the kettle cold on the stove top, no margarine left in the Frigidaire.

He'd spent an hour lying on the floor amongst the dust, eating every square of the chocolate wrapped in silver foil that his father kept in an old tobacco tin beneath his bed. Then the woman from next door had come knocking, standing on the threshold with her apron double tied.

'Where's your dad, then?'

'Don't know, miss.'

She had laughed at that. 'Just call me Mrs Butter and be done with it.'

She was a good woman, Mrs Butter, had squeezed out five children, all with ginger ringlets, boys and girls both. She'd put out her hand to Solomon then, as though to offer him a future.

'You'd better come with me till he gets back.'

And Solomon had allowed himself to be drawn towards a different kind of life. Milk bottles left open on the table. Children giggling in a corner. Comics and the smell of coal dust. But even then he had known that it would not last forever. Already a boy on his own in the world, only seven years old but like a soldier marching forwards, forwards, always forwards, never allowed to look back.

Two days later they had driven him north, seven years old and riding on the back seat of an old Ford, bumping and grinding its way from the heat of London to somewhere far beyond that. The driver had worn a felt hat with a brim, the woman sitting next to him a green one with gloves to match.

'Where are we going?' Solomon had asked as the sun sank lower and lower and the car drove further and further from everything he had ever known.

'To a new school,' the woman in the green hat had

replied, not bothering to turn, just continuing to stare out of the windscreen at the long straight road in front.

Almost sixty years on, the foundling school appeared to be deserted, no more boys mingling and tussling in the yard. Solomon peered through the gloom at a building that had seen better days, rather like him, water staining the stonework in great grey streaks. He realized that his hands and feet were clammy; every part of him, in fact. He knew, without being able to see, that beyond the quad there was a long field sprinkled with buttercups in summer. And beyond that, a river – a dark thing flowing swift in the night. He gave a little shiver, remembered the words of the Book Fetcher. *If it's business, that's one thing. If it's family business, that's something else.*

Behind him there was the sudden sound of footsteps on gravel, a boy watching from the shadow of the building, hair rumpled, knees dirty, a younger version of himself. Solomon started forwards, but the boy disappeared, sliding through a small doorway in the corner of the quad. The dog made to follow. Solomon hesitated, then he followed, too.

The corridor he found himself in was lined with wood, panel after panel fixed to the wall, a thousand names (or thereabouts) looking down at Solomon as he looked up at them. Head Boys and Prefects. Leaders of the First Eleven. Others who had won some sort of cup. The names were written in gold paint, all faded now. Solomon put a finger to the nearest, left a print in the dust, started to walk along the corridor tracing one lost name after another, until he came to the date when he had been a boy at this school, too. It was there that he found himself face-to-face with a man of his own age, wearing a felt dressing gown over a pair of trousers.

'Solomon Farthing,' the man said holding out both his hands. 'I knew you would come.'

It was the singing that Solomon remembered the most. A courtyard full of boys swirling and tumbling while from somewhere deep inside the old stone building a choir raised its voice.

> *The Lord's my Shepherd, I'll not want;*
> *He makes me down to lie*
> *In pastures green; He leadeth me*
> *The quiet waters by.*

Dropped from an old Ford into a school for boys of every size and disposition, abandoned by their parents to an uncertain future, not to mention the black hole of their pasts.

Solomon had come from a school in London where girls skipped and sang in the playground, while boys huddled in corners and bartered ha'pennies for a Black Jack or cards from packs of cigarettes. But here there was a courtyard and a chapel, the sound of boys singing percolating throughout the building from morning till dark. The evening Solomon arrived they had put him to bed in the sick bay beneath a blue blanket and a sheet stiff with the biscuity scent of starch. In the morning he had woken to an old woman bending over his pillow.

'It's time to get up now, Solomon.'

Whispering his name as though it was some secret they must keep between themselves. The woman had dressed him in borrowed shorts and a grey jumper striped with a V at the neck in pink. Then she had sent him to eat breakfast with a hundred other boys, all praying over porridge:

Our Father who art in heaven . . . give us this day our daily bread . . .

Each bowl stamped on the rim with a mermaid that was pink, too.

He had been at the school three weeks, maybe four, when he was summoned to the headmaster's office to find a man he had never met before standing beside the headmaster's desk. The man's jacket had been fastened, every single button, shoes polished as though it must be a Sunday. The headmaster had put his hand on Solomon's shoulder.

'This is your grandfather,' he'd said.

'We look after naughty boys now. The damaged ones.'

The man who had welcomed Solomon by name poured tea from a great, round pot into a mug stamped with a tiny mermaid on its lip. Aren't all boys damaged, thought Solomon as he watched the steam curl from the spout. One way or another. Or perhaps that was just him.

'They send them to us when no one else will have them,' said the man, nudging a mug of tea towards Solomon. 'A bit like when you were young. But for different reasons, of course.'

Solomon nodded, though after more than sixty years he was still waiting for someone to explain exactly how he had started, and what had happened next. They were sitting at the end of a long table in the school kitchen, somewhere Solomon had never been allowed to enter when he was young.

'Eddie Jackson,' the man had said when they first encountered each other in the corridor.

Solomon had replied as though answering to the morning register.

'Farthing, Solomon.'

'Yes, yes,' the teacher had said, as though that was only to be expected. 'Would you like some tea?'

The kitchen was a gloomy sort of place, cobwebs drifting from high corners, two huge sinks on one side and a metal counter running all along the other. There was the low stink of pizza charred along its edges, cheese burned on top. The dog sauntered into a corner to investigate while Eddie Jackson waved his arm towards a stack of unwashed plates in the sink.

'We let the boys make their own meals now. Chaos from order.'

'Are there no rules?' Solomon said.

'A few. But sometimes it's good to run free, don't you think.'

Solomon took a hot mouthful of tea, remembered his grandfather's instructions for a sensible kind of life. Polish shoes. Do not run. Always button your cuffs. He pulled the edges of his tweed jacket over the flap of his shirt beneath.

'How did you know I was coming?' he asked.

'Methven said to expect you.'

Solomon touched a finger to the half-walnut shell in his pocket. Somehow it didn't surprise him that this case had turned out rather like Edinburgh, a city in which one often reached the destination one wanted, without ever quite understanding the route.

'I'm trying to track down an old boy,' he said.

'We get a lot of old boys visiting.' Eddie Jackson nodded. 'Returning to the mothership, so to speak, once they reach a certain age.'

Solomon wondered then how it was that this man seemed to understand him, even though he barely understood himself.

'Mine's a bit older than most, though,' he said. 'From 1918, I think. A Thomas Methven. Though he might have started here as someone else.'

'Ah.' The teacher grinned then. 'Most of our boys begin as one thing and end as another. We count that as a success.'

After tea, Eddie Jackson led Solomon through a labyrinth of corridors towards the beating heart of the school – the room where all the registers were kept, counting all the lost boys in and counting them out again. The dog trotted along behind for a while, before wandering in a different direction, disappearing with a flick of its tail, didn't bother to look back. Somewhere, somehow, Solomon heard singing rise and fall.

It's a long way to Tipperary . . .

Or perhaps that was just inside his head.

The study was dark and dusty, full of books locked behind wire mesh that had not been removed for years. On one side there were the registers, row upon row of blue-spined journals that Solomon recognized from early morning roll-call. On the other a glass display case covered with a velvet cloth. To Solomon's surprise, the teacher made straight for the latter rather than the former.

'1918,' he said. 'The war generation.'

Drew the velvet from the glass.

The case was just like the cabinet of curiosities in Godfrey Farthing's pawnshop – full of stuff that somebody had treasured once. Solomon peered in to see a row of small dull plaques gazing back. Campaign medals. Distinguished service medals. Two Stars and a War medal, one for Victory, too. He recognized the last grouping from an old cardboard box of military memorabilia his grandfather used to keep beneath the pawnshop counter. Pip, Squeak and Wilfred, wasn't that what the old man had called them? Long since disappeared.

'Quite a few decorated soldiers amongst our old boys.' Eddie Jackson smiled down at the display. 'Something about the army, made them feel at home.'

'Where did you get these from?' Solomon asked, thinking of his own little silver cap badge, lost now in that city in the north.

'Donated. For the centenary. Amazing what people come up with if they're asked.'

1914–2014. Another celebration of mud, blood and wire. The war would be everywhere these next few years, thought Solomon. Devastation after devastation. Death after death.

Jackson moved further along the case to a display of photographs. Soldiers of every description – lanky and stout, dark-haired and fair. All with one similarity: none of them were smiling. As though they had known, before it happened, what would befall them all. Next to the photographs were some letters scrawled in pencil: on signal paper; on field postcards; on envelopes marked with the stamp of the censor in purple and red. Also a canvas pocketbook of some description splayed and pinned like a great Victorian moth. The pocketbook was a dirty thing, stained, one end folded back to reveal two rusty needles and something stitched in pink.

'What's that?' Solomon asked.

'Sewing kit,' said the teacher. 'A Housewife. All the men were issued them. What a way to fight a war, eh. With not much more than a needle and some thread.'

A sewing kit to repair what could be repaired, to stitch what could be stitched, a whole generation of men turned into housewives while the women at home machined the bombs they used to kill. Eddie Jackson pointed towards a photograph of a young man in uniform, rigid and precise, propped next to the Housewife.

'It belonged to my great-uncle. Do you recognize him?'

Solomon studied the soldier, impossibly young, with a cowl of black hair. He shook his head.

'No.'

'Try this one.'

The teacher indicated another photograph, the same man but older, wearing a master's gown this time. At once the blood rushed in Solomon's ears as he heard it again. That shout from across the field, a man in a black cape, its corners flapping, descending on him as though from the sky.

'The Jackdaw!'

'Yes.' Eddie Jackson laughed. 'My namesake. He taught here, too.'

Solomon bent to peer at his old teacher, the blur of something silver attached to the master's lapel.

'I'd forgotten he fought in the war,' he said. 'London Scottish, lion raising its paw.'

But Eddie Jackson shook his head. 'No, Bedfordshires I think. Hart crossing a ford, that's their emblem.'

How appropriate, thought Solomon, after everything that went on when the Jackdaw was old and he was still young.

The teacher drew the cloth back across the glass then, as though to consign the past to the past, and moved towards the blue-spined books instead.

'Now, let's look at the registers, shall we, see if we can find your old boy. What was he called again?'

'Thomas Methven,' replied Solomon, turning the walnut once more in his pocket.

'My great-uncle served with a Methven,' said Jackson. 'An accountant. Good with figures. That was what he said.'

Acumen and perspicacity. Sound husbandry of money. Rather like Thomas Methven, thought Solomon, if only he had not been too young.

'My Methven was born in 1918, I think,' he said. 'Once the war was done. He would have been taken out as a baby the following year, by a Mabel Methven, if my enquiries are correct.'

Eddie Jackson stopped searching then, as though disappointed.

'There's been a misunderstanding,' he said. 'We never took in babies. They went to the farm down the road first, came here at five.'

'The farm?'

'Belonged to a Mr and Mrs Pringle.'

WANTED: Home for a baby boy, 6 months old. Total surrender.

Solomon Farthing had a funny feeling then that if he attempted to trace Walter Pringle's family tree, he might end up here, too.

'Don't suppose you know anything about the Pringles, do you?' he asked. 'Or their farm.'

'Not really,' said the teacher. 'They ran it as a baby home for years. Noel and Dora Pringle. Well, he had the farm and she had the babies. Kept them warm until someone wanted to adopt. Unofficial, of course, like everything back then.'

Of course, thought Solomon. Like everything about this case. Not generating any of the kind of paperwork that would satisfy Margaret Penny of the Office for Lost People, yet somehow the correct route.

'All gone now, of course,' the teacher continued. 'Phased out after the first war.'

'Are there any records left from the farm?' said Solomon. 'I'm looking for a clue as to the child's real parents.'

'Ah, now. For that you will need our official archivist.'

And Eddie Jackson drew a whistle that Solomon recognized from his pocket, put it to his lips.

Up, up and up they went, then up some more, the Heir Hunter and the school's archivist shooed away by Jackson to the highest possible floor. When they got to the top, Solomon was practically on his knees. But he knew he had been there before, a room in a turret, with four windows, east, west, north and south. It was dark outside now, but Solomon was certain that in daytime he would be able to glimpse the river from here, buttercups like sovereigns all along the bank.

In front of the room's wooden door, the archivist turned and held out his hand to Solomon as though some sort of formal contact was required before they could proceed.

'I'm Peter,' he said.

Solomon hesitated, took Peter's hand in his own.

'Solomon Farthing.'

Peter's hand was small, soft boned. As they shook, Solomon found himself blushing, a fetching shade of rose.

Just like it had been years before, the room was furnished with leftovers. A stuffed armchair here. A pouf in fading leather there. On the floor was a rug, patterned at the edges, worn bare at its heart. On the rug lay a dog wearing a blue kerchief, nose tucked beneath its paw. The archivist grinned when he saw the dog, scampered across to give it a stroke. Solomon grinned, too. The archivist was one of Eddie Jackson's naughty schoolboys, eleven years old or thereabouts, hair mussed, knees scuffed, socks wrinkled at his ankles rather like the ones Solomon was wearing. Solomon bent to straighten his fuchsia socks, then looked around the room with all its treasures, understood that he was in Peter's den now.

The turret room was dominated by what looked like the headmaster's old desk, heavy oak with black feet and a green inlay all scuffed and torn. The desk was covered in a neat display of ephemera. A selection of ancient coins. A tray of mismatched keys. A single pair of spectacles fashioned from gold wire. Each item had been labelled, a small tag attached. Solomon waved a hand at the display. 'Is all this yours?'

Peter looked up from where he was crouching by the dog.

'It's my museum,' he said. 'I like to borrow things. Eddie said if I stopped I could look after this stuff instead.'

A row of pens with blunted nibs. An old tin containing the remains of a bird's egg, small shards of blue. Solomon felt for the walnut in his pocket. This room was a petty thief's paradise – all the pretty things.

Peter left the dog and came over to the desk, opened one of the deep drawers on the left-hand side and lugged out some sort of expanding file with *Pringle* written on the tab.

'Eddie says you want to know about the baby home.'

'Yes, please,' Solomon replied, leaned against the desk waiting to see what the boy might reveal.

The first thing out of the file was a photograph, not a farm with pigs and a muddy yard as Solomon had expected, but a house with gables and roses around the door. Outside the front of the house was a woman with a baby in her arms, several more on a blanket at her feet. On the gravel drive behind her stood another woman wearing a white cap; beside her, three deep-bottomed prams. At the edge of the photograph was a girl, fourteen, fifteen perhaps, flowers twisted about her wrist. Solomon flipped the photo over. On the reverse was a description:

Mrs Pringle's Home for Lost Souls.

Also a list of names:

Mrs Pringle. Elsie. Daisy Pringle.

And a date:

1918.

'Can I keep this?' he asked.

'What's it worth?' said Peter.

A boy after Solomon's own heart. Solomon suppressed a grin as he searched in his pocket, took out the sixpence and tossed it onto the leather inlay of the desk. Peter's hand was so quick Solomon almost didn't see it, darting out to slide the tanner away.

'Pre-decimal,' said Solomon, raising his eyebrows before the coin disappeared for good. 'Must be worth more than one photograph.'

Peter tried not to smile, delved into the expanding file once more. This time he produced a scrabble of paper slips all tattered and curled at the edges. Each slip was blank but for a number written across it in neat script.

'What are these?' Solomon asked.

'Admission dockets,' said Peter. 'Every baby got one when it arrived. They match the numbers in the book.'

Another register, with marbled endpapers this time, the name of the baby home inscribed on the front, inside lists and lists of the abandoned going back to well before the Great War. Peter slid the book across the desk so that Solomon could flick through the thick, woven pages. The entries began in the 1880s, each child's name prefaced by a number to match their admissions slip, followed by the name of whoever had adopted them, if they were lucky enough. It was a very thorough record, an Heir Hunter's dream.

Solomon turned the pages towards the end of the register, looking for the babies first signed for in 1918, left for a new life in 1919, the name of the clerk who had kept the record in those years inscribed alongside each:

Miss Evelyn Penny, Secretary.

Counting the babies in and counting them out again one by one. Solomon wondered for a moment if this Miss Penny was somehow connected to Margaret Penny of the Office for Lost People in Edinburgh, a woman who did her own sort of reckoning on behalf of the abandoned, albeit the deceased. But that was a whole other story and like all good Heir Hunters, Solomon knew not to get distracted. One wrong branch of the wrong tree, and his pursuit of Thomas Methven would be lost.

He checked all the names for 1918. And all those for 1919, too. But despite looking twice through Evelyn Penny's meticulous list, there was no record of a foundling boy handed over to a Mabel Methven née Kerr. Solomon was disappointed: another dead end, it seemed. But then he saw the spark in Peter's eyes, as though the boy archivist knew something that Solomon did not.

'Is there more?' he asked, closing the book and sliding it back across the desk.

Peter's grin almost split his face this time as he lifted a shoebox from the depths of another drawer, removed the lid and tipped its contents all over the old headmaster's desk.

Bits of ribbon. Bits of lace. Buttons and coins etched with crude lettering. Cheap jewellery and cut swabs of cloth.

The real treasure that was left.

'They came with the babies,' Peter declared. 'Aren't they pretty?'

Tokens, thought Solomon, heart skipping. All the things a mother left behind to prove a child was hers; just in case she ever wanted that child back.

The tokens were forlorn little things, each one a scrap of hope never realized, long since separated from its relevant admissions slip, nothing to identify the child to whom it had once belonged. Solomon picked through them. A sixpence with a hole in it. A single glass earring. A tinny medal inscribed with a heart. Each one waiting for a mother to return, with its matching pair. Solomon knew all about how a pawnshop operated. But he had never seen it applied to a child before.

'Did all the babies have tokens when they arrived?' he asked.

Peter shrugged. 'Don't know. But I've got one. Do you want to see?'

He reached into his trouser pocket and dug out a plastic figure, handed it to Solomon, a soldier shouldering his gun.

'My dad gave it to me,' the boy said.

Solomon didn't have anything left that had belonged to his father – nothing but a snatch of song hummed as he shaved of a morning. He felt suddenly bereft.

'My dad's dead,' said Peter. 'What about yours?'

'Mine too,' said Solomon. 'A long time ago now.'

'So do you have one, then?' Peter asked, sliding the plastic soldier back into his pocket. 'A token?'

Solomon was confused for a moment. What had his father left him but that fragment of singing in his head?

'Oh, no, I don't . . .'

But, of course, he did.

It took them several goes to find their match, a man in grubby corduroys and a boy with unbrushed hair, hands deep in the detritus of babies long since vanished into the mire. A patch stitched with a heart, here. A button from an army greatcoat, there. In the end it was Peter who saw it first, snatched it from amongst the jumble to hold it to the lamp. An admissions billet with a number scrawled in faded ink. *103*. And above that, two rusty holes where something had been held on by a pin once, long ago. Solomon could tell from the giddy *one two* of his heart that he had followed the right branch of the tree after all. He held up his token in reply. Thomas Methven's pawn ticket, no.125, two tiny holes matching two pinholes punctured through the admissions billet, to make a perfect four.

Solomon's heart was thrumming as Peter turned once more to the book with the marbled endpapers, ran his soft little finger down the lists of numbers and names. All those children deposited as one thing, ended as something else, just as Eddie Jackson had said. But when the boy came to it, the record was not for a child born in 1918, handed over six months later to a Mabel Methven née Kerr. It was for someone much older than that.

Child No.103.

Arrived with nothing but a pawn ticket. Also a name: *Sutherland, Alec.*

Deposited as a foundling in 1902. Left to be a soldier in 1918.

1918

One

The game would be played in the barn. Ten men arranged in a circle, the ground between them swept clean. Captain Godfrey Farthing the only one who would not join. Godfrey did not believe in gambles, but this was a bet he was prepared to take if it meant his men stayed safe.

7 November and the section ate breakfast in a thrum of excitement once Godfrey announced the news. He watched from the doorway of the farmhouse as they hurried to scrape egg from their mess tins, tossing the empty cans into the huge earthenware sink with a clatter as they rushed to complete their chores. Not much more than twelve hours before the attack was due and Godfrey had found another way to occupy his men's time. One more roll of the dice, until the bells pealed.

Mid-morning, washing sorted, barn swept clean and Percy Flint waited for the men to settle so that they could begin. Hair newly slicked with water, neat cuffs given an extra turn on his arm, Flint sifted the pack of cards from one impatient hand to the next. Alfred Walker sat beside him, pockets filled with whatever treasure he had previously purloined. George Stone had brought a handful of walnuts from the kitchen to throw into the fray. He chose a block of wood on the far side of the circle to perch on, stretched his feet in heavy boots, had taken off his apron for the day.

Next to Stone, Jackdaw and Promise, the A4 boys, huddled close, heads bent together in concentration as they pooled their resources. Buttons and pennies. A bird nest taken from a hedge. Bertie Fortune, the lucky man, was seated by the new recruit, Alec, so that he could help explain the rules. Everybody trusted Fortune to play fair even though he always came out on top one way or another, win or lose. Alec's dog nestled by the boy's feet, nose resting on its paws, as though it had belonged here all along. Then there was Second Lieutenant Ralph Svenson, sitting amongst the men as though he was nothing more than an ordinary soldier, rather than the officer who liked to win.

Godfrey had even persuaded James Hawes to play, summoning his temporary sergeant to the parlour earlier that morning once breakfast was done, all the men scattered to prepare for the day.

'Heard you lost a tanner to Promise on a game of chicken,' he said.

Hawes flushed, dirty freckles splashed on his neck, didn't deny it. 'Aye, sir.'

'Not like you to gamble, Hawes.'

'Needs must, sir.'

'Thought you might want to win it back.'

Godfrey fished inside the wooden box set on the parlour table, took out the leather pouch that contained the men's tobacco ration, pushed it across to Hawes. Both men stared at the little bag.

'What about the ration, sir?' Hawes mumbled.

Godfrey leaned back in his chair. 'It's not all of it, you fool. I'm not that stupid. Take it, I'll not offer twice.'

They both knew it wasn't a question so much as an order. Hawes reached for the pouch, plucked it from the table and held it in his fist. How solid his hands were, Godfrey thought. Beefy. Like the meat he used to saw for a living. He watched as his temporary sergeant left, dodging the muddy pools in the yard, and disappeared into the grain store. It wasn't like Godfrey Farthing to offer a bribe. But needs must, he thought. Both men understood that.

Now Hawes lay propped on a ground sheet on the edge of the circle, face and neck given a rough wash for the occasion, freckles bright once more. Just behind him Archie Methven sat on a chair brought in from the parlour, where he could see them all. Godfrey had only set one condition before they began – that Methven must be the bank. Just like Godfrey, the accountant never played, but unlike Godfrey, no game could go on without him. Despite the presence of an officer, it was always the accountant who had the final say.

As the men settled, Godfrey watched Archie Methven open his notebook in which all their names were listed. Godfrey had bought Methven the notebook out of his officer's allowance a year ago or so, a proper accountant's profit-and-loss account with its horizontal lines in blue and its verticals in red. He always had relied on Archie Methven to settle things for the men – whether they were alive, or whether they were dead.

They had agreed on the lang ten, Scotch Mist, as Alfred Walker called it. The first to catch the ten would be the winner – not *a* ten, but *the* ten dictated by the trump. As many rounds as they needed, Methven keeping the score. Two points for the queen. Three for the king. Four for the ace. Ten for the ten. And the knave as the prize that would beat them all. It would keep them busy the whole day until one man swept everything, or they ran out of things to bet and tallied the score. If there was no conclusion today, they would pick up again tomorrow. The game could be played continuously as long as the accountant dictated that it should. Or the bells pealed in the village. At least that was what Godfrey Farthing hoped.

He watched now as the men dipped into their pockets, deciding what to put in first or what to withhold. They might start with the trivial, but Godfrey knew that the game would end with each man gambling the most precious things he had. Six army buttons that went blue with the gas. An ace of spades from an incomplete pack. A needle. Some thread. A packet of Kitchener's Last. Once there had even been a plum cake, bid for by those left after Beach was gone. It had been made by the boy's mother, wrapped in newspaper to keep it moist.

Now that's really something.

Packed tight in a tin.

It arrived after Beach was dead, but before his mother got the letter. They bet and Stone won, carved out small slices of the cake and served it back to them with the ration of tea. None of them had felt it was the wrong thing to do. Beach was gone, but they could still enjoy the taste of sugar in his place.

The game began at 11 a.m., George Stone leading off. The old sweat and the eldest hand, put in one of the walnuts from the basket in the kitchen, then placed his first card in the centre of the playing area for all to see. Godfrey could sense it the moment the card went down – that thick air of anticipation that comes with winner takes all.

The men played in silence at first, nothing but the slap and scuff of cards, sawdust rising as they tossed their first bets in:

A matchstick;

A centime;

An old stub of candle.

As though the items being offered were only so much chiff chaff for all concerned. Outside the rain was falling again, cold seeping through the barn's wide door. From his position beyond the playing circle, half in the gloom, Godfrey could see the intensity of each man's gaze, adding it all up. Who might have a run of luck. Who a bad hand. Whose treasure could be won. And whose might be lost. But soon enough he also saw what he had been hoping for – that softening of the men's bodies as they began to relax. A shoulder eased here. A leg stretched there. A casual scratch at a forearm or the back of a neck. He could feel it in himself, too, uncertainty slipping from him like a greatcoat lifted from his shoulders after two weeks in a trench, no longer soldiers, but young men again, at play.

After three rounds, twelve noon been and gone, the comments began. Along with the jokes and the insults, the sly digs and the laughs. The men traded them across the circle, each one flying as fast as the cards.

'Bloody chicken feed,' said Stone when Jackdaw threw in a farthing. 'No use to anyone.'

'What, like that wrinkled fodder?' called Bertie Fortune. 'Walnuts for dinner again.'

The men all pretended to groan, but Godfrey knew

they didn't mean it. The walnuts were like everything else he had come across in this Eden – treasure of an unexpected kind.

It took Alfred Walker to offer something all the men thought was proper gold – the wishbone from the first night's chicken, tossed in with a grin to see where it might land. Must have bartered it with Bertie Fortune, Godfrey thought when he saw the little bone, wondered what for. He looked towards his lucky man sitting on the far side of the circle pulling at the corner of his moustache, received a slow wink in reply.

The men jeered when they saw Walker's offering.

'Starvation corner, mate,' said George Stone.

'White flag already,' laughed Flint.

'Thinks he's a dog, can win with a bone,' joked Jackdaw.

But Godfrey knew that Walker had made a good trade. He'd dug enough lucky charms out of dead men's pockets to understand that everybody carried something to protect themselves from the bullets if they could, had his own hidden in the straw of his mattress, in the attic room he shared with Ralph.

The men played for another hour non-stop, as outside the light arced across the horizon. Like the little sun rising then falling again on the grandfather clock in his mother's parlour back home. What would become of the clock if he did not return to claim it? thought Godfrey. He glanced at his wristwatch, remembered his father sitting at the head of the table with his teacup, the watch laid on a side plate as though it was a piece of shortbread rather than the last gift from his parents Godfrey would ever receive. When he'd left the house the following morning, Godfrey had never imagined he would ever return to those uninspiring fields where the middle of England seeped into the east. A place he had only wished to get away from, grasping war when it came with both his soft hands. But now, whenever he stood beneath that circle of trees and looked out across the empty fields towards the river, he realized he had returned to the landscape of his youth with barely a second thought.

'Bets in for the last round before lunch.'

Archie Methven called for order as the final game of the morning began. This time Percy Flint threw in his reel of pink thread. Jackdaw a button from an officer's coat polished to a shine. Bertie Fortune had a postcard with a picture of a church's leaning spire.

'Where's that?' said Hawes.

'Albert,' replied the lucky man lifting his eyes to Godfrey, before looking away. 'Bloody disaster that was.'

George Stone rolled yet another walnut towards the centre of the playing circle, while Walker offered a small square of chocolate, only nibbled at one end.

'Mice got to it,' he said when the men protested.

'Rat, more like,' mumbled Flint.

It was then that Promise tossed a silver shilling into the ring, the coin landing with a *plink* amongst the other treasure. The A4 boy's winnings from a game of chicken, for which the real prize never had been paid.

Godfrey was aware of a sudden silence amongst the men as they stared at the silver coin, before retreating again behind their cards. He glanced towards Promise across the ring, but the fair A4 boy was watching Second Lieutenant Ralph Svenson, as though to see what the officer might proffer in reply. It was Bertie Fortune who made the suggestion.

'You could match it, sir. Silver for silver. Let it all balance out.'

Ralph was very still for a moment, his strange eyes fixed on the playing area scattered with all its little treasures. Even Godfrey felt the heat in his boots, wondered if he was finally going to get a glimpse of the prize Fortune had mentioned, the one that had created all the fuss. But then Ralph gave a slight smile, laid down a Woodbine, and the game began once more.

The cards were dealt, laid one on top of the other, points won and lost, until the end of the round came and the shilling was lost to Alfred Walker, who laughed and tossed it in celebration.

'Heads I win. Tails I win again.'

The men all laughing, too. Except Ralph, whose blank face belied the cold in his eyes. Godfrey glanced again at his wristwatch, 1 p.m. and counting, indicated to Archie Methven to end the game there.

'All done,' said the accountant gathering in the cards, before sliding the pack into his top pocket.

And the men disbursed, a sudden lightness in their step.

Lunch was a round of tackety biscuits and tea brewed in the ancient kettle, half a boiled egg each, shells peeled by Promise in a basin of water so icy it coloured his fingers blue. Stone must have a secret store of them, thought Godfrey, hoarding till the last. The men stood and stretched as they waited to be served, gathered in the yard with their hands tucked under armpits to keep warm, breath clouding about their heads. The rain had ceased, the two remaining chickens *flittering* and *flapping* in the dust of the grain store, black eyes gleaming amongst the sag of blankets strung on makeshift ropes to air.

When the food came out, Godfrey watched Ralph as he sat alone in a corner of the yard, tea in one hand, biscuit in the other, crouched on the stump of wood they used for a chopping block. The game could have a balancing effect, that was what Godfrey had discovered, first one man on top, then another, in a constant ebb and flow. But Godfrey had seen the way his second looked at Promise's shilling, knew he must take care. Ralph had a way of calculating the odds that was ruthless and precise, a man who played only for himself.

Stone ended the meal with a flourish, a dish of some-thing they had not seen for months. Fruit stewed and slippery in a huge stoneware bowl stirred in with what looked like syrup, the single tin of Lyle's from the cellar come into its own, as though the old sweat knew somehow that the end would soon be here. The men thrust forwards with their mess tins clattering to be first. Promise followed with one of the precious cans of Nestlé's Condensed, each man adding a swirl to his portion of dessert.

'Hey up!' said Alfred Walker, taking the tin of milk first. 'This is better than Tickler.'

The army's standard jam. Walker poured out his share of the Nestlé's, then licked the lip of the tin before handing it to Jackdaw. Flint looked disgusted.

'You dirty bugger.'

But then Jackdaw did the same, passing it to Flint next so that the married conscript had to take his medicine or forego the treat. The moment Godfrey took a spoonful of the mixture he knew that Stone had added something illicit. Brandy, a low note of France's best, smuggled in from somewhere unknown.

After lunch, Godfrey left the men to play once more, forded the pond and walked some way towards the fold in the land instead. Everything was shaded, the afternoon mist closing in, shadows gathering beneath the hedgerows. Godfrey longed to head to the walnut grove so that he could stand amongst the silent trees. But he did not want to leave the farmyard and the men for the time it would take him to walk there and back. He looked across the fields towards the river hidden in the distance, wondered if the enemy were watching him, too.

In his pocket Godfrey touched Ralph's dice, turning them once, then twice. Zero hour was supposed to be dawn the next morning, attack as soon as the sun edged above the line. But Godfrey Farthing had already decided to let that moment pass, a gamble of his own, nothing written in his service diary but *Rain*, *Rain*, *Rain*, one day after the next, until the bells pealed.

On the hill, there was the sudden movement of a creature in the distance. A rabbit, Godfrey thought, leaping over one of Alec's simple loops of wire. Or a hare, perhaps, springing from its shallow form to frolic in the twilight, fur turning to white with the cold. But once again it was a boy, standing at the edge of the grove watching Godfrey from afar. Beach, this time, perhaps.

I'll be seeing you, then.

Waving to Godfrey from wherever he had ended.

Godfrey raised his hand as though to wave back, two soldiers saluting each other across the battlefield. Found the boy already gone.

Back in the barn Godfrey could tell at once that things had changed. Stone was out, had retired to the kitchen to prepare supper. Jackdaw out, too, no more shiny bits and bobs to play. Bertie Fortune had declined to continue, saving his treasure for later, no doubt, Godfrey thought. Or for barter with whoever might win.

'Quit while you're ahead.'

That was what the lucky man said, scraping together his small collection of winnings and refusing to play again. The men didn't mind. Bertie Fortune was Bertie Fortune, never would give it all away.

The paraffin lamp had been lit for the first time, all the men's faces cast in and out of shadow as they dipped back and forth. Percy Flint wanted to continue, but no one would sub him and he did not seem to have any further trinkets he was willing to bet for himself. He sat on the furthest edge of the circle, watching the rest of the action with a scowl. Alec had counted himself in for the end, but Hawes had not, glancing at Godfrey for a moment from across the field of play, no more small screws of tobacco to toss into the ring. Hawes had kept the game going all day with a seemingly endless supply, all wrapped in thin scraps of paper, some sort of print on both sides. All finished now.

'What about that book instead?' Alfred Walker joked.

But Hawes just ignored him. They all knew their temporary sergeant would never let *Old Mortality* go.

Godfrey's second sat in a casual slouch on the far side of the playing area with a whole pile of stuff laid before him. One day of the game and already Second Lieutenant Svenson had taken everyone else's treasure, thought Godfrey, made it his own.

'Final bet's in before supper,' called Methven, his face flushed like them all at the end that was near. 'Whoever wants to play.'

Ralph hesitated for a moment, flicked his eyes towards Flint who sat in the shadow at the edge of the circle, then leaned forwards and nudged Flint's spool of thread towards the centre of the playing area, all the men watching it unravel as it rolled across the flags. Promise shifted in his seat, card held tight against his chest as though he knew he had something worth playing, but wasn't certain whether to stick or fold. Godfrey's heart skipped with its *one two* beat at what might be about to happen, the last round of the day turning into a battle between his second and the fair A4 boy. It was funny how these things worked out.

Ralph nodded towards Promise. 'Your turn. If you dare.'

Promise's face was like chalk in the gloom compared to the other men, theirs all blotched and high.

'I don't have anything else to bet with,' he said, refusing to look at the second.

Ralph stretched his feet towards the playing area as though it was a fire to keep him warm. 'You can't play if you don't bet.'

'I know the rules.'

Promise's reply was sharp, but Ralph just nudged at the reel of pink cotton with the tip of his boot.

'You've a Housewife, haven't you,' he said. 'That would do it.'

'What d'you want that for?' Jackdaw was agitated, unable to keep still.

'Like a crow,' said Flint without looking at the darker A4 boy. 'Always cawing.'

Alfred Walker laughed then, a nervous release of tension. Godfrey watched as Jackdaw turned towards Promise, dark eyes shining for a moment in the glow from the paraffin lamp, as though warning his friend not to proceed. But Promise was staring at the second lieutenant, a boy only a few months older than he was, spots still on his jaw.

Ralph smiled his lazy smile. 'What's it to be, Promise? Play or fold.'

But Promise would not fold. Instead he held on to his cards the same way Hawes held his book with the red woven cover. Ralph shrugged, made as though to gather all his remaining treasure from the ground. Then Promise scrambled up, went over to his pack and pulled the Housewife from the pocket on the outside, brought it back to the playing circle and tossed it down.

'Have it if you want it. I don't care.'

Flint grinned. Methven's voice cut low through the tension.

'Play your cards.'

And the final round began.

Promise played his card first, body stiff with anticipation, kept his eyes low and hesitated for a moment, before darting his hand out and throwing the thing down. An ace. The ace of trumps. Godfrey's body washed with instant relief as a sigh rippled through the group of men. Promise's card would take some beating. The A4 boy might yet prevail. They all turned towards Ralph now, waited to see what he held in his hand. Godfrey's second took his time, rolled his head back on his neck so they could all hear the crick of his vertebrae.

'Good shot, Promise,' he said. 'But wide.'

His strange eyes were pinned on the A4 boy, unwavering in the gloom. All the men saw how Promise tried to stare back, then flinched beneath his lieutenant's gaze. There was a sudden prickle of tension amongst the men, bodies alert. Godfrey saw the raw flush on Promise's neck, the twitch in Jackdaw's hand. Then Ralph grinned, laid down his card. A ten. *The* ten. The ten of trumps. Ralph was the winner once more.

The men began to speak in urgent whispers, a huddle here, others there, Archie Methven, the accountant, adding up the final reckoning now the game was done. Godfrey watched Ralph gather in the men's prizes:

Hawes's tobacco.

Walker's wishbone.

Flint's reel of pink cotton.

Amongst other things.

Also Promise's housewife filled with needles and pins. A dirty thing. An ordinary thing. Not something normally counted as treasure. He couldn't understand why Ralph had suggested Promise bet it, felt a thread of anxiety thrum inside at the idea that the game was not all it seemed. Then his second bent forwards, flipped the canvas strip open, and Godfrey Farthing understood.

There on the playing circle, lit by the glow of the paraffin lamp, were two hearts stitched together in pink thread. Entwined with two initials. Jackdaw and Promise bright amongst the needles, everything they were to each other laid out for all the men to see.

There was a heavy silence in the barn, the stink of the paraffin lamp suddenly overwhelming, the dark void beneath the roof pressing down. Relations between two men of the kind displayed here were a punishable offence. Two years inside for indecent behaviour. Hard labour. Or worse. Something Captain Godfrey Farthing could not ignore if another man complained. He felt blood thumping in his ears suddenly at the thought of what might be coming, that ache in his chest. Then came a voice from the shadows.

'I haven't had my turn yet.'

Ralph's face was suddenly flushed with the fumes from the paraffin lamp.

'Who's that?' he said.

The men all twisted to peer towards the far edge of the circle, Alec the new recruit, counted in for the final game, not counted out yet, staring back. Also his dog. Godfrey saw how the dog's eyes glinted like small mirrors in amongst the gloom. Sweat prickled beneath his tunic then at the possibility of a different ending, no longer the second lieutenant holding all the cards. Ralph must have felt it too for he crouched forwards, razor spots vivid.

'I thought we were finished.'

All the men swivelled towards Archie Methven, perched on his parlour chair. Methven frowned at the notebook with its reckonings, its blue horizontals and red verticals, then nodded, turned to the new recruit.

'But you have to bet to play.'

Alec laid down his offering, as though it was nothing but a minor prize. For a moment the men stared as though it was something they had never seen before. Then a murmuring began, whispers around what remained of Godfrey's section. Here was a real gamble. Not pennies. Or buttons. Or rough tobacco in a little paper screw. But the chance of something much more special. A best Sunday suit. A pair of fine leather shoes. Or even better than that:

A gold ring.

A fur stole.

A diamond, perhaps.

Alec's bet was a pawn ticket, no.125. That small square of blue.

They all felt it then, the sudden thrill of the unknown. A bet on life rather than death, the possibility of survival. The boy played his card as though that was nothing special, too, laid it down amongst the chiff chaff for all to see. A knave. *The* knave. The knave of trumps. The new recruit had caught the ten. Game over. Winner takes all.

Two

It began with a fight as it always did, one man against another, everyone else standing around to watch, Godfrey's section threatening to collapse from the inside out now that the first round had been played. 8 November, nine men lined up in the yard waiting for Second Lieutenant Ralph Svenson to parade them for the day, no idea that this was the morning they were supposed to have been ordered over, crawling through a drainage ditch towards a certain death before breakfast had even been served.

The whistling was low at first, Percy Flint at the end of the section, cuffs buttoned, hair tamped down. It was an old song from the music hall back home, melody snaking along the line.

Who were you with last night
Under the pale moonlight . . .

Bertie Fortune jabbing at Flint with his elbow to make him stop. But Flint did not give up. The whistling soon gave way to song, a thin voice, unpleasant, stretching for the high notes:

'*Who were you with last night*
Under the pale moonlight?
It wasn't your sister
It wasn't your ma . . .
I saw yer, I saw yer . . .'

Flint could not sing well, but they all knew the words.

Ralph appeared on the step of the farmhouse, a grin growing on his face as the song grew, too. He leaned against the doorframe in his unbuttoned tunic to listen to Flint's clumsy crooning in the rain:

'*I saw yer*
I saw yer . . .'

Then he started to sing, too, a strong voice and pure:

'*Like a rosy apple red*
Out with Uncle Fred
I saw yer, I saw yer . . .'

The words rippling down the line all the way to Promise where he stood with his hair uncombed.

The fair A4 boy flushed bright as a coxcomb when he realized what they were saying, shifted to his right as though to disassociate himself from the singing, leaving a gap between him and the rest. Promise did not like to fight, would avoid it unless he was ordered. So it was left to Jackdaw to take Promise's place. He made a gesture, cupping his hand at the crotch of his trousers.

'You can have some if you want some, Flint. But you'll have to bloody pay.'

Flint stopped singing. 'You dirty little bastard. Could have you both on a charge.'

But Jackdaw just laughed. 'What, not the right kind of hole for you?'

'That's enough.'

Bertie Fortune grabbed the A4 boy's arm, tried to warn him. Not everyone was prepared to protect two boys who liked to tumble in the hayloft, whatever else went on. But Jackdaw shook the lucky man off, made a thrusting gesture in Percy Flint's direction.

'Some of that fancy soap should do it, Flint. Ease the way in.'

The gob of phlegm that splattered across Jackdaw's cheek then was warm, like the blood that had spurted from a chicken's neck. Jackdaw didn't even wait to wipe it from his face, launched himself at Flint instead, jabbing and pecking with his fingernails, scratching at Flint's eyes. Jackdaw might only have been eighteen, but he knew how to scrap, how to stick the bayonet in and give it a twist. Flint flung up his arms to cover his face.

'For fuck's sake, get off, man.'

Kicked out blind at Jackdaw's dodging, weaving body. The other men broke ranks, gathered round.

Fight, fight, fight.

All but Promise, who shrank from the brawl, hiding behind Alec and his little dog, as Jackdaw skipped in for one final rake of his fingernails down Flint's face before he danced away. The wound was superficial but impressive, raw in the pale light of morning. Flint was furious. He *dib dabbed* two fingers to his cheek, saw the blood.

'You fucking bastard, I'll do you for that.'

Lurched towards Jackdaw where he stood grinning in the rain. Bertie Fortune grabbed for Flint's arm, tried to stop him. Promise cowered. The dog barked, once, twice. Ralph just laughed.

'Flint!' Captain Godfrey Farthing stepped from the door of the farmhouse where he had been shaving in the back room, came over to the men. 'What the hell are you doing?'

Flint pulled away from Bertie Fortune's grip, jabbing a finger towards the darker A4 boy.

'He bloody started it.'

Godfrey turned to where Jackdaw stood on the far side of the pump, eyes alight with the damage he had caused.

'Private Jackson?'

Jackdaw didn't reply, stuck his hands into his pockets, dropped his head to stare at the mud on his boots.

Godfrey frowned. 'So who will tell me what's going on?'

Though he didn't really need to ask. There was an awkward shifting, each one of Godfrey's section glancing towards Second Lieutenant Svenson, before looking away. Godfrey came to stand in front of his second.

'Lieutenant Svenson?'

Ralph blinked once, his eyes almost translucent in the morning light. Then he shrugged, put his hands in his pockets, too. There was silence, one officer staring at the other. Then Godfrey stepped away.

'Back in line, everybody. You, there –' to Flint. 'You there –' to Jackdaw. 'Opposite ends this time. Hawes in charge.'

The men began to shuffle into some sort of order as Godfrey turned back to the farmhouse, Flint still cursing beneath his breath as he dabbed again at his cheek. But Jackdaw couldn't resist, hissing the insult as Flint slunk past.

'Stinking *Phyllis*.'

It was Bertie Fortune who laughed now, Archie Methven who grinned. All the men knew that Flint had been treated for syphilis twice that year alone. Flint turned on Jackdaw, body right up against the younger man's.

'Shut yer face or I'll give you something you won't forget.'

'You wish,' Jackdaw sniped.

'Which way do you want it? Up the arse or in the cakehole,' Flint jibed, before jerking his head towards Promise. 'Or shall I give it to your boyfriend instead?'

Alfred Walker cheered then, Promise shrinking even further behind Alec, Ralph with his arms across his chest grinning before he decided to take charge.

'Do as the captain says, boys. Back in line.'

As though he was not a boy himself.

Jackdaw stood for a moment, pushing the black cowl of hair from his face. Then, as he moved to retake his place, he bumped the young officer, grabbing for him as they fell. The men stood in silence this time as there in the mud they wrestled – Jackdaw slippery and wild, grappling at Ralph's clothes and his hair, Ralph rolling and scrabbling in an attempt to get on top. Two boys scrapping as though they were in a school playground again. Until Godfrey Farthing came running once more.

That morning the rain fell like it had on Noah during the flood. In the yard, Hawes was calling the orders, Ralph forced to watch as the officer in charge.

'Now men, as you're told.'

About turn. March. Halt. Then repeat. Men tracking through the mud, their heads bare, their hair and shoulders soaked. No more time for chasing chickens. No more room for larking in the hayloft. No more time for cards. Through the parlour window Godfrey noticed that Jackdaw and Promise stood at opposite ends of the line this time, didn't look at each other as they trekked through the mud along with the rest. He felt sorry for the A4 boys. He liked them. But he knew that together they were weak.

In the parlour, Godfrey took the orders from the top pocket of his tunic, read them over once again. He had woken early that morning with his heart in his throat, anticipating the enemy at the door. But when he rose to look, he'd found everything still. Low mist in the fields and the whole world covered in a glorious morning dew, sparkling across the roof tiles and the pump, the naked rosebush by the gate. The only sound had been the stream running through the pond and out again, a single blackbird singing in a hedge. There had been no sign of the enemy. Another day survived.

Now, as the men paraded in the rain, Godfrey took the battered tobacco tin from the wooden lockbox and eased off the lid. He tucked the orders behind a row of ten neat Capstans, replaced the lid again, fingers fluttering as though they'd never stop. Ignoring a direct order would be reason for a court martial, if he could not explain himself. Godfrey pressed two fingers to a spot just above his heart, felt the ghost of shrapnel shifting in his chest. The euphoria he'd experienced on rising to find dawn had already been and gone, had dissipated now after the fight in the yard, replaced by a small seam of anxiety worming its way in. He put the tobacco tin in the wooden box, was about to lock it when he heard a sudden cough, a shuffle of boots on the stone flags of the entrance hall. He looked up to find Hawes loitering at the door.

'Brought this back for you, sir,' said Godfrey's temporary sergeant. 'Don't think I'll be needing it again.'

He laid a small leather pouch on the parlour table – all

that remained of the men's tobacco ration. The two men gazed at the pouch, before Godfrey slid it towards him, lifted the lid of the wooden box and dropped it in. He and his temporary sergeant both knew there would not be another game. The brass key rattled in the hole as he locked the box again. There was silence for a moment before Godfrey spoke, a cold edge to his voice.

'Anything else I can help you with, Hawes?'

'Is there a script, sir?' Hawes said. 'For Jackdaw.'

The A4 boy's punishment. Striking a Superior Officer. Death in the worst-case scenario. Godfrey glanced through the parlour window at Ralph attempting to wash his face beneath the pump. He shook his head.

'Not this time.'

'The lieutenant won't like it,' said the temporary sergeant.

'The lieutenant can go hang.'

Hawes's neck pinked up then, his arms, too. Godfrey sighed.

'Do you think we're ready, Hawes?' he asked.

'A soldier's always got to be ready, sir.'

'Yes, but you know what I mean.'

'Is anyone ever ready, sir.'

It wasn't a question. Godfrey nodded, put his fingers on the top of the lockbox containing instructions to cross the river, engage the enemy, hold their ground whatever happened.

'Would you disobey a direct order, Hawes?' he asked.

Hawes coughed again then, a clearing of his chest.

'Not sure I'm the man to ask.'

*

It was Ralph who came to take Hawes's place once the
temporary sergeant had left to hand out chores for the
day. Godfrey's second lieutenant appeared covered in mud
and chicken shit, a cut on his brow from his fight with
Jackdaw, fury like a midnight fire lit in his eyes.

'Is that it, then,' he said, stamping into the parlour in
his dirty boots, 'no further action?'

Ralph the youngster demanding fair play.

'I'm assuming we're talking about Jackson here,' said
Godfrey.

'You have to punish him.'

'What for?'

'For fighting me,' Ralph said. 'Isn't it obvious?'

A dirty blond curl had fallen loose from Ralph's usual
parting, no hint of lemon oil now. Godfrey hadn't realized
just how wavy it was, the boy's hair, like that of some sort
of demented cherub. He ran a hand around the back of
his own neck, felt the soft prickle of an old man's stubble
even though he was not yet twenty-six.

'He was only defending himself, wasn't he. I heard the
singing.'

Ralph coloured. 'It was insubordination.'

'Really?'

'Striking an officer.'

Godfrey leaned back in his chair. 'Since when did you
become all concerned with protocol?'

The two officers stared at each other for a moment. It
was Ralph who looked away first. Godfrey tapped on the
edge of the table with his fingers. The cut on Ralph's
forehead looked deep, as though it might benefit from a
stitch or two. A war wound, Godfrey thought, something

for the boy to display. He touched his own forehead as though in sympathy.

'Does it hurt?'

Ralph was sullen. 'A little.'

'Alec could sew it for you. He says he's good with the needle.'

'No!'

Ralph's voice was cut through with something Godfrey had never heard before. Hurt. As though he was a child again. Godfrey frowned at his second then. It was hard to remember what Ralph had been like when he first arrived. A boy who grinned when they shook hands, who smelt of cut grass and candle wax, that high note of lemon. Now Godfrey couldn't help but notice how strong his second had become compared to the other young men, Ralph's body all muscle where theirs were all bone. Only a few weeks before Second Lieutenant Ralph Svenson had been soft, his shoulders and his arms rounded with a layer of fat that came from sweet living. But now he was lithe beneath his uniform. Godfrey wouldn't bet against him in a fight.

'Clean yourself up now,' he said, turning away as though the business between them had been concluded. 'Then I want you to get a work party together, dig a new latrine.'

'What about the game?'

Ralph still sounded hopeful, but Godfrey's reply held a warning, as though daring his young second to contest.

'No more games for now, Ralph. Not after this morning's little escapade.'

'But . . .'

'And tell Fortune I need him.'

'What for?'

Godfrey stood all of a sudden, exasperated. What was it about this boy that he couldn't take instruction? 'Just do as you're told. None of this would have happened if you hadn't been so gingered up about those damn chickens.'

Ralph scowled, a young lad still, retreated to the parlour door. Then he stood there in his muddy, crumpled tunic.

'I know what you're trying,' he said, strange eyes flicking from Godfrey to the lockbox and back again. 'It won't do any good.'

Bertie Fortune was up to his arms in the great earthenware sink, alone in the kitchen washing the mess tins, when Godfrey came to search him out. Godfrey had decided not to wait for Ralph to carry out his orders, realized that he couldn't rely on his young second to do what he asked now.

Fortune was whistling while he worked, a tune learned from the Americans they had encountered before the big spring push. Brand new men, all with swagger, marching up the line at just the moment Godfrey and the rest were bent so far backwards it seemed they must fall. Alfred Walker had taken to them straight away, spent all his time pestering with questions about dollars and candy, had been talking about the promised land ever since. Whereas Bertie Fortune had been much more practical, used the opportunity to enrich himself. Razor blades and eau de cologne. Fancy soap in waxed paper. English treasure for American gold, swapped again for French.

Now Godfrey watched Bertie Fortune for a moment

as he clattered the mess tins, the remains of the lye creating a scummy sort of lather, grease all about the lucky man's wrists. He wondered for a moment if he might be making a mistake. Godfrey was fond of his fixer, a man who grasped life and turned it to his advantage, would do anything for anyone if you made it worth his while. But he also knew that Bertie Fortune only ever delivered in strict order. Whoever paid first, came first. Unless someone paid more, in which case that trumped everything else. Godfrey Farthing turned his young lieutenant's dice in his pocket, knew the game wasn't finished yet.

In the attic room above the kitchen, Percy Flint stood with a bowl of water poured from Stone's black kettle, waiting as Second Lieutenant Svenson washed. Ralph's body glowed in the low November light. Flint was amazed at how much healthier the young lieutenant appeared compared to all the other men. He would have touched Ralph if he dared, just to see that it was real, the flex of muscle beneath the boy's skin. But an officer was an officer, no matter how young, not someone an ordinary foot-slogger like Flint ever wanted to cross.

Ralph splashed warm water on his face, ran his hands through his hair, then scrubbed at his head with an old scrap of towel. When he emerged he was in the pink again, the losses of the previous night all rubbed clean.

'Here you go, sir. I got this for you.'

Flint handed Ralph a fresh shirt, the lieutenant's second best, chicken blood scrubbed from its collar, washed and aired in the grain store. Ralph pulled it over his head and tucked it into his breeches, smoothed the front.

'You like to keep things nice, Flint,' he said.

'Yes, sir.'

Ralph took a pack of Woodbines from his trouser pocket, offered them up.

'You can have one if you want, Flint. As a thanks for helping me.'

'Sir.'

Flint didn't wait to be told twice, slid a tab from the pack. Ralph slipped the rest of the Woodbines back into his pocket.

'Sorry about your reel of thread, Flint,' he said. 'Didn't quite go the way we intended.'

'No, sir.'

Percy Flint sorted all the men's clothes. Washing every morning. Chat watch every night, smoking lice from the seams of their shirts with the flame of a candle. Flint knew all about who kept what where, including their sewing kits, often loaned out his pink thread to those who needed a repair.

Ralph glanced at the married conscript. 'You still got your fancy soap, Flint?'

'Not much of it, sir.'

'Got to pay for something like that, eh?'

Flint fingered the rim of the bowl, the water inside dirty now. 'Do you think we'll get a chance to play again, sir?'

Ralph lifted his tunic from a peg, shrugged it on, but didn't button it. 'I don't know, Flint. Doesn't seem likely after your stunt this morning.'

'What about the pop ticket, sir? I'd like to have a go at that.'

Pawn ticket no.125, that small square of blue.

'Me too, Flint. Me too,' Ralph replied. 'But I'm not sure the boy will play it again even if we could.'

'You could offer the cap badge, sir. That might work. All the men are waiting for it.'

Ralph shifted. 'Doesn't belong to me, Flint. Hadn't you heard.'

'Finders keepers, though.'

The second lieutenant blinked, took his hands from his pockets, looked at Flint with those strange eyes. 'That's right.'

From the entrance hall below there was the sound of boots on the step, Fortune and his captain murmuring together. The men in the attic were silent for a moment. Then Ralph bent to peer into a small triangle of mirror propped on a shelf, fiddled with his hair.

'I thought you'd be more interested in Fortune's eau de cologne than a cap badge, Flint.'

'Fortune won't bet that, sir,' said Flint. 'Keeps it for other things. He likes to barter.'

'You like to barter, too, don't you?'

'Depends what's on offer, sir.'

'This might be going begging.'

Ralph turned from the mirror and held a small tin towards Flint – a gentleman's pomade. Flint stared at the thing.

'And what might that be worth, sir?'

Ralph smiled, laid the container back on the shelf and began to button his tunic. 'I'm wondering about your idea, Flint. Another little game. Unofficial.'

'Sir?'

'One round, winner takes all. Do you think there'd be any takers? I could put in the cap badge to sweeten the pot, see if we can't tempt the new recruit.'

Flint grinned, teeth brown at their roots. 'Walker would, sir. Stone, too. Hawes definitely won't, might try to stop it.'

'Hawes is a coward, Flint,' said Ralph. 'He won't interfere.'

'Not sure Methven will want to be involved, sir, if the captain hasn't sanctioned it. But Jackdaw might if he thinks there's a chance of the badge. No idea about the boy, but worth a punt. He was keen enough last night, couldn't wait to take it all for himself.'

Flint and Ralph looked at each other for a moment, then Ralph brushed his hands down his tunic, tugged it straight at the bottom.

'In the grain store then, in an hour. You spread the word.'

'What about Fortune?' said Flint.

Ralph ran his hand across his hair. 'Leave the lucky man to me.'

An hour later, Bertie Fortune and his commanding officer walked out together, fording the overspill from the pond and climbing the field opposite as though they were two friends going for an afternoon stroll. They walked for a while as Godfrey explained what he wanted, Fortune nodding, a small pack slung across his back, his hands in his pockets, no attempt to make a note. Bertie Fortune never needed to write anything down. He was a man who didn't like to leave a trail.

At the fold in the land, when Godfrey could see the

grove of walnut trees small in the distance, they stopped and stood side by side, staring across the bare fields. The rain had softened, nothing more than smirr cloaking their faces and their tunics. In the distance a cloud of starlings whirled and wheeled. Godfrey noticed for the first time that his lucky man had not brought his rifle with him, as though he knew he would not be needing it anymore.

'What will you do while I'm gone, sir?' Fortune asked.

'We shall wait, Bertie. As we have done every other day of this bloody war.'

Twelve hours there. Twelve back. Until his lucky man returned. By nightfall tomorrow, that was what they had agreed, Bertie Fortune marching back to his section with the answer his captain wanted in his hand. Fortune pulled at the corner of his moustache for a moment.

'Will you let them play again, sir? While you're waiting.'

'I don't think so, Fortune,' Godfrey replied. 'Tried that once. Onto something else now.'

'The lieutenant won't like it.'

'Better return quick, then, hadn't you.'

Bertie Fortune didn't reply, stared out across the open fields. Then he turned towards his captain.

'But if you do decide to play, sir, you should let the lieutenant win.'

'And why's that, Fortune?' said Godfrey.

'So that he doesn't try another way.'

Godfrey sighed, unbuckled the new-fangled watch from his wrist, slid it into Bertie Fortune's palm.

'Keep it safe, Fortune,' he said. 'That's all that matters now. And make sure you get what I asked in return. The men are depending on it.'

'Sir.'

Fortune closed his fingers around the small disc of glass, slid his fist into his own pocket, brought it out empty as though nothing had gone on. They shook hands before he left, Godfrey holding on for a little more time than was proper, as though passing some secret between them. Then his lucky man was gone, walking away across the fields, Bertie Fortune in search of treasure, everybody's fate in his hands.

Three

This time the game was played in the grain store, six men hidden amongst the washing sagging on the line, door pulled shut bar a crack for light.

Flint.

Walker.

Stone.

Alec.

Jackdaw.

And Promise.

Their captain gone to wander the fields with his lucky man – Second Lieutenant Ralph Svenson finally in charge.

One round. Sudden death. The chance to win back everything the men had lost the day before. Or all that had never been paid. Their playing area was a small green cloth, thrown across the chiff chaff by George Stone. One side of the cloth was plain, the other patterned with the symbols for Crown and Anchor. But Ralph Svenson preferred aces and kings to dice for this game, the opportunity for calculation rather than random chance. Stakes high. Insubordination of a different kind.

Ralph dealt the cards himself, tossing a round to each of the men, then called bets in. It was the section's petty thief who led them off this time. Alfred Walker opened his hand and slid something onto the rough playing area.

A piece of green ribbon, a snake of perfection in amongst the muck. The men all stared.

'Where'd that come from?' said Percy Flint. 'Some lady's knickers?'

'You bloody wish, Flint.' Walker grinned. 'Came from a Jerry, that's what I was told.'

Beach's ribbon, the colour of an Irish summer, last seen attached to his pack like a pennant on a lance.

'Bloody miser,' muttered Flint, crossing his arms now. 'Why didn't you play it yesterday? Always keeping the best stuff for yourself.'

'I'm betting it now, aren't I?' said Walker. 'When I win, I'm gonna give it to my sweetheart, along with all the rest.'

'You don't have a bloody sweetheart.'

'I will have when all this is over.'

'What's she going to do with a bit of ribbon from a dead Jerry?' said Flint. 'Trim her knickers with it?'

For once Walker ignored the married conscript. 'She'll hang my picture from it. Or tie it in her hair.'

'What if she wants a different colour?'

'Then I'll trade it,' said the petty thief. 'Buy her a fox stole.'

'What?' Flint laughed, a mocking sound. 'Something dead to drape about her neck.'

'Now, now, boys,' murmured George Stone. 'Let's play on, or the captain will be back. My turn next.'

Percy Flint subsided, two spots of colour on his cheeks as they waited to see what the old sweat had kept for best. George Stone reached into his pocket and pulled out something the men had not seen for several months now. An orange, its skin a little wrinkled. Alfred Walker whistled.

'You bugger. Kept that quiet.'

Stone smiled, placed the orange in the centre of the playing area, leaned back with his arms crossed. They all knew that the orange was proper treasure, something every soldier would want.

Percy Flint went next, sliding his offering forwards – a gentleman's pomade, faint scent of lemon lingering around the edges of the small circular tin. The men shifted, uneasy. They all knew where the pomade had come from, wondered what might have been offered in return. Second Lieutenant Ralph Svenson smiled, then fixed his gaze upon Promise across the opposite side of the circle.

'What about you, Promise?' he said. 'Last chance to win.'

Promise blushed. 'I'm not playing this time.'

Ralph smiled his slow smile. 'What, gone the way of Hawes?'

Promise flushed, a raw colour at the base of his throat at the idea he might be a coward. Jackdaw couldn't help himself.

'Let's see yours then, sir,' he said, voice defiant. 'That's what we're here for.'

'Now, now, Jackdaw,' replied Ralph. 'No need to go off half-cocked. You first.'

The dark A4 boy scowled. Then he rummaged in his pocket, tossed Hawes's tanner into the middle of the playing field, where it spun for a moment before settling. A cheap thing won on a bet over a chicken, expecting silver in return.

Ralph Svenson touched a finger to the scar on his fore-head, glanced towards the fair A4 boy. 'Can't keep your treasure to yourself, eh, Promise.'

'You bloody—'

It was George Stone who held Jackdaw back. 'Keep calm, boy. Keep calm.'

But the second lieutenant had already turned towards Alec, anticipation lighting his strange eyes.

'Now you,' he said.

Alec reached forwards, dropped something on to the green cloth, sat back. The men all stared at the offering. A beech nut, safe inside its prickled shell.

Ralph swore. 'What the hell is that?'

'Nature's bounty,' said Alec.

Jackdaw laughed and Flint gave him a sour look.

'Bloody rabbit food,' he said. 'Where's the pop ticket?'

But Alec just shrugged, waited to see if the second lieutenant would take the bait or not.

In the bottom of a drainage ditch, a mile or so away, Captain Godfrey Farthing lay on his belly watching the river a few hundred yards ahead. The day was still damp, dew clinging to every leaf and grass stem, his uniform drenched, from collar to cuff.

As he studied the open ground on the far side of the water Godfrey could feel the *one two* beat of his heart at the thought of the afternoon sun catching on the buttons of his tunic, drawing the enemy fire. He had been lying in the ditch for an hour, now, maybe more, nothing to see but a spider running across its sodden web. But that didn't mean the enemy were not in front of him, across that dark rope of water, a slow continuous flow.

As the sun began to fall towards the horizon, Godfrey rolled onto his back and let his gaze wander into the sky.

A single crow flew steadily across his vision, grey clouds beginning to move above him, too. He closed his eyes, felt it seep through his body from beneath. Not cold, or damp, water oozing from every pore of the ground. But a strange peace coursing through every one of his veins; that terrible calm that comes when a man knows the end is coming, but not in the way he had imagined when he began.

It reminded Godfrey of that time when Beach was still alive, crouching beside his captain in the bottom of a trench, Godfrey stood on the fire-step staring at a newfangled watch strapped to his wrist as he counted down the minutes and the seconds, whistle cold against his lip. Next to him James Hawes had shifted in the mud, a nervous, twitching energy. Godfrey had reached out a hand and laid it for a moment on his sergeant's sleeve.

'You all right, Hawes?' he had whispered, eyes still on the glass face of his wristwatch.

Hawes's reply had been nothing more than a grunt. 'Sir.'

But Godfrey had smelled the fear rising from the ex-meat man, then, like the smell that rose from a carcass that had waited too long to be cleaved.

After Beach was gone and Godfrey had received that letter from his father's solicitor telling him his parents were gone, too, he'd stood on the fire-step once again and stared at the dark clouds shifting above him, thought how beautiful they were. The same stillness he felt now had settled on him then, as he gazed across No Man's Land towards the hidden enemy, knew what he would do. He'd waited five minutes, ten perhaps, to see if anyone might stir. But there had been nothing more than the quiet chat of men further along the line, the rasp of an illicit match struck against the sole of a boot, the *clink* and *jink* of a rifle as Hawes shifted in his sleep once more.

Godfrey had reached out, touched the ex-meat man's sleeve.

'Goodbye, Hawes. I'll be seeing you.'

Put a foot to the ladder, a hand to the top.

Then there'd been the wet slick of mud between his fingers as he scrambled over. One foot on the lip of the trench, then the other, until he was out. How marvellous it had been to stand untethered on open ground, body wide to the enemy, Webley still holstered, nothing between him and a sniper's bullet but the glint of a watch strapped to his wrist.

Now that's really something.

Waiting with his arms stretched wide for the men in grey to finally bring him down. Like Beach had been brought down, roses blooming across his second-best shirt, nothing left of the boy but those flat eyes staring at an empty sky.

Godfrey could still remember the smell of Hawes beneath him as his sergeant pulled him down. The stink, almost animal, like the mud that caked them all from skull to toe. Also the hammering of the ex-meat man's heart as above them a thousand bullets suddenly traced the sky. Then the cold shock at realizing he was hit, blood seeping through Godfrey's vest, through his shirt and his tunic, straight into Hawes's eye. Yet still Hawes had clung on, holding his captain like a mother might hold her child. Godfrey Farthing still had the shrapnel beneath his skin to remind him of what his temporary sergeant had saved him from. Punishable by death in the worst-case scenario. A self-inflicted wound.

In the grain store, Second Lieutenant Ralph Svenson tossed it down. Not a silver cap badge, small lion raising its paw. But a dirty thing. An ordinary thing. All stuffed with needles and pins. Promise's Housewife won on the turn of a knave the day before, but in the hands of their second lieutenant now.

'Bloody thief!' Jackdaw cried, jerking towards Ralph where he sat across the field of play.

'Leave it, son.' George Stone held on to the A4 boy by the collar as he scuffled and twisted, tried to get loose. 'Not worth the trouble.'

Ralph laughed. 'I think you'll find it's Walker who's got the sticky fingers. Specially when there's something in return.'

A ribbon, green as an Irish summer.

Alfred Walker blushed as Promise turned towards him, face shocked. But Jackdaw cared only about the second lieutenant.

'You bastard, Svenson!' he shouted. 'Where's the bloody cap badge? Flint said you'd play it. Why else d'you think we're here?'

'What badge?' shrugged Ralph. 'I don't have it. Frisk me if you like.'

He stretched his arms wide then, as though offering Jackdaw a target. The A4 boy swore again.

'I'll kill you for this.'

'Caw, caw, caw,' cried Flint.

But Second Lieutenant Svenson just laughed at the

spectacle he had created. 'You can try, Jackdaw. But then you might end up in front of a six-man squad. We can get Hawes to do it. I've heard he's good with the rifle.'

He turned his gaze to the crack in the grain-store door where James Hawes stood watching from the other side. Ralph stared at the temporary sergeant for a moment before turning back to scuff at Promise's Housewife with his boot.

'This is your chance, boys. Retrieve the evidence. Or shall I call Hawes in, have you locked in the shed?'

'You fucking bastard –'

Ralph glanced once more towards the door, nothing to see now but a pale slit of light falling across the stone. Then he turned back to the A4 boy, his face a sneer now.

'Well, Jackdaw. Do you want to play, or not?'

An hour later, the land on both sides of the river was quiet as Godfrey Farthing wriggled away, crawling through the drainage ditches and the water meadows until he was back where he began. He stood on the brow of the fold in the land watching the spot where his lucky man had left, Bertie Fortune getting smaller and smaller until he was swallowed by the afternoon mist, nothing but emptiness stretching out on all sides. The land here was beautiful, Godfrey thought, hardly a sign that only a few miles back the world had been devastated beyond repair. Nothing left but a landscape like the surface of the walnut he turned now in his pocket, all its tunnels and grooves.

Godfrey stared across the bare fields, imagining Bertie Fortune returning tomorrow with treasure in his hand. One more night to keep his men safe, until the end came.

Then he turned to walk away himself. Back towards the farmhouse with its grain store and its two remaining chickens. Back towards the basket of walnuts in the kitchen. Back towards the water running in and out of the pond. He made it halfway home before the rain began.

Then he heard the shot.

1957

Jackdaw

The day dawned brighter than the last, buttercups sprinkled along the riverbank, two kinds of clover blooming in the field. Jackdaw watched from the windows of his turret, east, west, north, south, staring over the hayfield, bright in spring sunshine, towards where a river was hidden in a fold of the land. In his pocket his fingers searched for the prick of a tiny silver cap badge, time passing across his skin like water across shingle, all its little runnels and rills.

The latest war was over, nothing but a skirmish in the desert at Suez, a squabble over a canal. Still, it had left all the men disgraced, nowhere to look for consolation but the fact that none of their sons might have to fight again. Once Jackdaw had crouched in front of weapons powerful enough to kill several men at a hundred paces, one squeeze of the trigger, spray it all around. But even he knew that war was a matter of atomics now, something nobody could stop with a machine gun and a tank.

For Jackdaw this was meant to be a new beginning, too. A school for foundling boys, orphaned or abandoned. Or for those whose parents simply didn't have the time. Sent up from London, not even sixty but already an old man, tired right through to the centre of his bones. When he'd arrived he had walked into the empty quad with its silent spear of stone, seen all the names. What was it, he had thought then, that made one go on in the face of disaster? This school was meant to be a safe berth for him, after another kind of disgrace. Yet somehow Jackdaw had known even then that his time was already long past, no chance of resurrection now.

He peered down from his turret window towards the boys he was supposed to be supervising in the quad, a rabble seething and roaring, no scuffle worthy of his attention until it involved bruises on both sides. He watched as one of the older boys, stolid and unimaginative in his taunting, came to stand over a new arrival only appeared the night before. The new boy was a small thing wearing a school hand-me-down, much too large. He hunched on the steps of the memorial, picking at the names carved into the stone. Jackdaw had seen them come over the years and he had seen them go, boys of all descriptions trying to be men. But he knew the moment he saw this boy that he was different. A solemn little thing, barely grown yet, but already old inside.

Down in the quad the older boy, Bothwell, plucked at the bottom of the new boy's second-hand jumper, the pink V on the front practically to his knees.

'Where d'you get this from?' he said.

'His mummy knitted it,' another boy shouted.

'Maybe he knitted it himself,' Bothwell said.

They all laughed.

Bothwell began to tug at the jumper. 'Let's have a shot, then.'

The new arrival squirmed as the two boys grabbed him, dragged the V-neck over his head, began to toss the borrowed jumper around. Bothwell threw it a few times, too, then dropped the bedraggled thing to the gravel, kicked it away.

'What's he got on underneath, d'you think?' he said, pulling at the new arrival's shirt, tiny buttons pinging across the gravel, *one, two, three.*

They didn't see him coming.

'That's enough!'

Descending with his gown flapping like his namesake, warning them to scatter, which they did. Some laughing. Some cawing. Jackdaw didn't know how, but they had his name already, flown from the metropolis as though on silent wings. He got in a slap or two before they vanished. One of the reasons he was *persona non grata* at the school he had just come from. Amongst other things.

'Are you all right?'

Jackdaw lifted the jumper from the gravel, handed it to the new arrival. The boy was dirty about the knees, hair all mussed. Jackdaw frowned at something familiar in the child's face, a fleeting glance. Then the boy took the jumper and pulled it over his head, got in a tangle. When he finally emerged, his face was tight with hot tears. They stood together in silence, one old man, one young, before the boy began again with his picking, scraping moss from the names of dead men on that old familiar plinth.

'*Old Mortality*, eh,' Jackdaw said.

'Sir?'

The boy knew how to be polite at least.

'From the book. Walter Scott. He liked gravestones, too.'

But the boy did not know his Scott. At least, not yet.

'What's your name?' Jackdaw asked.

'Solomon, sir.'

'Solomon what?'

'Farthing, sir, like the coin.'

And Jackdaw knew at once what it meant. His captain returned to haunt him, for a debt that never could be paid.

In the staff common room that afternoon, Jackdaw listened as the young male teachers whispered and laughed from behind their registers as the old matron, Miss Janie, began with her list. All the boys who were confined to the sick bay. All the boys who had been released. Miss Janie had been at the school since before the first war. Another relic, like him.

Solomon Farthing turned out to be one of her latter charges, delivered to them overnight from London and deposited in the sick bay because there had been nowhere else for him to go. The headmaster was looking for a volunteer to take the boy into their house, but no one was offering. Solomon Farthing was asking to be preyed on. They could all see that.

Jackdaw heard the men behind him start again with their whispers.

'His father took a dive, that's what they're saying.'

'What?'

'Didn't bother to swim.'

'He was a C.O., wasn't he. Conscientious Objector. Wouldn't go and fight.'

'Bloody coward,' one of the teachers muttered.

'I heard he got sent to prison,' said another.

'Got what he deserved, then.'

'Bloody conchies.'

Jackdaw felt in his pocket for the small silver cap badge, put his fingers about it as though to keep it warm. He always had wondered if he would have the guts to do it himself – refuse to lift a gun if asked a second time, take the hard labour instead. Thank God he hadn't been fit enough for the second war when it came, got through it all as a fire warden, nothing more dangerous than that. He'd become a vegetarian when he returned from the first, had damn near starved the first few winters. Nothing to eat but dried milk and turnips shrivelled on their stalks. Another reason for the younger generation to laugh behind his back. Still, Jackdaw never could forget the blood on Promise's shirt, the way that chicken had danced across the mud.

Now he pricked the silver pin against his thumb, once, twice, thought of all the things he had fought for once, all the things he had lost.

'I'll have him.'

He hadn't meant to say it. Had intended to keep his head down, listen to the boys sing in the chapel as he waited for retirement, nothing to do then but read poetry with his feet up by the fire. But life was life, wasn't it. One more spin of the dice couldn't hurt. Wasn't that what Fortune always said?

The staff room went quiet, all eyes turned to the old man at the back. The headmaster paused for a moment, as though uncertain whether to accept. But nobody else was offering so he bowed to the English teacher as though they were in some sort of court and Jackdaw was, for that moment, king.

*

That night, Jackdaw could barely breathe as he paraded up one row of beds and down the other, boys stretched before him from the window in the gable, to the door at the far end. Once it had been the best part of his day, the evening after lights went out, strolling amongst his tiny flock, boys with hair like flax and burdock, their faces smoothed by dreams. It always reminded Jackdaw of Promise, asleep in the hayloft with his arm flung out, a boy all angles and shadows, the bloom of cold air pinking up his cheeks. Jackdaw remembered lying beside Promise. Shirt cuff to shirt cuff. Wrist bone to wrist bone. Hip next to hip. That one time when he had truly lived – with danger every single day.

Now he felt suffocated by it – the stink of little boys. Filthy hair on lumpen pillows. The odour of unwashed bodies drenching the air like a terrible perfume. He smelled it in the night just before he woke, flailing beneath his blanket. Cordite. Then that lingering scent of lemon oil gone sour. Jackdaw could smell it again now as he moved towards the end of the dormitory, one boy's fear rising from the bed sheets as he approached. He could hear the voices whispering in the dark, too. Little tongues darting like fish in a river, calling to the new boy across the gap between their beds.

'Hey, you. Farthing. Where you from?'

'Is your mother dead?'

'What does your father do?'

'Is he dead, too?'

Jackdaw hoped that Farthing would stay silent, as the boy's grandfather had done for all of these years. But when it came, Solomon Farthing's voice was thin in the echo of the dormitory's rafters.

'My father was a soldier.'

More than ten years since it had ended and still the stick by which they were all measured. The other boy made a strange noise in the darkness, half-laugh, half-disgust.

'I heard he was a conchie.'

Farthing's voice was plaintive. 'What's a conchie?'

'We'll show you, if you like.'

Jackdaw saw them then, two of the little bastards sliding from their beds, pyjamas pale in the darkness, hands already pulling the blanket from Solomon Farthing so as to leave him in the cold. Jackdaw moved quick, ready to intervene, smelled it before he got near. That burst of urine, hot on a small boy's crotch. The others smelled it too.

'Christ!'

'He's peed!'

'Dirty bugger.'

And Jackdaw felt the shock of it again – that slur to which he had become accustomed, normally aimed at him. He could hear Farthing crying as the other boys scuttled back to their own beds, sheets warm and dry. He hesitated for a moment, before he retreated, too.

Two weeks later and the older pupils were practising for the pageant in the chapel, some sort of summer ritual that required one to be voted the prince of them all. The person who was chosen had to strip and drape himself in a cloth, while all around him boys who were fully clothed processed with fronds of greenery as they sang. No one ever admitted that he wanted to be the one to disrobe. But every boy desired to be chosen. That was just the way of things.

Jackdaw found Solomon Farthing sitting on one of the wooden benches at the back, scratching at the underside of the pew in front. He stopped when Jackdaw approached, folded his fingers over whatever was in his hand.

'Do you like it?' said Jackdaw, indicating the boys at the front.

'I like the singing.'

'*An endless picture-show,*' Jackdaw murmured.

'Sir?'

'Nothing.'

Solomon Farthing was too young for Sassoon, Jackdaw thought, wouldn't understand. He glanced at the bruises on the boy's legs, saw how he drew them away from the teacher's gaze beneath the pew, turning something in his hand so that it caught and glittered in the candlelight. A thruppenny bit for tuck, given to the boys who had nothing, so they would not feel left out. Solomon Farthing had polished it on his short trousers. Jackdaw smiled. He, too, liked shiny things.

'Not want to play with the others?' he asked. 'They're out in the yard now.'

Farthing dipped his head.

'No thanks.'

'Want to see something special instead?'

'Yes, sir.'

The boys were singing:

The Lord's my shepherd . . .

As Jackdaw placed his hand on Solomon's shoulder, felt the warmth of young skin beneath the boy's shirt, took it away again. The boy's hair was as fair as the sun on the hayfield as Jackdaw walked Solomon away. Just like the old man's was grey.

Up, up and up again they went, all the way to the top of the turret, towards a square room with a solid wooden door. Inside the room was hazy with evening light filtering in east, west, north and south. Farthing exclaimed, ran to one of the windows, knelt on a big oak chest to see. Jackdaw grinned, came to stand beside him.

'There's the field,' he said. 'Two kinds of clover if you search for them. And beyond that the river, buttercups all along the bank.'

'We're not allowed by the river, sir.'

'Who says.' It wasn't a question. Jackdaw shrugged as the boy glanced at him. 'We've all got to live.'

He moved towards the desk with its drawers and its green leather inlay, the carpet beneath starting to get worn at its centre, the stuffed armchair in the corner taking all the room.

'Want to see my treasure trove?' he said.

Solomon Farthing turned from his perch by the window. 'Yes, please, sir.'

'Over here, then.'

Jackdaw gestured towards the desk, pulled out the top drawer for the boy to see. Together they peered inside at a few shiny plaques on colourful ribbons. Jackdaw's campaign medals, Pip, Squeak and Wilfred. Also a cross in cloudy, tarnished silver, crowns on its tips east, west, south, north.

A Military Cross.

For Gallantry.

Or something like that. The boy's eyes shone in the low summer light as he stared at the treasure. Solomon Farthing had probably never known a hero, thought Jackdaw. A man who fought his way through the worst of it all and came home with a medal on his chest to cover the hole.

'Is this yours, sir?' Solomon asked, pointing to the cross on its purple and white striped ribbon.

Jackdaw shook his head. 'It belonged to an old boy, I think. Found it in one of the drawers downstairs, in the library.'

'What did he do for it, sir?'

'What all men do in war,' said Jackdaw. 'They fight.'

Solomon was silent for a moment. 'Can I hold it?'

'Don't see why not.'

Jackdaw slipped the cross from its case, handed it to the boy, warm in his hand. Solomon Farthing held the medal for a moment. Then he asked. 'What's a conchie, sir?'

Jackdaw sighed, took the cross and replaced it in its little box, closed the drawer again.

'A man who doesn't do his duty,' he said.

A man who would not even pick up a stick, let alone a gun.

'Did you fight in the war, sir?'

'Yes,' said Jackdaw. 'The first one.'

'Did they give you a medal?'

The old man's face changed then. 'No, not like this. But my friend had one. Would you like to see?'

In the common room the next day he heard the headmaster discussing Solomon Farthing's fate with the other young men, a boy who wet the bed almost every night, shunned by the other boys, constantly being called to the laundry to wash out his sheet.

'He seems to attract trouble,' said the headmaster.

'The boys know that he's weak –' one of the younger teachers stirred his tea – 'they take advantage.'

'We'll have to beef him up, then. See what he can do.'

'He won't do well here,' said the games teacher. 'Does he not have any family to take him?'

'Not that we know of.'

A true Oliver Twist.

He would not survive. That was what Jackdaw thought. All of Solomon Farthing's soft edges sharpened, or worse. Until there was nothing left of the boy he was now – a child who liked shiny things, who wanted to play amongst the flowers on the riverbank and listen to other boys sing. If he stayed here, Jackdaw knew that Solomon Farthing would become a man just like him. A husk of a thing, always ready with a slap or a caustic remark, someone who had learned to hide from the vicissitudes of life beneath a brittle exterior, spent his whole existence pretending he was something he was not.

Jackdaw thought of the bird's nest Promise had found when the end was near, a perfect thing bound together with moss and straw, long since abandoned in the hedgerow. The new recruit had showed them where to look, lifting it from the thorns to place in Promise's hands. Inside the remains of the nest there had been the remains of an egg, one life inside another, broken apart now. But Promise had lifted the pieces out as though they were the most important treasure. A young man playing in the back field as though he was a boy again, nothing to do in life but that.

Jackdaw tipped a spoon of sugar into his tea, then another, thought of the things he could do for Solomon Farthing. Show him how to punch. Show him how to scratch. How to dig the weapon in. Or return him to the family he had lost somewhere along the line, make his life anew. He turned from the trolley of tea things, cups, saucers and spoons, realized the other teachers were discussing him now, their voices low as though he might not hear.

'He's friendly with the new boy. I saw them together in the chapel.'

'What do you mean, friendly?'

'I don't know. He's had him in his room, though.'

'You know he's one of them, right?'

Dirty bugger.

'What was it about last time? At the school he came from, I mean.'

Another nest, Jackdaw thought then. Of vipers and intrigue. Whispering behind their registers, watching him always. Jackdaw hated bullies, would bring them down if he could.

'I know someone who might take him.'

Jackdaw's voice was louder than he had intended. He watched them turn in surprise towards where he stood alone by the tea trolley.

'Who's that, then?' asked the headmaster.

Jackdaw circled the spoon once in his teacup, heard the scrape of sugar on china.

'His grandfather,' he said.

*

Solomon had made it to the river at last, escaped from lessons and left to play on his own, no other boys to spoil his fun. He stood on the small crescent of shingle, staring at the thick current of water before him where it ran and glittered in the sun. All along the bank buttercups were just beginning to unfold their petals to the sun, butter beneath his chin. Soon it would be summer. Who knew what that might bring?

'What are you doing?'

Solomon turned and squinted towards the bank where a boy had suddenly appeared, older, flesh thick about his waist. Bothwell, come to play his games. Bothwell leered at Solomon.

'Are you playing with yourself?'

Solomon flushed, took his hands from his pockets. 'No.'

'What is it, then?'

'Nothing.'

Bothwell came sliding down the bank, grit on his sandals. 'Come on, conchie. Let's see.'

'No.'

Grabbed at Solomon, twisting Solomon's arm around his back, prising apart his fingers till he had the treasure in his hand. A small thing, glinting in the sunlight. A silver cap badge with a lion raising its paw.

'Where did you get this?' said Bothwell.

Solomon flushed again, face hot. 'It was my dad's.'

'No it wasn't. Your dad was a conchie.'

'Give it back.'

'Did Jackson give it to you?' Solomon's silence told Bothwell that this was true. He laughed. 'He gives it to all the boys he likes. You're nothing special.'

'How do you know?'

'I just do. He's disgusting. Why do you think he left his other school?'

Bothwell stuffed the little cap badge into his pocket, grabbed at the rope that hung from the tree instead, a thick plait hanging down to touch the surface of the water, ready to swing out.

'Shall we go on the rope?' he said.

'I don't want to,' said Solomon, his face pinched. All the boys were warned to stay off the rope.

'Don't be a scaredy.'

'I'm not.'

Though it was clear that he was.

'Go on, I dare you.' Bothwell grinned. 'I'll give you the badge back if you do it.'

Solomon felt it then, the heat that rose all through his body. He stepped towards the rope, felt it huge between his hands. His little heart was galloping *one two one two* at the thought of the water, how cold it must be, how deep. He heard Bothwell laughing, was about to drop the rope again, step away, when the shove came, the other boy's hands rough on his back, the sudden swing out. Then his feet dangling over nothing. Water deep beneath him, glittering in the sunlight. The sound of air rushing in his ears as he felt his hands slipping, his voice a high shriek.

'I can't swim!'

Somewhere behind him Bothwell laughing. Then everything falling as he finally let go.

Solomon landed with a thud on the shingle, breath forced from his lungs, grit all along his thigh. He lay for a moment, winded, nothing but the sound of the water rushing on and on. He could feel the sting of a graze on his elbow, blinked as a shadow cut across the sun. Bothwell grinned above him, offered a hand, took it away again as Solomon reached out, laughing as he tossed the little cap badge towards the river instead. That was when Solomon Farthing made his move, just as the Jackdaw had taught.

The older boy cried out as he went down, Solomon upon him, knees clamped in like a bony vice, feet dug into the damp and shifting shingle, one small arm after another punching and punching, fists small ridges of bone. Then he was pushing and pushing at Bothwell's face, the older boy's head suddenly in the water, bubbles on his lips. Bothwell's legs thrashed as he twisted and scrabbled, tried to get free. Solomon punched again then, as though it did not matter anymore. That his mother was dead. That his father was dead. That there was no one left in the world for him. Then he rolled away, lay on his back amongst the shingle, watched the sunlight ripple and refract through the trees.

After a moment, Bothwell tried to get up, blood smeared across his cheek as though he had put on make-up for a play. He stumbled in the shallows, then again, staggering as he slipped on a hidden stone beneath the surface, went down. He splashed like a hooked fish as the current pulled him under, one hand waving. Like the little silver cap badge, thought Solomon, lion raising its paw.

He watched as the boy disappeared beneath the dark water, one glimpse of his face pale amongst the river reed, then nothing, the surface of the water suddenly smooth again. No sound but a bird singing from the branches, the water running on and on, Solomon standing on the shingle, feet dug into the ground.

Then came the shout from across the field.

'Boy!'

That black cape flapping, an old man descending on him as though from the sky. Pulling on Solomon's shoulders as he shoved past him to plunder the water, grasping for Bothwell. By his ankles. By his shirt. By anything he could get his hands on. Feet. Belt. Or hair. An old man ducking and ducking and ducking again, until he came up for air. Solomon watched as the Jackdaw rose from the river with Bothwell in his arms. Then he crouched to pluck something from the shallows. A silver cap badge rescued from its little shingle grave.

PART FOUR

The Charge

Godfrey Farthing
b.1893 d.1971

Solomon Farthing
b.1950 d.

Archibald Methven
= Mabel Kerr

(adopted)

Tom
b.1913 d.1918

Thomas Methven
b.~~1920/21,~~
1918? d.2016

2016

One

Solomon woke in the very early morning to a dawn washed clean by night-time rain. Outside a lark was singing as though its tiny lungs might burst. He lay listening to its solitary call, wondered if somewhere over the border Walter Pringle was listening, too.

The Mini had refused to start when the time had come for him to leave. Six boys pushing in the dark, alongside Eddie Jackson in his dressing gown, and still the little car had stalled. They had given Solomon a blanket to sleep under instead, blue with a white trim across the edge.

'We've put you in the sick bay,' Eddie Jackson had said. 'I hope you don't mind.'

Solomon had undressed as though he was a boy again, folding his corduroys with care before laying them on a nearby chair. When he'd got into the bed he'd known that somewhere far in the hidden dormitories of this great building other boys were lying beneath blue blankets, too. He'd gazed towards the ceiling, thinking of the river at the bottom of the hill, the way the sun sparkled from its surface as though refracted by a hundred mirrors, the dip and glide of the swifts. As he fell asleep he was sure he could hear the boys singing,

The Lord's my shepherd . . .

All their small mouths raised to the chapel roof.

The next morning the sun was barely over the horizon as Solomon stood at the window looking down into the quad, wondering if Alec Sutherland had ever made it onto the glory rolls. The war memorial was a dark presence, lichen creeping across all of its tongues and its grooves. Solomon could feel it still, the cold touch of the stone as he scraped at the moss, sixty years passing through his fingertips as he waited for a man in a black cloak to come billowing over and present his new name. He had a sudden memory of all the poems he had ever learned from that man, crowding now inside his head.

There is some corner of a foreign field . . .
Dulce et decorum est.
A drawing-down of blinds . . .

The war to end all wars, wasn't that what they had called it? Nothing more than a series of poems for men like him.

Solomon stared through the window, beyond the school buildings, to a long slope of grass running towards a river hidden at the bottom of the hill. The field was grey in the low light of dawn, waiting for a beautiful day to warm it. The banks of the river would be studded with buttercups at this time of year, clear water lapping at the fringes. There would be a tree, its branches stretching as though to touch the other side. Then that place in the middle where the water suddenly ran dark.

Take care, boys. Only ever stay in the shallows.

But what sort of life was that.

Beyond the courtyard on the far side of the war memorial Solomon realized there was someone staring back. A boy with fair hair, his shirt all untucked. As Solomon watched, the boy lifted his hand to wave, waited for Solomon to raise his in reply.

Mid-morning, breakfast done in a scatter of sugar pops and burnt toast and Eddie Jackson leaned into the window of the Mini, small dog once more adorning the back seat.

'So you're off to visit the castle?' he said.

'Regimental Archive,' Solomon confirmed. 'Where all the old soldiers go to rest.'

The most likely place to find Alec Sutherland, a boy soldier born and raised in the local hayfields, must have joined up somewhere nearby.

'They have a knight's quest, too, if you fancy it,' said the teacher. 'George spearing the dragon.'

Emblem of the Northumberland Fusiliers. Solomon thought again of his lost lucky charm.

The schoolboys cheered as the Mini's engine rattled into action at the first turn of the key this time, the dog giving a sharp bark as though to join the general fun. As Solomon released the clutch, let the little car begin its roll upon the gravel, Eddie Jackson tapped on the window, slid something in.

'Everything that came with you the first time,' he said. 'Then got left behind. My great-uncle kept it for you all these years, in case you ever returned.'

Some sort of tin wrapped in plastic. Solomon took the parcel, laid it on the back seat of the Mini next to the dog. The dog gave the tin a cursory lick, curled its body about the package as though to keep it warm. Eddie Jackson was about to withdraw, then he hesitated.

'By the way,' he said. 'You're not the only one who's been asking.'

The vibrations from the Mini's engine suddenly jangled up and down Solomon Farthing's spine.

'Oh yes?'

'A man came by yesterday before you arrived. Wore a smart suit.'

'I don't suppose he gave you a name, did he?'

'Oh, I try not to do names if I don't have to,' said the teacher. 'But he drove a big car. Grey, it was, and shiny. Do you know it?'

Yes, thought Solomon. He knew it all too well.

They had fleets of them now, Dunlop, Dunlop & Dunlop. And all the rest. Retired police officers in hybrids, relaxing in lay-bys as they waited for the phone call that would send them into the breach. Doorstepping long-lost relatives. Polite but persistent requests for ID. Checking empty properties to see whether they were worth the chase. One million. Two million. Sometimes even three. Solomon understood these men from the bottom of their sensible shoes to the tips of their ballpoint pens. He, too, was of the door knocker persuasion – liked to do the dirty work himself.

'What was he after?' he asked now, as though he didn't know.

'Old boys,' said Eddie Jackson. 'Just like you are.'

'What did you tell him?'

'I told him the records were confidential.'

So there were still good men in the world. Solomon held his hand out the window of the Mini, found it all aflutter.

'Thank you,' he said. 'For everything.'

'You're welcome,' said Eddie Jackson, grasping Solomon's fingers and holding them still for a moment. 'Come back any time.'

The local castle was just what any boy would expect. Ramparts. And cannons. A dungeon and a keep. Plus plenty of turrets on which to fly a flag. Solomon approached via lanes edged with cow parsley and Queen Anne's Lace, skirting the fringes of the nearby market town in an attempt to avoid any sleek grey cars that might be lurking there. He was half a mile from his target when he drove past a sign that said: *£16 at the Gate*. It was only then that Solomon realized he might actually have to pay to view a soldier's record; with money that he did not have.

The boy appeared at the same time as the castle, a head of muzzled hair ascending into the small rectangle of the rear-view mirror, just as the castle ascended the horizon in front. Solomon swerved the wheel.

'What the hell . . . !'

The Mini scrunching on mud and gravel as he pulled into the side of the road. Solomon turned to admonish the stowaway only to find him sitting with his arm around the dog. Peter, the acquirer of pretty things, had acquired Old Mortality now. Peter grinned. The dog emitted a low growl of warning. It wasn't meant for the child.

'I love castles.'

That was the boy's explanation.

'I have a season ticket.'

That was his opening bet.

Solomon phoned the school from a call box, using a pound coin borrowed from the stowaway.

'Oh, he does that all the time.' Eddie Jackson was bluff. 'Usually finds his way home. Why don't you keep him for the day. His parents won't mind.'

'I thought he was an orphan.'

'No. A confabulator.'

'So his father's not dead, then?'

'Comes to visit him every two weeks.'

'What about his mother?'

'She comes too.'

Solomon left the Mini in the castle car park, Peter at his side, approached the entrance by way of a path past a treehouse and a huge plastic swan. When they got to the front of the Pay Here queue they were ushered through with barely a nod – a grandfather and his grandson, camouflage of a sort. As they passed beneath the Lion's Arch, Peter slipped his hand into Solomon's, gave a small skip. Solomon's heart skipped in reply. Whatever he had expected from his search for Thomas Methven's long-lost kith and kin, it had certainly not been this.

They left the dog on the back seat of the Mini, curled around an old tobacco tin, met the other on the way in. Stuffed. Like the three dead finches on Walter Pringle's mantelpiece, but with a less inquisitorial gaze. The dog's name was Sandy, to go with its sandy hair, the Mascot of the Northumberland Fusiliers, welcoming them to the Regimental Museum. Solomon stood close to the case and looked the dead dog in the eye. The dog gazed back, its pupils like tiny mirrors. What was it about soldiers that they would take a dog to war? he thought.

Peter was excited.

'It's real, you know.'

Solomon could tell that the boy would have liked a stuffed dog of his own to add to his museum. Along with everything else around them, too. Telegrams sent to grieving widows. A New Testament with a bullet hole through its heart. A dead rat and a piece of one-hundred-year-old bread. Outside it was dragon quests and archery with rubber tips. But Solomon knew that inside this single turret was where the real soldiering took place.

The exhibition on the ground floor of the Regimental Archive paid homage to the Northumberland boys who had fought the Great War. Farmers' sons and labourers. A footman and a gamekeeper. Men who dug turnips and polished shoes for a living, before heading off to shoot their fellow man. Some of them probably could have got away with staying behind, Solomon thought, like the older Mr Methven had suggested. Tend the land and keep it safe, not to mention themselves, too. But what young man would do that when adventure was at hand? To leave. Or to remain. That must have been the only question then. As it was the only question now.

Peter was already going around the displays pointing at all the treasure. A tin helmet that was twice the size of his head. A metal spike to stab the enemy in the eye. There was even an officer's gun, primed and ready, bullet standing close.

'I'd like to have a gun,' said Peter.

'What for?'

'To shoot someone, of course.'

Solomon saw it again then, that look on his grandfather's face when Godfrey Farthing found him standing by the open cabinet in the pawnshop, pearl-handled pistol in his hand. As though he thought Solomon would shoot him. Right there. Right then. A bullet in the eye, blood and brain matter splattered all over the baize counter like the sparkle from a ruby. Then the fear, a sudden dose of mercury running through Solomon's bones, as his grandfather took the ladies' gun, pointed it back at him.

By the time they reached the third floor of the turret, Solomon felt as though he had been to war himself, such was the array of memorials to the fallen both up and down the stairs. As Peter studied yet another Fusilier mascot, shot and stuffed in a way they never would for a man, Solomon stood at the high window to recover, looked down into the Outer Bailey where two rows of young people were facing each other, holding what looked like broomsticks between their thighs.

'What on earth . . .'

'They're learning to fly,' said Peter, coming to stand close. 'Like the boy wizard.'

But it wasn't the would-be wizards that Solomon was exclaiming over. Rather a man in a smartly tailored suit exiting from the staterooms as though he had been casing the joint. Silk tie, check. Striped shirt, check. Highly polished shoes. Solomon stepped away from the glass, put a hand out to pull the boy away too.

'Shit.'

Peter giggled. 'You swore.'

Solomon looked at him, a wriggle of a thing in short trousers, just like all the boys running around outside. He knew he ought not. But what was camouflage for if not to add advantage? Besides:

You scratch my back and I'll scratch yours.

Solomon put his hand on Peter's shoulder, as he imagined a grandfather might.

'I need you to do something for me while I check the archive. Keep watch, maybe create a distraction.'

'Can I take the dog with me?'

Solomon wasn't even sure why Peter was asking. The dog did as the dog did. Not anything Solomon could control.

'Yes, you can take the dog.'

'Who am I looking out for?'

Colin Dunlop of Dunlop, Dunlop & Dunlop, haunting Solomon's every step south.

The actual archive was in the next turret along. No tin helmets. No medals. No Bibles with bullet holes through the heart. Just the real thing. It was a small room, dominated by a table covered in felt, surrounded by floor-to-ceiling cabinets, each drawer neatly labelled, a single computer in the far corner.

'We normally require an appointment to be made in advance,' said the archivist when Solomon announced himself, having set Peter loose to play a game of his own.

'Yes, of course,' said Solomon. 'But my car broke down and I was diverted by your splendid displays and . . .'

When in doubt, Solomon Farthing had always found flattery useful. Also the contents of his pockets, which he offloaded on to the table now. A pawn ticket, no.125. An advert for the sale of a child. The flyleaf of a Bible, torn out when the Reverend Jennie made the mistake of turning her back. Plus a crumpled piece of paper with a growing family tree, the name *Thomas Methven* inscribed at the foot, Archibald and Mabel Methven above. No archivist could resist the sight of paperwork, Solomon understood that.

The archivist stared at the little pile of detritus on his desk. Then he sighed.

'All right, Mr Dunlop. You win. Service number and battalion.'

Solomon smiled. He'd used the name Dunlop in the hope that should its real owner show up, the archivist would consider him the fraudster, rather than the other way round. Now he attempted some of the famous Farthing charm.

'I don't have either, I'm afraid. But perhaps your expertise can help me with that.'

The archivist pouted. 'But you do have a name?'

'Alec Sutherland. Born 1902, went for a soldier in 1918.'

'Well,' said the archivist. 'We don't hold the Records of Service here, I'm afraid. You'd have to go to the National Archive at Kew for that. Or look up the summary online. But I can see what we do have, if you don't mind waiting a few minutes.'

'No problem,' said Solomon.

And the archivist disappeared through a door stamped 'Staff Only', as though to discourage any suggestion that Solomon might follow and help with the search himself.

The moment he was gone Solomon took his chance, moved across to the computer and logged on using the Post-it note with the password stuck beneath the lip of the desk. He accessed the National Archives website via the archivist's Favourites tab, typed the name into the search box for the WWI service records and waited for him to appear. Alec Sutherland, the foundling boy, made sudden flesh on the computer screen. Five foot ten. Fair hair. Good teeth. A farm worker who had enlisted in the Northumberland Fusiliers, February 1918, in the market town Solomon had skirted earlier. The next step back on Thomas Methven's family tree, perhaps.

The details came from a medical report made when Alec Sutherland had first signed up. Solomon frowned at the screen, double checking the dates. Alec Sutherland had almost certainly lied about his age, he thought, if the record from the foundling school was to be believed. Onscreen it said he was eighteen when he enlisted. But the boy had been deposited at the school as a baby in 1902, went to France in April 1918 in time for the last Big Push. Sixteen, if that, nothing but a farm boy weighed down by a pack almost as big as himself. What was it about a society that called them heroes, Solomon thought, when all it ever did was use boys as fodder for the guns.

There was no address given for Alec Sutherland other than that of the school for lost boys where he'd grown up, with its field of buttercups and two kinds of clover, a river at the bottom of a hill. More disappointing, there were no next of kin listed on the service record either, other than the headmaster of the school at the time. Still, Solomon reached for his piece of paper that started with Thomas Methven at the bottom, yet only stretched as far as Archibald and Mabel Methven née Kerr at the top, scribbled the boy's name and his dates next to theirs and pondered the connection. It was Thomas Methven's real parents he was attempting to track, Alec Sutherland his only lead so far.

As he was about to fold the paper again, Solomon's eyes lingered for a moment on the space where he'd scribbled his grandfather's name. *Godfrey Farthing b.1893 d.1971*, standing at the counter of the *Borders Observatory* in his khakis cancelling an advert for the sale of a child. Solomon hesitated, moved the cursor to the search box, was about to try for a new record when the door marked 'Staff Only' swung open once again.

The archivist appeared, blinking from behind two smudged lenses as though he knew something untoward had happened in his absence but couldn't be sure quite what. He was carrying a brown envelope, disappointing in its thinness, tied with a neat piece of string.

'Not much, I'm afraid,' he said.

'But there is something,' Solomon replied, standing by the edge of the table as though he'd been waiting there all along.

The archivist nodded, untied the knot with delicate fingers and tipped the envelope upside down. A piece of card slid out and lay on the felt between them like a landed fish. The archivist turned it over for Solomon to see. He recognized what it was immediately. A field postcard from the first war, written in pencil, sent by an Alec Sutherland of the Northumberland Fusiliers. The card was dated:

8 November 1918.

On one side, *I am quite well* were the only words not yet crossed out. On the other, the address of a farm that took in babies. But it was not that detail which got Solomon Farthing's heart leaping. Rather something else inscribed on the card. There, above the address, the name of someone he had encountered before. On a black-and-white photograph dated 1918, two ladies with babies all about their feet. Also a girl not that much younger than Alec Sutherland had been at the time. Fourteen. Fifteen, perhaps, flowers about her wrist.

Daisy Pringle.

A soldier's sweetheart left behind in the hay.

Two

Kew was a garden of delights. A vault of every possible document one could imagine. Then some more. Solomon arrived having driven half the day and through the night from a castle in the north. No dinner but the remains of a packet of orange tic tacs. No documentation to ensure entry but the ID card of a man called Colin Dunlop, secured before he left the castle by a certain sleight of hand. The morning of the third day into his search for Thomas Methven's living next of kin, and already Solomon had landed at the mothership. If he'd bothered to keep her informed, Solomon was certain that DCI Franklin could not fail to be impressed.

The National Archive was an ark of MI5 proportions, three floors with plenty of glass, all the proper treasures hidden from view. Just like at MI5, an emptying of pockets took place at the door. Pens and bags. Coats and food. No suspicious items allowed should one wish to proceed. Solomon laid what remained of his life on the floor of a small metal locker in order to secure entry. One dead Nokia. One walnut shell rubbed to the nub. A sad state of affairs. Yet as he made his way towards the Document Reading Room, his fingers started with their flutter against his corduroy trousers, his heart with its *one two* skip beneath his tweed. The Internet was all very well, but this place was the holy grail of Heir Hunting. A physical manifestation of all life's weft and weave.

At the entrance to the inner sanctum on the second floor, Solomon handed over his recently acquired ID to receive a Reading Ticket in return.

'Mr Dunlop,' said the man at the desk, cross-referencing the official documentation with his computer file. 'Not been in for a while.'

Thank goodness, thought Solomon, for the virtual. No reason for Colin Dunlop of Dunlop, Dunlop & Dunlop to plough his furrow in person when he could do it all from behind a screen. As he passed through to the next level, Solomon wished for a moment that he had the where-withal to attempt a hack on his fellow Heir Hunter's National Archive account. One swift bypass of an en-crypted password and he could find out what the Edinburgh Man was really working on that required him to trace every one of Solomon Farthing's steps. A parallel investi-gation, perhaps. All the answers to the truth about Thomas Methven already connected, Colin Dunlop right now sipping tea at some old lady's table as she signed for fifty thousand – minus commission, of course. But Solomon was damned if he was going to let his dead client go that easily, still had a couple more rolls of the dice.

Solomon had come to London because he had a feeling that all of life led there. Not just the remains of Alec Sutherland's full service record, hidden somewhere deep in the stacks. But also the girl he had left behind. Daisy Pringle, last seen on a black-and-white photograph from 1918, flowers about her wrist.

Cherchez la femme.

Wasn't that what all good Heir Hunters said? Always

easier to trace the female of the species, if only through births, rather than the male, who had a higher tendency to disappear. But as he'd driven south towards the truth of it all, Solomon Farthing had known deep in his belly that there was more to it than that. He had come to London to uncover everything he'd left behind when he was seven years old, riding north on the back seat of an old Ford accompanied by a woman wearing gloves and a man wearing a grey felt hat.

Solomon's trip in the opposite direction, almost sixty years on, had been somewhat more comfortable, his hands on the wheel of a sleek grey car 'borrowed' from Colin Dunlop, his fellow Heir Hunter not aware yet of the favour he had done. It was Peter who had facilitated the handover, meeting Solomon near the exit to the castle, ice cream dribbled down his T-shirt, the remains of a cone skewered on the dog's whiskers, too. Both of them had looked guilty. Solomon had decided not to ask.

'He's in there.'

Peter had pointed towards the castle's famous Poison Garden, and it had seemed appropriate somehow to Solomon that Colin Dunlop of Dunlop, Dunlop & Dunlop was spending his time in the north checking all those deadly plants.

'Did you get it?' he'd asked.

Peter had grinned as he slid a car key into Solomon's hand – the result of a distraction involving a dog escaped into the castle's motte and bailey, the creature creating argy bargy amongst the visitors while a boy practised the art of pickpocketing as everyone looked the other way. Solomon had felt bad, if only for a moment, about a fellow

Heir Hunter's loss. But there was no way his aunt's Mini would have made it all the way to London, let alone back again. Besides, what else was a ward from a naughty boys' home for, if not a naughty kind of deed?

Peter had cheered as they drove out of the castle gates on seats clad in leather and an engine that purred, the dog yipping, too. Even Solomon grinned as they glided down lanes stuffed with cow parsley and Queen Anne's Lace, no wind whistling about their feet this time. There was something satisfying about robbing those who had all the advantages, in order to help out those who did not.

But Peter had not been cheering when instead of turning on to the A1, Solomon had turned in at the gates that marked the beginning of that long drive to the foundling school.

'I thought we were going to London,' the boy said.

'I am,' Solomon replied.

'What about me?'

'You live here.'

'My parents live in London.'

'I thought they were dead.'

Peter had subsided then, pouting as though he was the one who had been wronged. But ten minutes later when the schoolmaster arrived to fetch him, the boy deserted Solomon with a grin on his face and barely a backward glance. Solomon's whole body had been sore as he watched Eddie Jackson take Peter by the hand. A father *in loco parentis* to his temporary son. The afternoon had been closing in as he began to put the miles between them again, getting dark as he crossed from the north of the country to the south. As midnight rose with the road, Solomon had tried to sing:

'It's a long way to Tipperary . . .'

Given up ten minutes in when the absence of the dog became too loud.

The boy had bought the dog. At the end of the long drive as they'd waited for Eddie Jackson to appear, Peter had stopped sulking and laid out his opening offer on the edge of the car's front seat instead. An ID card for the National Archive slipped from Colin Dunlop's pocket, along with the car key, while everyone around him chased after a dog on the loose. Solomon had been tempted, of course, but still he had refused.

'I'm not taking you to London.'

A city for boys. But only once they were grown.

But Peter had not given up at the first refusal, offered Solomon something else. A petrol card registered to a Mr Colin Dunlop. One swipe of its chip and gallon after gallon could be at Solomon's fingertips, enough to get there and back again twice over should he feel the need. Solomon had refused once more, despite the sudden *one two* leap of his heart at the thought of fuel on demand.

But the boy would not give up. He turned to nod towards the dog where it lay on the back seat, asleep for once and snoring.

'We could toss for it,' he'd said, eyes bright. 'See who gets lucky.'

Rummaged in his pocket and brought out the little tarnished tanner that Solomon had given him the evening before. Solomon's fingers had given a wild flutter at the thought of a gamble he might be prepared to take. He'd tried to imagine the coin falling the wrong way, letting the dog go, adding another debt to all those he had yet to repay. On the other hand, it would only be doing what all proper Edinburgh Men did. Gambling with other people's money, rather than their own.

Ten a.m. and despite an empty feeling inside at the absence of anything resembling breakfast (or, perhaps, the dog), Solomon Farthing discovered that luck, or happenstance, or perhaps an Heir Hunter's instinct, was about to serve him well.

The first document he had requested from the depths of the National Archive was an extract from the 1911 Census, just to check there really had been a Daisy Pringle resident at a baby farm in the north. When it arrived Solomon held the paper to his nose and sniffed. Supposition was one thing, pawn tickets and crumpled pages from a Bible. But this was evidence. A document smelling of sawdust and old carbon, the real stuff of life.

The first entry on the Census record was for a *Mr Noel Pringle*, head of the household and proprietor of the actual farm next door. Stacks in the fields and manure in the yard, cows, dogs and pigs, as opposed to gables and babies crying, warm milk sliding from a wrist.

The second name was that of his wife, *Mrs Dora Pringle*, signing off the schedule with a flourish that suggested she must have been the one who was really in charge.

The third was a *Miss E. Penny*, Secretary to Mrs Pringle. A name Solomon remembered from Peter's register with the marbled endpapers, counting the abandoned in, then counting them out again in one neat account.

The next three names on the Census were all nursemaids

who slept in – an Elsie, an Ingrid and a Jane. Solomon blinked, remembered the whisper of an old woman waking him from beneath a blue blanket at a school for foundling boys. Hadn't she said that he could call her Janie? The last remnant of a previous generation, perhaps.

At the bottom of the list of adults was a man named *Tony*, some sort of travelling salesman who had arrived at the baby farm that day and been allowed to stay the night.

But the rest of the 1911 Census record was taken up with children. Those who had died. And those who had lived. Thirteen babies, all of indeterminate origin, listed and named as foundlings, amongst other things. Solomon ran the tip of his finger over the names, considered what might have become of them. Turnip farmers. Or footmen. A lady's maid or a teacher of girls. Either way they were the lucky generation, he thought. Too young to fight the first war. Too old, perhaps, for the one that would come next.

But his main interest was not in the foundlings listed on the Census, rather another child who appeared alongside. Noel and Dora Pringle's daughter, Daisy. Eight years old in 1911. Making her fifteen when the photograph Solomon had in his pocket was taken. And judging by a field postcard sent towards the very end of 1918, the nearest thing Solomon had found to Alec Sutherland's next of kin.

Before moving on to his second document, Solomon did a little checking to solidify what he had found out so far. He sourced a record for the marriage of Noel and Dora Pringle. Then a certificate proving the arrival of Daisy, a happy moment in 1903. Noel and Dora's marriage had been witnessed by one of Noel's brothers, a man called

Walter who came from somewhere across the border. Solomon smiled. He knew that if he pursued that branch of the Pringle family tree he would find a newspaper proprietor and his ledger at the end of it. A favourite uncle, perhaps, just when Daisy Pringle needed one the most.

But it was with the second document Solomon Farthing had requested that he struck real gold – still a day to go before DCI Franklin would be expecting a result and here it was,

Ding
Ding
Ding!

Solomon almost stood and cheered when he read through the paper, then read it again, practically shouted it to the rafters:

He's here!

Like those interlopers at New Register House in the Athens of the North. For the second piece of paper was a birth certificate for a baby boy, born in the district of Northumberland in which the Pringles' baby farm once resided – a piece of paper that contained the following truths:

Date of Birth: *November 1918*
Place of Birth: *Mrs Pringle's Home for Lost Souls*
Sex: *Male*
Mother's name: *Daisy Pringle*
Father's name: Blank

All signed off by a *Miss E. Penny, Secretary* in December 1918. Proof that Daisy Pringle once had a child of her own, when she was still a child herself.

But it was two other lines on the birth certificate that

told Solomon Farthing he had followed the correct branch of Thomas Methven's family tree after all. The first came almost at the bottom, as though it was the most insignificant thing:

Father's occupation: *Soldier*

And the second, nearer the top. One more line completed in neat handwriting instructing the world as to the name by which Daisy Pringle wished her child to be known:

Forenames: *Alexander (Alec)*

Alec Sutherland and Thomas Alexander Methven linked once again. Not only by a pawn ticket, no.125, this time. But also by a name. One man's legacy to his only son.

Three

It was lunchtime when Solomon Farthing quit the National Archive at Kew, his future in one pocket, his past in the other, Old Mortality caught somewhere in between. Outside the sun shone hot as he left the mothership behind and entered the neighbouring green. He made his way across the grass to stand on a bridge overlooking a river. The water here was clear, rippled with weed wending its way back and forth like a mermaid's hair. So easy to slide into, Solomon thought. If only he dared.

His first trip to London in more than ten years had been a success. Not only had he evaded the attentions of his fellow Heir Hunter, shaking Colin Dunlop from his tail somewhere between here and the north, but he had also found what every person in his industry sought – a birth certificate for his dead client, Thomas Methven. And like all good Heir Hunters, Solomon Farthing knew that a birth certificate almost always led to a living relative, somewhere along the line.

As Solomon stared into the water, sunlight shifting and refracting off its surface, he was satisfied that he had completed his task. Nothing left to do but doorstep the lucky recipient of all his digging and get them to sign, commission on fifty thousand within his grasp at last.

And yet . . .

In the right-hand pocket of his jacket he had other

news, the details of which filled his heart with sorrow rather than the joy that usually came with the knowledge that someone else's treasure was almost within his grip. The findings from another file ordered from deep within the hidden stacks. Not *Pringle* this time. Or even *Alec Sutherland*. But *Farthing*. All that remained of Solomon's father, on which he might rebuild.

Solomon had known as he reached to flip open the Farthing file that reading it would be to nibble at forbidden fruit. A family tree that had thrived like the blossom of an Edinburgh cherry in spring – full fling one moment, swept into the gutter the next. Grandparents long dead. Parents chopped down, too. Nothing left now but Solomon Farthing standing alone at the foot. All he had ever known about his family was that both his father and his grand-father had been soldiers once. Only to discover when he was seven years old that at least one of those facts might be a lie. That his father was never a hero. Only ever a coward, just like Solomon had turned out. That his father had been too afraid to lift a rifle when the moment came, as once Solomon had refused to take three steps into a river and save another boy's life.

As he'd laid his hand upon the documents pertaining to his father's war, in search of absolute proof, Solomon had wondered if this was the real reason his father and his grandfather had become estranged. One man spent his young life leading his men over the top, only to discover that when his son's turn came to do the same, he had refused. A man who had never driven a tank, or charged towards the enemy across a beach in France. Who'd taken the easy way out when it all became too much. Straight down into the river. *Like an arrow*. Caught in its muddy churn. Nothing left of him but that fragment of singing lodged inside Solomon's head.

Now, with final evidence of his father's cowardice in his pocket, Solomon put one hand on the top rail of the bridge and tried to imagine what courage it must take to follow with his foot. To stand on the far side and contemplate oblivion, as his father had once done, consider all the things he had ever done right. And those he knew he had done wrong. A life spent ducking and diving and bartering his way to and fro, fleeing the moment any trouble appeared, rather than standing to fight.

'You're not going to jump, are you?'

The boy was so close that Solomon could feel the heat off him, the child's legs dusty with whatever earth he had been ferreting in while Solomon had been indoors digging up his own. The boy's hair was almost white in the sun, eyes like tiny slices of mirror as he squinted up at Solomon, while Solomon squinted down at him. Solomon wasn't sure what he should reply. Yes. No. Maybe. But as though to allay his confusion, the boy didn't insist upon a reply, laid one hand on the rail very close to Solomon's instead. Solomon couldn't help noticing that while his fingers were fluttering, the child's hands were still. Together they stood staring into the water, nothing but the sound of the river meandering beneath. Also the call of a blackbird somewhere in a tree. Eventually, the boy spoke.

'Are you going home now?'

Solomon looked at the long stretch of water as it flowed forever onwards towards the city. London or north? There was only ever going to be one way home. Just one more thing to do first.

It took Solomon Farthing an hour before he arrived at his next destination, somewhere south of the river, deep in the heart of Battersea, surrounded by a tall iron fence. A graveyard of a different sort of green to Kew, haphazard and choked with weeds, not far from the bridge from which Solomon's father had taken that fateful fall. The cemetery's burial land had been exhausted in the 1960s, given over now to butterflies and trees, insects and other creatures flitting amongst the stones. Solomon entered by the gate on the main road and was quickly subsumed.

He wandered south through the graves. No map. No guide. Just a myriad of paths and a reference scribbled in biro on the back of his hand. The cemetery reminded Solomon of his favourite burial ground back home – hundreds of gravestones laid flat amongst the shorn grass at one end, hundreds more buried by nettles at the other. It too was a haven for wildlife – the wren, the magpie, the dog fox and his vixen. Not to mention a thousand tiny mammals tunnelling their way through leaf mould and the crumbled bones of the dead. Edinburgh's 'secret garden', that was what they called it, the nearest thing Solomon had to what could be called a family plot. The perfect cruising ground for the low flight of the tawny owl. And the glorious boys of his youth. The place where he had first met Andrew, standing in the twilight by a soft-grey tomb, all its carving eroded by the rain.

Solomon remembered escaping from the silence of his

grandfather to lie amongst a forest of obelisks and stone crosses, ivy snatching at his feet. Sixteen and dreaming of another life, the soft black of an Edinburgh night cut through by the rustle of a thousand rodents in amongst the undergrowth, human and animal both. The grass had been tall. It had been wet. Cuckoo spit smeared across his shirt. His head had been thumping with an overdose of adrenaline. Or perhaps the stolen sherry he had drunk. Above him the planet had spun on its axis. Beneath him he'd felt the damp embrace of the earth. He remembered doing his count:

One leg;

Two legs;

Two arms;

Five fingers . . .

Just as Godfrey Farthing had taught, lifting Solomon to sit on the draining board in the scullery that very first night, checking one limb after another as though to make sure the boy was safe. Solomon had lain in the cemetery for an hour, perhaps, waiting with his heart in his throat to see what might happen next. Then Andrew had appeared and his life had taken a whole new turn.

Now, he searched for an hour with no luck, mopping at his forehead with a blue kerchief taken from his pocket, before starting again. It seemed an age since he had lost his lucky charm between the floorboards of a dead man's house, torn shirt flapping about his wrist. Solomon wondered if he would ever see the cap badge again. Or whether he might have to make his own luck from now on.

Eventually, the day grew too hot and he sat to rest amongst the grasses, pulled the last of the paperwork he had secured at the National Archive from his inside pocket. All that remained of a Captain Godfrey Farthing, such as it was.

His grandfather's service record had been blank. Or as good as, given the information it relayed. No dates or details of enlistment. No dates or details of discharge. No personal correspondence or information about wounds. Originally in three parts, the record had been decimated over the years, filleted first by judicious civil servants who had needed the space, then the remainder obliterated by enemy action in a second war, bombs falling on the very place where all the information about a country's previous heroes had been kept. Even from this distance, Solomon had felt the irony in that.

There had been nothing left of his grandfather but a name:

Farthing, Godfrey

And a rank:

Captain

And a regimental number:

3674.

Sent out to war as a young man to make sure his men did their duty. Came back an old man, never did know how to keep a lost boy warm. Nothing to suggest he had ever met or known that other lost boy: Alec Sutherland, vanished into the mire at the very end, never did return.

Solomon had looked for secondary evidence, of course. First amongst the Silver War Badge rolls – those men discharged for wounds or illness – thinking of that pucker of scar tissue hovering over his grandfather's heart. But there had been no sign of Godfrey Farthing amongst the sick. Nor on the campaign medal index. A Star. A War medal. One for Victory, too. Decorations doled out like sweeties to all the men who had fought.

'Probably didn't apply for them.' That was what the expert he spoke to said. 'Not every man did.'

Godfrey Farthing, the hero, fought for four years and came out standing, didn't even want the honours to show. An old man who wore flannels until they were baggy at the knees. Who washed in the bowl at the sink every evening, rather than in the bath. Someone who raised Solomon to know exactly how to behave, but barely spoke a word himself. A mystery to Solomon when he was a boy. And still a mystery now.

Solomon had the sudden sense then that everything he had ever understood about his grandfather was not quite right. That perhaps he never had been in the war to end all wars, or at least not in the way Solomon had imagined, a hero rushing the enemy's barbed wire. That just like his son twenty years later, perhaps his grandfather had kept his head down, too, rather than raising it above the parapet, the little medals beneath the counter in the pawnshop belonging to someone else all along. Another soldier who had fought and survived, pawning his glory in return for a Sunday suit or a decent Friday dinner, never bothering to buy the medals back.

But still Solomon could never forget how his grandfather marked the end of the cataclysm year after year. Lit a candle in the little chapel at the side of the great grey church by way of remembrance.

*Our Father who art in heaven . . . forgive us our tres-
passes as we forgive those . . .*

Never wore a red poppy. Only ever a winter rose.

The sun was playing out its long fall from the sky, as
Solomon Farthing began again with his search, lingering
over a carved angel here, attempting to decipher a name
vanished from a tomb there. He had lost sight of the way
back to the cemetery gates long before, could feel sweat
gathering beneath his tweed jacket at the prospect that he
might have come all this way, only to fail at the last.

It was not until the sun was descending beneath the
top line of the trees that he found what he had been looking
for all of his life. There, in a tangle of London grass, a
splash of white amongst the green:

His father, Robert Farthing.

His mother, Else Farthing née Gold.

Dirtied somewhat by the years that had passed. Solomon
stood for a moment feeling the earth tip beneath his feet.
Then he pulled the dog's blue kerchief from his pocket,
licked at its corner, began to scrub the stone clean.

After, he lay beside his father, beside his mother, for
the first and last time. The grass was sweet in his nostrils,
the scent of cut hay. Solomon lay so long that he heard
his father singing. So long that he saw his mother's shadow
move behind the curtain. So long that he felt their hands
upon his hair.

When he sat up again he unwrapped the treasure given
to him by Eddie Jackson at the foundling school. A tobacco
tin all scratched and battered, rather like him. The tin was
the one his father used to keep his chocolate in, hidden

beneath the bed. As Solomon eased off the lid, the sudden aroma of old-fashioned tobacco loosed into the air. But the tin did not contain Woodbines, or even Capstans lined like bodies in a bed. Instead it was stuffed with articles clipped from a newspaper in 1957 about a man who jumped into a river. Because he was drunk, perhaps. Or because he could not live without his wife. Or because he was trying to save a young lady. The first thing Solomon slid from the tin was a cutting that said, *Hero*. He didn't bother with the rest.

1918

One

Godfrey ran. Two fields over behind a fold in the land and it sounded, sudden and loud. A single shot. The commencement of battle. Followed by a second. The enemy's reply.

At once Godfrey started as though the whistle had been blown. *Over the top.* Tumbling across empty fields full of ruts and troughs of wet earth, slithering in and out of muddy dips, urging himself forwards, forwards, always forwards, stay upright, stay upright, just follow the man in front. All he could hear as he ran was blood thudding in his ears, the frantic *one two one two* of his heart. And the ring of those two shots, over and over, puncturing the air.

Above him a scattering of starlings wheeled in the grey, swooping and circling as Godfrey stumbled on, all the worst things rippling from the soles of his feet to the roof of his skull. A misfire while polishing a trigger. An argument amongst the men. Or the arrival of the enemy. A surprise attack from across that river, one man down already, a single shot, execution style, followed by the next. It wasn't until Godfrey was almost home that another thought flitted through his brain. Perhaps it had been a warning shot sent up by Ralph – their own company arrived at last. Captains and lieutenants. Corporals and sergeants. Soldiers marching down that lane expecting Godfrey Farthing's section to be ready. Found instead men playing chicken in the yard and the officer in charge disappeared to wander amongst the trees. Desertion. Punishable by death in the worst-case scenario. Not even there when the moment came.

Godfrey sucked in great gasps of cold air as he got as close to the farmhouse as he dared. All around him there was a merging of sky and land, the outline of the farmhouse hazy, its accompanying buildings indistinct. Everything was still. The mist low in the hedgerows. The birds silent. No commotion as he approached, crouched low to the earth to avoid the sniper's eye. Instead it was as though the two shots had only happened in a dream, the backfire of a charabanc on the parade at Hastings, nothing but an ordinary accident waiting to happen if one got in the way.

Godfrey huddled on the far side of the stream, pain pinioning his lungs, waited for his heart to steady before he moved forwards again. It was some time since he had been required to run that far, scrambling and dodging as shrapnel splintered all around him. How quickly he had become accustomed to something more sedate. A line of smoke from the farmhouse chimney traced the sky. There was the brief glitter of the pond in the gloom. In front of Godfrey was a new latrine pit, half dug, a dark hole in the ground just waiting for him to step inside. He waded through the water, the cold of it soaking through his boots, stepped out the other side with ice already in his veins.

When he got to the yard, at last, it was empty. No men stood in a semi-circle with rifles to their heads. No chicken *scritch scratching* at the entrance to the grain store, fixing Godfrey with the black bead of its eye. He crouched in the shadow of the barn, heart beating a loud tattoo upon his ribs. The last time he had spoken to Beach had been in a yard just like this one, mud and a huge heap of slag in one corner, the boom of the guns echoing like a distant thunderstorm calling them to play. What had happened to the boy, he thought, once he was in the ground. Rotted like the rest who had met disaster, or floated from the earth somehow to follow his captain around forever after, reminding him always of all the boys he had lost.

Across the yard, the door to the farmhouse stood open, warm light spilling on the step, welcoming all comers to whatever carnage they might find inside. Godfrey put a hand to the wound above his heart, felt the shrapnel shift. His revolver was in the attic room beneath the rafters, lying greased and ready to fire. He had left it beside his bed for days now, preferred to walk unarmed amongst the trees. Abandoning one's weapon. Another offence that drew the ultimate sanction.

Then came the voices.

'What the damn hell?'

Heard Jackdaw protesting.

'It wasn't my fault.'

They were in the kitchen, gathered around the long table, the remains of Godfrey Farthing's men. Godfrey couldn't help but count as he stood in the doorway. One, two, three . . . four, five, six . . . like the chimes of his father's clock. Eight soldiers at the reckoning. Plus Ralph standing at the head.

Godfrey felt wild, as though the whole world had begun to tilt, anger bubbling in his chest. Or perhaps it was relief.

'What happened?'

The men turned towards him as he spoke, eight faces caught in the middle of something in which he had no part. Alfred Walker and the two A4 boys huddled together on one side of the table, along with Alec, dog close at his feet. On the other, Percy Flint and James Hawes were gathered around Archie Methven, George Stone standing somewhere behind. They stared at their captain's sudden appearance, uniform all streaked with mud once more. Except Ralph, who turned his gaze towards the stove for a second as though searching for his supper, before looking back. For a moment, no one said anything, then Ralph stepped forwards.

'It's nothing,' he said. 'A prank.'

Holding out his hands as though to appease an angry father. What was it, Godfrey thought then, that always threw him into that role when he was still a young man himself?

'A prank?' he said, clenching his left hand to quell its flutter.

'The grey.'

And Ralph stood aside.

There on the table lay the remains of a chicken – feather and bone, the hard scales of its feet. It had been obliterated by a gun shot, nothing left of its head. A bloody mess laid out on Stone's scrubbed surface, like the rabbit in the trap that Godfrey and Alec had found laid out on the hill. Standing over the dead bird was George Stone, huge metal pot already in his hands. For soup, Godfrey thought, cock-a-leekie. Perhaps even a jar of prunes dug from a secret supply in the cellar, packed tight in their sweet juice before the war had even begun.

'Christ.' Godfrey pushed a hand through his hair, left a streak of mud from cheek to brow. 'I thought someone had been shot.'

Ralph laughed. The men stayed silent.

'Who got it?' Godfrey said.

Eight men and Ralph circling in the yard.

This way. Grab it!

Laying bets on who would catch the chicken first:

A button.

A matchstick.

A centime for the grey.

Godfrey's second throwing in a twist of officers' tobacco when the other bets fell away. Sometimes Godfrey thought war was all a game to Ralph, nothing more than a toss of the dice and a chase after a chicken until the mortal bullet came. Then again it was a game for all of them, wasn't it? A war that amounted to nothing more than waiting and waiting, the only respite a skirmish from which many would not come out alive.

'It was my fault.'

Jackdaw stood forwards all of a sudden, collarbone in sharp relief beneath his filthy shirt.

'Jackson!'

It was strange hearing Jackdaw's real name, a warning in Ralph's voice. The younger man faltered, fell back to stand next to Promise. Godfrey noticed that the two of them stood apart from each other now, no more touching at the hip bone. Nobody spoke. Godfrey rubbed at his forehead again, made the muddy streak worse.

'Well, what the hell's going on? Hawes?'

But Second Lieutenant Ralph Svenson was the one in

charge now. He stepped forwards to stand right in front of Godfrey, spoke softly as though they were sharing an intimacy that must not be passed to anyone else.

'Look, it was an accident. Too much high spirits. My fault really. Got carried away, took a pot shot.'

'You shot it?'

Godfrey stared at Ralph. Discharging a weapon outside of battle was a punishable offence. The boy could be cashiered before his career had even begun. But Ralph didn't even blink, just nodded his head, those strange translucent eyes staring back.

Godfrey woke in the night knowing that something wasn't right. He lay for a moment beneath the rafters of the farmhouse. The rain had stopped, no more constant *pitter patter* on the roof. He looked across to the far side of the attic room, knew at once that Ralph's bed was empty, blanket pushed aside to expose the mattress stuffed with straw. He listened again for the sound that had woken him. A cry. Like a creature caught in a trap. It came again, more muffled this time, Godfrey's whole body suddenly alert, the sound somewhere inside the farmhouse, not outside as he'd first thought.

Immediately, Godfrey was up, swinging his feet over the side of his narrow bunk, pulling on his trousers. He tried to light his candle, one match, then another, his hands too shaky to get the wick to take. He left it in the end and crept down the narrow stairs in the gloom, his feet bare. In the small square of hall, he stood to listen once more.

The door to the parlour stood open, Ralph's wooden

cup on the mantelpiece, Godfrey's writing things on the table by the stain. Opposite, the kitchen was cold, the faint smell of embers rising from the stove. There was a dark patch on the table where Stone had attempted to scrub away the chicken's blood. Godfrey frowned at another smell he recognized. Not woodsmoke or the faint stink of cabbage being boiled into soup. But skin and fat roasting, the unmistakable scent of burning human flesh.

He found them beneath the floorboards, the rug in the back room rolled away to reveal a thin square of light. The trap door to the cellar, once loaded with boxes of apples hidden in sand, now stacked in sparse formation with the few rations they had left. The three men were gathered towards the back of the empty space. On a shelf next to them was a paraffin lamp, its low glow seeping towards Godfrey across the beaten earth floor.

Archie Methven was sitting on a wooden chair salvaged from the parlour – the one Godfrey normally chose as his own. Methven's shirt was pulled to his waist, trapping his arms, as though he was wearing a straitjacket. His shoulders were exposed, muscles rolling beneath his skin. Godfrey could see the wound, below Methven's collarbone on the right-hand side. Livid. A raw mess. Like all that had remained of the rabbit once it had gnawed its foot away. Archie Methven's chest was palpitating, one rapid breath after another as he gripped the seat of the chair. His knuckles formed a tight ridge of bone, white tipped, on either side. His mouth was stuffed with a stick to stop him biting his tongue right off.

George Stone stood behind the injured accountant, a hand clamped each side of Methven's head to hold him still. He was wearing his apron again, but not for cooking this time. An old-style barber surgeon, Godfrey thought, someone who would trim a man's hair in return for two cigarettes, then pull his teeth for three. Ralph Svenson stood next to Stone, holding something metal in his hand.

'What's going on?'

Godfrey's voice reverberated around the dark walls. Archie Methven made a gargled sound in his throat, flashed his eyes in Godfrey's direction. Ralph's face was stark in the glow from the paraffin lamp. He suddenly looked much younger than his nineteen years – a boy again, frightened of what his father might say. Stone didn't even look at the intruder, just bent his mouth towards Methven's ear.

'Careful now,' he murmured. 'Careful.'

Then he nodded at Ralph, who moved in towards Methven, touched the tip of his metal instrument to the other man's flesh. At once the accountant jerked and struggled, the sweat cold on Godfrey's back as he watched Stone stroke Methven's hair over and over.

'It's all right now,' the cook kept saying. 'It's all right.'

As though he was the man's mother, come to comfort him in the night.

'What the devil?'

Godfrey's eyes were wide in the pitch and gloom of the cellar, the flicker of the lamp throwing shadows all around the walls. Stone released Methven, whose head rolled back on his neck, took the metal instrument from Ralph and moved away towards a corner, a sudden hiss rising from a bucket of water near the floor. Then the old sweat turned, wiping his hands across his apron, eyes steady when he glanced at Godfrey for a moment before moving back towards the shelf where he had an emergency kit laid out. Field dressings and a couple of sachets of Lamels for the pain. Tape, gauze and a bandage made of crepe. Stone began tidying the kit as though it was nothing more than the remains of a supper. Ralph came to stand by Godfrey at the bottom of the cellar steps. The boy's hands were trembling.

'The accountant's been shot,' he said.

'What?'

'I told you. An accident.'

'I thought that was the chicken.'

Ralph blinked, a flicker of his normal demeanour. Godfrey understood at once. The chicken was the alibi, so that he would not find out.

'Who was it?' he said.

Mishandling one's weapon was a grave offence. Shooting a fellow soldier even worse. But Ralph didn't say anything. Godfrey nodded towards Archie Methven stripped and sweating on the parlour chair.

'What the bloody hell were you doing to him?'

'Trying to take out the bullet,' said Ralph. 'It was Stone's idea.'

Of course, George Stone, the old sweat, seen it all before.

'Did he get it?' Godfrey asked.

'I think so.'

They both looked towards the shelf. Most of Stone's makeshift surgery was already gone, disappeared beneath the folds of his apron or into some secret cupboard carved from the wall. But there on a mess tin brought down from the kitchen Godfrey could see the remains of the bullet, a smear of blood glistening in the paraffin glow.

'Why the red-hot poker treatment?' he said.

'Cauterizing the wound.'

It was Godfrey's turn to be silent now. Subterfuge was not unknown amongst the men – for card games or Crown and Anchor, for illegal rum rations or an extra round of tobacco. But this was of a different order. One man shoots another and a senior rank tries to cover it up.

'There will have to be an inquiry,' he said.

'No!' Ralph put his hand on Godfrey's arm, the first time they had touched since they shook hands on his arrival. 'You know what it means.'

Ralph's grip was tight, that of a man much older than nineteen. Godfrey looked into those clear eyes for a moment. They both knew exactly what it meant for one of their men to be blamed for the shooting of another. Then Archie Methven groaned and Godfrey shrugged Ralph away, moved to crouch by his accountant instead. For a brief moment he laid his hand on Methven's head, a man who had served with him for almost eighteen months now. Then he looked across the dark space towards Stone, found the old sweat staring back at him.

Later that night, while Archie Methven tossed and pitched on a pallet bed made up by the kitchen stove, Godfrey stood in the doorway to the farmhouse breathing great lungfuls of cold air to escape the impending scent of rot inside. He stepped away from the stone porch, into the yard, realized suddenly that his feet were bare, icy mud oozing between his toes. He had nothing but a shirt and a pair of breeches to cover him as he moved towards the lane down which he had marched his men to safety only two weeks before.

Would it never end, Godfrey thought as he watched a thread of light seeping over the horizon. This constant effort to do the right thing – ignore the mistakes and punish the wilful, keep the men together at any cost. He had realized long ago that he was not the sort of leader to make his own decisions; a captain who left it to others to tell him what to do. Dispatch. Retrench. Attack. Defend. But here in this small slice of paradise, there had been no one but him to decide. And it had come to seem almost impossible now.

Godfrey turned back to stare across the empty yard, the taste of something bitter in his throat. What would happen, he thought, if he was the one to go next? Eight men left behind to defend against the enemy. Or fight it out amongst themselves. Nothing left of him but a walnut shell and a set of crumpled orders that he should have acted on but had not. Disobeying a lawful command given by his superior officer. Penal Servitude. Or worse. Six men from his own unit fiddling with their rifles until they were given the order to shoot.

It was then that he saw it, hidden in the shadow of the barn. Two boys touching. Another small gesture of defiance in amongst the muck.

Jackdaw had his hand on the back of Promise's neck, as the other boy bent to retch and retch again into a pile of old straw, eyes glittering like a sick fox in the night.

'We have to tell, Ned,' Promise was saying. 'We must.'

Jackdaw held the other boy's shoulders, pressing his thumbs into the bone.

'Why should we? You know what'll happen if we do.'
'The captain won't let it.'

'That's not what Stone says.' Jackdaw's reply was fierce. 'And he's the one who should know.'

The two boys were silent then, standing close, face-to-face, hip bone touching hip bone, wrist touching wrist. Then Promise's lips glistened in the moonlight as Jackdaw leaned in. Godfrey found his heart beating like a wild thing as one boy kissed another, Jackdaw and Promise merging into shadow as they fell back against the barn's dark wall.

Two

Captain Godfrey Farthing woke from a dream that told him the end had come at last. Bertie Fortune, walking towards him across the walnut shells, salvation in his hands. The shells crunched beneath the lucky man's feet, shifting and rattling like the bones of a thousand dead men piled up year after year.

'Have you got it?' Godfrey heard himself saying.

But Bertie Fortune didn't reply, just got closer and closer, holding something in his hand. A walnut shell, perhaps, freshly cracked to reveal its tiny brain. A wristwatch forever keeping time. Or that little silver cap badge, glimmering in the sunlight.

Strike Sure.

As a lion raised its paw.

Godfrey could feel it then, shrapnel shifting beneath his skin, the wound in his chest swelling and spreading as he waited for Bertie Fortune to reveal his treasure for all to see. The lucky man's eyes were upon him like two dead pebbles. Like George Stone's in the cellar. And James Hawes looking at him from across the field of play. Three men staring at their captain, as though Godfrey was the enemy and they held the guns. There was the sudden stink of cordite in his nostrils, the pound of his heart as if it might break free. Then the sweat on his neck, though Godfrey knew that the air outside was cool, rain pricking his skin as a man's thick hands were placed upon his sleeve.

'Sir?'

Waking to grey light filtering from the window high on the gable wall.

James Hawes was standing by his bed in the attic. Godfrey lifted his head from his pillow, heard the sound of men in the yard, the rattle of dishes being washed in the kitchen as though it was just another normal day.

'Is it Fortune?' he said.

But Hawes shook his head. 'No, sir. It's Methven. I think you'd better come.'

The accountant had got worse in the night. Wrapped in Godfrey's thick coat, he sat by the range in the kitchen shivering and shivering, nothing to stop the convulsions that ran through his body from his crown to the soles of his boots. Breakfast was already long past as Godfrey crouched next to him, tried to ignore the heat pulsing from the injured man's skin. Stone had improvised well, but there was no doubt in Godfrey's mind that Methven's wound would start to rot from the inside out soon enough. There would be nothing left to do then but cut his arm right out of its socket, watch their accountant die from loss of blood if they could not get him to a field surgeon first.

He slid a glass phial containing three grains of morphia from his pocket, showed it to the injured man.

'We'll have you in clean sheets before you know it, Archie.'

Methven gazing at his captain as though Godfrey was

an apparition – the Angel of Mons, perhaps, reincarnated from the very beginning of the battle to the very end. Godfrey saw the way Methven's eyes flicked to the glass bottle in his hand, like Second Lieutenant Ralph Svenson, always seeking something that was out of reach. Glory. Or salvation. Or medicine for the here and now. Godfrey held the phial close to Methven, the tablets inside like tiny crystals of salt.

'You can have some, Archie. But tell me first. You won't get anyone into trouble, I just need to know.'

A Jackdaw.

A Promise.

A Second Lieutenant.

The name of the man who had wielded a rifle, then melted in amongst the rest.

A tangle of words and phrases unfurled from Methven's lips. A name, followed by another name. And another. And another after that. Men long gone, disappeared into mud, into shell holes filled with rifle oil and the remains of a corpse, the slick taste of clay on their lips. Men loaded onto trains back to England, or left to rot in graves marked with nothing but a stick. Archie Methven was doing the reckoning. Counting them in and counting them out again as though his whole war had been nothing more than a profit-and-loss account, a fevered recitation of the lost.

Godfrey placed a hand on Methven's arm to try and still him, his own fingers fluttering as though to match the trembles of the sick man. He felt in one pocket of Methven's tunic, then the other, held something out for his accountant to see. A little notebook with its blue hori-zontals and red verticals – the record of who owed what to whom. Godfrey saw Methven's eyes focus for a moment, flare in recognition, then slide away to gaze at something over his captain's shoulder instead.

Godfrey turned, found Second Lieutenant Ralph Svenson standing in the kitchen doorway. There was the faintest scent of lemon oil gone sour, the glint of a belt buckle polished to a shine. Godfrey found he couldn't help himself.

'The enemy will see you a mile off in that thing,' he said. 'Take a pot shot.'

Ralph flushed, the raw colour of a boy. Most officers had long ago given up wearing anything that would identify them as such. It was a sign of Ralph's ignorance that he was nutted up, flashing on his cuffs. But also a sign of something else, too.

Godfrey felt a ridiculous satisfaction at having embarrassed the young man, if only for a second. Archie Methven rolled his head towards the window, began again with his stream of babble. But it was Ralph who spoke clearly this time.

'What shall we do with him?'

'What do you propose we do with him?'

Ralph just shrugged. 'We won't be able to take him with us when we go.'

'What makes you think we're leaving?'

Ralph smiled then, his strange eyes sliding towards the floor. 'We'll have to go eventually. Can't stay here forever.'

Why not, thought Godfrey. It was as good a place as any to take a last stand.

'No one's going anywhere,' he said. 'And certainly not with a man left behind.'

'Fortune's left, hasn't he.'

Heat prickled then, all along Godfrey's collar. What did his second know about the arrangement he had made with his lucky man?

'Fortune will be back this afternoon.'

Ralph was silent for a moment, then he said, 'You can stay with Methven if you want. I can take the rest.'

Godfrey felt it then, fear curdling in his stomach. He knew that part of Ralph wanted this to happen – to march the remaining eight to the top of the hill and let fate make its call. Godfrey knew that most of the men would go if they had sight of the orders. Would rather take their chances on the battlefield, than face a bullet from their own side. Mutiny. Punishable by death, execution style. A single shot to the heart.

Next to Godfrey, Archie Methven shivered, body rippling with a fever that came from a bullet fired by his own side, too. Godfrey placed his hand once more on the injured man's arm as though to quiet him, stared at Ralph for a moment. How had it come to this, he thought, that his men could be so easily parted, cleaved down the middle by a boy barely out of school?

None of the men had confessed. Not Godfrey's cook or his temporary sergeant. Not his petty thief or his two A4 boys. Not even his new recruit. He had called them one by one to the parlour after breakfast, stood them in front of the table as he sat behind.

It was just a game gone wrong. A mistake. An accident. An attempt to bet on the chickens. The last but one. The grey.

They all said it, the same version of the truth. Until

Godfrey felt it rise within him, his old man barking and thumping on the arm of his chair because Godfrey had failed to wipe his shoes at the door again, or bring his homework back from school. How was it, Godfrey had thought, as one after the other of his men slouched away, that he had become the accuser and his own men the accused? He couldn't even rely on the A4 boys, two young men who had the most reason to let Ralph take the blame. Godfrey had tried Jackdaw first, a boy who found it difficult to keep his mouth shut if there was an injustice to be solved.

He asked him straight out.

'Did Second Lieutenant Svenson shoot the accountant?'

Watched the boy bloom red.

But even Jackdaw had insisted. An accident. A misfire. A slip of the thumb. Would not be moved however much Godfrey pushed. One A4 boy, joined at the hip bone with the other, never was going to let go.

Promise's mouth had been pinched when he was ordered in to stand before his captain, blanched about the lips as though trying to keep the truth in. But when Godfrey asked, he shook his head, too.

'He didn't mean to do it.'

That was what he said.

Still, Godfrey made the A4 boy turn out his pockets just in case. A search for the prize Fortune had mentioned – whatever it was that had set the chickens running in the yard. But Promise wasn't carrying anything that could have been regarded as proper contraband, just the spoils of a town boy let loose in this strange place. A couple of pebbles from the stream. A piece of shell from an egg. The kind of things Alec Sutherland might forage from a hedgerow. Stuff of no value, but here in this forgotten Eden, the most important treasure of all. What was it about war, thought Godfrey, as Promise returned his small treasures to his pockets, that it always came back to the little things. The stuff no man could do without.

That afternoon, Godfrey watched Alec sew Archie Methven's wound. The boy had not been lying. He was good with the needle, one careful thread after another until a neat line of pink was stitched into the older man's skin. But beneath the boy's repair, Methven's arm had gone black. No longer the pallor of a man injured in winter, but a deep purple running from his fingertips to his heart. The heat on the accountant's skin was like a furnace, almost too hot for Godfrey to touch.

George Stone had done the cutting and the draining first, prodding and pressing at Archie Methven's swollen shoulder until any pus they could squeeze from the wound had dribbled and oozed down the accountant's chest. The liquid had been clear, but Godfrey had known it would not be long before they could all smell it. That sweet stink of impending putrefaction. Like the men's feet after they'd stood in a trench filled with water week after week. The kitchen would be saturated with it, Godfrey thought. One day. Two days at most, before it was too late. Only Methven was oblivious to the danger, numbed by a slug of illicit brandy supplied by Stone.

'Fortune got it for me,' the cook had said as he slid the quart bottle from a hole in the kitchen wall that would normally house a Bible or a sprig of rosemary to ward off the blight.

The bottle of brandy was a squat thing, French glass thick at the base, the contents gleaming like an amber jewel. Godfrey hadn't asked what Bertie Fortune had been given in return. Instead he'd gestured to Alec to come forward with his needle, thread borrowed from Percy Flint. The boy had promised him a steady hand and as Godfrey watched him make one careful stitch after another, he'd realized what a relief it was to have a soldier who did exactly as he said.

Afterwards he took Alec to the parlour and thanked him.

'You did a good job.'

'Yes, sir.'

'Have you ever stitched a man before?'

'No, sir. But I've helped with a sheep.'

'You'll be looking forward to going back soon, eh. Start a flock yourself.'

'Yes, sir.'

The boy blushed, cheeks flaming. The colour made him look even younger than he was, a lad already walking out with his sweetheart. Godfrey rose from the table and came to stand in front of the new recruit, put his hand on the boy's shoulder.

'You didn't tell, did you, Alec. About the orders.'

It wasn't a question. Alec flushed again, shook his head.

'No, sir.'

Godfrey believed him. What else could he do? As he turned away the boy slipped something from his pocket, held it out.

'Like you suggested, sir. In case something should happen.'

A field postcard, addressed to a girl at a place some-where in the north, *I am quite well* the only words not yet crossed out. It was Godfrey's turn to flush then, two spots of colour on his cheeks.

'Nothing's going to happen, Alec.'

But the boy insisted. 'Just in case, sir.'

The two men stared at each other for a moment. Then Godfrey took the card, flipped it over.

'Is this all you want to say? I can give you a sticky jack, if you want, keep your message private.'

Alec shook his head. 'She'll know what I mean.'

Godfrey nodded. Then he put his hand on the boy's sleeve. 'I'll keep it for you, Alec. But you can deliver it yourself.'

As he watched the boy head back to the barn across the muddy yard, Godfrey felt it within him then. Fury at his second lieutenant burning beneath his breastbone, like the poker that had failed to cauterize Archie Methven's wound. All Ralph had ever wanted was to go to war, flash his pistol at the enemy, while his men stuck the bayonet in. And yet all the devastation he had caused had been here amongst his men. Fighting. And betting. And strutting the yard like one of those chickens until they were all tip and turn.

Godfrey thought of Ralph's face two nights before when he'd flipped open Promise's Housewife, the pleasure his second had taken in bringing another man down. He looked again at the field postcard in his hand, thought of his wooden lockbox, inside the letter Archie Methven had written to his son. Evening the odds, that's what a gambling man like George Stone might have called it. Playing his own game, that was how Captain Godfrey Farthing thought of it now.

Three

The punishment began at 1600 hours and took place in the yard so that all the men could see. Godfrey took the prisoner's red identity disc and left his green, as though he was dead already, nothing to do but write and inform the next of kin. He removed the boy's tunic, left him shivering in his shirt. All the other men watched as though it was some kind of theatrical performance, couldn't believe what they saw. But what else had Godfrey been doing for the last four years apart from maintaining discipline and ensuring the chain of command? It wasn't difficult to get soldiers to do what one wanted in war, Godfrey had found. It was more a question of choosing one's moment and acting when it came.

Godfrey had written the order while Hawes waited, used a piece of paper scored out on one side:

Dear Mother and Father . . .

Flattened all its crinkles and wrote on the reverse.

His hand fluttered as he detailed his decision, felt the naked patch of skin on his wrist where only recently the watch had kept it warm. No need to verify, or to send for further instruction, petition for court martial as the rules allowed. They were in the blue. This was an emergency. Nothing to do but preserve discipline and carry out the necessary punishment. It might be one man's say against another's, but Captain Godfrey Farthing was still in charge here.

'You can lock him in the chicken shed after,' he said as he handed the order over to his temporary sergeant. 'Keep him there for a night on a diet of bread and water.'

'What will the men think, sir?' said Hawes.

'What have the men got to do with it?' Godfrey slid the lid on his pen, put it in his pocket. 'I'm the officer in charge.'

There were all sorts of punishments available had Godfrey chosen to enforce the army rules these last two weeks, rather than let his men dance with the chickens and gamble amongst themselves. Penalties for men who no longer kept curfew. Who failed to wear their tunics for parade. Men who didn't shave for two days if they didn't feel like it, bartered work duties when they wanted a change of shift. Godfrey could have punished them all. With a ten-shilling fine. Or a reprimand. A mention in dispatches, and not in a good way. Or perhaps simply confinement in camp. For loss of personally issued clothing. Not saluting correctly. Breaking into a house in search of plunder.

But wasn't it he who had requisitioned the farmhouse with just that intention, to eat all the cabbages and use someone else's furniture as his own? Besides, they were already confined to camp – eleven men reduced to nine without the enemy even in their sights. One injured beyond repair by his own side. The other wandering the fields. Their lucky man, Bertie Fortune. A talisman Godfrey Farthing had let go.

Godfrey looked through the parlour window at his makeshift Eden as Hawes went outside to prepare, saw it suddenly through different eyes. The mud. The piles of

rubbish beginning to accumulate. The overflowing latrines.
It reminded him of the trench he had once shared with
Beach, a mess of rat bones and lice, men's bodies festering
on the rancid leftovers from Plum & Apple, the stench
where men had relieved themselves rather than fight their
way to the officially sanctioned pit. How far he believed
they had come, this close to the end, hidden in their own
little oasis against the never-ending disaster outside. Only
for Godfrey Farthing to discover that they had not come
far at all.

Inside the farmhouse as four o'clock approached, Godfrey
went through his belongings item by item deciding what
to take and what to leave. The black half-walnut he had
meant to set loose on the pond had spilled on the floor
and he retrieved it and put it on the table to remind him.
He didn't like the idea that the tiny boat would never get
to journey, when that was what he had intended all along.

He turned out each of the pockets of his tunic, tossing
away odd bits of this and that, added the whole walnut
to the half one, slid the accountant's notebook and letter
into his top pocket, hesitated before adding Alec's field
postcard, buttoned it all down. He kept a pen and a stub
of pencil, a box of Vestas and a pinch of French tobacco
that he had bartered once with Ralph. Ralph preferred the
rough stuff that they got with the ration, never seemed to
smoke more than a blink. He used the ration fags for
gambling instead. Along with everything else.

Godfrey packed his pouch with ammunition for his
revolver, stuffed his bag with binoculars and whistle. He
added two field dressings and some bandages, the last grain

of morphia, secured the clasps and buckles. If this was to be his last stand, he wanted to be ready. Who knew what the next few hours might bring?

At three fifty-five he had Hawes call the men to order, paraded them for the second time that day. He could tell they were wary. The youngsters Jackdaw and Promise kept glancing at him as though he might lock them in the lean-to. For fighting or worse; kissing behind the high barn wall. Flint wouldn't look at him at all, staring into the distance and scratching at the cut on his face where Jackdaw had scraped him. Alfred Walker's casual charm was gone, given way to a furtive sort of fiddling with whatever he had in his pocket. Even Alec seemed suddenly vulnerable, his eyes cast to the sea of manure about their feet as the dog watched from the barn door. Only George Stone had a more resolute look about him, as though he was someone for whom the worst had already happened a long, long time ago.

Godfrey had spoken to Ralph first, called his second lieutenant into the parlour to let him know a sanction was coming. For fighting. For brandishing a weapon when the enemy were nowhere in sight. He'd handed the young officer his two dice back, watched Ralph grin, a sudden sight of the boy's former self.

Once he had the men gathered, Hawes stepped back towards the middle of the yard, heels together, yelled:

'Parade!'

Seven men lined at the pump to see what might happen next. Beside them Second Lieutenant Ralph Svenson was all dressed up, flashing on his cuffs. He kept glancing at

Jackdaw with those strange translucent eyes, smiling as though he knew what was coming.

Stealing. Punishment by confinement to barracks. By a fine of ten shillings or, in the worst case, dismissal.

Disobeying a lawful command given by his superior officer. Penal Servitude.

But striking a superior officer, as Jackdaw had done to the second lieutenant. Death. Or at the very least humiliation.

Godfrey saw how Ralph's eyes flickered with confusion as he came to stand before him instead. Tunic on. Belt on. Cap, boots and cane.

'Second Lieutenant Ralph Svenson, I am charging you with the negligent discharge of your weapon occasioning false alarms in camp. Also the wounding of a fellow soldier. Please surrender your weapon and come with me.'

It rained for the whole afternoon. For once even the birds were silent. Lashed to the pump wearing nothing but his second-best shirt, Ralph's hair was soon plastered to his face, flattening over his forehead and his cheeks, the blond curls turned dark, streaked with the constant run of water into and out of his eyes. At first he tried to shake his hair to keep it from bothering him, but eventually he gave up, just bowed his head further and further, let the rain *drip drip drip* from every part of him until it made a pool in his lap.

They released him at six when it was already dark, Hawes untying the knots as the men continued to sit guard in the barn. The second lieutenant could barely walk as Hawes dragged him to the chicken shed and shoved him inside. At seven the men ate in the barn, watching through the open door while George Stone brought their officer food – a hard biscuit and a tin of water. The old sweat held the tin to Ralph's mouth, an awkward gulp as some of it slid down the boy's throat and the rest sluiced down his chin. Godfrey stayed indoors and ate in the parlour, a glass of water and a piece of cold chicken. The last remains of the grey. Afterwards he cracked open one of the walnuts that he kept in his pocket, took his time to chew on the creamy contents, a bitter aftertaste lingering on his tongue.

James Hawes came to see him once the deed had been done. 'When do you want me to let him out, sir?'

A good man, Hawes, despite his fear of blood. Tried to do the right thing whatever the circumstances.

'Leave him,' Godfrey said. 'We'll keep him there for the night at least.'

'He won't forget, sir.'

'None of us forget, Hawes.'

There was an uncomfortable silence between the two men before the temporary sergeant spoke again. 'Are you sure this is the right way to go, sir?'

'Well, let me tell you, Hawes,' said Godfrey, 'humiliation is a two-way street. I think Second Lieutenant Svenson needs to understand that.'

'What next, then, sir?'

'What do you mean?'

'Are we going over?'

Godfrey pushed back his chair with an abrupt shove, stood up.

'No, we're not fucking going over, Hawes. Not tonight. Or tomorrow. You're staying here and all the men are staying here, including Second Lieutenant Svenson, and you're going to keep your heads down until they sign the bloody papers and the whole thing is done.'

Hawes stood rigid. 'It wasn't him, you know, sir. Who did the shooting.'

'Who was it, then?'

Hawes was silent. Godfrey took off his cap and ran a hand across his stubble of hair. Asked another question, more direct this time.

'Did Jackson shoot the accountant?'

'Why don't you ask him?'

'He won't say, will he.'

'Jackson couldn't hit a cow's arse with a banjo, sir.'

Godfrey turned away. 'In which case we'll have to take Lieutenant Svenson's word for it and leave things at that.'

Early to bed in the barn, the men all bedded down by ten, the rain dissipated until it was nothing more than a soft patter on the roof. Ralph had been taken to the latrine by Hawes before being shoved into the lean-to with a rough cloth to dry himself and a blanket to sleep under. Godfrey watched from the parlour window. He didn't bother to speak to his second. What man would want to listen to his abuser at just the moment he had been freed to curse?

At eleven, Godfrey called Hawes into the parlour. On the table before him lay the little brass key for his lockbox, the orders tucked safe inside the tobacco tin, hidden beneath the rest. Also Ralph's Webley in its holster. Hawes stared at the gun. Godfrey didn't bother with a preamble.

'I'm going to take Methven, Hawes. If we wait, he'll die.'

'What about Fortune, sir?'

Godfrey paused. Twelve hours there. Twelve hours

back. A few more for misadventure. Bertie Fortune should be home by now. But there was something about the emptiness that had settled on the farm and its yard since his lucky man had gone, which suggested to Godfrey that Bertie Fortune might not be returning any time soon.

He looked directly at his sergeant. 'Would you trust Fortune, Hawes?'

Hawes shifted, dipped his head to the floor, didn't reply. Godfrey slid the brass key across the parlour table to the temporary sergeant.

'Keep this. It's got the men's pay books inside, if you need them. Also their letters, just in case.'

'Sir.'

Hawes took the key, slid it into one of his tunic pockets. Then Godfrey picked up Ralph's Webley, held it out towards his temporary sergeant.

'You're in charge now, Hawes. Make sure to keep them busy. Leave Lieutenant Svenson in the lean-to until I return. I'll be back by nightfall tomorrow.'

'I don't like guns, sir.'

'None of us do, Hawes. But I trust you to handle it wisely.'

Godfrey waited until Hawes held out a reluctant hand, slight tremor in his fingers, placed Ralph's revolver in his sergeant's grasp, watched him stuff it into the back of his waistband. Then he held out his hand again and dribbled six bullets into Hawes's open palm.

'Try not to use them,' he said. 'But if you have to, don't hesitate.'

He marked up his diary before he left. It was the ninth of November. The rain had ceased at last.

1948

Fortune

Bertie Fortune returned with treasure. Not two-string pearls for his wife. Or a brooch for the bride-to-be. French champagne for the wedding breakfast. Or cigars for all the men. Not even a suit with a lining dark as midnight. But a conscience as clear as the day he first took up his rifle. At least that was what he liked to think.

They had sent him out to gather in the laundry – no use for a man in the house when a wedding was in the air.

'Get a treat, too,' shouted his wife, Annie, as she closed the front door behind him. 'For a celebration. You'll know when you see.'

They left him on the step with nothing but the laundry tickets in his hand. For his wife's dress with the silk collar. His son's best shirt. Stockings and undergarments. His own lucky suit. But Bertie Fortune knew that he could not return until he had acquired some other sort of treasure, something with which to make the party swing. What the women requested, the women got. Bertie Fortune's motto for a long and satisfying life.

The wedding was to go off at noon the next day, all the outfits waiting to be collected so that they were spick and span. Annie was already laying out the china, wiping the rims of the saucers, polishing the spoons. Their daughter Alice was in the kitchen with her sleeves rolled up and her apron tied double, making pastry with real butter. It still amazed Bertie to see so much in a single bowl. Perhaps he should bring oranges, he thought as he buttoned his coat. Fresh from the Canaries, a sudden burst of colour to make them feel alive. Or maybe even a pineapple, with its prickled skin and golden flesh. Something they used to dream of through those long despondent years.

'I'll get married when you can buy me one of them, Mr Fortune,' his future daughter-in-law Iris had once declared.

That'll be never, then, he remembered thinking. Cost more than a month's wages – if you could get your hands on one, that was. Bertie Fortune was a man who could get his hands on most things, but it had been hard enough to find an apple then, let alone a pineapple, that terrible winter of '47. He'd almost lost it in those never-ending months, felt age pressing on his bones in a way he never had before. Annie had looked bad too, skin the colour of the tea they used to drink during the first war. Grey. Stinking of chlorine. And yet they'd drunk it all the same.

But now the second war was over and things were looking up. A pineapple – that would make a good catch. That was what Bertie Fortune was thinking as he stepped away from his front door, tipped his hat at a neighbour, set off down the street.

The wedding party was for Bertie's youngest. Billy Fortune. Come back alive from the second war Bertie had lived through; what more from life could a father want?

But now Bill was disappearing again, into the arms of this young lady, Iris. Not much more than nineteen, come down from somewhere in the north to seek her fortune in the big city now that all the bombs were gone. Bertie had only been introduced to her a few months back, possessor of a blue hat with a tweak of netting at the front, like a boat sailing on the neat roll of her hair. The hat was jaunty and so was she, wearing a skirt that swung out when she turned. Bertie thought it was extravagant, but he could see that Annie was impressed.

'Did you see what she was wearing?'

Whispering with Alice as they warmed the teapot, casting glances at the smart young lady with a typing job and a room in a hostel for women who did not have a husband yet. Where had she come from, this girl sitting at his kitchen table with her pretty legs crossed, that was what Bertie Fortune wanted to know. The daughter of a mother she never mentioned, and an airman who had crashed and burned?

'Don't ask,' said Annie.

Alice giggling from behind her hand.

So Bertie had not. What use was it delving into the past, when he of all people understood that the past was often better left alone? Bertie knew he should be happy to see Bill and Iris together, a young woman who winked at him as she lifted the milk bottle from the table to top up her cup. They were part of the new society, all anyone talked about now. Pensions and a National Health Service.

We're all in it together.

Whereas Bertie Fortune had made his money by keeping it to himself . . . unless he could bargain for something better, of course.

Where would he go to find a pineapple, Bertie thought now as he wound his way towards the heart of London, dodging cabs and trams as he crossed the streets, narrow and wide. To Covent Garden, perhaps, barrows laid high with fruit and veg of all descriptions, flowers of every possible colour and shape. Or to the Lane with all its stalls – bric-a-brac and mackerel, sherbet, and sausages hung from string. It was always possible to find treasure, if you knew where to look, that was what Bertie Fortune had realized, digging into other people's leftovers, never knew where they might lead.

He had learned that when he was a young man, just back from the fields of France. Start with something that can win every game, then grow a business from the ground. Not French tobacco and papers that disintegrated in the damp. But scrap metal and hand-me-downs. Pots, pans and nails. A rag-and-bone man with a single cart, buying from some and selling to the rest. There wasn't anything Bertie Fortune wouldn't take a punt on when he'd first started out. Built it up from there.

He was worth a fortune now, by name and in cash terms, too. Bertie's Fortune. An old, old joke. One of the lucky ones, at least that was what everyone said, came back from disaster untouched, spent all his young life building up a cash reserve. Bertie was in his fifties now, getting towards being an old man. He wondered, sometimes, what he would do with it all. The warehouses and the trucks. The money sitting in the bank. He would have handed the business to Reg, in the natural way of things, his eldest son and heir. But Reg had gone and got himself shot, in the desert, never did make it home. Got himself buried there, too. No different from all the boys in France, Bertie supposed when they told him. But he minded more than he was prepared to admit, used to go and sit on the bench in the cemetery just so he could pretend.

No wonder we have a restless world, Bertie thought as he crossed the street at Piccadilly, Eros finally returned to his perch. All those dead people trying to get home to where they belonged. A bit like Europe these last few years, refugees and prisoners-of-war, soldiers, sailors and candlestick makers all trying to get to somewhere other than the place they had ended up. Whereas all he and the rest of the lucky ones had done was get onto a boat for Southampton, came on a night crossing once the bells pealed in the village, arrived home next morning to find his father having a jar of tea at the table before his early shift. Twenty-four hours give or take, but sometimes Bertie thought it was the longest journey he'd ever taken. They hadn't even sung to pass the time on the way back.

It's a long way to Tipperary . . .

Had some intimation already that perhaps they weren't quite so lucky as they'd thought.

An hour later, Bertie was headed towards the east of the city, river glimpsed from between the gap sites, wondering if it really was worth visiting the Petticoat to look for treasure, or whether it would be the same as what he had found so far. Empty birdcages and bargains pulled from derelict houses, twenty-two tiny mother-of-pearl buttons laid out on a tray, to match some girl's twenty-two-inch waist.

He had collected the laundry already, just to make sure, got the book stamped before watching as they tied the neat paper package with string. His wife's dress. His son's shirt. His own lucky suit, of course. Blue as a starling's egg, three buttons, neat lapels. Also some lilies of the valley for the men's buttonholes. But he still didn't have any treasure to take home for the ladies. No pineapple to balance on a special stand next to the wedding cake, all three tiers.

The woman at the Garden had told him to try the docks.

'Get down there quick and you might pick up a bargain.'

Bananas stacked in crates. Perhaps even a coconut. All the treasures of Jamaica and the Canaries, ready to disburse. But even she had shaken her head at the idea of a pineapple still in its prickly skin. She could get him a can, she'd said. Rings or chunks. But not a fresh one. Only the very deepest pockets could get those.

Bertie Fortune used to be the one with the deepest pockets, that's what he thought as he set off for the ships. Walking away across the fields of France, one stuffed with walnuts, the other with an orange, only a little wrinkled despite having been buried in a box of sand in the cellar for several weeks by the time it came to him. The orange had been a treasure Bertie could not resist. The most valuable thing the farmhouse had to offer as far as he was concerned. He had used it to barter for a bed as he waited for the bells to ring in the village. A few glasses of wine in an estaminet, and somewhere to hide until the end came. George Stone had already owed him for the brandy – a squat quart bottle, contents gleaming like the best sort of amber. And when Bertie Fortune had needed it, the favour had come good, Stone equipping him with everything he'd required to barter his way to the coast. Food and drink always were the best kind of currency in war time, oranges some of the highest-value things it was possible to get.

Now, as Bertie Fortune arrived at the docks, he found them stuffed with oranges, men shouting the odds over boxes crammed full. As he passed one of the crates, he plucked an orange from the top, tossed a shilling to the vendor in return, inhaled the glorious scent. Thick citrus peel stained his fingernails yellow, as he dug into the pith.

Alfred Walker had liked oranges, that was what Bertie Fortune remembered. Had one in his pocket when Bertie bumped into him that time at Mulholland's, trying to get a job. Ten years after the first war was done. Maybe more. Didn't even mention what had gone on.

'Did you get your girl?'

The very first thing Bertie asked the boy. And the grin on Walker's face told Bertie that he had. Not just a wife, but a daughter too. Clementine. That was what they called her, oranges in a brown-paper bag in Walker's pocket ready to take home for a treat. He'd told Bertie that his wife, Dorothea, was expecting again, baby due any moment. Alfred Walker was hoping for a boy.

'Little Alfie,' he said. 'That's what I'll call him.'

Walker had laughed at that, Bertie joining in, knew the hubris of naming a boy after oneself, only for him to go on and prove all sorts of dishonour.

And yet . . .

'They're the future, now,' Walker had declared. Before telling Bertie that they were all off to America soon. The promised land. 'Can't wait. You can do anything there.'

After he shook Alfred Walker's hand, said goodbye,

Bertie had gone to the pub on the corner, drunk three dark pints, smoked to inhale. Perhaps he should consider America himself, he had thought then. Ship them all over. Annie, Bill, Reg and Alice. He'd even agree to Annie's mum going, too, if that was what she wanted. Got as far as checking on the price of tickets, wrote a letter off in speculation to some sort of distant cousin settled in a place called Nova Scotia. It had seemed like the right way to go in the lean years, when business had become all sorts of struggle. Never did get a reply.

But ever since he'd got his feet back in the dirt of England Bertie Fortune had been reluctant to dig them out again. Alfred Walker was a dreamer, always had been. It was his natural state to want to wander. But Bertie was more solid than that. An entrepreneur and a businessman, knew to hold on to where it all started, in case it all fell apart. A little strip of a yard. A horse and a cart. Something other people wanted. Alfred Walker chased dreams, but Bertie Fortune chased money. It had come out good so far.

Now Bertie dodged and weaved amongst the clamour of the docks, searching here and there for that elusive pine-apple, something more special than what was to hand. He had tried all the usual suspects, the afternoon winding on towards tea, before he realized he might have to go to a spiv in the end. One of those men who did their business down the back of the alleyways rather than at the top.

Bertie supposed he was a spiv himself, really. The world was full of favours to be done, after all. Things to be swapped. Or bartered. Brandy for an orange. An orange for a bed. He had pawned the captain's wristwatch for the suit he was carrying now. Did it that same week he arrived home on the overnight sailing to Southampton. Took the watch to the pawnshop and bought the suit with the cash. Blue. Three buttons. Turn-ups. All the rage then, still doing him well now. He'd had *Fortune* stitched into the collar, wore it every Sunday when he first started out. A gentleman riding a rag-and-bone man's cart, only ever going to ascend.

Bertie had redeemed the wristwatch after his first three or four cartloads, never needed to pawn it again. He'd been keeping it for Reg, some kind of memento. Until Reg was killed, of course, no use for telling the time now. Perhaps he should give the watch to Bill, Bertie thought as he pushed his way through the mass of dockworkers and vendors. Let him count down the minutes and the seconds like young men do. Bertie didn't need to count the hours himself anymore, knew already that he was out of step with the future. Just as he had been when he came home in '18, discovered no one really wanted to know what he had been doing those past three years. All of Bertie's youth gone in an instant.

What was it Captain Farthing had called it once?

A great lacuna of time.

A fancy way of putting it. But that was how Bertie saw it now, too, the first war. Like some great death machine still operating somewhere in the never-never, churning up and spewing out and churning up and spewing out over and over, while somewhere else the next generation got on with what the next generation always did. Dancing. And drinking. And dazzling each other with the swing of their skirts. Whereas Bertie would only ever be that man walking away across the fields knowing that freedom was stuffed into his pockets if he dared.

Besides, Bertie had no use for trinkets anymore. Not wristwatches. Or even silver cap badges, small lions raising their paws. It had bothered Bertie then and it bothered him still now. How the second lieutenant had tossed that little badge into the ring as though it was nothing but a gewgaw, rather than the remains of a man. Ralph Svenson never did have any idea where the badge had come from. But Bertie Fortune knew. Always had thought it ought to have been sent back to where it belonged. Or added to the pot along with all the other things, right from the start – let the rest of the men have a square go. Or perhaps what Bertie Fortune really minded was that he had been expected to take part.

Bertie shoved his way through the ever-increasing crowds on the dockside, found himself caught in a flow of people all trying to see something going on by the quay. Another old man like he was, offering bargains to the world. The man was standing on an orange box, great hull of a ship looming behind, shouting some sort of scripture as he pulled things from beneath his filthy coat. A scrubbing brush. A cheap gold chain. Preaching about the fire that would come from heaven to burn them all if they did not confess. The man's neck was thick with dirty freckles, his clothes barely held together by a stitch or two of thread, standing there with holes in his boots shouting and shouting about forgiveness:

Our Father who art in heaven . . . forgive us our trespasses as we forgive those who trespass against us.

Until he produced the prize. A fruit, all prickled on its outside, all golden inside, summoned from amongst the folds of his long coat as though it was some kind of rabbit held aloft for all the world to see. Bertie could hear the murmur ripple through the crowd as they realized what the man was showing off, felt himself press forward along with the rest. He tried to fight his way to the front, grappling with the younger men, got pushed back instead. But even from three or four deep Bertie Fortune suddenly knew who the man was, the stink of him like a carcass hung too long before it was cut. The ex-meat man. The man who used to work in an abattoir but couldn't stand the sight of blood. James Hawes, shouting like the day of reckoning was upon them, staring at Bertie Fortune from across the heads of the crowd.

Bertie Fortune came home with treasure. In the front door and straight through to the kitchen, handed Iris the pineapple, all prickled skin and spiky top. Oh, how her face lit up, just like those fountains on VE Day.

'Why, Mr F. You really are a treasure.'

Twirling round right there about the table so they could all get a look at her legs. How they'd laughed then, the women, passing the pineapple from one to the other as though a new dawn was upon them, kept touching it in amazement before whirling off to make the tea. It made for quite a celebration in the end, not the wedding, but the night before. Ale out. Sherry out. Even a bottle of French champagne Bertie had been saving for when Reg might say, I do.

Annie was furious when he told her later what he'd swapped the pineapple for.

'But that was your lucky suit!'

All cleaned and ready for a wedding. Blue as a starling's egg. Lining dark as midnight. Three buttons, turn-ups, neat lapels. Given away to an old comrade who couldn't even pay a ha'penny. Got a pineapple in return. Annie's face had been stricken where she lay upon the counterpane, as though now that the suit was gone all their luck would run out, too.

But Bertie had felt lighter after, as though he was young again, ready for it all, wandering back through the highways and byways of London with a conscience clean as that first glass of water he had drunk the day he walked away. Standing at the water fountain in the middle of a village, orange on the edge of the stone, waiting to see what he might be offered in return. He had known he was safe then, after everything that had happened. Nothing left to do but find a bed for the night, put his feet up and his head upon a proper pillow, listen to the birds sing as he waited for the bells.

Bertie could still hear them singing now. Sitting in the kitchen of an evening while through the wall the women *chitter chattered* like starlings gathered on a chimney pot, all those young men's voices between his ears, too.

It's a long way to Tipperary . . .

Singing like his own son must have sung as he rode a tank into the desert until he met that German bullet, fell into the sand. Or perhaps they had come up with new songs, for a new war, their own kind of comfort, each generation making way for the next.

Either way it *was* a long way to Tipperary, that was what Bertie Fortune thought now, somewhere he had never

been. No time left for that. He was here in this house for
the duration now. Nothing left for him to do but stay at
home and get old, read the rest of that poem he had started.
Eliot.

The moment of the rose and the moment of the yew.

Might try the other one, too, if there was enough time
left. What was it they called it?

The Waste Land.

Not a bad description of his life.

PART FIVE

The Reckoning

Godfrey Farthing
b. 1893 d. 1971
|
Robert Farthing
= Else Gold
|
Solomon Farthing
b. 1950 d.

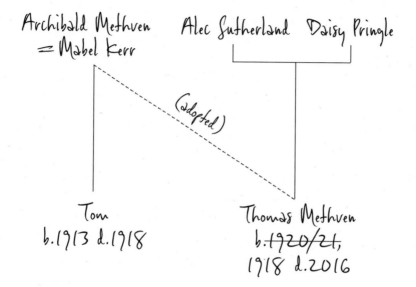

Archibald Methven
= Mabel Kerr

Alec Sutherland   Daisy Pringle

(adopted)

Tom
b.1913 d.1918

Thomas Methven
b.~~1920/21,~~
1918 d.2016

2016

One

He came home in another man's car, Solomon Farthing driving through the night once again until Auld Reekie appeared out of the dawn. The air was warm as he slipped into Edinburgh, its castle and spires rising from the haze, a city waking to all its glory, drawing a grateful resident to its dusty, scented heart.

The news from Kew had been just as Solomon expected – bad mixed with good. The good news was – they had an address for him. The bad news – it was in Edinburgh. Only Solomon Farthing knew how to turn bad news into gold.

He'd driven north in Colin Dunlop's hybrid, enjoying all the benefits it conveyed, stopped at a castle in Northumberland sometime in the early hours to see if his aunt's Mini was still waiting for him there. Needless to say, the Mini had vanished, disappeared into the ether with its rust holes and its string. Solomon had considered stopping at the school, lured by the idea of laying his head upon a blue blanket. Then he'd thought of DCI Franklin and the favour she was doing him, in return for the favour he had once done her.

Not many hours later and here he was, five minutes from Thomas Methven's only living relative, not far from the nursing home in which his client had breathed his last. A strange juxtaposition, Solomon thought as he parked

Colin Dunlop's car in a nearby cul-de-sac (misdirection, of a sort). Then again, Heir Hunters like him understood all about the odd ways people turned out to be connected. Especially in a city like Edinburgh, where somewhere along the line everybody knew everybody else.

Solomon's quarry was a woman called Iris Fortune. Widow, never any children, lived most of her life in London but originally from the north. He arrived on her doorstep at 8 a.m. hoping to surprise her. Only for her to appear before he'd even had the chance to knock. An old lady with hair all teased about like a stick of candyfloss, she caught him blowing his nose with one hand and trying to palm a gritty tic tac with the other. Good impressions mattered if one wanted to leave with a contract signed and sealed.

'Can I help you?' she said.

'Mrs Fortune?'

Solomon held out his hand, but Iris Fortune didn't take it.

'Who wants to know?'

'Solomon Farthing.'

'Like the money?'

A quarter of a penny once, the lowest denomination possible. Why was it that even on the doorstep of a stranger, Solomon was reminded of his net worth. He attempted gravitas despite the crumple of his shirt.

'I have some news for you, about a relative.'

'They're all dead.'

Solomon touched a hand to his dishevelled hair, realized he had been bested somehow before he'd even got into Iris Fortune's hall.

'Yes, well, maybe . . .' he replied. 'But one of them has left something behind.'

Indoors things were much as he expected. China ornaments. Vertical blinds. Three-piece suite in beige. It should be easy, Solomon thought. Famous last words. On the television set in the lounge there was a first-person shooter frozen in the middle of a game. He couldn't hide his surprise.

'Is someone else here?' he asked.

'Oh, no,' Iris Fortune laughed, 'my great-nephew showed me how. Runs through our family like a streak of raspberry ripple.'

'Sorry?'

'Death by shooting.'

And Solomon knew at once that he had come to the right house.

The tea Iris Fortune offered was Earl Grey. Solomon had been hoping for a sherry, or at the very least a coffee. But somehow this old lady knew just how to keep him on a leash. She sat opposite him on the sofa turning the pages of the contract he had cobbled together by the photocopying machines at Kew, a small crinkle in her forehead.

'So who exactly is dead?' she said. 'I can't help if I don't have a surname.'

An old Heir Hunter trick. Get the client to sign before confirming full name and d.o.b., plus anything else that might mean they could claim the estate themselves. Solomon knew that Iris Fortune was looking for elucidation. But he wanted to obfuscate as long as possible until he was sure the commission on fifty thousand would be his.

'I'd rather we agreed it was a case worth pursuing together before we go into all the boring nitty gritty,' he replied.

'But how can I decide if I don't know the name?'

Like everything in life, Solomon thought, you take a gamble. Still, he gave her the spiel.

'Well, I'm pretty sure of the connection. You can check my credentials, if you like, speak to one of my previous clients.' A gamble of his own. 'But really it would be an acknowledgement of the unpaid work I have carried out on your behalf so far, an agreement that we will tackle the rest of the case together. And share whatever we find.'

Solomon liked to think it sounded as though he was offering some sort of partnership when he said this, rather than holding a relative's legacy to ransom so that he could take most of it for himself. But still Iris Fortune had questions.

'Five figures, you say? Split how many ways?'

Solomon wriggled a little in his chair thinking of the Reverend Jennie Methven's enormous family tree. And the much smaller one in his pocket, which he had sketched himself.

'An eighth is common,' he said. 'Perhaps a sixth. But I suspect there could be significantly less once we investigate. Do you have a lot of cousins?'

Iris Fortune frowned as though counting out the cousins for herself. The one who wore her hair in pigtails. The one who ran away to sea. The one they cremated and sprinkled in the rose garden. All on the wrong side of the family, of course. *C'est la vie.* Or *c'est la mort.* That was just the way life and death worked. It was Mrs

Fortune's next remark, however, that made Solomon's heart skip.

'And why would I not just pursue it myself? You can get everything on that web thing these days, can't you.'

Yes, Solomon thought. You can. Along with Colin Dunlop and all the other Heir Hunters knocking on your door and shouting through the letterbox, leaving constant phone messages the minute the case appeared on the QLTR list. Solomon tugged at the flap of his cuff, tried to stop his fingers starting with their incessant fluttering this early in the day. He was certain he had seen Colin Dunlop following him around Edinburgh's bypass in his aunt's stolen Mini. Then again, he could have been hallucinating. Half a bottle of Fino drunk to the bone while he was lying in a London graveyard the night before might have had the same effect.

'You could spend a lot of time following the wrong path,' he said, now attempting sincerity. 'Only to find someone else has got there first. I would be saving you the trouble.'

A knight in muddy corduroys.

'And what was your name again?'

'Solomon,' he said. 'Solomon Farthing.'

Iris Fortune blinked then. 'You'll be related to Godfrey.' It wasn't a question.

'My grandfather,' he replied.

They still asked him sometimes, Solomon's clients. Where'd my watch go? How about that coat? What did he do with those earrings my mother used to have? As though it wasn't them or their relatives who had bartered their worldly goods, but some stranger who had taken everything from them on the promise of a return, only to run away and never come back. It was over forty years since Godfrey Farthing had died and still people spoke about him as though he was hiding somewhere with everything they had ever owned.

'I'm sorry,' Solomon said, holding out a somewhat leaky biro acquired by deception from the National Archive. 'I just need you to . . .'

But Mrs Fortune laughed then like a child skipping round a maypole, as though there could be nothing better in life to do than that.

'Oh, son, I don't think that's necessary. I've been watching that programme for years now. You know the one.'

And he did.

'*Heir Hunters*,' she said. 'So interesting. Got to be careful, old women like me all on our own. Don't know who might come calling.'

Solomon couldn't stop the flutter of his fingers then as fifty thousand began to slip from his grip. He tried to rally.

'Well, there are always things that we can bring to the table . . .'

But Iris Fortune just shook her head as though she was doing him a favour rather than the other way round.

'Oh, don't you worry about that. I've got that web thing through the back. Would you like to see it? Ancestry dot com.'

'Ancestry dot com,' Solomon echoed, understanding that his five-figure commission was about to disappear like dust off the mantelpiece.

He pulled a blue kerchief from his pocket, patted at his forehead, felt, all of sudden, every single crush, spit and crumple of the last few days. He missed the dog, that was what it came down to. The way it used to lean against his leg at dispiriting times like this. But the dog was long gone, lost to a boy in Northumberland who had won him with the toss of a coin. Just as Solomon would be long gone, too, once Freddy Dodds's men realized he was back in town. Solomon had a sudden premonition of his return to that basement flat in the crescent, no camouflage of any sort to protect him now, his first visitor one of those Edinburgh Men of an unsavoury disposition come to welcome him home. With a brick. Or a bat. Or the toss of another coin to see which of his limbs they should threaten first. Freddy Dodds standing in the hallway, calculating what he might get for the grandfather clock. While Colin Dunlop slid seamlessly into the seat in which Solomon sat now.

It was then that Iris Fortune held out the unexpected hand of an Edinburgh kind of friendship.

You scratch my back and I'll scratch yours.

'Now son, I may be able to help you,' she said, patting the seat on the sofa next to her. 'But let's start again, shall we. And give me it all this time, chapter and verse.'

Thomas Methven (deceased) was her brother – or half one at least. A baby boy born to a Daisy Pringle in November 1918, abandoned to a Mabel Methven née Kerr six months later to make up for the child she had lost. Along with a pawn ticket, no.125, of course, not the kind of evidence Margaret Penny of the Office for Lost People might appreciate, but the only real proof Solomon Farthing had of Thomas Methven's roots.

It hadn't been hard to trace Daisy Pringle through the

records after that. An only child who had lived a life of full abandon once the war to end all wars had finally run its course. Her paper trail had proved fulsome even on an initial, speculative surf. Marriages. And divorces. Her signature on a couple of death certificates, too. Solomon knew that once he did some proper digging, all sorts of shenanigans might appear.

Daisy Pringle, it turned out, had been one of the lucky generation. Bright Young Things, wasn't that what they called them? Girls and boys who only ever wanted to dance. Left home as soon as she could and made for London, champagne cocktails and skirts at the knee. No wonder she gave away her first-born child, Solomon had thought as he wrote it all down. Who wants to move into a new era with a constant reminder of the previous one hanging on your hip?

And yet, the real treasure had not been Daisy Pringle, but the other child she left behind. A daughter called Iris, born ten years after the first. The product of a short-lived marriage to an airman who had later crashed and burned. And even better, the daughter was still alive; and sitting before Solomon now.

'Oh no, son,' said Iris Fortune, dismissing the rough family tree Solomon had sketched by way of demonstration. 'I've never had a brother.'

Solomon was not surprised by this reaction. It wasn't uncommon for Heir Hunters to know more about a family than the family knew themselves.

'Your mother may not have mentioned it,' he said. 'She was very young at the time.'

'My mother told me everything,' said Iris Fortune. 'A very voluble woman.'

And judging by Daisy Pringle's paper trail, Solomon thought this was probably true.

'I did have a brother-in-law though.' Iris Fortune sat a little straighter. 'And nephews, too, by marriage. If that's any good.'

She began to tick them off on her fingers as though she was doing the reckoning for herself:

Reggie Fortune. Brother-in-law. Shot in the desert.

'Some time in 1943, I think. Not that I ever knew Reggie. Only from photographs, of course.'

A great nephew. Iraq, the first time. Wounded by Friendly Fire.

'Imagine going all that way only to get it from your own side. He ended up with that thing they all talk about . . .'

Iris Fortune fished for the word.

'Gulf War Syndrome?' Solomon suggested.

'No, the one you get after.'

Relief, Solomon thought. That you are still alive.

'Stress,' Iris Fortune declared, as though it was something you got after a bad day at the office. 'Post Traumatic . . .'

Then there was Uncle Bob.

'Belgium, 1917. One of the doomed.'

And his twin brother, James.

'Shot by some sniper a month later when he stood up to go to the toilet. You'd think he'd have learned by then.'

Iris Fortune paused at that, as though only now considering the devastation.

'Imagine losing two sons in the same year. How awful.

My father-in-law was the only one left after that. Albert Fortune. Though everyone called him Bertie. Thank God he came home or his mother would have shot herself, too, probably . . . through the back in the larder.'

With a ladies' gun, thought Solomon, pearl inlay on the handle.

'She spent a lot of time in there, polishing her china,' Iris Fortune continued. 'Always was a doomy sort of person.'

She brushed a crumb from her lap as though to dismiss all those who had been stupid enough to end their days floundering in the mud of a battlefield.

'Quite a military family, really. All on my husband's side, of course.'

Solomon glanced again at the television screen frozen in a moment of madness. He had never been interested in war, not the way that other boys were. The make-believe sticks. The belts strung across the chest. Running along that riverbank as though it was a canal in the desert they never would get back. The only wars his generation had ever been called to were on the barricades. Anti-Vietnam. Pro-abortion. Gay rights. You name it, they marched. Culture wars, wasn't that what they called it in America now? They were all obsessed with guns over there. Black. White. Old. Young. Men and women both. Even children knew how to pull a trigger. Whatever had become of those crusading years?

Solomon felt melancholy settling on him at the thought that life was nothing but brutal in its brevity, whereas Iris Fortune seemed revitalized now that she had accounted for all the deaths by shooting in her family tree. She put a hand to her perfumed hair, the scent of geraniums rising in the warmth of the living room.

'I can show you some photographs, if you'd like?'

Solomon sighed. He preferred to sign the deal before he got caught in albums and family stories that often turned out to be untrue. Then again, he had already decided he must not leave the house without Iris Fortune's signature on his contract. What other chance did he have with Freddy Dodds? Not to mention DCI Franklin. So he slid back into the depths of the sofa.

'Pictures would be good.'

They looked through albums until Solomon thought he would go cross-eyed. Then she brought it out. A black-and-white photograph of a group of men – soldiers, all lounging on the grass as though oblivious to the big guns that must have been firing just beyond the ridge. Solomon could tell at once that it dated from the first war rather than the second. There were the leg straps and the flat tin helmets, the brass buttons and the belts.

'This one's George Stone,' said Iris Fortune, pointing to an older man at the end of the line. 'He went all the way with my father-in-law.'

She moved her finger along.

'I don't know who he is, the man with the book. But the boy here is called Beach. And this one . . .' She indicated a man standing in the background in the shadow of a tree.

'This one is your grandfather, I think.'

Solomon started. What was it about this case that wherever Thomas Methven led, Godfrey Farthing followed? A story Solomon had not been able to untangle yet. He stared at the photograph of his grandfather as a young man, barely into his twenties, not much older than Solomon had been when the old man went into the ground. He wasn't sure he had ever seen a picture of his grandfather at this age before, felt all of a sudden as though he had been playing a game his whole life and now, without warning, realized it might be over before he'd properly begun.

Iris Fortune was pointing further down the line of men at a soldier with a cheery smile and a very neat moustache.

'This is Bertie, my father-in-law.'

Both Solomon's hands were trembling as he touched a finger to the twenty-something Bertie. Then to Godfrey Farthing, where he stood beneath a tree.

'Did he know my grandfather well,' he asked, 'your father-in-law?'

But Iris Fortune shook her head.

'No idea. Bertie hardly spoke about the war at all. Said once that the walnuts were bitter. But I've still got the watch he wore then.'

She pulled back her sleeve to reveal a small thing with a rim of gold that glinted in the morning light.

'He gave it to my husband for a wedding present. Said it would bring us luck seeing as it had survived, too.'

Solomon blinked at this relic of an old war, still ticking away after all this time. Then Iris Fortune let her sleeve drop and turned again to the pile of albums, slipped out one with hard covers and black sugar-paper pages. She flipped open the front and showed Solomon a photograph of a young woman laughing on the steps of a registry office.

'That's me,' she said. 'On my wedding day.'

Next to her, a man with the same gold watch on his wrist and a spray of lilies of the valley pinned to his lapel.

'That's my Bill, Bertie's youngest.'

Pointed out her mother-in-law, Annie. Her sister-in-law, Alice. And next to them an older man in his fifties, somewhat awkward in an ill-fitting jacket. Iris Fortune ran her hand across the front of the photograph.

'This is Bertie,' she said. 'He was supposed to wear his lucky suit for the wedding, but the laundry lost it the day before. Ended up wearing one that belonged to his dead son instead. It was strange, the luck just ran out of him after that. Lost all his money, kept on giving it away.'

Solomon frowned at the dapper man in the crumpled suit, wondered what his grandfather would have made of Bertie Fortune if they'd ever stayed in touch. He noticed a woman at the very edge of the wedding group wearing a hat with a huge curled feather. The elusive Daisy Pringle, perhaps.

'Is that your mother?' he asked.

But Iris Fortune shook her head.

'Oh no, we weren't speaking then. But I do have a picture of her somewhere.'

She began turning the pages of the album back and back again, the photographs getting smaller and smaller as she folded time away. Two boys in a yard. Some women sitting on a lawn. Then a picture of a girl, fourteen, maybe fifteen, standing in a field of tall grasses, behind her a house with gables and roses round the door.

'This is my mother,' Iris Fortune said.

A bedraggled chain of flowers circling the girl's wrist. Solomon didn't even attempt to stop the *flitter flutter* in his fingers as he rummaged amongst his own paperwork, pulled out the photograph of the baby farm he had acquired from Peter's archive at the foundling school, placed it next to Iris Fortune's picture so that she could see. The old lady bent low over the two images, her mother's face on one, then the next. When she looked up her eyes were shining.

'Where did you get this?'

'From the home where my client was born.'

Thomas Methven (deceased); Daisy Pringle's son.

After that, Iris Fortune turned the pages of her album more slowly, pausing over every scene as though they had taken on a different significance now. Babies in deep-bottomed prams. A tree stretched across a river. A young woman with a register in her hand. It was not until the very last page that she rotated the book for Solomon to see. A miniature thing, barely one inch by two. Another photograph of her mother, standing next to a boy this time, in a field of hay. The boy was five foot ten or thereabouts. Good teeth. No more than sixteen. Even in black and white Solomon could tell that his hair was as golden as the sun under which he laboured. Iris Fortune touched a finger to the boy in the photograph, as she had touched her mother's picture, too.

'Mother always did say she had a sweetheart who went to the war,' she said. 'Got himself shot, right at the very end, that was what she told me. Firing squad.'

Oh.

'Cowardice.'

Oh.

'Or desertion.'

Suddenly Iris Fortune took on the look of a lost child, haunted by a whole flurry of ancestors who should have been there but were not.

'Or perhaps that was another story. There were so many ways.' Her eyes were shiny again as she raised them to Solomon Farthing. 'I never knew his name.'

They both looked again at the boy standing in the hay field, smiling back at them from one hundred years before.

'Alec,' said Solomon. 'Alec Sutherland.'

Summoned to life once more.

Half an hour later, Iris Fortune waved Solomon Farthing off from her doorstep, seeing him down the garden path until he made it to the pavement beyond. They'd spent a happy thirty minutes swapping anecdotes, before she had shown him the door. She'd even offered Solomon a morning sherry by the end. Brown and syrupy, in a tiny crystal glass. The sherry had not been Solomon's favourite, but it was proof of a connection between them. At least that was what he'd thought.

They had clinked the glasses before they drank, in memory of Iris Fortune's mother, Daisy Pringle. And her sweetheart, the long-lost Alec Sutherland. Also their son, Thomas Methven (deceased). Then Solomon had offered up his contract once again, along with the leaky biro, hope blooming in his chest this time.

But as Solomon made his way down Iris Fortune's garden path, all he felt was a deep slurry of disappointment at how his detective work on behalf of Thomas Methven had come out. Four days of searching for a dead man's true origins and he had been left with nothing to show once again. No closer to the fifty thousand than he had been at the foot of Greyfriars Bobby when DCI Franklin first dropped in her note.

'The money . . .' Iris Fortune had said as she folded her father-in-law, Bertie Fortune, and Solomon's grand-father, Godfrey Farthing, and her mother, Daisy Pringle, back into the past. 'Do you know where it comes from?'

'I'm afraid not,' Solomon had replied.

No serious Heir Hunter ever asked that. Money was money, regardless of its origins. As long as it wasn't crim-inal, of course. But Iris Fortune had not been satisfied with that explanation, clicking off the television set and zeroing the tip of the soldier's frozen weapon to black as though to indicate it really was the end.

'Well, that's that, then,' she'd said, rising from her sofa to show Solomon the door. 'Wouldn't want to inherit anything dirty. Never can get rid of the stain.'

Two

Solomon Farthing left Iris Fortune's house with an unsigned contract in one hand and a loose cuff hanging about the other, knowing that he had failed yet again. Flying the flag for insolvency, he thought as he walked away, the emblem of his life to date. Outside it was a perfect Edinburgh morning, buildings slanted with light. But despite having eulogized it only an hour or so before, Solomon was feeling its colder side once more.

What was it Iris Fortune had said about her father-in-law after he lost his suit?

All the luck ran out of him.

Exactly how Solomon felt now. Nothing left for him to interrogate but a dead man lying in a coffin, adorned in his burial gown. He patted at the pocket of his jacket, felt again the loss of his lucky charm. Then he stopped abruptly by a rose bush growing over a wall, surveyed his own attire. Second-best shirt. Crumpled tweed. Muddy corduroys. An outfit said a lot about a person, that was what he thought. Especially one with fifty thousand sewn inside.

Solomon's heart hammered against his ribs like a little mallet as he hurried towards Colin Dunlop's stolen car hidden in a neighbouring cul-de-sac. He must return to the nursing home, he thought, go back to those care assistants with their e-cigs and their anecdotes, have another go at picking their brains. Or maybe visit the funeral parlour first, get acquainted with Thomas Methven and his suit for himself, find out where it came from. There had to be a reason why the money had been sewn inside that particular item of clothing, as opposed to anything else. And Solomon didn't want the evidence to be destroyed before he'd had a chance to assess it for himself, the whole lot handed over to Margaret Penny from the Office for Lost People so that she could see it all burn.

He rushed round the corner, aimed Dunlop's car key somewhere in the vicinity of the hybrid, certain that this was a final branch of the tree worth pursuing – his ultimate roll of the dice. Then he saw it. Someone aiming back at him. Not his grandfather standing in the pawnshop pointing a ladies' gun at Solomon's heart. Or an old lady with a console in her hand, first-person shooter blazing away. But one of his own misdemeanours, returned to haunt him at the last. There at the kerb, right in front of where he had parked his getaway car, was a Mini that had seen better days. Rust holes in the floor. String holding the bonnet down. And behind it, Colin Dunlop of Dunlop, Dunlop & Dunlop smoking as he leaned against the trim of a sleek grey motor, caught up with Solomon Farthing at last.

Colin Dunlop took the driver's seat as he gave Solomon a lift to his second reckoning of the day, a smooth run round the stretch at Seafield, on their way to the north of the city now. As they passed the Edinburgh Cat and Dog Home, Solomon released the window so that he could hear the barking. He understood now why a soldier might take his dog to war.

'Long time no see, Solomon,' Colin Dunlop had said when they were finally face-to-face. 'Give you a lift?'

It wasn't a question. Still, Solomon had attempted to wriggle his way out.

'Not sure I'm headed in your direction, Dunlop. If you don't mind.'

Colin Dunlop had grinned, tossed his fag at Solomon's feet, tip still burning, crushed it with his shoe.

'But you're going to see Freddy Dodds, aren't you. Said he'd invited you to tea.'

Of course, Solomon thought then, sweat all along his grimy collar. Not content with stealing his case by stealth, Colin Dunlop had covered the expense of his pursuit by doing another man's dirty work as well. He sighed, considered running in the opposite direction, understood that the time to flee was long past. Then he tossed the car key towards Colin Dunlop as Dunlop had tossed the cigarette butt towards him. Whatever the destination it did have a certain élan to it, riding into the fire in a rival's chariot, hoping that for whatever reason they might be immolated, too.

'You never bloody stand still, do you,' said Colin Dunlop now as he pressed the button on his side to make Solomon's window rise again. 'Been chasing you around like some sort of butterfly these last couple of days.'

Solomon held tight to his folder with its unsigned contract, Thomas Methven and all his antecedents and descendants inside, written out on a rough family tree. He was quite pleased to discover there was still something of the slippery about him, even in his somewhat diminished state.

'Why do we need to go to Dodds's anyway?' he asked, to divert attention from what Colin Dunlop was really there to steal.

'Everyone ends up at Dodds's, don't they,' said Colin Dunlop. 'Especially when there's money looking for a home.'

They arrived just in time for elevenses, turned into a garage tucked away in a dead-end street to find five men and one woman dressed in navy boilers, sitting around on whatever they could find. A firing squad, thought Solomon as they pulled up, should it come to that.

The radio was singing out over the small forecourt, a muddle of chat and advertising jingles, the raucous sound of pop. The whole place stank of rubber and diesel, a sign advertising same-day turnaround on brake pads and oil transfusions fluttering in the breeze. But Dodds didn't just service exhaust pipes and deliver certificates for dodgy MOTs. All of Edinburgh knew that.

One of the mechanics came to assist Solomon from the car. Dodds was famed for his approach to service – anything one wanted, just ask.

'What can I do for you, gentlemen?' she said.

'We're looking for a place to exchange,' said Colin Dunlop.

'Thomas Cook might do it.'

'Not a favourable rate.'

'And what rate might you be looking for?'

'That depends.'

Colin Dunlop nodded towards Solomon. The mechanic looked the Heir Hunter over, took in the fuchsia socks and muddy knees.

'I'll get Freddy, then.'
Solomon didn't even need to ask.
You scratch my back and I'll scratch yours.

Freddy Dodds was a fence. The best in the business.
Everybody in Edinburgh knew that. Never had seen the
inside of a prison, let alone a police cell in Gayfield on a
charge of Breaking and Entering . . . with Intent to Steal.
Dodds turned stuff that had been stolen by other people
into money. Just as Solomon's grandfather once took the
everyday and turned it into the stuff of life. Old shirts and
fur coats. Signet rings and watches. Boots. Blankets. And
Sunday suits. All transformed into rent money or betting
slips, weekend pints or a trip to the cinema for the kids.
Whereas Freddy Dodds turned anything and everything
he could get his hands on into cash.

But even Solomon knew that Freddy Dodds had
branched out well beyond fencing now. His garage might
have been covered in grime, but it could be a very effective
laundry when there were dirty things needing a wash. The
proceeds from casinos. The takings from slot machines.
The income generated in a betting parlour while the punters
shouted the odds. Anywhere that took cash over the
counter and returned the punter something less valuable
instead. Money laundering, that was Dodds's métier. When
it came time for Freddy Dodds to retire, Solomon knew
that his son would rise to even greater heights. He had
trained as an accountant. What better cover could a true
Edinburgh Man need?

Freddy Dodds came out now from behind his glass enclo-
sure, slow and steady, rather like Solomon's grandfather

drawing treasure from his case. Solomon wasn't certain exactly what it was that Colin Dunlop owed to Dodds for which he had become the pawn, but as the fence ambled over, Solomon had a sudden realization of how these businessmen saw him. Not as a fellow professional, but as a debt to own or trade.

'Well, well,' said Freddy Dodds, shaking hands with Colin Dunlop and then Solomon, as any proper Edinburgh Man must. He jerked his head towards Dunlop's car. 'Having trouble with the Mini, Solomon? Your aunt mentioned something about it needing done.'

Solomon twitched inside his tweed jacket. His aunt who wasn't really his aunt, the other person in Edinburgh who had put a summons on his head.

'She could do with a once over, Freddy, if you don't mind.'

'No bother.' Dodds held his hand out for the keys. 'I'll send someone to get her, shall I. Where is it now?'

Last seen round the corner from Iris Fortune's house. Solomon was reluctant to offer up the location. But Colin Dunlop had no such qualms.

'It's on the Southside, Freddy. Parked it there myself.'

Freddy Dodds grinned, gave Solomon a flash of gold – an incisor glinting for a moment in the morning sun. The story in Edinburgh was that the tooth had been fashioned from the proceeds of Freddy Dodds's first ever deal. Cash for gold. Or perhaps it was gold for cash. Either way would work. Dodds took the keys to the Mini from Dunlop and slipped them into his pocket as though sequestering Solomon's last tangible asset with no intention of ever handing it back.

'I heard you were working on a new case, Solomon,' he said. 'Something hot?'

Yes. No. Maybe. Why did Solomon find it so difficult to answer one definitive way or the other, choose to dissemble instead.

'It's a police matter.'

Freddy grinned again. 'They given you a warrant card, have they?'

'Just a favour for a friend.'

Solomon knew there was no point quoting the DCI's name here to warn the fence off. Dodds would always be able to go higher, probably fixed the chief constable's timing-belt.

Small talk completed, the fence turned to the real business in hand. 'Seems you have something of mine, Mr Farthing. Needs returned.'

Solomon tried to ignore the five men and one woman in boiler suits who had moved to stand in a semi-circle around them now.

'I can't imagine what,' he said.

One thousand. Two thousand. Three thousand and counting. Not forgetting all the rest. But Freddy Dodds didn't even mention money. He was after something else instead.

'Small. Wears a blue kerchief. Last seen in the vicinity of Greyfriars Bobby.'

Solomon could not contain his surprise. 'The dog?'

Nor could Colin Dunlop. 'A dog?'

The real reason Solomon Farthing had been ferried to Freddy Dodds's garage without so much as a by your leave.

'Aye.' Freddy Dodds seemed peeved now. He poked a

finger into Solomon's chest. 'Word has it he's with you. That's why I sent Dunlop.'

'But the dog belongs to Mr Scott, doesn't he?'

A beggar man and his trusty hound.

'No. He's mine.' Freddy was annoyed. 'Scottie hires him by the day to increase his turnover. But I'd like him back now, if you don't mind.'

The fence's tooth was gleaming again, but with something more like malice than joy. Still, Solomon held his ground. He knew when he was in business. Word around Edinburgh had it that Freddy Dodds loved animals even more than he loved gold.

'I don't have the dog,' he said. 'Dunlop will vouch for that. But I can get him back for you. If you do something for me.'

Freddy Dodds blinked. 'Oh yes, and what would that be?'

'A certain debt accrued on the Lucky Sevens,' said Solomon. 'Amongst other things.'

It was Freddy Dodds's turn to be incredulous now.

'You are joking, aren't you? Ten K for a mongrel. Nobody would pay that.'

The proceeds of Solomon Farthing's love affair with the puggies and the roulette wheel, tossing cards at a green square of baize.

'What!' Solomon wasn't surprised at the debt, so much as the amount. 'It can't be that much, can it? I thought it was nearer five.'

'My son's been keeping a tally,' said Dodds, gold tooth winking. 'Very good with numbers.'

There was silence for a moment, nothing but the tinny

clatter of the radio playing a happy song. Then Solomon shrugged, his Heir Hunter insouciance coming to his aid. Or perhaps the recklessness of a man who had nothing more to lose.

'Oh well, then, I'm afraid there's nothing I can do. Unless you want to toss for it instead? Your money or your dog.'

He dipped into the pocket of his jacket, brought out a small coin. A sixpence gifted to him by Peter after Solomon had lost the dog in a bet. Dodds stared at the coin glinting in the morning sun. Then he cursed.

'Bloody bastard.'

And it was Solomon's turn to grin. Freddy Dodds might like to deal, but he wasn't a gambling man, at least not in the precipitous manner Solomon Farthing was accustomed to. All of Edinburgh knew that.

Dodds grimaced, rubbed a hand across the back of his neck.

'Ten per cent off the debt,' he said. 'And that's me being very generous indeed.'

Solomon felt a little kick of glee inside at the knowledge that Freddy Dodds was prepared to deal.

'Fifty. And I'll need a receipt.'

'Twenty. Last offer.'

'Not a dog lover, then.'

'Thirty,' said Dodds, lips pinched.

Solomon did a quick calculation. Thirty per cent off ten K brought it down to seven. Easily payable with a twenty per cent commission on fifty thousand, leaving the rest for him. If Solomon could get Iris Fortune to sign, of course. But Freddy Dodds wasn't finished yet.

'You'll get a receipt when the goods are delivered. Not before. And I want him back tonight, no question, or the arrangement's off.'

Solomon began to sweat again beneath his tweedy jacket.

'I can get them both,' he said, taking a blue kerchief from his pocket and wiping it across his face as though to make his point. 'The money and the dog. But I need a vehicle to secure them.'

Freddy Dodds spread his arms wide. 'Well, you've come to the right place, then, haven't you.'

A Lada. A Skoda. A Fiat towed in from Portobello. Except all of them were out of commission right now. Instead the fence was indicating another vehicle, just pulled up to the garage forecourt. Polished. All its trim sparkling in the sunlight. Solomon stared at his new ride. He hadn't known that Freddy Dodds was in the funeral business. Dodds was smiling again, glint of gold appearing from behind his top lip.

'The driver's got a job to do first. Take you where you need to go after.'

'A funeral?' said Solomon.

'Aye. Some old soldier. They wanted all the spit and polish.'

Solomon's heart played its little dance. 'I don't suppose you know his name, do you?'

Freddy Dodds frowned. 'Methven. If I had to guess.'

Three

Solomon Farthing rode to his final reckoning in a hearse, polished wood and silver fittings, glass on three sides wiped until it gleamed. He sat in the passenger seat, holding tight as they bumped and bounced over the Edinburgh sets. He had expected the hearse to proceed at a stately pace. But the minute they'd pulled away from Dodds's garage, the driver had put his foot down.

'Sorry about this,' he said as they lurched around corners and flew over potholes. 'Meant to have collected him at least an hour ago. Don't want to keep the furnaces waiting. Trouble if they get backed up.'

But just when Solomon expected the hearse to plunge uphill towards the centre of the city and out the other side, it veered right instead.

'This isn't the way to the crematorium,' he said, clutching at his folder of paperwork.

'Not going to the crematorium yet,' said the driver. 'Got to do the pick-up first.'

The hearse accelerated towards its destination, deep into a Tory suburb of the city, houses that belonged to Edinburgh Men who wore beige and frequented the Probus, amongst other things. Solomon's heart was pounding so loud he thought all of Edinburgh must hear it as the hearse drew alongside a property he had been to before. Generous driveway and French windows at the back. A lilac blooming on the far side of the road. The house belonging to a dead man. And the original scene of the crime.

As Solomon followed the driver through the front door and into the hall, soiled leather shoes sinking into that familiar pile, he had the startling sense that he might be about to meet himself coming the other way. An Heir Hunter, hair wild about his face, torn cuff flapping, the stink of Fino on his breath, sneaking down this very corridor as he tried a bit of breaking and entering in an attempt to turn his luck. His fingers were fluttering like a thousand butterflies as he entered the living room, found them staring back. Three women sitting in a ring around the dead man as though they were already in a church. Margaret Penny of the Office for Lost People. Margaret Penny's mother, Barbara. Her friend, Mrs Maclure. The remnants of Edinburgh's Indigent Rota, delivering a new service to the needy of the city.

Sitting in.

Wasn't that what they called it? Holding vigil for those who did not have anyone else to see them safely on their way.

Also, there, in the middle of the room, propped on two chairs upholstered in brocade, a coffin with the lid being screwed down at that very moment. And inside that the mortal remains of Solomon's client. Thomas Methven (deceased).

It began with a fight, as it always did, about who owed what to whom and why, three Edinburgh Ladies against an Heir Hunter. It was never going to be a fair fight. The first to mount the battlements was Margaret Penny of the

Office for Lost People, rising from her chair the moment Solomon appeared and positioning herself in front of Thomas Methven's coffin as though she knew Solomon's sole intention was to strip the dead man of all he had left.

'What are you doing here?' she said, adjusting what looked like a fox stole tucked beneath her summer coat. 'This is my case now.'

Solomon edged further into the room, clutching his folder containing Thomas Methven's family tree high on his chest as though to prove his prior claim. Though even he knew his general air of dishevelment did nothing to aid his cause.

'DCI Franklin put me in charge,' he said. 'Suggested there might be a delay at the QLTR end. Paperwork backed up.'

There was the slightest flush on Margaret Penny's neck then, as though she had been caught in something she had tried to hide. An inefficiency at the office, perhaps. Or an attempt to expedite the growing backlog at the mortuary by spiriting Thomas Methven away before he'd been officially signed off. Or maybe it was just because she was wearing a fox around her neck in the warmth of a summer day – her funeral outfit, Solomon presumed.

Either way, Margaret Penny placed her hand on one end of Thomas Methven's coffin as though to reinforce her advantage as an actual government official, rather than someone who was simply doing a favour for somebody else.

'This isn't a police matter,' she said. 'Nothing suspicious in an old man's death.'

'It's his outfit I'm interested in,' said Solomon. 'How the money got inside.'

'The suit?' Margaret Penny frowned. 'What's that got to do with anything?'

'Might mean nothing. Could mean a lot.' Solomon slid a hand into his pocket to hide its flutter. 'Simply attempting to secure Mr Methven's inheritance for the rightful next of kin.'

Margaret Penny waved an indignant hand towards the driver of the hearse, fastening the last screw on Thomas Methven's coffin.

'Well as you can see,' she said, 'it is too late for that.'

Margaret Penny was wearing shoes with a strap across the ankle. The shoes were red. An invitation. Or a warning. Solomon Farthing couldn't be sure. Either way, she was proving an admirable adversary, he thought, in defence of the deceased. He felt his fingertips suddenly hot at the thought that together he and Margaret Penny might rule this city . . . if they could only get on. He flicked his eyes towards the driver of the hearse, wondered whether he might be able to wrestle the screwdriver from his hands and let the dead man out. But when help arrived, it was not in a form Solomon had anticipated – all that remained of Edinburgh's Indigent Rota coming to his aid.

'What inheritance?' said Barbara Penny from her seat in the depths of a dead man's sofa. Barbara Penny was old – well over eighty – was wheezing slightly with every breath, a grey NHS stick clutched in her hand.

'Fifty thousand, that's what I heard,' said Mrs Maclure, blinking from behind wire-rimmed spectacles.

'But I thought he was an indigent.' Barbara Penny sounded indignant.

'Apparently . . .' said Margaret Penny, eyes sliding

towards her mother, then away again, 'we were misin-formed.'

All three women turned to look at Solomon Farthing then, as though accusing him of something he had not even begun to understand. Solomon considered offering them a slice of his ever-diminishing commission as a way to get them to agree to set Thomas Methven free. But then he thought better of it. Whatever their peculiarities, Edinburgh Ladies (unlike Edinburgh Men) were not renowned for being bought or sold.

'I need to find out if the burial suit has something to do with where the deceased's money came from,' he said, trying a different tack. 'If we cannot confirm, all of his cash goes to the Queen.'

'Oh,' said Mrs Maclure, brightening. 'I love the Queen.'

Solomon noticed that she was holding a small posy in her hands, three spring roses.

'What?' Barbara Penny stumped with her stick on the carpet. 'The Queen's got enough already, hasn't she? Let the man see, Margaret, for goodness' sake. No harm in that.'

'Oh no,' cried Mrs Maclure, reaching as though to touch the end of Thomas Methven's coffin, before thinking better of it. 'Don't disturb him now that he's at rest.'

'He's not at rest until they've put him in that furnace,' said Barbara Penny, chest giving off a little whistle. 'Burned him to a crisp.'

'Oh, for pity's sake . . .' Margaret Penny slapped the coffin, a gesture that startled them all. 'If we don't get a move on, he'll miss his bloody slot.'

'Language, Margaret. Please!'

Barbara Penny rattled her grey NHS stick again and they all subsided. The old lady frowned at him, then at Margaret, as though they were children.

'Now,' she said. 'What makes you think this suit is what you need, young man?'

'Just want to find out where it might have come from,' Solomon mumbled.

All three of the women glowered at him then, as though he was a man at the end of a firing squad just before the hood went down.

'Why on earth didn't you say that when you came in,' Margaret Penny demanded. 'Could have saved ourselves this trouble.'

'So you know where Thomas Methven acquired the suit, then,' said Solomon.

'Yes,' said Margaret Penny.

'Sort of,' muttered Barbara Penny.

'Oh no, dear,' said Mrs Maclure, smiling and bobbing her head. 'It wasn't Mr Methven who acquired the suit. We got it from your aunt.'

She arrived then as though she was the Queen, Solomon's aunt who wasn't really his aunt, all dressed for a funeral. And after that, a wake. She swept into the living room like a latter-day Frida Kahlo, hair piled high on her head gleaming like freshly polished steel, speared at the top with a turquoise clasp. She was wearing some kind of robe, black, with Chinese embroidery cascading down the trim. Every one of her knuckles was adorned with a lump of silver. Solomon was sure that he recognized her earrings from his grandfather's old cabinet – two heavy drops of jade.

'Apologies,' his aunt announced as she came through the door. 'I was delayed by some business.'

Turning cash into gold. Or gold into cash, perhaps.

'About time too,' said Barbara Penny thumping her stick. 'We need you to explain to this young man—'

'Ah, you are here at last, Solomon,' his aunt pronounced. 'Dunlop found you, I presume.'

You scratch my back and I'll scratch yours.

Solomon pulled at the edges of his jacket as though to straighten himself out now that his aunt who wasn't really his aunt had arrived. Margaret Penny stepped forwards as though to explain, then subsided as her mother gave her a stare that could have put them all in a coffin. Perhaps he and Margaret Penny had something in common after all, Solomon thought then.

His aunt moved to stand in front of the dead man's wooden box, Solomon Farthing and Margaret Penny parting like the waves to make way. She placed both hands on the top as though she was about to pray over Thomas Methven, sing him on his final journey.

'So here he is, then, Mr Methven. All ready to go.'

'Hang on . . .' Solomon felt a sudden agitation in his chest at the idea that now his aunt had arrived Thomas Methven might disappear into the furnace, no more questions asked. 'What about the suit?'

'What about it?'

'I need to know where it comes from.'

His aunt who wasn't really his aunt turned slowly towards him, frowning as though the answer was obvious and he was the stupidest one in the room.

'It comes from my stockpile, of course.'

Black shoes. Trousers that had seen better days. Sunday gabardine.

The remains of Solomon Farthing's inheritance, piled into his aunt's spare room and kept for forty years, just in case he should ever change his mind.

'It's all still there,' said Solomon's aunt, a graceful wave of her hand.

Blankets and seed pearls. An otter in a case.

'Minus a few items we deemed necessary to donate, of course. For charity, you understand. We didn't think you'd mind.'

'For charity,' breathed Solomon.

As though he was not a charity himself.

All of Godfrey Farthing's worldly goods turned over to the indigent of his adopted city. Another service on behalf of the dispossessed – anything the abandoned might need to go out in, once the end finally came, but did not own themselves. Shoes. And waistcoats. Jackets. And shirts. Or in Thomas Methven's case, a suit, blue like a starling's egg, lining dark as midnight. The perfect burial gown.

Mrs Maclure clasped both hands together now as though she too was praying. 'Such a wonderful man, Mr Methven. It was the least we could do.'

'You knew him, then?' said Solomon, staring at the coffin of his deceased client as though willing him to open the lid from the inside out so that he could explain.

'Of course,' said Mrs Maclure. 'We all knew Thomas Methven.'

'He sold me a life insurance policy once,' said Barbara Penny from her corner of the sofa.

'I didn't know you had life insurance,' said Margaret.

'Protection from thieves.' Barbara frowned at Solomon then. Or, perhaps, at his aunt.

'A stalwart of the flower and vegetable shows.' Mrs Maclure smiled. 'Loved his roses almost as much as his wife.'

She indicated through the living-room window towards flowerbeds crammed with great blooms in pink and orange all up and down the path. Both Solomon's hands had begun with their agitated flutter now.

'So this is Thomas Methven's house?'

'It used to be,' replied his aunt. 'Sold it long ago. But I have an estate agent friend, told me it would be empty. We thought Mr Methven would like to rest somewhere he once belonged before he departed. A small gesture from his friends, in memory of a long and happy life.'

Estate agents, thought Solomon sinking onto the corner of one brocade chair, Thomas Methven's coffin occupying the other. Another type of Edinburgh Man, not that far removed from the Heir Hunter end of things.

'I knew it was you.' Mrs Maclure's eyes widened at the memory of her previous meeting with Solomon Farthing in this very room. 'What a fright you gave me. Thought you'd come to pay your respects. Until you ran away, of course.'

'Nothing new there then,' muttered Solomon's aunt.

Solomon blushed a furious red as all four of the Edinburgh Ladies impaled him with their gaze. His aunt put a hand heavy with silver rings to her hair, as though to adjust it.

'Well, now that's sorted, we can get on with things. Don't want to keep Pastor Macdonald waiting at the crematorium any longer than we must.'

But Solomon Farthing was not an Heir Hunter for nothing. Knew where his loyalties lay.

'What about the money?' he demanded. 'If you provided Mr Methven with the suit, you must know where it came from. It was stitched inside after all. Very neat, too. That's what I've heard.'

'What?' Margaret Penny sat down on the edge of the other brocade chair. 'I thought they found it in his room. Or some bank account or other. I didn't know it was inside his suit.'

'Sewn into the lining,' said Solomon. 'Like a second skin.'

'Absolutely nothing to do with me,' said Mrs Maclure, bending towards Solomon as though about to offer him a bowl of tea.

'Don't be ridiculous,' said Barbara Penny, wheezing again. 'Nobody thought that it was. We all know your sewing's terrible.'

'I arranged it.'

They all looked towards Solomon's aunt then, standing beside Thomas Methven's coffin with the air of an evangelical preacher ready to call down the fire. Except it wasn't a prayer she was opening with, but the truth about Thomas Methven's legacy. Or one version of it, at least.

'You arranged it,' Solomon repeated, his voice faint now.

'Yes,' replied his aunt. 'After we chose the suit for him, I arranged for the money to be sewn inside. There was no other way to get rid of it.'

She did at least have the courtesy to blush then, a slight colouring of her cheeks at the audacious nature of her claim. All of them could imagine a better way to get rid of fifty thousand pounds than sewing it into a dead man's suit and casting him into the fire.

'But why did you need to get rid of it?' said Margaret Penny.

'He didn't leave a will, did he.' Solomon's aunt was somewhat flustered now, fiddling with a great silver ring on her middle finger. 'Unless I've been misinformed.'

'No,' said Solomon. 'You were not misinformed. Thomas Methven did not leave a will. Why on earth do you think I have become involved?'

It was then that Solomon's aunt who was not his aunt showed why she was feared throughout the city – from the east to the west, from the southside to the north – rising in a mighty flame of indignation, earrings jangling, robe swirling as she sought to put her putative nephew in his place.

'And why on earth did you not come and see me when I asked, Solomon Farthing?' she declared. 'I sent word four days ago when I realized you'd been put on the case. Did you bother to come and visit? No, you did not. If you had, everything would have been cleared up at once. Instead I was left to my own devices and this is the result. Poor Mr Methven yet to go to his rest. And the debt still unpaid.'

There was general astonishment in the living room then, the ladies of the Edinburgh Indigent Funeral Rota open-mouthed at this display of wrath from the one member of their little band who was normally so self-possessed. Margaret Penny looked scandalized by the whole intrigue. Barbara Penny, amused. Mrs Maclure a little bewildered at this strange turn of events. Solomon Farthing felt sick like he'd never felt before at what might be coming.

'What debt?' he said.

His aunt who wasn't really his aunt leaned against the coffin.

'The one your grandfather owed to Thomas Methven, of course.'

1918

One

Godfrey Farthing left in the early, early morning like the coward they probably imagined him to be. He had fed Archie Methven all that remained of Stone's brandy to prepare him and wrapped the injured man's shoulder in a fresh field dressing, binding the tender livid flesh until the wound disappeared. Methven was the most lucid he had been for some time, no longer whispering those long strings of names. Instead he followed Godfrey with his eyes, the way a baby watches its mother. Godfrey was not comforted by the injured man's stare. Archie Methven believed his captain would save him. But they had both seen enough carnage by now to know it was impossible for one man to carry that burden alone.

Once Godfrey was done he blew out the flame on the candle, let the smoke trickle into the air. Outside the rain had ceased, the first grey light silvering the walls. It would be a good day for walking, that was what Godfrey hoped. In the semi-darkness he attempted to help Methven from his chair.

'Can you walk, Archie?'

Methven looked back at him, two black eyes searching, before he closed them for a moment, took a breath, pushed from his knees. Then together they were up, swaying, before Godfrey steadied them against the table's edge. They stood there for a moment like some sort of statue sculpted by the faintest early morning light. Then Godfrey led Archie Methven to the door and they began their slow shuffle into the dawn.

George Stone brought out breakfast at 8 a.m. Not bread and water this time, but a last egg fried with fat scraped from the top of last night's broth. Ralph did not look as though he had spent the night considering remorse. His breeches were covered in chicken shit, but when Stone unbarred the door of the lean-to, the second lieutenant was lounging on a pile of filthy straw as though it was the best room in the house. Stone handed over the plate of food, leaned on the door to watch Ralph eat. He noticed that despite appearances, the young second lieutenant's fingers trembled with the cold.

'Where's the captain?' said Ralph between mouthfuls, yolk dribbled on his sleeve.

'Taken the accountant,' said Stone.

Ralph wiped at his mouth with the back of his hand. 'Who's in charge, then?'

'Hawes.'

'Hawes!' Ralph licked chicken fat from the rim of his spoon. 'He couldn't bloody organize a slaughter in an abattoir.'

George Stone didn't smile. He had seen boys like the second lieutenant before, just lads really, full to the brim with bravado until the guns began. Ralph ran a finger round the edge of his plate, sucked it clean. Then he winked at the old sweat, cheeks fresh with the morning air.

'Let me out, Stone. You know it isn't fair.'

'Orders, sir.'

'Whose bloody orders? I should be in charge here.'
Ralph handed Stone the empty plate, held on to it a little
longer than was necessary. 'I'll make it worth your while.'

Outside in the yard James Hawes dismissed the men
from parade in front of the pump, let them fall out for
breakfast. Flint and Walker. Jackdaw and Promise. Not
forgetting Alec Sutherland, the new recruit. A section that
had once been eleven, now reduced to eight. Hawes was
wearing Ralph's revolver tucked into the waistband of his
breeches as he went to check on the second lieutenant still
locked in the shed. The men huddled in a group around
the entrance to the barn as Stone appeared from the kitchen
to join them, carrying the huge black kettle of tea. It was
Percy Flint who brought it up, the matter of the prisoner.

'What shall we do about the sub? Can't leave him in
the shed forever. Apart from anything else it's bloody
freezing.'

Flint was right. All across the countryside there was a
thick cloak of frost – the roof, the fields, the pump all
aglitter. For once the ground was hard underfoot.

'Captain Farthing's orders,' said Stone. 'He'll be back
tonight to sort it.'

'That's what you think.'

Stone whipped round. 'Who said that?'

The men all stared back at him, five pairs of eyes. It
was Alfred Walker who dared to speak.

'It's true though, isn't it. He's left us to sort ourselves
out.'

Stone put the kettle down on the frozen mud, came to
stand right in front of the petty thief. 'Shut your gob,
Walker. It's not up for discussion.'

Jackdaw following up. 'We should wait for Captain Farthing to return, see what he says.'

'Caw caw caw all you like, little boy.' Percy Flint spat. 'He's not coming back, is he. He's done a runner, just like Fortune.'

'Flint!' Stone's bark was sharp.

'We could vote.' Promise's voice was shrill in the cold air. 'Those who want to let him out and those who want to wait for Captain Farthing.'

Flint turned on him. 'This isn't bloody Parliament, you know. Anyway you're too young, even for that.'

Stone put out a hand to stop Promise from responding. 'Captain Farthing ordered Second Lieutenant Svenson should stay in the lean-to until tonight when he returns and that's what's going to happen.'

'He's not the ranking officer right now, though, is he.'

The men all looked towards another soldier approaching from across the yard. James Hawes the ex-meat man, returned from checking on the prisoner to rejoin the fray.

'Christ, Hawes,' hissed Stone. 'You know what he'll do if we let him out. March us up the bloody hill and not down again, just for the fun of it. Set one against the rest.'

'He's done that anyway, hasn't he,' said the temporary sergeant, daring them to disagree.

The men were silent then, shifting their feet on the frosted ground. They all knew that was true. Jackdaw flicked at the black cowl of hair hung across his eyes.

'What do you suggest then?'

Hawes touched his hand to the butt of Ralph Svenson's revolver, let it drop away.

'I don't know,' he said. 'But I won't take a friendly bullet. Not for any man. Not anymore.'

'What the fuck does that mean?' said Flint.

Hawes flushed then, freckles bright on his neck, didn't reply.

'What are you not telling us, Hawes?' Stone's dark eyes were glittering.

Hawes looked away, fingers *tip tapping* for a moment against his leg. 'Ask the new boy. He knows.'

The men all turned to Alec where he stood at the edge of the circle, dog tight at his feet. The boy stared back, said nothing. George Stone moved to stand in front of the new recruit.

'Well?'

Alec shrugged, flicked his eyes away. 'I don't know what he's talking about.'

James Hawes scowled, his eye twitching now. He rubbed a hand across his face as though to stop it. 'There was meant to be an attack, all along the line. That's what the orders said.'

'What!'

The men gathered in.

'Who says?' exclaimed Jackdaw.

'Bloody hell,' Alfred Walker swore. 'And the captain ignored it?'

'He must have had his reasons,' Stone growled. He turned to Hawes. 'Let's see the damn things if you're so certain they exist.'

Hawes touched his pocket then, where he kept his book with the red cover safe and clean.

'I don't have them,' he said.

'But you're happy to rile us up and let the lieutenant go,' snapped Stone. 'What makes you think we want to know about the orders anyway?'

Hawes stilled then, eyes boring into the old sweat as though to drill a hole. 'You of all people know the penalty for disobeying a direct one, Stone. Or have you forgotten?'

Stone glared at Hawes then, muttered, 'Fucking coward. Don't know what's best for your own men.'

Hawes stepped forwards, thick shoulders bunched, neck tight, the colour on him high. 'Say that again, Stone, and I'll put you in the chicken shed, too. Or worse.'

'You can fucking try, soldier.'

Two men nose to nose now, ready for a scuffle. But it was Percy Flint who decided in the end, for them all.

'Let's have a game,' Flint said. 'Call it rec time.'

Ducked over to the lean-to and lifted the bar before anyone could stop him. Not chickens flapping out this time, released at last for their morning scrape. But Second Lieutenant Ralph Svenson, sauntering into the pale sunlight as though he'd had the best night's sleep of the lot.

'Morning, boys,' he said. 'Ready for some fun?'

Captain Farthing and Archie Methven walked and rested and walked and rested until the sun rose over the fields. A thin line of violet stretched out across the horizon as Godfrey stared at the way ahead, one mile further, then another after that, a long vista of beaten dirt and crushed stones disappearing into the distance, nothing to see on either side but endless, empty fields. Their progress was slow, a limping, shuffling gait. It was cold, the rain of the last few weeks turned to frost. As daylight arrived they were off map and Godfrey was starting to wonder if they might simply walk their way back into the trenches from which they had once come.

Mid-morning and as eleven stole near, Methven was resting for much longer than he walked, shivering as though he would never stop. His face was grey, like the tea they used to drink in the trenches, stinking of petroleum or whatever canister it had been carried forward in. Godfrey waited for his accountant to catch his breath once more, thought of that second night in camp, the men gathered around a paraffin lamp aglow with borrowed fuel. He remembered the scent of the barn, cut hay and dirty straw, Archie Methven's voice low from the shadows as Second Lieutenant Ralph Svenson asked him what he planned to do once the end came.

'What's his name, Archie?' Godfrey said, Methven heavy on his arm. 'Your boy back home.'

Methven sagged against his captain, breath harsh in his throat. 'Tom, sir.'

'How old?'

'Five.'

'He'll want to see you again, then, won't he. If you can hold on.'

The accountant gripped tighter then, fingers digging through Godfrey Farthing's greatcoat to the flesh beneath, began again with his dragging, stumbling walk. But by noon they were still out on the open road and Godfrey knew that they could not go on. He stopped to gaze at the empty fields all around them, not a soul for miles. Above them the sun was at its highest point, only a few hours until darkness descended once again. Next to him

Archie Methven's breath came in short, ragged gasps, a man exhausted by his attempts to keep alive.

'Lay me down, sir,' the accountant said. 'Where I can still feel a bit of warmth.'

Godfrey helped Methven to the ground at the edge of the road, the injured man sitting pitched a little to one side, aquiver with tremors from his top to his toe. Above them the curled orange leaves of a beech hedge quivered, too. It was cold, freezing air finding every crevice. Godfrey knew they would not be walking any further now.

'What should we do, sir?' said Methven once his captain had got him comfortable with a greatcoat for cover and a gasbag to lean against.

'I must leave you here, Archie, and continue.'

'What for, sir?'

'To find help, of course.'

Archie Methven was silent at this. They both knew he was used to doing the reckoning. He did not need soft words to understand how things were adding up now in the profit-and-loss account. They were quiet together for a while, the sun's rays stretching towards them across the fields. Everything was covered in a cobweb of frost, the sun too weak to diminish its glitter. It was beautiful, thought Godfrey. Nature's way of excusing man's destruction, whatever lay beneath. He thought of the rabbit that had gnawed through its leg. Then of Alec Sutherland's field with two types of clover, buttercups all along the riverbank. What were the men doing now, he thought, released from their chores? Playing cards in the barn, perhaps, James Hawes keeping order with an officer's pistol on his hip.

Archie Methven slept on his shoulder for a bit and Godfrey drifted, too. When he woke, the sun was low on the horizon once more. He roused Methven with a gentle touch on the sleeve, fed him some water from his canteen, the final half-grain of morphine. The two men sat in silence for a bit longer, until the accountant broke the spell.

'The orders, sir. That the boy brought . . .'

'What about them?'

'What were they?'

Godfrey looked away. Did it matter now, that one of his men knew he had tried to keep them safe?

'To attack,' he said. 'Across the river.'

Archie Methven coughed then, flinched with the pain. 'Will you carry them out, sir? When you get back.'

Godfrey rubbed at a stain on the edge of his tunic. 'I must confirm before proceeding.'

'Isn't that what Fortune went for?'

'I don't trust Fortune.'

'You paid him though, didn't you. For the right answer.'

Godfrey hesitated, taken aback even now at Methven's boldness. What did his accountant know about his request to Bertie Fortune for orders to withdraw? A forgery, perhaps, if he could secure one. In return for a watch. Or a new letter from a superior officer who saw that the end was coming and understood the reasonable thing to do. Either way Godfrey had paid. But not enough, he thought.

'Not that it's done me any good,' he said.

'What did you ask him for? Orders to withdraw?'

Godfrey didn't say anything. Methven began to laugh, a thin rasp in his throat. 'They could have you at the end of a six-man squad for that if they find out.'

'It doesn't matter now, does it.'

'He wouldn't have come back anyway,' said Archie Methven. 'Whatever you asked for.'

'What makes you say that?'

'You're the one who said you didn't trust him.'

'We've known each other a long time, me and Bertie Fortune,' said Godfrey. 'I thought he would do what I asked.'

'Too long, perhaps.'

'What do you mean?'

Methven laughed again, a thin wheezing sound. 'The second lieutenant will have paid him more.'

In the yard, amongst the sharp nip and slide of frost, Second Lieutenant Svenson got Promise to work the pump once again. The A4 boy heaved on the handle till his shirt was splashed and soaked. Ralph ducked and ducked his head again, silver droplets scattering all over as he shook chicken shit from his hair. He rubbed himself dry on a cloth brought out by Percy Flint, shrugged on his tunic. Then he came to stand in front of Hawes, held out his hand.

'Give me the pistol, Hawes. Or have you forgotten what we discussed when you visited the chicken shed earlier?'

Still Hawes paused, glancing towards the other men, Promise shivering and shivering as Ralph's body softened into its usual languid superiority.

'You know the punishment for desertion, Hawes,' he said, his voice threatening.

The temporary sergeant flushed, a painful crimson all about his neck. 'I'm here, aren't I.'

'Cowardice, then.' Ralph waved his hand towards the

remains of the section. 'Or would you rather I did a French on them.'

The decimation of a battalion, one man in ten shot on an officer's orders, for the mutiny of a few.

'What!'

Jackdaw couldn't help himself. But Ralph just laughed, pushed a hand through his damp curls.

'Or maybe I'll get Promise to do it instead. Seems like he could be a decent shot.'

The men flinched then, shifted on the icy ground. Behind them Stone swore, a low curse.

'Bastard,' as Hawes uncurled his fingers from the butt of the pistol, slid it from his waistband and held it out to the second lieutenant as though relinquishing a toy. But Ralph just smiled, took the weapon and shoved it into his holster. Then he reached into the pocket of his breeches, pulled out a crumpled sheet of paper.

'Now, men, here are the orders we've all been waiting for.'

Flipped the paper open in the cold air.

Out on the road, huddled beneath a hedge as the day began to turn, Archie Methven shivered and shivered until he stopped. Then he shivered some more. Godfrey laid his accountant down, with his gasbag for a pillow, covered him in his greatcoat to try and keep him warm.

'You'll remember, sir,' Methven whispered. 'What I asked you. About visiting my wife and boy.'

'Of course, man,' said Godfrey. 'Of course. Till you see them for yourself.'

'And the account, sir?'

'I have it here, Archie. I have it here.'

The notebook with the profit-and-loss account, all written out on neat horizontals, divided by red. Godfrey slid the book from his pocket and held it up for Methven to see. The accountant gazed at it for a moment, closed his eyes before speaking again.

'You must go back, sir,' he said. 'Otherwise Lieutenant Svenson might do it himself. Fire into the grey, I mean. Take the men, too.'

Godfrey put a hand to Methven's arm, as though to reassure him. 'Second Lieutenant Svenson is locked in the lean-to with the chicken, Archie. I don't think we need to worry about him.'

Methven raised a faint smile at this. He had seen Ralph's glee at winning too many times not to take some satisfaction in the second lieutenant's temporary demotion. But they both knew that the lean-to was nothing compared to a desire to win.

'He won't like it, sir,' said Methven. 'Best go back and let him out.'

'You were the one who was shot, Archie. Don't you want to see him punished?'

'It wasn't him who shot me, though, was it.'

'Who did then?'

Methven closed his eyes again. 'It was an accident, sir. I got in the way.'

'In the way of who?'

'Jackdaw, sir.'

'And why did Jackdaw shoot?'

'He got in the way of Promise.'

One A4 boy protecting another. Just as they'd been taught.

Godfrey was silent for a moment. Then he shifted, turned to his accountant. 'Why was Promise waving his gun? He must have known it's not allowed.'

Archie Methven breathed out, a long sigh into the frosted air. 'The second lieutenant wouldn't pay, sir. Only so far a man will let another get away with that.'

'Pay what, Methven?'

'The cap badge, sir. The one you took from Beach.'

The orders had come from the company commander. To attack across the river. To engage the enemy wherever possible. To hold their ground whatever happened. To be the first over. The last to return. It was the end, but not as the men had hoped for, turned by the stroke of a general's pen to dust.

After Ralph had read them aloud there was absolute stillness in the yard, the men staring at the mud frozen now beneath their boots, all around the hard glitter of the frost. Ralph returned the orders to his pocket, buttoned them down, came to stand in front of George Stone, the old sweat, eyes lit with a strange, translucent glow.

'We go now, Stone. Do a recce, get ourselves in a good position. Wait the night then attack at dawn. We'll have their machine gun and a few more souvenirs in time for breakfast tomorrow.'

George Stone stared at his second lieutenant, gave a slow shake of his head. Ralph stared back. Then he turned towards the rest of the section.

'Any man who doesn't want to play can stay in the lean-to. Wait for the battalion to arrive.'

The men shifted inside their heavy boots. They all knew what the battalion meant. Court martial. Every single one. It was Percy Flint who made the first move, shuffling out of the line towards the second lieutenant, leaving a gap between him and the rest. Alfred Walker followed next, a quick step to stand beside Flint. Then Arthur Promise darted across, eyes down.

'Don't—'

Jackdaw's cry was sharp in the cold air. Stone looked at the A4 boy with his cowl of black hair.

'It's all right, son. You can go, too.'

Watched as Jackdaw hesitated, then moved to stand by Promise again, hip bone to hip bone, cheeks stained the colour of wine. The second lieutenant had covered for the A4 boys once. They all knew he wouldn't do it again.

Ralph turned to Alec.

'What about you? Coming to join us? Or going to wander the fields with the rabbits?'

The new recruit didn't say a thing, just stayed where he was, feet firm on the frozen ground, as though he had been planted there long before. Ralph laughed, a single high note.

'Tell you what,' he said. 'We'll play for it. First to pull an ace gets to stay behind. I think you can help with that, Flint.'

The married conscript slid a pack of cards from his trouser pocket, handed it to Ralph. The cards were decorated with black-browed ladies, pink roses in their hair. Ralph grinned.

'Nice pack, Flint.'

Flint flushed. 'What's mine is yours, sir.'

'Thank you, Flint. If the accountant was here, I'm sure he'd agree.'

Stone spat into the manure heap to the side of the barn door. 'What's going on, Hawes? Thought you were meant to be in charge here.'

Hawes didn't reply, fixed his eyes on the tips of his boots instead, fingers twitching as though they would never stop. Ralph ignored the old sweat, sifted Flint's cards from one hand to the next. A soldier's pack – the Almanac and Bible. A ten for the Ten Commandments. A four for the four evangelists. Two for testaments Old and New. And the ace of course, the one true saviour, God in all his glory handing down the luck. When he was done, he fanned the cards out before Alec.

'You first,' he said.

Alec shook his head. 'No thanks.'

'I insist.'

'Not bloody likely.'

There was a sudden burst of cards in the air, so quick none of them realized Alec had done it, knocked aside Ralph's offer and set the pack a-sail. Tens and sevens. Fours and aces. Queens. Knaves. Hearts. Clubs. Diamonds scattering amongst the frozen muck. Ralph stood for a moment staring at the cards about his feet, a boy again, anger in his eyes. Then he blinked, two patches of colour high on his cheeks, reached for his gun.

The dog began to bark. A sharp *yip yip* sound bouncing off the stone buildings of the yard, over and over. Ralph turned the Webley once in his hand, then lifted it and pointed it at the new recruit.

'Keep that dog quiet, can't you.'

A casual kind of gesture, as though he was about to shoot a chicken. All the other men froze, Percy Flint slipping on the icy ground as he twisted his body from the second lieutenant as though to avoid a blow. But Alec stayed standing, hands at his sides, chest open to the barrel of the gun. The barking of the dog crescendoed, a loud *yap yap* puncturing the air like a gun of its own. Ralph scowled, pale eyes fixed on the new recruit.

'Shut that bloody thing up, I said.'

But still Alec didn't move. So Ralph turned and lifted the revolver, shot the dog instead.

The dog tumbled on its back, yelping and squealing, squirming like a rabbit caught in a trap. Promise squealed, too, turned away. Hawes cried out, *flitter flutter* hands upon his ears. Alfred Walker laughed, a high, nervous pitch. George Stone went white as a dead man. Alec made for the dog.

'You bastard!'

But Ralph pointed the gun at him again, arm straight out as he'd been taught.

'Why don't you lead,' he said. 'They like fresh blood, the Jerries. That's what I've been told.'

Methven's skin was like ice when Godfrey said goodbye. Like the sweat across Godfrey's back as he imagined Second Lieutenant Ralph Svenson's fingers in and out of all his precious things. Picking through his captain's stuff like some sort of pocket thief, searching for treasure. Because he was bored. Because war was not what he had imagined it might be. Because he liked to play. Nothing more than another boy soldier. Like Alec. Like Beach.

Now that's really something.

Lying dead in the filth, just as Archie Methven was lying on the empty road now.

'I still think it would be better to get help, Archie,' Godfrey had insisted, as his accountant leaned more and more to the side. 'Hawes will keep the second lieutenant at bay until I've returned. Then you'll see your boy again. And the rest of us will wait it out till the end arrives. It must be near now.'

But Methven had lain back then as though the whole world was lying on him.

'Hawes won't stop him, sir,' he said. 'If it comes to it.'

'What do you mean?'

'They did a deal, sir. Him and the lieutenant.'

'What deal?'

'Safe passage,' the accountant replied. 'For when the moment comes.'

Archie Methven was still breathing as Godfrey walked away, his cheeks and his lips furred as though frost had already set in. It was only from the small puffs of vapour escaping from the accountant's mouth that Godfrey could tell his man was still alive. He watched for a few seconds as he stood in the middle of the road, waiting for one, then another, no more than a heartbeat in between. Then he looked down the road towards where they had been going. Set off back the way they had come.

Two

It began with confusion and ended in disaster. The crawl through a swamp to a river they could not breach. Water too deep to wade through. Nothing on the other side but a bare field of stubble to cover their approach. Some of them had seen worse. Men drowning in mud while their friends walked by. Others left to hang upon the wire. But Ralph could not be persuaded. He had never seen anything like that.

In the end it was George Stone, the old sweat, who went first, squirrelling along at the head of the section, crawling through the frosted grass with his second lieutenant close behind. Stone did not trust any of the younger men to do a reckoning that was worth the name, wanted to make sure that whatever happened they had the best advantage in the end. It took them half an hour of walking, and half an hour of sliding and squirming, soaked from the belly down within ten minutes of setting out. By the time they got to a reconnaissance position, heads down in the grass as they tried to catch their breath, their helmets were like ice, fingertips sticking to the rim. But their bodies were slick to the skin with the sweat of it. An assault on the river at last.

'You are fucking joking.'

Despite what he had seen and done, even George Stone could not believe what lay ahead once he surveyed the task. Less than a mile from the target, the low land in front, the slow incline on the other side. There were bushes and clusters of grass at the top of the hill opposite offering plenty of cover – but only for the enemy. And between them the river, slow and deep, a skein of silver grown on top now.

Stone hawked into the cold ground.

'They'll have us like the chickens.'

'Not if we surprise them.' Ralph's voice had taken on a breathless air.

'With what, sir? A wishbone to keep the bullets off? Or a white bloody flag.'

George Stone had made sure they had both. Wouldn't let Ralph leave until they'd at least got in some supplies.

'We can't fight a sortie without them,' he'd said. 'We'll be blasted.'

Organized the makings, such as they were. Biscuits and tobacco. Ripped sheets for field dressings. Knives sharpened against the handle of the pump.

'And grease your bloody Enfields,' he'd instructed the men. 'No room for jamming.'

If they were going to walk into battle, Stone had thought, they might as well be prepared.

In the yard, the men had packed and repacked, laid out weapons on the straw. Lee Enfields and knobsticks. What ammunition remained. There was even a knife, glimmering in the afternoon light. Officially they still used bayonets, eight daggers gleaming in the dawn as they stabbed and gouged. But most of the men preferred German souvenirs if they could get them. Short-bladed things, nicked and pitted, bought from behind the lines or scavenged on a trench raid, like the one Fortune bartered with Methven, long ago.

Once it was all laid out, George Stone had surveyed the weaponry spread on the ground. A ragged collection of arms, he'd thought, just as they were a ragged collection of men. An assortment of young boys and an old sweat held together by clothes borrowed from dead men, knew that it was a disaster just waiting to unfold.

While the men organized themselves outside, Ralph sat in the captain's parlour, Webley at his hip. His heart pulsed in his throat as he began counting down the hours until twilight, as he counted out his treasure, too.

A wishbone.

A tanner.

A reel of pink cotton.

Laid along the edge of the parlour table, next to the water stain.

The heel of Ralph's boot *tap tap tapped* on the stone floor as he rubbed one finger across the cut on his forehead, the wound a little swollen. Then he began stuffing his pockets with the little treasures, all his own now.

Ralph had made Hawes do the job, lined the men at the pump after the dog had been shot, got them to empty their pockets so that he could see who still had what. In the background the dog had writhed and whined as the temporary sergeant frisked each one, produced the usual medley of matches and pennies, a small screw of tobacco here and there. He got the green ribbon from Alfred Walker. A handful of walnuts from George Stone. Jackdaw had tossed in a shiny brass button, Promise a couple of hips from a hedgerow. Percy Flint offered his gentleman's pomade. Ralph had watched as it all came out, then made the men stand by as he picked everything through. Until he came to Alec Sutherland's contribution. A beech nut in its prickled shell.

Ralph had leaned towards the temporary sergeant then, whispered, Hawes right in Alec's face as he demanded to know:

'Where's the bloody pop ticket?'

Percy Flint shouting, 'Walker, you thieving bastard. Let's see it.'

Alfred Walker pulling his empty trouser pockets inside out for all to see, nothing but a tiny piece of stiffened orange peel dropping to the ground. Beside him Jackdaw had jittered, his black cowl of hair dark against his pale skin. Next to him Promise looked as though he was dead already, his eye sockets huge, his jawbone pressing through. He had a greenish tinge to his face as though he had been sick once that day, wouldn't take that much for him to spew again. But Alec just stood impassive, refused even to flinch.

Hawes had gone to it then, without even being asked. Thick fingers into every pocket and fold of the new recruit's clothes, pulling Alec's shirt from his waistband, forcing his tunic off. As though the boy was the enemy, rather than a man on their own side. When the temporary sergeant was finished, he'd turned to Ralph and unfurled his fist to reveal a pawn ticket, no.125. That small splash of blue.

Ralph took the ticket from Hawes's palm, grinned as he held it to the sun, two tiny eyes shining back. Then he wrapped it carefully in a piece of waxed cotton to keep it dry, slid the slip into his top pocket, next to the orders, buttoned them down above his heart.

It was George Stone who held on to Alec as the boy

struggled and slid on the frozen mud, trying to get his property back, the only thing he had left of his mother. They could all hear him crying as the old sweat held tight, Stone's grip strong enough to leave a crescent of finger marks along Alec's wrist, should the boy live long enough for them to bloom.

'Don't do it, son,' Stone hissed. 'Or he'll shoot you here and now.'

The dog, crying too, had already dragged itself halfway across the yard towards the barn as though to safety when Ralph turned on his heel. Returned to the parlour with its wooden lockbox and its table with the water stain, to lay out the treasure for himself.

Later, when the men were packed and loaded, Alec tending to the dog's wound as best he could while the rest waited until the sun went down, Hawes came to see Ralph in the parlour to let him know they were ready. The second's face was hollow, cloaked in the grey of twilight, strange eyes flicking here and there. Hawes stood at the parlour door as though he didn't want to enter.

'Are you all right, sir?' he said.

'Of course.'

Ralph didn't look at his temporary sergeant.

'We can wait if you want to,' Hawes said. 'See what happens tomorrow. When the captain returns.'

'Why would we do that?'

Ralph's voice was sharp. Hawes looked away.

'The men are ready, then, sir. When you are.'

Ralph nodded. Then he shoved his chair back, an abrupt push, went out in the yard.

All the men were watching as Ralph took Hawes by

the arm, escorted him to the chicken shed, pushed the temporary sergeant inside, dropped the bar across the door. Second Lieutenant Svenson did not want a man who was afraid of blood causing trouble on his foray. But more than that, he had learned one thing on this whole adventure.

Pay one's debts.

James Hawes had sold Ralph the captain's orders. In return for safe passage when the moment came.

Now, with darkness drawn around them like a cloak, Ralph Svenson lay on the bank next to Stone staring across to where the enemy were staring back at him. He could feel it still, fear hammering against his breastbone as he fumbled for the dice in his pocket, turned them over and over again.

'Are they even there, do you think?' he whispered to Stone.

'Let's bloody hope not,' Stone replied. 'Cos if they are, we're buggered.'

Ralph shivered, a sudden ripple up and down his body. 'Why don't we stay until midnight, take them then.'

'And see with what?' said Stone. 'No fireworks here, sir. End up shooting each other.'

'So we wait,' said Ralph. 'Cross just before dawn.'

'We might be dead by then, sir,' said Stone. He wasn't joking. There was ice all across the river, everything stiff with the cold.

Ralph was silent for a moment, considered the relief of retreat, whispering the order to the men. *Pull back. Pull back.* Returning to the farmhouse, the kitchen still warm with the last of the embers, the barn waiting with its soft mounds of hay. Nobody would know, he thought, except the men here. And they would do whatever he wanted now. He squeezed his eyes closed, opened them again to grass grey on the ground in front, frost on his tunic sleeve. All around the darkness pressed against him, while above the sky soared like the roof of a great cathedral open to it all. Ralph shivered again, blood frozen in his fingertips.

If this was not living, what was?

'Dawn it is,' he said. 'The beginning of a new day.'

They waited. And they waited. As though they were in the trenches again. Six men and their commanding officer, huddled together trying to keep warm.

Flint.

And Walker.

Stone.

And Jackdaw.

Promise.

And the new recruit.

Enough for a firing squad, should a firing squad be required.

They attempted to sleep top to tail, like rabbits in a burrow. Hands tucked into armpits. Feet curled beneath their coats. Their breath clouded above their heads as the single stars came out above them, pricking at the sky. Near midnight George Stone handed round a ration and they nibbled on the edge of hard biscuits, took a tot of water mixed with brandy from a flask passed between them before they bedded down again. Soon enough their lips were frosted, their ears and their fingers numb, rifle triggers slippery beneath their fumbled hands.

Stone lay at the edge of the group, listening to the slip and sigh of the men's breath coming over and over as they sat out the hours. He counted in his head. One tin of M&V. One of Nestlé. One pack of tea. Thought of the eggs Promise used to bring him, warm and speckled, held in the flap of the A4 boy's shirt. Next to him he could feel Percy Flint twitching and shifting beneath his coat, praying for the bugle no doubt, that long cool note that would signal all was well. Beside Flint, Walker would be dreaming of the promised land, traversing its golden pavements with a girl on each arm. And Alec, the new recruit, walking in the clover, rabbit trap in his hand.

Stone rubbed his frozen hands against his thighs, blew onto his fingers and thought of Hawes shivering in the chicken shed. That fucking coward. Worse than a pervert or a thief, wasn't even here to see what he had done. What would it take, Stone wondered, to stop the young lieutenant making a martyr of them all? A slow withdrawal, one man after another sliding back through the swamp to the safety of the farm before Svenson woke. But Stone had seen the price for desertion close up, smelt it in his nostrils every day since. Whatever happened next, he didn't want that to be his legacy once the thing was done.

In the end it was Alfred Walker who started it, the men awake again, restless and shifting in amongst the frozen grass as the clocks ticked down to dawn.

'I vote we go back,' he said, his teeth an unstoppable *chitter chatter*, still an hour to go. 'No way we can stay out any longer. Come back once the sun is up and take them then.'

'Shut up, Walker,' hissed Flint. 'We're here now, aren't we.'

Jackdaw joined in, his voice hoarse from the cold. 'I knew we should have waited for Captain Farthing.'

'Why didn't you just stay away, then,' said Flint. 'You had your chance. Could have hidden in the chicken shed with Hawes.'

'What, and get myself bloody shot?'

'You'd know all about that,' Flint sneered. 'If you hadn't shot the accountant the captain would never have left and we would never have been here.'

'You fucking bastard, Flint. You're the one always playing warm-up to the second.'

'We'll all get shot if we stay here.'

Alec's voice was low in the darkness. All the men were silent for a moment. Then Promise spoke, voice shaking, as though to make a joke.

'I bet there aren't even any Jerries over there.'

Flint was suddenly aggressive. 'Want to test it? I dare you.'

'Shut up, you idiots.' Stone crawled over. 'Keep your bloody heads down and be quiet or you'll wake the lieutenant.'

Too late now.

At the edge of the group, Ralph moved beneath his coat, raised his head an inch or so from where he'd laid it on his pack, blond curls in disarray.

'What is it?' he whispered. 'Stone? Are they here?'

Flint was dismissive. 'Promise thinks the Jerries aren't even over there.'

Ralph rubbed at his face with the back of one hand, his fingers too numb to feel. 'Maybe they aren't.'

Stone shot a quick glance at Svenson, saw the boy's face bleary in the grey. 'We could wait, sir, till we know.'

But Jackdaw was too agitated to stay quiet. 'What's the point of this, then, sir? We should go back.'

'Bloody faggots, bloody cowards.'

Flint's face was hard in the low light. Stone looked towards the married conscript, saw Ralph looking at him, too. Ralph blinked, touched his Webley, turned his gaze upon the two A4 boys, their faces drawn with cold.

'Right, well, maybe we should go and find out.'

'What! No, sir.' Stone put out a hand, grabbed at Ralph's tunic. 'It's too dark. We won't find them before they find us.'

Ralph shook him off. He slid his Webley from its holster, the grip cold against his palm.

'Not me, you idiot.'

He turned to where Promise was huddled in the grass behind Jackdaw and the new recruit, pointed his gun at the A4 boy as the A4 boy had once pointed a gun at him.

'It's Promise who wants to know.'

He slid onto the ice like some sort of creature, edging on his belly towards the end of the world. The ice groaned and shifted with his weight, black darts appearing across the silver sheen every time he moved. Behind him, six men lay silent on the bank, the hairs on their arms, on their necks, standing to attention. They could all hear Promise sobbing as he crawled forward inch by inch.

'I can't swim. I can't swim.'

His voice the thin call of an animal crying softly in the night.

'Shut up, Promise,' hissed Flint. 'Or they'll hear you.'

'Bloody bastard,' cursed Jackdaw, spitting the words towards Ralph. 'Let him come back.'

Stone held Jackdaw by his arm. 'Calm down, son. No room here for a fight or we'll have them all shooting before you can say kingdom come.'

'That's enough now, isn't it?' Walker's teeth were *chitter chattering* again. 'We get the joke.'

Ralph crouched at the lip of the riverbank, eyes wide. His heart was hammering again, but his head was suddenly clear.

'You can do it, Promise,' he said, excitement lighting his eyes. 'Keep going.'

The fair A4 boy, limbs spreadeagled, trying to grab at anything to help keep him safe. They all heard the ice as it creaked and shifted once more, the low groan of a beast woken from its slumber. Stone slithered on his belly through the frosted grass to Ralph.

'That's enough now, sir. Let him back.'

'But he's nearly there!' Ralph's voice was eager, the excited whisper of a child.

'Call him back, sir,' said George Stone, his voice serious now. 'Or the other side will hear and start shooting.'

Ralph turned his head to the old sweat, eyes huge and pale. 'Are you frightened, Stone?'

'It's not a game, sir.'

The two soldiers stared at each other in the dark, a young lad and a man old enough to be his father.

'All right. All right, Stone. Just a bit of fun.' Ralph began to call, a low voice thrown out across the skein of ice. 'Promise! Promise! Come back now. That's an order.'

'He's scared,' Jackdaw hissed. 'He won't make it back on his own.'

Flint spat into the grass. 'Bloody coward.'

Ralph lifted his head a little to take a look. Promise was nothing but a shadow now hunched in the dark. Ralph glanced back at Stone, the old sweat's eyes upon him. Then he fumbled at his side to release his revolver, laid it on the frozen grass.

'Look after this for me, will you.'

Began the slow slide out onto the ice himself. But Jackdaw was ahead of him already, crawling into the darkness on his belly to rescue his friend. The ice heaved and creaked with the weight of them, tiny lines appearing hither and thither. Stone cursed, pushed himself forwards too, felt the surface crack beneath him.

'Watch out, lads. It's going!'

Scrambled and slithered back to the bank. He only just made it when he heard the *woomph*. Great chunks of ice upending. The dark water suddenly revealed. The river was deep, flowing swift and strong beneath, closing over the heads of the A4 boys and their second lieutenant, the water a sudden maelstrom of ice and men.

Promise rose to the surface, thrashing like a child tossed into the sea. 'I can't swim! I can't swim!'

Jackdaw gasping and splashing as he tried to grab his friend, reaching for Promise's arms, his sleeve, his webbing, pulling the boy through the thick freezing water, clawing for the bank. Stone and Alec reached, too, grabbing for the fair A4 boy. Dragging and hauling him out of the water, Jackdaw following, retching and coughing, his whole body in a spasm with the cold. Promise was hardly able to open up his fingers when they finally got him clear, grip fixed like a chicken's claw, Jackdaw shivering behind. Stone began rubbing and rubbing at Promise's hands.

'It's all right, son. All right. We've got you.'

Then the gunfire began.

They lay together, faces buried in the frozen earth, six men with their hands over their heads, live fire falling on them like sudden April rain. Bullets bounced off the ground by their heads, off the ice, zipped through the water and stung the grass all around. It went on for three minutes. Then, just as suddenly, it stopped.

The silence then was huge, nothing but blood rushing in their ears, their faces pushed into the muck. Stone's heart pounded in his chest as he twisted his head, tried to do a reckoning. A Jackdaw. A Promise. Lying hip bone to hip bone, one arm around the other. Flint to his right. Alec to his left. Alfred Walker next to him. Then he gave the order.

'Withdraw! Withdraw!'

The men slid and crawled away, wriggling back through the grass to the safety of a willow tree not yet cut to a stump. It was only after a few minutes had passed, the black confusion in their heads clearing, the high-pitched ringing in their ears lessening to a low whine, that they heard the call.

'Stone! Stone! Come and get me.'

Second Lieutenant Ralph Svenson's voice floating towards them from somewhere on the opposite bank.

George Stone cursed, lifted his head a little to take a look, saw the shape of the second lieutenant crouched in the water on the far side of the great black stretch, nothing showing but the pale halo of his head.

'Swim back,' called Stone. 'Swim back.'

'I can't,' came the voice. 'I'm injured.'

George Stone peered over his shoulder at the other men, shuddering and trembling in their soaking uniforms.

'Go and get him, Flint.'

'You bloody go and get him, Stone. This is your shout.'

'You let him out the sodding lean-to.'

'Following orders, just like you were.'

George Stone looked over at Walker. Alfred Walker looked away. There was another burst of gunfire, bullets pattering around their second lieutenant in the gloom. They all heard Ralph's cry as one struck the bank right by his head, throwing up shrapnel and chunks of frozen mud.

'Stone, Stone. Come and get me!'

'Swim back, you fucker,' Flint hissed beneath his breath.

The two A4 boys, Jackdaw and Promise, huddled together, their faces like ghosts. Stone cursed again, dipped his face to the earth, the weight of four years pressing down.

'Christ,' he hissed. 'I can't swim either.'

He looked again at Percy Flint. At the A4 boys. Then at Alfred Walker and the new recruit, all staring back at him.

'What?' he said. 'Do you want to bloody toss for it?'

There was silence for a moment. Then Walker reached into the top pocket of his tunic, pulled something out. A farthing, glinting for a moment in the dark.

The petty thief's voice was so quiet they could barely

hear him. 'Heads we get him, tails we retreat, wait till morning.'

'Walker . . .' George Stone sounded a warning. 'What about the orders?'

'Sod the orders,' said Walker. 'They can wait another day. Waited long enough already and nothing's gone wrong.'

George Stone dropped his head to the cold ground for a moment.

'We can't leave a man behind,' he said. 'What if someone finds out?'

'So what?' said Walker. 'It's only his own rules.'

'He'll freeze to death in the sodding water.'

The men were silent. Then Jackdaw spoke.

'I'm with Walker.'

Flint nodding too, Alec saying nothing. Stone closed his eyes for a moment, then opened them again, looked at the other A4 boy where he shivered and trembled.

'What about you, Promise?' he said. 'It's on your say. We won't do it if you don't agree.'

The fair A4 boy stared at the old sweat, his teeth rattling and rattling as Jackdaw put a hand to his arm.

'You don't owe him now.'

Then Promise nodded – one quick dip of his head. Alfred Walker was looking at Stone as he flicked the farthing into the air. They all watched it turn, once, before the drop. The coin landed beside Walker on the grass, a black spot amongst the frost. Even in the dark they could see it.

Tails.

Three

He came back as dawn approached. 11 November and Godfrey Farthing on the long march home at last, walking down a road that seemed to come from nowhere and go to nowhere, just as the war to end all wars did, too. He knew that somewhere he had failed. Let one man walk away. Left another to die beneath a hedge. But all in the hope that he might yet save the rest from slaughter, before it was too late. A slither through the marsh. Then a wade through that river. Squirming in the grass until they met the falling bullets, one, then the next. It would only be the same as every other day his men had spent on this patch of raw earth, going forwards, forwards, always forwards, doing their duty until the bullet that was meant for them arrived. But now that the end was almost upon them, Godfrey could not help but think of what should come next instead.

He had left a knife with Methven, just in case it should be useful. A German souvenir acquired by his accountant from Fortune, in return for God knows what. The knife was sharp, its blade stocky. It would make a good weapon if it came to self-defence. Methven had insisted Godfrey keep it for himself. But Godfrey Farthing did not want something that he knew had been acquired by Bertie Fortune – every last souvenir, every last piece of notepaper, every last bet or promise his lucky man had ever made tainted now by his failure to return.

Instead Godfrey had tucked the knife beneath Methven's coat, buttoned the notebook and all it contained into his own. He had shaken Methven's hand before he left, the accountant's fingers just like Beach's had been that time. Cold, as though he was dead already, nothing left to do but remove his red disc and leave the green, walk away once more.

Godfrey had been cold, too, as he walked into the twilight, the country he had fought over for so long laid out before him like an uninviting bed. Empty fields. Scrub huddled along a ridge like a grey cloud. The rise and fall of the hedgerows, black and stumped in the gloom. Far in the distance he imagined he could see the silver ribbon of a river calling to him. Beyond that, a fold in the land. And beyond that again, a simple ring of trees.

As darkness began to fall, Godfrey stopped to rest. He sat by the side of the road, on the edge of a ditch, his feet on the frozen remains of moss and dead leaves. He took a couple of walnuts from his pocket, cracked the shells against his knee, let the pieces fall to the ground. The nuts were bitter, the last of a good crop. He washed them down with a piece of ice taken from the ditch, smashed with the heel of his boot, sucked until his lips were numb. When he set off again it began to rain, soft prickles against his skin. It was then that he came upon him. The man who told Godfrey Farthing that the end had come at last.

The man was a soldier just like him, walking towards Godfrey out of the gloom. Not Bertie Fortune returned with everything Godfrey had asked for, but someone carrying treasure nonetheless. The man slowed as he saw

Godfrey approaching, just as Godfrey slowed, too. Unlike Captain Farthing's khaki, this man was wearing grey.

They stopped a few feet apart, staring at each other as though neither had ever seen such a man before. A Fritz, out of space and time, thought Godfrey. Just as he was out of space and time, too. Godfrey hesitated, the thought flickering in his brain of reaching for his pistol, safe in its holster beneath the wool of his coat. Then he saw that the man was walking closer, his empty hand held out.

'*Guten Abend*,' said the soldier when he came to stand with Godfrey. 'Good evening.'

His English careful, but precise.

'Good evening,' replied Godfrey.

He took the man's proffered hand and shook it once. The man slid his hand into his pocket, Godfrey's heart giving a little stutter, before he saw that the soldier was offering him something else now. A piece of cheese cut close to the rind. Godfrey stared at the cheese, dipped a hand into his own pocket and brought out a walnut, offered that in return. Then the two men stood in silence and ate together until all that was left was a scattering of rind and broken shell on the road.

When they were finished, the man held out his hand once again, pulling at the sleeve of his uniform. The man's skin was yellow, like the cheese, the bones blue beneath. He was pointing at a wristwatch, second-hand, the strap worn.

'*Morgen*,' he said. 'Tomorrow. *Kaput*.'

'Sorry?' Godfrey shook his head, confused.

The man kept jabbing at his watch. '*Morgen*.'

'Tomorrow?'

The man began to nod, a grin splitting his face. He pointed again at his watch, at the eleven, let his sleeve fall. He was still grinning as he held out his hand again. They shook once more, the man reaching to pat Godfrey's shoulder. Then gone. Walking away towards the enemy. Except by the time the man arrived, they would not be the enemy anymore.

At the river, as dawn approached, the men slid away from their second lieutenant one, by one, by one. Jackdaw and Promise went first, the fairer A4 boy shivering uncontrollably, his pack all a-jingle, rifle rattling on his back.

'Christ's sake,' Flint cursed from somewhere behind. 'Can't you keep him quiet. Have bloody Fritz at us again.'

Alfred Walker hissed, his teeth chattering, too, 'Shut your mouth, Flint. You're the one who'll bring them down on us, always complaining. Should have put a bullet in you when we got the chance.'

Four men slithering and crawling slowly through the frozen grass, soaked to the bone, their uniforms stained. Alfred Walker pushed from behind, sliding on his belly, trying to put as much distance between him and the river as he could without giving the enemy a sign. Behind them George Stone began with his check, as the rest retreated. One man. Two men. Three men. Four. Counting his men out, just as earlier he had counted them in. When they'd moved away, no more than shadows in the grass, retreating now, he turned back towards the riverbank, to where his second lieutenant lurked somewhere on the far side. He stared across that dark stretch, touched his forehead to the grass for a moment, before he began to slide away himself.

He only made it a few yards before he heard a soft call ahead, Alfred Walker somewhere in the gloom.

'We're missing one, Stone. Is he with you?'

'What?'

'The boy, Alec. Is he with you?'

George Stone looked back towards the river to see a shape moving low to the ground. Alec the new recruit looping his rifle over his head, laying it down on the frozen earth.

'Christ.' Stone began to slide back. 'Alec, what are you doing?'

Ahead of him on the lip of the river Alec had begun to unbutton his tunic, shrugging it from his shoulders until he was wearing nothing but a shirt. Stone moved forwards on his belly again, grasped for Alec's wrist. From across the water there was a call once more, a disembodied voice floating across the ice.

'Stone, Stone. Come and get me. I'll make it worth your while.'

George Stone gripped tight to the new recruit's arm.

'You don't have to, lad,' he said. 'He'll get back.'

'No he won't,' said Alec.

And they both knew that he was right about that. Suddenly Alfred Walker was at Stone's side once more, all agitated now.

'What the fuck's he doing?' he hissed.

George Stone didn't reply. He could feel his teeth chattering, cold in the very centre of his bones. Alec turned to them both, face pale in the grey light, hair a shock of white.

'I'm going over for him,' he said.

Walker swore. 'Don't be bloody stupid. Fritz'll get you.'

But before they could stop him, Alec slid into the river, head first, like an otter, like a boy who was used to swimming wild. Stone and Walker watched, hearts racing in their chests as Alec sliced through the cold surface, and disappeared into the current beneath.

He came home as dawn approached, hot beneath his uniform as the farmhouse chimney loomed from the mist at last. As he turned in from the road Godfrey Farthing remembered that first time, his heart in his throat at the thought of carnage, only to discover Eden, cabbages covered in sacking and chickens strutting in the yard. He thought of his men who were left, what they would do when he woke them and gave them the news. Nothing to do now but count the hours till the bells rang at last. Flint hanging his washing in the grain store. Walker sweeping chiff chaff from the barn. Jackdaw and Promise larking in the hayloft. Stone plucking the last chicken to make them all a feast. Then there would be Hawes hiding in the barn with his book, turning and turning those pages. Alec, his new recruit, wandering the hedgerows with a pawn ticket in one pocket and a rabbit's foot in the other, searching for autumn treats. And not forgetting Ralph, of course, Godfrey's second lieutenant, tossing his dice high in the air and laughing as they fell. Godfrey Farthing's men, safe in their Eden, nothing to bring them harm now.

Godfrey was almost at the yard when he heard it, a sort of shuffling and a dragging, a low whine as he approached. Some sort of creature creeping towards him beneath the hedgerow. He couldn't understand what it was at first. A filthy thing, matted. Perhaps a hare injured in one of Alec's traps. Or a fox grown thin over the winter, pitted and scarred. He was wary, uncertain whether to approach. Most foxes if cornered preferred to fight, would rather bite than surrender. It was only as the thing got closer that Godfrey was able to see that it wasn't a fox, but something more familiar. The new recruit's dog.

Godfrey couldn't remember the dog's name, if he'd ever been told it. He walked towards the creature and it halted in its progress as though aware all of a sudden that someone was there. The creature lay, its flanks lifting in and out and in again, a small cloud of white around its muzzle. For a moment it reminded Godfrey of Archie Methven laid out beneath a similar hedgerow many hours' walk back along the way.

Godfrey crouched, ran his hand across the dog's head, held up its jaw for a moment so that he could look into its face. The dog's eyes glinted, a pair of tiny mirrors as Godfrey reached for each notch of its backbone, one, two, three. The dog gave a soft whine as Godfrey touched its back legs, left femur shattered, bone sticking out from amongst the skin and muscle. The dog had been shot at, just like Methven. No one left behind to stitch its wound.

The yard, when Godfrey got to it, was skimmed with frost, ice turning the mud into some sort of frozen wonderland as a hint of dawn began to show in the sky. Everywhere was silent, nothing but an abandoned mess tin lying by the pump. Godfrey stood with the dog in his arms and listened to the stillness, knew at once that he had returned too late.

He looked towards the sky, a faint echo of grey. It was difficult to know exactly what time it was, whether the men would have gone over already or were still waiting for the clock to tick down. Godfrey wished then that he had not given his wristwatch to Fortune, probably bargained away long since for his passage home. Then he heard a rustle in the dirty straw.

Godfrey found him in the shed, the last man standing, nothing on but a shirt and a pair of britches, chicken shit all over his boots. He had lifted the bar from the door hoping to find his second lieutenant, found Hawes, his temporary sergeant, instead.

Hawes was shivering like he would never stop, a ghost at the far end of the coop. When Godfrey opened the door, Hawes lifted his hands to his face as though ashamed to be seen. Godfrey knew what had happened before he opened his mouth. Archie Methven had been right. Hawes had sold the men to Ralph in return for safe passage, not even there when the moment came.

The temporary sergeant turned away as his captain approached, would not look him in the face.

'They're coming back for breakfast, sir,' he said. 'Once they've shot the rest.'

'Shot who, Hawes?'

But Godfrey didn't really need to ask. Three miles there and three miles back, a fire fight on the far side. If Ralph had taken the section to the river they were either dead in the field on the other side by now, or bogged down and frozen to the earth arguing about who should go first. He came to stand close to his temporary sergeant, could smell the fear lifting from the man, the stink of him like that time in the trench.

'Who shot the dog, Hawes?'

But Hawes just shook his head over and over, fingers *tipple tappling* on his thigh.

'I don't like blood, sir. I couldn't help it.'

A man worn down by war until there was nothing left of what he had been. A man no use to Godfrey, or anyone else. And yet, out of all of them, he was still here. He was still here.

Godfrey left Hawes in the shed because his temporary sergeant would not come out. He knew what he must do. A wade through a swamp. A scramble through a drainage ditch. A crawl to the banks of a river for a reckoning, count out whatever remained. Before he left he climbed the stairs to the attic, brought down a blanket and draped it over his temporary sergeant, placed the dog in his lap, too. He left Hawes a knife taken from the kitchen, the one Stone used to slice the necks of the chickens, wasn't prepared to see one of his men go unprotected again. Also that book with the red woven cover, fetched from Hawes's pack in the barn.

Old Mortality.

Battle pages ripped out at the end.

At the river, George Stone and Alfred Walker lay flat on the bank, straining to see. The water flowed silent in the semi-darkness, ice floating on its fringes, the current strong in the middle where Alec had disappeared. On the far side they heard Second Lieutenant Ralph Svenson calling once again.

'It hurts, Stone. It hurts. Come and get me.'

Another boy in the grip of the freezing water, would not last long now. Stone could hear Walker breathing next to him – in out, in out – the rapid beat of his own heart as though it must burst. Then the petty thief's grasp on his arm.

'There!'

As halfway across, Alec bobbed up again, fair head pale against the grey. The two men watched as the new recruit rose from the water like some sort of merman rising from the sea. The boy's breath was a small cloud against the dark water as he breathed out, then in again, prepared to disappear once more.

On the bank, George Stone held his breath, too, tried to stop his teeth rattling in his skull. He could feel the grip of Walker's fingernails through the rough wool of his tunic sleeve as Alec vanished into the dark water again. Nearly there, he thought, one boy swimming to save another, bringing him home so that Stone could account for them all.

On the far side of the thick rope of water, there was a sudden splash, followed by another. Then a voice calling louder this time as a figure emerged from beneath the lip of the bank.

'Stone? Stone? Are you coming? I'm here.'

'Keep down, you idiot,' Stone hissed between his teeth. 'Keep down.'

But Second Lieutenant Ralph Svenson could tell that something was different now. He moved from his hiding place, buttons glimmering in the semi-dawn, flashing on his collar and his cuff visible as he raised his arm.

'I'm here, Stone! Here!'

His voice louder now.

'Keep back!' Walker cried.

Too late.

George Stone ducked his head, face buried in the frozen grass, as down it came. Lead falling from the sky once again, *pitter pattering* the surface of the river as though it were nothing more than rain. Walker ducked, too, calling out as the bullets struck the water, the grass, the earth all around. And on the far bank, within sight of the prize, Alec Sutherland the new recruit rose from the dark water, straight into the hail.

1921

Stone

They had gathered so that they might get the best view: a thousand men lined each side of that slab of grey stone in the middle of the parade, one empty coffin stacked on top of another and another, all piled on a plinth. Ex-soldiers three deep either side, men pressed front to back and front to back again, as though they were waiting to board a train to France. George Stone could smell them as he stood pressed tight. Damp wool and cheap cloth, stale hair oil and the sweat of folk who did not wash every day. The men were thin, their coats hanging from their limbs as though from a clothes horse. They looked starved. Not surprising after everything they had seen.

The first year it had been a cardboard sarcophagus. Last year, the unveiling of the plinth before him now. One more monument to all the men who had fallen, those who were left standing silent, as the Generals and the politicians marched past. Men who came home to find themselves begging with tin cups, wheeling themselves on trollies where their legs had once been. Or standing on street corners holding trays of matches — one box for 3d, don't strike it above the parapet – all that was left of their hopes and of their dreams. This year, for the first time, it was splashes of colour on all the men's shoulders. Red. Like the flowers in the cornfields. Like Beach when he went down. Stone tried hard not to look, but the poppies were everywhere, stains upon the lapel.

As they waited for the commemoration service to begin, George Stone stared over the heads of those in front towards the memorial, its great grey bulk. He imagined it full of men buried one above the other, a whole pile of them reaching into the sky. But he knew that the coffin on top was empty, like all their hearts were now. In his pocket he fingered the means by which he made his living – two dice and a piece of green cloth – wondered how the game would go tonight. Armistice Day always did prove rich pickings. All those old soldiers used to gambling with everything they had.

It was the scuffle that caught his eye, a bit of argy bargy on the far side of the street. Stone strained his neck to see as one man in a smart coat turned to a silent group on the edge of the pavement opposite.

Disgusting. Shouldn't be allowed.

The men did not respond to the slur, stood silent, shoulders tight against each other, as though they were about to go over the top. But it was something else that caught Stone's attention. Not a flower on their lapels, but small flaps of paper attached there instead. Some pink. Some blue. Pawn tickets pinned above their hearts.

Stone had heard that there might be protests, but he had not expected this. Something that suggested it was not the coats the group were wearing that were for sale, but the men inside them too. He let his eyes wander along the row and back. For a sudden moment he was sure that one of them was Percy Flint, hair smoothed down, parting a white arrow on his scalp. But when he looked again he knew that he was wrong. Flint would never do anything as dignified as this.

*

Parade done, wreaths laid, and the dancing could begin. From London to Liverpool and back again, the most popular celebrations were those in the victory halls. Bands with their trumpets and their big bass drums. Girls with gin rickeys. Beer spilled on the floor. George Stone had already decided to try his luck in the East End, knew there would be less police there. Plenty of ladies wanting a thrill. And ex-servicemen looking for a throw.

He set himself up in an alleyway, down the side of one of the dancehalls not far from the Thames, back pressed against the wall, an old sweat crouched above a playing area swept clean with the quick brush of his cuff. Not cards this time, but dice. Crown and Anchor – the soldiers' sudden death. Stone throwing out his patter.

'Put a little snow on it . . . Make it even on the lucky old heart . . . Are you done, gentlemen, are you done?'

Urging any revellers who appeared at the end of the alleyway to place their bets on his square of patterned cloth. George Stone shook the little coloured dice in his hand, trickled them onto his playing field as he waited for his first round. He sometimes offered three dice to even the odds. But Stone did not want to take any unnecessary risks here. Crown and Anchor was his livelihood now that all the other jobs were gone.

He began at six, as the band was warming up and the beer was beginning to flow. By seven things were tipping his way. By nine the clientele were flushed and swaying as they attempted to throw. George Stone was quids in, the bank flourishing, knew that it would be a very good night. He understood how to put on a show for them – all the young men and girls. Rolled up his sleeves and crouched over the game, hands quick, spewing out the chat.

'Who'll make it even on the diamond or the meat hook . . . I touch the money but I never touch the dice.'

Just as he had when he took the ship home across the Channel once the bells had pealed, tossing the dice against the gunnel until he made enough for a meal. A steak fried in butter. Mashed potato on the side. Now he hunkered beneath the lamppost, cast in its weak pool of light, waited outside in the cold November evening for his latest prey, while inside the boys and girls danced beneath a glitter-ball.

It was the shoes that made George Stone pause. A pair of men's sharp-toed brogues, two tone. Next to him, two women wearing T-bars, one black, one cream, buckles glinting in the light. One of the women was saying something.

'Oh, do let's, Alfie.'

The man laughing, in a way that made you want to join in. 'Why not. Might as well have a whirl.'

Stone recognized the laugh at once. Alfred Walker, the section's petty thief, come out to play with a girl on each arm.

'Stone! Bloody hell.'

The look on Walker's face when Stone stood to show himself was worth the loss of a game or two. Both men shook hands as though they might never stop while the ladies giggled behind. It was a small reunion, but the first George Stone had ever had. It was strange, he thought, staring into the face of this boy he used to know so well, how Walker had become another person altogether, his past self some sort of ghost from which he had walked away. When they were done being amazed, Stone turned to introduce himself to the girls.

'George Stone, ladies.'

'Dorothea.' The girl with the black shoes held out her hand for Stone to take. 'Dottie for short.'

Dorothea was young, nineteen perhaps, hair that fizzed in the lamplight, a fox fur draped about her neck. She had a ribbon tied around her forehead. Green, of course. The other girl was younger, barely eighteen, perhaps not even that. Cream shoes and a skirt skimming her knees. Walker said she was a friend of Dorothea's, come to celebrate the Armistice like all the young folks of the day.

'Daisy,' said the girl, holding her hand out for Stone to take so that he could see the bangle shining gold about her wrist. 'Daisy Pringle.'

As though she was some sort of flower herself.

'The ladies want to throw, Stone.' Alfred Walker laughed again. 'Treat them gently, won't you.'

Then they began.

Walker placed a tanner on the diamond, a penny on the club. The two ladies both put down a thruppenny bit, one on the heart, one on the diamond, too. The coins had been polished so that they glinted in the lamplight, made Stone think of Jackdaw and all his shiny things. Stone handed Walker the dice first. The petty thief shook them in his hand, pretending to blow on his fingers before throwing, made a score on the club, got back his penny, plus a penny from the bank. Both girls took their turn,

Daisy winning with a squeal, Dorothea losing with a small frown. Then they played some more.

The game wound on in a swift to and fro of bet and counter bet, George Stone's hands quick, lining his treasure along his side of the cloth so that they could see. Pearl buttons. A half-crown. A small round of scented soap.

'Come and put your money with the lucky old man . . . are you done, gentlemen? Are you done, ladies? Are you all done?'

Then, towards the end, he drew it from his pocket. An orange, bright amongst the grey.

Walker whistled when he saw the fruit. 'Where'd you get that from, you bugger?'

Stone just smiled. He had his ways and he had his means. Dorothea and Daisy giggled, urged Alfred to have another go. He paused for a moment, then opened his jacket and took something from the inside pocket. A wishbone, tied at the end with a piece of pink thread.

'Is that it?'

Daisy's voice had a little whine to it. But Dorothea hushed her with a grip to her arm. George Stone stared at the good luck token, a sudden quiver in his hands. The old sweat could feel the cold contraction in his heart as he saw again the men that were left standing in a circle beneath the naked trees. The crackle of walnut shells beneath their boots as Godfrey Farthing gave the order. The silence as one by one they knelt to rummage in a dead man's clothes. Stone's fingers felt sticky as he remembered the treasure:

A wishbone;

A tanner;

A reel of pink cotton.

Wiping his hands on his tunic again and again before they dug the hole. Their knees had been black by the end, after they'd taken turns to scratch out the grave, rolled a dead man into it face first before covering him over.

None of them had spoken of it after. Not when they walked away across the fields. Not when they met Hawes standing on the far side of the pond. Not when the bells rang out across the empty land later that morning, even though it wasn't a Sunday, the end suddenly arrived. That had been the deal, George Stone thought as he dipped a hand into his own pocket now. No one says a thing. Not now. Not ever. Nothing to do but let it eat the soul. And each item returned to the man to whom it had belonged, as though in payment for everything they had done wrong. Except the wishbone, of course, property of one Bertie Fortune, who never did return to save them, from wherever he had gone.

George Stone stared at the wishbone where Walker had laid it on the diamond. Then he took his own treasure from his pocket and laid that down, too. They were all silent as they stared at the old sweat's offer. A cap badge, glinting in the lamplight, small lion raising its paw.

Alfred Walker swore.

'Bloody bastard. You had it all along. Where'd you get it?'

'Fortune had it,' said Stone, staring at the petty thief with his black eyes. 'Got it from the lieutenant in return for news about the orders. Swapped it with me for an orange and a tin of syrup.'

'For Christ's sake, Stone.' Walker's eyes were wild now. 'Why didn't you give it to Promise? Or back to Svenson. Could have saved the whole bloody mess.'

'Nothing was going to save us,' said Stone then, gathering in his dice, the green cloth by its corners. 'That boy always wanted to go to war. He got what he deserved.'

The three young folk left without playing a last round. Alfred Walker, the petty thief. His girl, Dottie. Her friend, Daisy. Hurrying away into the future, whatever that might be. Stone stayed for a few minutes gathering in his treasure. A penny and a thruppenny bit. A cigarette and half a crown. He left as he had arrived, sliding from the alleyway into the crowd, a heave and swell of young men and girls swirling in front of the dancehall, sweaty and elated at the thrill of being alive. He was almost home, down on the far side of the river, when he came across another ghost. Coming out of a pub alive with men holding pint glasses and beer bottles, jostling against each other in a raucous, jovial crowd. Jackdaw. His face pale, eyes huge, still lost somehow without Promise by his side.

George Stone knew that this pub was one where men came to meet men, seeking solace, amongst other things. He'd often come here and waited on the far side of the street, to see if the boy would appear. Now his hand tightened around the little cap badge in his pocket as he began to follow Jackdaw through the crowd. Jackdaw was quick, a young man slipping between the gaps, disappearing then appearing again, his sleek cowl of black hair. Stone pushed his way through, stocky shoulders pressing against damp wool here, the stink of sweat and coal. He thought he might not be able to clear the space between them, would watch Jackdaw vanish like all the young men who had gone before. Then there was a sudden cheer as men with pawn tickets on their lapels appeared to join the throng, marching in a mock parade towards the bar. Jackdaw hovered for a moment on the edge of the crowd, looking for a way through, and Stone caught him then, brushed against the younger man's coat, felt it once beneath his thumb before he let it go.

Jackdaw always had been the one who wanted a medal. Not for him, but for his friend. Except George Stone knew it was never soldiers like them who got the brass. It was men like Second Lieutenant Ralph Svenson. Or Captain Godfrey Farthing. Silver crosses with a crown on each corner, a ribbon in white and purple silk.

For Gallantry.

Or something like that.

There weren't many things Stone could do to make things better. But he could do this. A small thing, dropped into a pocket, back where it belonged at last. A lion raising its paw and the motto of the London Scottish.

Strike Sure.

PART SIX

The Inheritance

Godfrey Farthing
b.1893 d.1971

|

Robert Farthing
= Else Gold

|

Solomon Farthing
b.1950 d.

Archibald Methven   Alec Sutherland   Daisy Pringle
= Mabel Kerr   = Airman

(adopted)

Tom   Thomas Methven   Iris
b.1913 d.1918   b.~~1920/21~~,   = Bill Fortune
                    1918 d.2016

2016

Records, if one can be bothered to dig, tell their secrets, all laid out in black on white. Who paid whom, with what, and when. Sometimes even why.

Solomon Farthing recognized the book immediately when his aunt who wasn't really his aunt pulled it from beneath her Chinese robe. One of Godfrey Farthing's ledgers, a thin volume with an ancient leather spine, inside the truth about Thomas Methven's fifty thousand. Or at least a version of events.

'I found it after you left, Solomon,' said his aunt. 'When I was clearing the place.'

Of a shirt without a collar. A fur coat made of squirrel. A brass cornet dented at one end.

'But I studied his ledger at the time,' Solomon protested. 'There was no mention of a debt owed to a Thomas Methven.'

His feet in their fuchsia socks were roasting now at the idea that he might have missed fifty thousand back in 1971, for a completely different start in life.

'That was a different account,' his aunt replied, placing her hand on the book's cover as though to demonstrate her prior claim to whatever it contained. 'Godfrey kept this one hidden in the glass cabinet, on the shelf beneath the ladies' gun.'

Pearl inlay for a handle, dark eye pointing at Solomon's heart. Camouflage of a sort.

'But what has this to do with poor Mr Methven?' Mrs Maclure sounded bewildered.

'Probably nothing,' Barbara Penny muttered from her seat in the depths of the sofa.

Solomon's aunt frowned at this interjection, flipped the ledger open to the first page, smoothed it down with one sweep of an embroidered cuff. Her hair was gleaming like a freshly sharpened blade as she fixed her eyes upon the small congregation.

'Well,' she declared. 'Do you wish to see or not?'

All the ladies crowded round then. Margaret Penny in her red shoes, dead fox draped about her neck. Mrs Maclure still clasping her posy of spring roses, somewhat wilted now. Even Barbara Penny, grumbling and wheezing like an old accordion as she heaved herself to a standing position with the aid of her grey NHS stick. Solomon had to fight for his place by the coffin – a dishevelled Heir Hunter and the remnants of Edinburgh's Indigent Rota gathered around Thomas Methven's wooden box as though whispering a few parting words to the dead man before he was finally carried out. But it wasn't prayers or even secrets they were concerned with at the last. Rather row after row of copperplate – all the *Ins* and all the *Outs.*

The first page of the ledger contained one neat entry after another in Godfrey Farthing's careful script. Each line began with a total inscribed on the left, a sum copied across from the ledger Solomon used to watch his grandfather tot up at night. This was followed by a simple calculation – one tenth of the week's takings deducted – then a new balance noted on the far right of the page. The next page was the same. And the one after that. A tenth of everything Godfrey Farthing ever earned, siphoned off over fifty years of running his pawnshop, until the old man got a cough one day, was laid out in his own coffin the next.

'It must be thousands,' breathed Mrs Maclure.

Possibly fifty, thought Solomon. Or something very near.

'But what does it mean?' said Margaret Penny, fox head dangling close to the ledger as though it wished to get a good look, too.

'Can't you tell?' Barbara Penny stomped her stick on the carpet. 'It's a tithe, of course.'

'For the church!' beamed Mrs Maclure, raising the three spring roses to her cheek. 'He always was very devout, Mr Farthing. Went every week.'

Our Father who art in heaven . . .

Incense and candles dripping. Grey stone rising. The touch of an old man's finger to the cold of the martyr's cross. But despite the truth of Mrs Maclure's declaration, Solomon Farthing could tell by the giddy eddies of his heart that this was not the reason his grandfather had set aside one tenth of all he'd ever earned, year after year, after year.

As though to confirm that his instinct was correct, Solomon's aunt dismissed Mrs Maclure's suggestion with a snort.

'Don't be ridiculous,' she said. 'No one gives their money to the church anymore. Too many bad apples, spoiled it for the rest.'

'Who did he leave it to, then?' Margaret Penny demanded.

But her mother was ahead of them all, as befitted an old lady who had spent her life making every penny count. 'Someone called Mabel. That's what it says here.'

There, at the bottom of each page, a running total of all the deductions. And next to that the name of the intended recipient.

Mabel Methven née Kerr.

Money set aside for a rainy day, perhaps. Or a new hat. A smart pair of gloves. Or to pay for a child that never had been hers. Beneath his fluttering fingers Solomon Farthing felt the rough weave of a folder of paperwork, inside a newspaper cutting offering a child for sale.

WANTED: Home for a baby boy, 6 months old. Total surrender.

As though signalling the end of a war.

He saw again his grandfather standing on a village green, still wearing his khakis, handing over a child to begin a new life.

'I'm assuming this Mabel is related to our Thomas?' said Margaret Penny, her voice as dry as the finest Fino.

Solomon looked up, found himself face-to-face with Margaret Penny's fox, black eye winking at him as it caught the light. Yes, no, maybe, he thought.

'Sort of,' he replied.

Everything came out then: all Solomon Farthing's carefully acquired paperwork spread across the top of the dead man's coffin. A birth certificate for a boy born to a Daisy Pringle in 1918. A field postcard from a soldier to the girl he left behind. An advert cut from a newspaper in 1919 offering up a child. Then there was the flyleaf from a Bible detailing an unofficial baptism – a baby boy who came in as one person and left as someone else. Also a pawn ticket, no.125, that small slip of blue, the prize that connected it all.

'Goodness,' said Mrs Maclure, peering at the treasure trove strewn across Thomas Methven's last resting place. 'You have been busy.'

'What's all this rubbish?' demanded Barbara Penny, her chest whistling with a single high note, as though she preferred the past to be hidden, rather than laid out on display for all the world to see.

But Margaret Penny seemed enlivened by the ephemera of Thomas Methven's life. As though suddenly he had become a real person, rather than just another case.

'Is this his family tree?' she asked, indicating Solomon's crumpled piece of paper with the rough sketch of where Thomas Methven had ended and how he had begun.

'Yes,' said Solomon.

No point in hiding anything now.

Margaret Penny traced her finger from Thomas Methven's dates up the dotted line to those of his adoptive mother and father, Archibald Methven and Mabel Methven née Kerr. Then she ran it horizontally towards the names Daisy Pringle and Alec Sutherland, Thomas Methven's real parents as far as Solomon Farthing was concerned. After that she came back down, one solid vertical line descending from Daisy Pringle to her second child – a girl called Iris Fortune, Thomas Methven's half sister, his living next of kin.

'So you found a relative to claim the money, then,' Margaret Penny said.

For a moment Solomon Farthing could not tell whether she was happy at the outcome, or somehow bereft at losing a client she had believed her own.

'Well, Mrs Fortune hasn't signed yet,' he mumbled. 'A small matter of provenance to sort.'

'What do you mean?' Margaret Penny's reply was sharp.

'She wishes to know where the money came from,' said Solomon. 'Whether it's dirty or whether it's clean.'

'Oh, Iris,' sighed Mrs Maclure. 'Now there's a difficult woman. Always will say black if you say white.'

'Well,' said Barbara Penny, giving her stick a shake. 'If the cash did originate with Godfrey Farthing, it couldn't have come from cleaner hands.'

Solomon tucked one flapping cuff inside the sleeve of his tweed jacket as though compelled to smarten up now that his grandfather's good name had been invoked.

'You knew him, did you?' he said, though he didn't really need to ask.

'Oh, yes,' said Barbara Penny. 'Used to give me an excellent rate for my silver apostle spoons whenever I was short.'

'Very generous with the poor.' Mrs Maclure nodded her agreement. 'Always let them have their coats back for a Sunday service.'

'Told a good story,' said Solomon's aunt, her face suddenly soft.

Solomon felt affronted then, as though he was a boy again, left out of some secret circle of acquaintance in which his grandfather had been another man entirely from the one that he recalled.

'What stories?' he said. 'He never told me any stories.'

Not at bedtime. Or at any other time, if it came to that. His aunt made a dismissive gesture in his direction.

'You only had to ask, Solomon. But you were too caught up in your own business most of the time.'

Scrapping. And thieving. And trading cigarette cards for ha'pennies. Throwing jacks against the wall. An orphan boy in short trousers ducking and diving his way through the closes and passageways of Edinburgh, while the girl who was supposed to be looking after him sat on the steps of a pawnshop licking at a lollipop, eavesdropping on her mother and an old man telling it all.

'Well, the story I want to know is why Godfrey Farthing left his money to Thomas Methven's mother,' said Barbara Penny. 'What was their relationship anyway?'

It was then that the young man appeared.

He arrived all out of breath, holding a packet of pink wafer biscuits to celebrate an old soldier's last moments before the coffin and its occupant were burned for good.

'Am I too late?' he said.

'No,' said Solomon's aunt, a wry tone to her voice. 'Mr Methven seems to be having trouble getting to his ultimate destination. He has been delayed by this gentleman.'

She indicated Solomon, where he sat leaning against the corner of Thomas Methven's coffin, mopping at his forehead with a blue kerchief. The young man blinked at the unexpected guest. Solomon Farthing, not part of the Edinburgh Indigent Rota. At least, not yet. He came over and held out his hand.

'How nice to see you again,' he said. 'Pawel. We met at the nursing home.'

The boy with the lovely brown eyes.

'And what might your role in this drama be?' demanded Margaret Penny, tucking her fox inside her lapels.

'Pawel did the honours with the needle,' said Solomon's aunt, small gleam of a smile. 'He's got a very neat stitch.'

Pawel blushed at the compliment. 'Just a favour, for a friend. We all loved Mr Methven. Wanted to help at the end.'

'Why on earth did you sew the money inside his suit anyway?' asked Margaret Penny. 'Couldn't you have just handed it over? It would have paid for his funeral, at least.'

'And my new hat,' grumbled Barbara Penny.

'And the flowers,' said Mrs Maclure. 'They cost an absolute fortune these days.'

'Who would I have given it to?' said Solomon's aunt, raising her arms to the ceiling as though to call on a higher power than even she might wield. 'It belonged to Mabel Methven. She never took it, so it belongs to Thomas Methven. And Thomas Methven is dead.'

They all looked toward the coffin then, as though to remind themselves of that fact.

'You could have kept it,' mumbled Barbara Penny. 'I would have done.'

'If you'd told me about it back then, I might have been able to help get it to the rightful owner,' Solomon complained.

He still felt aggrieved at the idea that his grandfather had accrued a fortune and not passed it on to him.

'Oh, for goodness sake!' Solomon's aunt who wasn't really his aunt dropped her hands and rapped them on the coffin lid. 'I tried to get in touch with you at the time, Solomon. But who knew where you were, always flitting from one place to the next. In the end I wrote Mr Methven a letter offering the money to him. Never did get a reply. Probably tore it up and scattered it on his compost heap, if those rose bushes are anything to go by. They look as though they've been well fed.'

There was heavy silence in Thomas Methven's living room at the idea that the dead man had once turned down a fifty-thousand inheritance to cultivate his roses instead. Then Mrs Maclure sighed.

'I still don't understand,' she said. 'Why would Mr Farthing save all his money to give to Mabel Methven. Was she one of Mr Farthing's customers?'

'Not quite . . .'

They all looked towards Pawel then as he rummaged in his pocket, took something out. A notebook, its pages stiff with age, blue horizontals and red verticals inside, amongst other things.

'It belonged to Mr Methven's father,' Pawel said, handing the book to Solomon. 'His name's on the inside cover. You were asking if he'd left anything else behind. I found it after you'd gone.'

A notebook hidden in the underwear drawer of one of the nursing home's other inhabitants.

'Mr R. had it,' said Pawel. 'Seems he likes to borrow other people's stuff.'

Solomon remembered it then, an old man winking at him as he shuffled down the corridor at the nursing home, eyes a sudden startling blue. He turned the little notebook in his hand, saw how it fitted neatly in his palm.

'Do you know what it is?' he asked.

'It's a story,' Pawel smiled. 'I'll tell it, if you like.'

Records, if one can be bothered to dig, tell their secrets, all laid out in black on white. Who served with whom and when and why. Sometimes even what they did next.

It was Pawel who did the explaining, as the ladies of Edinburgh's Indigent Funeral Rota drank it all in.

'I helped Mr Methven with the research,' he said. 'All the men his father served with. What happened to them in the end.'

Ten men, plus their commanding officer, of course. Captain Godfrey Farthing in charge till the last. Ten lines on a tree that spread for some and withered for others, none of them knowing from day to day what might come next. Not a chart fully tabulated, all boxes complete. But a story that would resonate down the line if anyone chose to tell it, speaking across the generations to people who weren't even conceived of yet.

It was like doing the Reckoning, Solomon thought, as he turned the stiff pages of the little notebook. All the soldiers he had stumbled across on his journey into Thomas Methven's past, counted out then, counted back in again now.

Archibald Methven, married to Mabel. An accountant after all, just as Eddie Jackson at the foundling school had suggested, if the neat record in the notebook was anything to go by, a thorough list of who owed what, to whom, and why.

There was the school teacher's namesake, Private Edward Jackson, listed in the notebook as Jackdaw, just as Solomon had known him, too.

Also Bertie Fortune, Iris Fortune's father-in-law, the man with the cheery grin and the ill-fitting suit, a section's lucky man.

Somehow it didn't surprise Solomon when the next name he came to was *Hawes, J.*, breath catching for a moment in his throat as he remembered Andrew making his mark, with those strange 'i's and odd 't's, noting the acceptance of a suit in return for a lucky sixpence. Plus three medals. A Star. A War medal. One for Victory, too.

Everybody was connected, one way or another, that was what he thought.

There were several other men listed in Methven's notebook whose names Solomon did not recognize. A Private Percy Flint, owner of a reel of pink thread. An Arthur Promise and a George Stone – someone who only ever bet walnuts, as though that was all the men had to eat at the end. Also an Alfred Walker, bet a wishbone, won a green ribbon.

'Alfred Walker you say?' Barbara Penny wheezed and flapped her hands from the corner of the sofa at this news, had to be calmed with one of Pawel's pink wafers before they could go on.

'The second lieutenant went by the name of Ralph Svenson,' Pawel said. 'One of the only men to receive a medal. Mr Methven and I found him in the victory rolls.'

A Military Cross. Silver, on white and purple silk, four crowns on the four tips, east, west, south, north.

'What was the medal for?' Solomon asked.

'Gallantry,' said Pawel. 'Or something like that.'

A skirmish at the last. Two dead. Bloody unlucky.

'Your grandfather was cited for one, too,' Pawel said,

glancing towards Solomon with those soft eyes. 'We found an extract from the *London Gazette*. Seems it was never claimed though. Sent to a school in the north of England instead, near the border. Do you know it?'

A school for foundling boys, thought Solomon. Counted out, then counted in again. He read out the last name in the notebook:

Alec Sutherland.

Bet a pawn ticket. Lost it all.

'Thomas Methven's real father,' said Margaret Penny, eyes alight. 'Do you know what happened to him?'

'Vanished,' replied Solomon. 'According to his service record at Kew. One of the missing, his body never found.'

Solomon's aunt took a deep breath, then exhaled, laid her hands to rest on the coffin lid, heavy with their silver rings.

'Well,' she said as though everything was sorted now. 'That explains it.'

'Explains what?'

'Why your grandfather was paying.'

The debt, of course. The debt. Fifty thousand sewn inside a dead man's burial gown, in return for the loss of a father who never would come home.

'This doesn't prove anything,' Barbara Penny grumbled, waving towards the little notebook. 'Only that they knew each other, played a game once.'

Solomon's aunt put a hand to her hair. 'Yes, but it chimes with a story Godfrey told, to my mother. About what happened at the end.'

'What story?' Barbara Penny said. 'One can't decide about money on a story.'

'That he shot a man once,' said his aunt, readjusting the spear of her turquoise clasp as though it might prove a useful weapon. 'Murder. That was what he called it.'

Godfrey Farthing, not a hero after all.

1918

The land lay flat and silent as Godfrey Farthing finally got near. A mile away from the river. Then half. Then a bit closer still. The ground was frozen as he approached, grass grey about his feet. Nothing to hear but a single bird singing above him, somewhere out of sight and reach.

Godfrey stopped when he had a few hundred yards of marshland to cover, wound throbbing beneath his shirt as he wondered whether to go forwards or whether to go back. He knew it was his duty to try and bring them home, whatever remained of his men. Their red discs and their green. Their cap badges and their pocket books. Uniforms. Belts. And bones. But Godfrey Farthing's heart was in his throat now at the thought of what might greet him – just as it had been when he'd first marched his men to safety down that muddy lane. Not cabbages, or an apron flapping on the line this time. But all that was left of his section slaughtered like the chickens, laid out upon a river's edge.

Godfrey pressed his belly to the bottom of a frozen drainage ditch, trying to calm the frantic *one two* of his heart. For the first time since he had crossed that short roiling Channel in a boat full of men, he understood. This was what his mother must have felt when she watched him march away to war. That small thread of fear inside that the worst might happen before her boy could make it home again.

He reached for his weapon, released it from its holster, put the cold grip in his hand. All around an early morning fog had gathered, everything indistinct, nothing to see but the immediate ground in front. As Godfrey began to slither forwards again, something dug into his side – the black half-shell of a walnut, forever in his pocket, never yet set sail on the pond. It was then that he saw them. Ghosts heading in his direction, moving silent through the frozen grass.

Mist clung close to the ground like gas in a trench as Godfrey peered towards the apparitions inexorably sliding his way. Khaki or field grey? Old men or boys? He found it impossible to tell, nothing to hear but the soft *clink* and *jink* of weaponry sounding through the foggy air as they slid by, barely a yard or two in front. Godfrey held his breath as they passed, started with his counting:

One soldier.

Two soldiers.

Three.

Praying it was all that was left of his section on which a captain could rebuild. Rather than the enemy on manoeuvres, crossed the river for one final skirmish before the bells began to peal. Men in *Feldgrau* headed towards the farmhouse and James Hawes in the chicken shed, guns held out in front. The soldiers were almost gone, Godfrey about to turn and follow, when he felt the knife at his throat. The prick of a blade all nobbled and pitted on the handle, sharpened to a glitter at the top.

'Not a word, or I'll gut you.'

One slice across his neck, like a chicken bleeding out.

Thick fingers tasting of dirt and the faintest hint of apples, forced his face into the earth. Then there was the breathing right in his ear, as though it was inside Godfrey's own head, his sudden realization that this was where it was going to end. Never would live long enough to hear the clear note of the bell ring out across the empty fields. Or to celebrate, champagne mixed with brandy, cherry on the side. Nothing left of Godfrey Farthing but a body laid out in a drainage ditch, blood all along his collar, a field postcard and a notebook buttoned over his heart.

Then the weight suddenly lifted, Godfrey's whole body light as the blade disappeared, too. He choked and touched a hand to the chill of his bare skin, as beside him another man fell back, eyes wide in the grey light as though he had seen a ghost himself.

The two men lay gasping on the frozen turf as though they were fish landed from a river, almost drowning in the air. It was Godfrey who spoke first, his voice ragged, words hoarse as he spat dirt from his lip.

'What the hell, Stone.'

The old sweat sprawled next to him, white rime about his mouth. Between them a knife lay abandoned on the ground. George Stone swore, his voice a rasp.

'Christ, sir! Didn't realize. Thought you might be one of them.'

The enemy, crossing the river further up, perhaps, coming for them now. Godfrey wiped at his face with his tunic sleeve, tasted damp wool and soil as he twisted in an attempt to see the ghosts once more.

'Where are the rest?' he whispered.

But the men were gone, vanished into the mist, making their way forever forwards, forwards, never looking back. Stone rolled over, lay on his belly, panting.

'I told them to withdraw,' he said.

'How many?' said Godfrey.

Stone hesitated. His voice was low when he said it. 'Four.'

A Jackdaw.

A Promise.

Percy Flint.

And Alfred Walker with his dreams. Plus George Stone, the old sweat, of course, survived from the beginning right through to the end.

Godfrey pressed his cheek to the ground for a moment, sick feeling in his stomach, the scent of lemon oil suddenly in his nostrils.

'What about the second lieutenant?' he said.

George Stone's face was all shadow, hard to see.

'The lieutenant got caught on the far side of the river, sir,' he said. 'We had to leave him. Too much damn lead.'

'Was he injured?' Godfrey whispered.

Stone hesitated. 'That's what he said, sir. Not sure it wasn't a funk though. Too scared to swim back.'

'Christ!' Godfrey was the one to swear now. 'He'll be dead before the sun's up then.'

George Stone turned his gaze to the horizon, grey light rising. 'What happened to Methven, sir?'

There was silence then, before Godfrey shook his head.

Together the two men lay on their bellies in the drainage ditch, breathing in and breathing out, breath clouding over their heads to mingle with the mist. Somewhere above them a bird began to sing a few notes, then stopped. Beneath them the ground was chilled. Between them nothing but the sharp blade of a knife. When the bird did not call again, Godfrey gathered himself, checked his holster, the cold grip of his pistol in his palm.

'We have to get him, Stone,' he said. 'Can't leave him there. You go, call the men back and meet me at the river's edge. I'll lead from there.'

But George Stone cast his dark eyes to the frosted earth, refused to look at his captain, shook his head. 'Tried that already, sir. Didn't work. Men chose to leave.'

'What do you mean "chose"?' said Godfrey, staring at his cook. 'Who gave the order?'

George Stone shifted, rolled over to stare back.

'They tossed for it, sir,' he said. 'Heads or tails.'

Godfrey Farthing saw it then, a coin falling in the grass, deciding who would live and who would die. Five ordinary soldiers taking their chance, just as the officer in charge had taken his chance with them. He breathed in frost, the sweet nip of grass frozen beneath his fingertips, reached to touch a hand to his old sweat's sleeve.

'All right, Stone,' he said. 'You catch up with the others and take them to the walnut trees. Wait for me there.'

'What will you do, sir?' Stone's voice was nothing more than a rough murmur amongst the sough of the willow trees.

'I must go forwards,' Godfrey replied. 'Find the lieutenant.'

George Stone hesitated, adjusted his Enfield on his back, fingers trembling with the cold. He turned towards where the rest had vanished into the mist. Then he looked to his captain again.

'We need a story, sir. If you get him.'

'A story?'

'About what happened.' Stone's eyes were black now. 'You know what he'll say if we don't.'

It was only as they parted – the old sweat disappearing in pursuit of the remains of the section; Godfrey Farthing ready to cross the river at last – that Godfrey realized they had missed one at the reckoning, turned back to call.

'Stone! Stone,' he hissed. 'What about the new recruit? Was he with you?'

Heard the answer float towards him across the frozen marsh.

'He's in the river, too.'

What does it mean to love a man? That was what Captain Godfrey Farthing found himself asking as he crawled and slithered across the few frozen yards towards the river, nothing but saplings and stubby reed beds, a grassy field on the opposite bank waiting to become a killing ground; the perfect place in which to shoot a man dead. Beneath his shirt he could feel the shrapnel shifting, a ghost beneath his skin. He had spent four terrible years pondering that question and the closest he had got to an answer was watching two boys kiss in the shadow of a barn.

Godfrey had never tasted love himself. At least not in a way he had imagined it might be. With a girl who swung her skirts and dared to show her ankles, someone he could have taken home for his mother to meet for tea. But now, as first light started silvering the willows, Godfrey wondered if in fact he had understood love only too well. Here in this Eden, crawling through a drainage ditch to save who might be left. And before, amongst the mud and oily soup of a trench, men of every shape and distinction lying about his feet. Godfrey had understood it then and he understood it now, that feeling deep inside that once released might keep him from having the courage to stick the bayonet in. Like Hawes. Like Beach.

Now that's really something.

Shine on a young man's eyes.

Or perhaps, Godfrey thought, he had understood it right from the start. With the touch of an old man's hand on a son's shoulder as he showed him how to wind the clock at night. Small sun descending. Moon rising. Time passing as it must.

The river ran swift and dark, ice gathered on its fringes as Captain Godfrey Farthing approached to salvage what was lost. A young man with two dice in his pocket. Or a new recruit with nothing but a rabbit's foot in his, a boy Godfrey had sworn he would keep safe. As he lay within feet of the target, water flowing swift and silent in front as dawn approached, Godfrey felt his old wound aching as though the bullet had only just gone in. All around him the early morning mist rose from the grass like a wraith. From the earth. From the surface of the water. A kind of miasma making it hard for Godfrey to see. He touched his forehead to the cold ground, teeth clenched, hand gripped on the handle of his weapon. It was when he looked up again that he saw it. Another ghost, approaching through the grass.

The ghost was coloured grey like the enemy, uniform stained dark with the water it had waded across, rising from the lip of the river and drifting towards Godfrey in silence. Godfrey pressed himself to the earth, felt its cold seep into the very marrow of his bones. Through the haze he caught a glimpse of *Feldgrau*, the scatter of broken walnut shells trailing at the ghost's boots. Then he looked again and it had hair bright amongst the grey, a boy walking towards him out of the dawn as though sauntering through a field of clover, buttercups all about his feet.

Relief flooded Godfrey's limbs, the sudden tingle of blood in his fingertips at the thought that it was Alec walking towards him out of the morning vapour, as the boy had walked towards him down that muddy lane only a few days before. He put a hand to the breast pocket of his tunic where a field postcard was fastened down, felt the shock of a frozen brass button beneath his thumb.

Then he looked again and saw that it was Beach ahead of him, arm raised as though to wave.

I'll be seeing you then.

Those flat grey eyes.

Godfrey closed his eyes again, counted:

One leg;

Two legs;

One arm;

Five fingers.

Opened them to see Second Lieutenant Ralph Svenson sauntering towards him across the frozen field. A young officer who had led a forlorn brigade in the absence of his captain, come out whole-skinned on the other side with a story of his own to tell. Of mutiny. Of men who would not follow orders. Of desertion at the last. The wound beneath Godfrey's shirt burned like ice as he breathed *out out out*, tasted a boy's palm stained with berry juice, caught the silver glimmer of a cap badge tossed amongst the chiff chaff as though it was nothing, heard the sound of a bullet firing, one man shot to warn the rest.

The bells had still not rung in the village as Godfrey stood, holding his revolver as he'd been taught. Arm straight. Back straight. Directed at the enemy – a ghost walking towards him out of the past. Second Lieutenant Ralph Svenson looked bewildered for a moment when he saw his captain there. Then Godfrey Farthing pulled the trigger. Aimed for the heart.

2016

Blood money. That was what it amounted to, Godfrey Farthing's debt. One man shot to save the rest, before the end had come.

'Murder!' thrilled Mrs Maclure, crushing three spring roses against her breastbone.

'Expediency,' declared Solomon's aunt.

'An accident,' said Margaret Penny. 'Unintentional.'

Or just something that happened in a war.

Either way Solomon Farthing knew what it meant. Thomas Methven's legacy was tainted. Definitely something that would leave a stain. He perched on the corner of the brocade chair that was propping up his dead client, pondering the likelihood of Iris Fortune signing now that he had established where the fifty thousand began. Forty per cent? Thirty per cent? Or something much lower than that. It was Barbara Penny who interrupted his reverie, always ready with an opinion where money was concerned.

'It's not right,' she insisted. 'To burn that much cash, wherever it came from. Whatever it was for. Iris Fortune must be persuaded to see sense.'

But Solomon's aunt who was not his aunt, refused.

'Absolutely not,' she insisted. 'It was Thomas Methven's when he was alive. And it's Thomas Methven's now that he is dead. The money should accompany him into the fire.'

'Margaret!' Barbara Penny stamped her stick on the

carpet for the thousandth time. 'Can't you intervene here? Don't you need payment for the funeral at least?'

'Well, yes,' her daughter replied. 'I can insist on that. But not the rest.'

Solomon Farthing perked up at that. Perhaps he could petition for expenses, at least. Present himself at the Office for Lost People with an invoice for a four-day search east, west, south and north.

'Fifty thousand,' sighed Mrs Maclure. 'That'll create quite a blaze.'

'Fifty?' said Solomon's aunt. 'What do you mean, fifty?'

But it was a new voice entering the fray that silenced the lot.

'None of you will be getting anything if we can't find the actual cash.'

DCI Franklin, resplendent in a coat with a peach lining, leaning on the doorframe of a dead man's living room. PC Noble standing behind. And bringing up the rear, Colin Dunlop of Dunlop, Dunlop & Dunlop, come to find out what had happened to a stolen dog.

The money was gone. Disappeared from the safe at the nursing home, fifty thousand in used notes lifted in the night. DCI Franklin hadn't bothered to ask around, she'd come straight to the sitting-in for a dead man.

'Something told me the answer might be here.' She pointed towards Thomas Methven hidden in his coffin. 'Where all this rigmarole began.'

'Not me,' said Solomon, getting in first with his alibi. 'I wasn't even in the country. Just for the absence of doubt.'

'Do you have any proof of that?' said the DCI.

Solomon attempted to look outraged, knew there was no point. He could have got her to check the PNC database for licence plate recognition showing him driving south one night, north the next. But both of the vehicles he used had been stolen, didn't want to give DCI Franklin an excuse.

'I was at Kew,' he said. 'Searching the records for our client's next of kin.'

Though even that had been conducted under a false identity. Solomon glanced towards his fellow Heir Hunter, wondered for a moment if Colin Dunlop might verify the deceit for him. Decided he probably would not.

'And did you find any?' asked the DCI.

'Yes,' said Solomon, brightening now that he had something to show for her faith in him. 'No. Well, maybe. She hasn't exactly signed yet.'

'Good thing considering the money has been stolen.'

The inscrutable PC Noble, sticking in the knife.

'It wasn't me,' said Mrs Maclure genuflecting towards the police officers.

'Don't be ridiculous,' wheezed Barbara Penny. 'Nobody thought that it was.'

'Why would I rob my own client?' said Margaret Penny. 'The council always need the cash.'

They all looked towards Solomon's aunt who wasn't really his aunt. But the way she was fiddling with her turquoise hair pin made them realize that a false accusation in that direction might be a dangerous precedent to set.

'Well somebody's taken it,' said DCI Franklin. She came

to stand in front of Solomon where he was perched by the coffin. 'Empty your pockets.'

'What! I said it wasn't me.'

'You're the only one with a police record, though, aren't you.'

It wasn't a question. Though Solomon was sure that Margaret Penny flinched then, a small tell, but a true one. Wondered what it was that she had done wrong in her life. Still, he knew it was best to appease the DCI.

You scratch my back and I'll scratch yours.

For one final time he dipped his hands in. To the pockets in his trousers. To the pockets on his jacket. Not forgetting the one above his heart. He laid what he found along the edge of Thomas Methven's wooden box.

An empty packet of orange tic tacs.

A dead Nokia.

A walnut shell rubbed to its bones.

Everything he had come into this case with. Everything he had taken out. Also a blue kerchief that belonged to a dog he had stolen, albeit inadvertently, reminding him about the other debt he still owed, time running out to settle that one, too.

DCI Franklin studied the paltry remains of Solomon Farthing. Then she studied the rest as though she might find the answer there. The ladies of Edinburgh's Indigent Funeral Rota stared back. Apart from Mrs Maclure, who nodded towards Mr Methven in his coffin, faint flush on her cheeks.

'Shall we try the suit?'

*

In the end they cut him open, unscrewed the lid of Thomas Methven's coffin and took a pair of scissors to his burial gown. The suit was still blue as a starling's egg despite all the years that had passed. Three buttons, turn-ups, neat lapels. Solomon would not have been surprised to find *Fortune* stitched in at the collar, if he'd dared to look.

But it was the ladies of the Indigent Funeral Rota who were wielding the knife. Up one seam, down another, until PC Noble took over and dipped her hands in. The young officer pulled it out piece by crumpled piece, banknotes of all descriptions stuffed into the lining of Thomas Methven's going away outfit, sewn together in neat pink stitch. Tens here. Twenties there. Purple notes. And brown ones. Even black and white. The women stared at the treasure trove as it showered to the floor, eyes shining like everyone's does when cash is thrown around. Used notes. Dirty notes. Ten shilling notes. A sea of paper money all long past its use-by date.

'I remember the brown ones,' exclaimed Mrs Maclure, dropping her roses at last. '1960!'

'This one goes back to 1953,' said Margaret Penny, picking a pound note from the carpet and frowning at it, front and back.

'The green is from after the war, isn't it?' asked Solomon's aunt. 'The second one.'

'Look at the white.' Mrs Maclure's eyes were wide behind the gold rim of her spectacles. 'Isn't that from 1921?'

Paperwork collected over three generations by Godfrey Farthing, piece by precious piece. Never did pay it into a bank. Or entrust it to the Co-operative Society. Kept it hidden beneath his ladies' gun instead. Thousands squirrelled and secreted over fifty years. All in honour of a debt that never could be paid.

DCI Franklin looked both disgusted and astounded at what had been revealed.

'They never told me it was in old currency,' she said. 'What a waste of time.'

'Must have been a mistake at the funeral home,' frowned Margaret Penny.

'Not even legal tender,' grumbled her mother.

'Can't you swap it?' said Mrs Maclure. 'Take it to the bank and they'll give you face value at least. A pound for a pound.'

'Hardly fifty thousand though, is it, either way?' said PC Noble, dampening even the slightest idea of any profit.

More like three, thought Solomon, doing a quick calculation as he gazed at the ocean of paper about his feet. Or three and a half, if he was lucky. Thirty per cent of which was not much more than nine hundred quid. The funeral parlour had got it right, though. Three grand in 1971 when his grandfather finally laid down his ledger, probably was worth about fifty today. Unlike any of them standing in Thomas Methven's former living room now, seduced by the glitter of false promise, somebody, somewhere had done the right sum.

After DCI Franklin had departed, indignant at the waste of woman hours, PC Noble by her side, Pawel served a round of tea and biscuits, pink wafers balanced on each saucer, as the ladies of the Edinburgh Indigent Rota finally got around to actually counting the cash.

One hundred.

Two hundred.

Three hundred.

Four.

'I never said it was fifty thousand,' Solomon's aunt was still insisting as she gathered in the ten shilling notes. 'A silly mistake on the part of the funeral parlour.'

'Or the nursing home,' said Margaret Penny. 'Got lost in translation.'

'Either way, poor Solomon here got sent on a wild goose chase,' complained Barbara Penny. 'Found the next of kin, only for her to be robbed at the last.'

Solomon's aunt sniffed then, as though all the largesse she had bestowed upon the city of Edinburgh in her various to-ings and fro-ings had been sorely misunderstood.

'Pawel and I made an executive decision,' she said rising once again to stand over the coffin. 'On behalf of poor Mr Methven. Expedited the money's return to where it belonged.'

'Stole it you mean,' muttered Barbara Penny.

'That's one version of the story.'

'Oh, I love a story,' said Mrs Maclure, sorting the cash into pre- and post-war. 'This will make a good one.'

The Edinburgh Indigent Funeral Rota, disputatious to the last.

Meanwhile, upstairs in the back room, away from all the flurry and fuss, the other new arrival laid it all down. Colin Dunlop of Dunlop, Dunlop & Dunlop explaining the real reason he had pursued Solomon up hill and down dale for the last few days.

'Been chasing your family tree,' he said. 'On your mother's side.'

'Oh yes?' Solomon wasn't sure he wanted to hear this. But what could he do. All Heir Hunters liked to command the room with a story to tell if they could.

'Did you know you had an aunt?' said Colin Dunlop.

'Yes,' said Solomon. 'She's downstairs now sorting things for Thomas Methven's funeral. We had to get another slot from Mortonhall.'

'Not that aunt. A real one. Your mother's sister, Judith Gold.'

Another name to add to that little patch of white, in amongst the green of a London cemetery.

'My mother's family are all dead,' Solomon replied.

Swept away in the second war to end all wars, the bitter aftermath of which eventually swept away both his parents, too.

'No.' Colin Dunlop was smiling now. 'Well, yes. Well . . . only recently.'

Solomon Farthing's real aunt survived on the wrong side of the Iron Curtain, lived her life accruing whatever she could, so that something would be left for any others who remained.

'It's a reasonable amount,' Colin Dunlop went on, withdrawing his paperwork from his briefcase and spreading it across the mattress for Solomon to see. 'Several thousand, perhaps. Maybe more.'

How many thousand? thought Solomon. But he knew that Colin Dunlop of Dunlop, Dunlop & Dunlop wouldn't tell him. Not until they had agreed commission, of course.

'What makes you think I couldn't sort it myself?' he said.

Colin Dunlop just smiled. 'My international reputation and expertise.'

Solomon sighed, knew that this Edinburgh Man was correct.

'Five,' he said.

'Fifteen.' Colin Dunlop adjusted his cuff. 'And I'd be doing you a favour.'

But in the end they settled. On ten per cent, of course.

Solomon signed the contract, then stayed in the spare room to rest while Colin Dunlop made his way to the kitchen to secure a cup of tea. Despite all his years as an Heir Hunter, Solomon realized it made him feel warm inside – the thought that he had done a fellow Edinburgh Man a favour.

When he came back downstairs to rejoin the funeral crowd, he found them wielding a screwdriver, ready to fasten Thomas Methven in once again.

'Anything you want to put with him?' said Margaret Penny, firmly in charge now. She had already removed every single scrap of cash from inside Thomas Methven's suit, waited for it to be counted, before hiding it beneath her own. To pay for the hearse, she told them. And the flowers, perhaps even a stone. Not to mention Pastor Macdonald's eulogy, chapter and verse. Solomon had watched as she did it, realized Margaret Penny's fox was watching him back.

There wasn't much to put alongside Thomas Methven in his wooden box. Mrs Maclure placed her three spring roses on the dead man's breastbone, where they lay like Walter Pringle's three dead finches.

Father, Son and Holy Ghost.

Solomon's aunt who wasn't really his aunt sacrificed one of her heavy silver rings in memory of Thomas Methven's long departed wife. Barbara Penny fished a small coin from her purse, slipped that in at the foot.

'To pay the ferryman.'

While Pawel tucked a reel of pink thread into the dead man's pocket.

'Just in case he needs to do a repair.'

'What about his father's notebook?' said Margaret Penny, its cover stiff with age, blue horizontals and red verticals all faded now. 'You'll want to keep that, won't you, to secure the inheritance for the next of kin? Or at least explain.'

But Solomon shook his head, let her slide the notebook down the inside of Thomas Methven's coffin, too. He was ninety-nine per cent sure that Iris Fortune would never sign for the cash now, if even half of his aunt's story turned out to be correct.

When it came to his turn, Solomon put in the most precious thing Mr Methven ever owned:

A pawn ticket, no.125.

That small slip of blue.

It was funny what turned out to be valuable in the end.

'There is one last thing,' said Mrs Maclure, just before the final screws went in. 'I found it wedged between some floorboards in the downstairs loo when I was sitting in one night.'

A silver cap badge belonging to a member of the London Scottish, little lion raising its paw.

'He was in the war, wasn't he, Mr Methven,' said Pawel. 'I think it must be his.'

'Toss it in then,' insisted Solomon's aunt.

And before Solomon could interject, Mrs Maclure flipped the badge over the lip of Thomas Methven's coffin, where it landed with a soft *plink* amongst the detritus of a life well lived.

Strike Sure.

There was one thing Solomon Farthing was left with at the end though, delivered to him by the men who turned up from the funeral parlour to help see Thomas Methven on his way at last. They handed it over as they slid the coffin onto one of their neat folding trolleys, wheeled Thomas Methven down the garden path between his roses and into the back of the hearse.

'Did our boss a favour once,' the undertaker said as he offered it to Solomon. 'Kept him for you, just in case.'

A box rimmed with dust, sticker on the top.

Godfrey Farthing
1893–1971

His grandfather's ashes, returned to Solomon after more than forty years away.

1919

Godfrey

Godfrey Farthing came home to find spring spreading like a rash across England. Six months since the war had ended, and demobbed at last. He didn't stop in London. Nor in the east. Not even in Hastings to visit his parents laid beneath their stone. Instead he stayed one night in a boarding house close to the port where he landed, then got on a train headed for the further reaches of the country, somewhere deep in the borderlands where England and Scotland touched.

He had come to deliver a field postcard that he carried always in one pocket, *I am quite well* the only words not yet crossed out. Also a pawn ticket, no.125. One mother's legacy to her only son. He brought a dog with him that walked with a limp now, back leg smashed beyond repair. But Godfrey Farthing thought the dog might prove popular amongst the boys where he was headed – a school for foundling children near the border with Scotland. A bonny place to live.

Godfrey arrived when the sun was already long past its peak, the only one to disembark at the small station, train steaming on ahead. To the Athens of the North, he thought, as he tucked the dog beneath his arm, checked the directions scribbled on a scrap of paper. Somewhere that might be worth a visit one day.

He walked to his destination through a land of rolling

fields, before turning down what seemed like a never-ending drive. It was the beginning of a warm evening and he carried the dog looped over one arm, wondering what he might encounter when he arrived. Tea, perhaps, poured from an urn. Boys running in the yard. The sound of laughter as children played their ordinary games. Or maybe a field with buttercups and two types of clover, river running swift at the bottom of the hill.

The shadows grew sharper as he approached, the sun starting its long fall from the sky as he came to it at last. A tall building hidden behind a fold in the land, grey walls and a turret, every little boy's dream. But as he entered the courtyard, Godfrey Farthing knew from the flutter in his fingers that once again he was too late. Found the old home shut and boarded, all the windows covered, no men left to run it anymore. There were weeds poking through the gravel in the quad. Godfrey walked about the building one way, then about again, found nothing but emptiness and dilapidation, rather like the buildings he had left behind in France.

The girl was sitting on the stump of an old tree by the gate as Godfrey finally took his leave.

'I like your dog, mister,' she called to him.

He stopped to let her pet the thing, the creature turning its dark eyes upon her as she rubbed and coddled its head. The girl was fair, like Alec had been fair, her hair cut in the new fashion Godfrey saw all about him now. Bobbed, barely skimming her ears. At her feet was a basket covered in a cloth and a thousand little daisies, or thereabouts, pierced by her thumbnail, one attached to the next.

'My name's Daisy,' the girl said when she saw Godfrey looking at the flowers. 'Daisy Pringle.'

And Captain Godfrey Farthing touched the pocket where he kept a field postcard, knew he had arrived at the right place at last. He was about to deliver his bad news when the girl got in first.

'Have you come about the advert?' she asked, eyes bright with hope.

'What advert?' replied Godfrey, confused for a second.

Daisy Pringle pulled a newspaper from where she'd been sitting on it to keep her dress from getting stained.

'This one,' she said.

The newspaper was from Scotland – the *Borders Observatory* – front page covered from masthead to foot in advertisements of all kinds. Martins for quality bread. The Pavilion for variety. Coal deliveries and spring goods. Godfrey noticed one offering home-sewn flannels, realized he might need some new trousers for himself now that the thing was at an end. Then he saw what Daisy Pringle was pointing at, a small text written out on a single line:

WANTED: Home for a baby boy, 6 months old. Total surrender.

Like the ending of the war. Then she pulled back the cloth covering the basket at her feet. And Godfrey Farthing peered in to find a child, smiling and kicking, hair bright as flax and two grey eyes looking back.

The village that was home to the *Borders Observatory* was barely thirty miles further north, on the cusp of the line that separated England from the rest. Godfrey arrived the next morning to find flowers blooming in all the gardens, clematis and spring roses, as though nothing untoward had gone on. He asked about for the address, found it with no problem, knocked on the door then stood back to wait. He fiddled with a small notebook in his pocket as he waited for someone to answer. When the woman appeared, they stared at each other for a moment as though they could not believe that the other existed, before Godfrey held out his hand.

'Captain Farthing,' he said as they shook hands across the step. 'How's your boy?'

Watched Mabel Methven's eyes fill like the sea.

The entire time they sat and drank tea together in Mabel Methven's front room, all Godfrey could think about was the *tick tick tick* of his father's old clock in the parlour at home. He must get the clock back from wherever it had gone, he thought, before he moved on to wherever he might go next. North, perhaps, away from the flatlands of his youth. Somewhere with hills and surprises round every corner, a place where one could not see what might be coming next. He realized at some point that Mabel Methven was talking about the north, too. About Edinburgh. How she might move there some day, to join her cousin who ran a shop.

'Plenty of folks needing the pawn these days,' she said, running a hand across her dress. 'It's a disgrace really, after what we've been through.'

Godfrey touched his breast pocket then, thought of the small slip of blue paper tucked above his heart. He must return it, he thought, didn't want to repeat the mistakes of the past.

Before he left for the station, heading south once again,

Godfrey stood next to Mabel Methven in the pretty churchyard and looked at the small stone nestled in the grass. The carving was bright, sharper than a blade at a chicken's neck, despite being six months old. It had weathered its first winter, thought Godfrey, just like the boy in the ground.

Thomas Archibald Methven
1913–1918

Taken by the influenza like so many others, never did get to see his father again. Godfrey put his hand to the stone, felt how warm it had grown in the morning sun, unlike Archie Methven who had grown so cold. It was then that he said it.

'I know of a child that needs a mother.'

That was all it took.

Godfrey cancelled the advert at the local paper that afternoon, refused the 6d refund that was due, made all the necessary arrangements. A baby handed over on a village green because one girl was too young, and another had grown too old. Before he departed, he handed Mabel Methven the only inheritance her new child had. A pawn ticket, no.125. That small slip of blue. Also a notebook with its horizontals and its verticals, thick grey pencil lines cancelling out the debt.

There was a story hidden amongst those pencil marks if only he wanted to tell. But Godfrey Farthing had sworn he would stay silent. As had all the men who were left. They had agreed on a different version of events as they stood beneath a ring of trees, ground crackling beneath their boots. The tale of a man who had led from the front and taken a bullet to spare the rest, given a hero's burial beneath the walnut shells. That was how Godfrey had thought of it then. He wasn't so sure now. But it was who told the story that mattered, not what really happened. Until a new page was turned.

It was on the train back to England that Captain Godfrey Farthing turned the next page of his story, standing in the corridor to get a breath of air, a woman smiling at him as she attempted to pass. The train rocked them together as if they were soldiers caught in a truck. The woman wore a hat with a ribbon threaded round the crown, her skirt well above the ankles, blouse nipped in at the waist. Godfrey thought of the light in Mabel Methven's eyes when he'd told her about Daisy Pringle's child. Saw the same light in this woman's eyes as he offered her a Capstan by way of apology, held the battered tin out. The woman smiled with amusement. Then she said it.

Yes. Yes, please.

And Captain Godfrey Farthing knew that he was about to taste another sort of love, at last.

A *coup de foudre.*

That was what he called it later, when he told the tale. A disaster waiting to happen, never should have taken the leap. But after the cigarette they had gone to the dining car to drink a cocktail. Champagne, with brandy at its heart.

All their short time together Godfrey dreamed only of what might be coming next. One live boy to shift the cold of the dead. But even after his son arrived safe and well there were always two other men who walked with

Godfrey Farthing, day in, day out. Waking beside him every morning. Lying down to sleep with him every night. The first was a young man who smiled as he foraged for berries in the hedgerow, small dog at his side. The second was a boy called Beach.

PART SEVEN

The Legacy

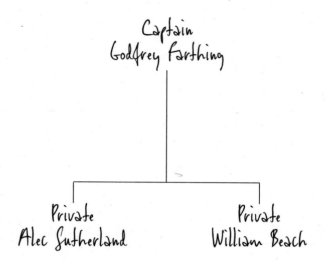

2016

It was November, leaves wet against the pavements, the haar rolling in. The vote had been taken, the decision had been made. Nothing to do but settle the terms and bury any differences, see what the future might hold.

Solomon Farthing drove his aunt's Mini south through the borderlands, dipping in and out of the autumn mist. He was headed towards a school for foundling boys: a place for children who had somehow lost their parents, or parents who had somehow lost their child. When he arrived, they gave him a bed in the sick bay, where he lay beneath a blanket with a blue trim listening to the singing as it rose and fell. In the morning, before all the boys were up, he wandered across the field towards the river and searched for him there.

Edward (Jackdaw) Jackson
1900–1978

Lying hidden in the grass. Dead buttercups where his head must once have been, a forest of weeds at his feet.

The Jackdaw's stone was small amongst the remains of the summer hay, his name chiselled in letters that were clouded with lichen. As Solomon scraped them clear, he remembered a man standing on a riverbank with a boy in his arms, pulled from the dark water, choking and coughing, so that Solomon Farthing might not have to take the blame. He had thought the old man ancient then, a relic of the past appearing from out of the sky as though he was already a ghost.

Ash on an old man's sleeve . . .

Burnt roses . . .

Dust in the air . . .

But he must have only been fifty-six or so, in line with the century. How young that seemed to Solomon now.

He walked back to take breakfast with the other boys, through the long grass, wet seeds clinging to his trousers and his sleeves. The field was like the place where he had finally laid his grandfather to rest. Deep in the wilderness of that wide open cemetery, spread over a great area from a leafy Inverleith suburb to the dark covered walkways of the Water of Leith. Edinburgh's 'secret garden' – that was what they called it. And Solomon Farthing's family plot now.

He had taken Godfrey Farthing in by the gate and left him there. Scattered right. Scattered left. Landing in amongst the nettles and the ivy, silvering the grass. When the box was empty but for a thin layer of dust, Solomon had lain amongst the ivy, too, started with his check. One leg. Two legs. Two arms. Five fingers . . . Counting them out and counting them in again; all the layers of bone and loam upon which his grandfather had finally come to rest.

Second Lieutenant Ralph Svenson, shot as he attempted a raid across the river. A hero at the end.

Alec Sutherland, vanished into the deep current, never reappeared. Left behind a pawn ticket just in case it should ever need redeeming. And a baby boy with sunny eyes.

Lance Corporal Archibald Methven, died from his

wounds on a lonely road in France, nothing left but a man standing in a photograph, dead son at his side.

Private Percy Flint, came home to drive a lorry, lived a long life.

James Hawes, temporary sergeant, roamed the world preaching about the Fall from his orange box, fell asleep beneath a lychgate one night, failed to rise again.

Private Alfred Walker, emigrated to the promised land. Went out in 1937 according to the passenger lists, never came back.

Private Arthur Promise, coughed his last in a transit camp while awaiting demob, Spanish influenza. Didn't make it home.

Private Edward Jackson, known as Jackdaw, with his swooping black cape. Cancer, of the oesophagus, spent his last days in the corner of a hospital where the visiting hours were two till four. No longer able to *chitter chatter*. No longer able to fight. No longer able to recite poetry as once Solomon Farthing had heard him do. Just lay on the pillow, his head as small as a bird's skull, smiling as one boy after another came to sing him out.

And Corporal Bertie Fortune, the section's lucky man. Died in his bed, of course.

Then there was Thomas Methven, the boy who started as one person and ended as another, served in a different war to all the rest. Came home and kept other people's money safe, grew roses till his wife died, then he grew some more.

'He was the best of them all.'

That was what Pawel said.

Or just the one who lived the longest, perhaps.

*

Solomon returned from his walk by the river to sit in the chapel, waited for the service to begin. That annual commemoration of the boys who left for war and never did return. He sat at the back listening to the rustle of the pupils as they entered, the creak of wood joints easing as they pretended to close their eyes. Next to him sat Peter, the boy archivist, holding a tiny bird's egg in one hand, something shiny in the other. A pound coin, fake gold glittering, ready for whatever adventure might come next. Behind Peter's feet, hidden from all who might start a commotion, was a dog. Dodds's faithful companion, loaned out for the day. The dog had yelped when it saw Solomon pull up at the garage in his aunt's Mini, leapt on to the back seat and rested its nose on Solomon's shoulder the whole drive south. Now, as a small procession of boys took their place amongst the choir stalls, ready to lift their mouths to the sky, Solomon could feel the warmth where the dog was leaning against his leg, felt contentment settle in his chest.

As he waited for the service to begin, he thought of the name newly chipped onto the war memorial outside.

Sutherland, Alec.

The letters bright now compared to all those that had gone before. Old Mortality, Solomon had thought as he watched stone dust blown from the plinth by a man wielding a chisel. He had paid for the carving with the proceeds of his windfall, courtesy of an aunt who really was his aunt this time. But not until he had settled his other debts, of course.

People loved to mark things, that was what he'd learned. A gravestone. A bench. An honours board in a school, boys' names written up in gold alongside their cricketing scores. Solomon had never thought that it mattered before, leaving something behind that couldn't just be washed away. But even men like Private William Beach had their memorials now.

Solomon touched the pew in front, ran his fingers along its underside, could feel it still, even after sixty years. *S. F.* His own initials. *I was here.* The boys around him bowed their heads then and Solomon felt that familiar stillness take hold. He looked for a moment out of the stained-glass window, beyond the quad, beyond the field, beyond even the river, towards where those who had been lost lay now. There was always a before, he thought. And an after. But it was what you did at the time that mattered the most.

Then the prayer finally began and he bowed his head too.

Our Father who art in heaven,
Hallowed be thy name.
Thy kingdom come,
Thy will be done,
On earth as it is in heaven.
Give us this day our daily bread
And forgive us our trespasses,
As we forgive those who trespass against us.
Lead us not into temptation and deliver us from evil
For thine is the kingdom, the power and the glory
For ever and ever . . .

THE END

It was summer. 1916 and the war was everywhere. Devastation after devastation. Death after death. Men were being slaughtered in the east and in the west, no room for boys such as Private William Beach who could not stand the noise of a bombardment and ran in the wrong direction the moment the whistle came. Six weeks of nothing but marching and being encouraged to stick the bayonet in. Six weeks of waiting for the orders to arrive. Six weeks of huddling at the bottom of a trench by his captain's feet listening to the guns, until the moment came.

Afterwards they said the captain didn't have to do it, that he could have changed his mind. But he had just been following orders: Godfrey Farthing's role in life. He argued for the boy, of course, refused to wield his weapon until all the appeals had been heard. Three months of waiting, only to be let down in the end, Beach blinking in the pale autumn light as Godfrey explained. Just the way it was at times like those when everything was out of kilter, a mess of gas and mud. No meaning to any of it other than kill or be killed.

They did it in the yard of a farmhouse in which they had been billeted, waited till the last day before moving out. All the men were gathered on the road with their packs and their gasbags as Godfrey had everything prepared, legs strapped and boots laced, while over the hill the big guns were booming, just out of reach. Beach was shivering when he was brought out, his whole body rippling with it though it was a fair day, leaves still dancing on the trees. There was a single blackbird singing in a hedge as they marched him to stand in front of the outhouse they had used as a latrine, next to the sooty remnants of a slag heap where the farmer and his wife once tossed the embers from their fire. Opposite him six men fiddled with their rifles, hot fingers on cold metal, had drawn the wrong straw.

They looped the rope round Beach's wrists and round his ankles, pinned an envelope over his heart to secure the aim. The boy was wearing his second-best shirt, Godfrey noticed, chicken shit smeared on the hem from the shed they had locked him in. He came to stand by the boy for a moment, looked into his grey eyes.

I'll be seeing you then.

That was what Beach said.

Think of your mother.

That was what Godfrey replied, before the hood went down.

At least one of them shot wide, brick dust flying. Or didn't shoot at all.

Gun jammed, sir, nothing I could do about it.

George Stone frowning at his rifle after as though there must have been something wrong.

Bertie Fortune had the blank, they'd all made sure of that. Didn't want the man who got them stuff to be put off his game. Besides, they'd known he'd take care of whatever was left after. The boy's plum cake and his green ribbon. There was money to be made, even out of murder. Not that any of them called it that in those days. Only afterwards, perhaps.

It was Hawes who never got over it. Shot true, like the

marksman that he was. A single wound clean through Beach's stomach, where it would hurt the most. The boy didn't even shout, just grunted with the impact of it, lifting his head beneath the hood for a moment as the smoke rose from their rifles to mingle with the mist. When it cleared Godfrey Farthing was standing with his hand still raised as though he hadn't already given the order, all eyes on him as he began his walk across. He leaned in to Beach as though to speak to him, four roses blooming, blood on the boy's shirt. Godfrey listened for his breathing – *in out in out* – called for the medical officer to check, too. The young officer walked over to listen for himself. Then he nodded, before stepping back.

After that Godfrey Farthing turned away for a moment and the other men thought it was all over, until their captain unhitched the leather clip on his belt. He drew the Webley from its holster, held it to his chest as though to check its safety, the rest of the men standing with their rifles waiting to be dismissed. Then Godfrey walked right up to Beach, just as they were encouraged to do when practising with the bayonet.

Be swift, boys. Hold him like your sweetheart.

Right arm held out straight, the pistol like an extension of his hand. He put the barrel close to the boy's temple – a gun to behead a buttercup.

Took aim.

Fired.

James Hawes always remembered the blood. George Stone the smell of cordite. Bertie Fortune the steadiness with which Captain Farthing carried out the deed. Not a single hesitation, or a turn to look. Nor any discussion with the other men who were there: the minister from the village; the medical officer by his side. Captain Godfrey Farthing had his opportunity and he took it. Walked straight up to the boy, then pulled the trigger.

Afterwards he made Hawes and Stone do the burying, had them wait while he cut off Beach's tags and rummaged in his pockets. He took the boy's cap badge for himself. A small thing, silver, with a lion raising its paw. Also the motto of the London Scottish.

Strike Sure.

Acknowledgements

The words of Harry Patch (the last of the British WWI veterans) in the epigraph were taken from an exchange with a BBC interviewer, as quoted in *Aftershock* by Matthew Green.

The phrase, 'It's a long way to Tipperary' is taken from the music-hall song, 'It's a Long, Long Way to Tipperary' by Henry James 'Harry' Williams and Jack Judge.

The lines quoted on p. 232–33 are taken from the music-hall song, 'Who Were You With Last Night' by Fred Godfrey and Mark Sheridan.

The line, 'An endless picture-show' on p. 264 is taken from the poem, 'Picture-Show' by Siegfried Sassoon.

The lines, 'There is some corner of a foreign field', 'Dulce et decorum est' and 'A drawing-down of blinds' on p. 278 are taken from '1914: The Soldier' by Rupert Brooke, 'Dulce et Decorum est' and 'Anthem for Doomed Youth' by Wilfred Owen.

The line, 'the moment of the rose and the moment of the yew' on p.349 and the lines, 'Ash on an old man's sleeve', 'Burnt roses ' and 'Dust in the air.' on p.494 are taken from 'Little Gidding' from *Four Quartets* by T. S. Eliot.

Throughout the writing of this book I read many accounts of men's experiences both during and after WWI. These ranged from the classic to the obscure, and I have no doubt that all of them, in some way, are reflected in the text. But I'd particularly like to acknowledge the inspiration and influence of Pat Barker and her novel, *The Ghost Road*.

Thank you: Clare Alexander and all at Aitken Alexander Associates; Maria Rejt, Josie Humber and all at Mantle; Natalie Young, Ami Smithson, Rosie Wilson and all at Pan Macmillan, with particular thanks to Gillian Mackay; my fellow writers in Ink Inc, especially Pippa Goldschmidt and Theresa Muñoz; Shirley Obrzud of GenGenie Research for introducing me to the world of family finding and New Register House in Edinburgh; Daniel Curran and Emma Johannesson at Finders International for their essential assistance in understanding the world of probate research north and south of the border; PC Emily Noble of Police Scotland for lending me her name; the Imperial War Museum, London; Alnwick Castle and the Fusiliers Museum of Northumberland; Christina Paulson-Ellis and Peter Brunyate for the WWI letters; my family and friends for their ongoing faith and support; and Audrey Grant for her love, encouragement and companionship on this crazy journey we have embarked upon.

As befits a story about men and boys, this book is dedicated to my wonderful son, Jack. But also to my father, Michael Paulson-Ellis. During its writing my father and I spent some months exploring his family tree, where we discovered several ancestors we hadn't fully known before (including some WWI soldiers) and I learned a lot more about him. Sadly, while my father was there at the start of this book, he didn't live to see its end. And yet, he runs through it still. Thank you, Dad, for introducing me to books, to history, to the love of reading and finding out how people used to live. And, of course, for your love and support always. Wherever you are now, this book is my memorial to you.